I0788444

Burn Up in Victory
Jennifer R. Donohue

Burn Up in Victory ©2025 Jennifer R. Donohue
Cover photo Shutterstock
Cover design Jennifer R. Donohue

Ebook ISBN: 978-1-945548-35-2
Hardcover ISBN: 978-1-945548-36-9

These violent delights have violent ends
And in their triumph die, like fire and powder,
Which as they kiss consume: the sweetest honey
Is loathsome in his own deliciousness
And in the taste confounds the appetite

Romeo and Juliet, act II, scene vi

Author Note

What you hold in your hands is very technically a novel-length sequel to a short story. "Mistempered Weapons" appeared in the Summer 2022 of Kaleidotrope, and you can read it online before or after reading *Burn Up in Victory*. You can skip it entirely! I do mean for this book to stand on its own. But if you want to know ahead of time who Marco is, if you want an introduction to this magical city in which you will find yourself, you can find it online for free.

If you've read my other books and are surprised that I've written a romantasy, yes, me too! If you are a romantasy reader and this is how you are coming to my books, welcome! I've done my best with these characters and their relationships. My intent for this book was for it to be fantasy first, romance second. But then again, the working file's title was "duelist enemies to lovers."

Content warnings for *Burn Up in Victory* include:

Psychological abuse

Parental abuse

Sword violence

Blood and injury

Chapter One

Serafina of House Galeazzo

There is a society dinner, and I'm descending the stair when my mother says with swift and casual venom, "Wear something you can fight in, you ridiculous girl." I stop, skirts in motion a moment longer. Of course, everything has changed. She's in stays and skirts, veteran and victor of many a dinner-duel, but I am not my mother. And while I have all manner of practice clothes, I do not have clothing suitable for fighting in should the mood at dinner turn, and I stand stricken, staring at her in my surprise. "Your brother was a close enough fit," she says, turning away from me with a dismissive clack of her fan. This is the first she's mentioned him in weeks. The horses and coach wait outside already, and my father as well, certainly. "Change now, don't keep us waiting on you long."

I gather my skirts and flee back up the way I came and down the hall. I don't want to fight at dinner tonight. I don't want to wear my brother's clothes. My mother isn't wrong; Marco and I were of similar builds, he a bit taller and broader in the shoulder. His boots would be far too big, but I have some that are perhaps too plain but would do. Nobody will be looking at my boots. Everybody will be looking at my boots.

Entering his rooms is like entering a tomb. I'm certain the servants have still come in here to clean, it isn't dusty or stale, but the doors have remained closed, the curtains drawn, the bed made, his remaining belongings undisturbed. I come up short in the doorway, but I'm crying and don't want anybody to see, servants or no, but especially not my mother.

There on the polished dresser, his remaining brushes, his cologne, the gaps where he removed items starkly empty. Of course he packed. He packed and he selected horses and a carriage and departed as though he'd told everybody, succeeding through the sheer casual brazenness of the act. I wish he'd taken me with him. That he left me is a wound I'm not sure will ever heal.

I open one wardrobe and then the next, shying away from the gaps where he took things away, my thoughts abuzz. I can scarce remember how I would be expected to dress for this dinner, in these clothes, and finally my hand happens upon a heavier jacket with nicer buttons, formal but not too fancy. Like armor, my mind babbles, and I take it and a pair of more formal breeches and then I can't stand the still air any longer and I flee to my rooms, banging the door shut behind me, and almost turning a heel in my silly shoes that are ill-suited for duels.

I'd dismissed my maid already, of course, and clumsily shed my dress, and bodice into a puddle of embroidered silk onto the floor, misbutton and then fix a shirt over my stays, step into the breeches. My jewelry will be either too much or invisible with the coat and I scratch myself in my haste at opening my necklace clasp and stop a moment, shaking, look at my pale face in the mirror. We are going to dinner to a family we have visited many times before. There will be few, if any, strangers at this event. I will not have to make explanations to anybody, for surely everybody will already know. I press a finger briefly to my smarting skin and look at it; no blood.

I finish buckling my sword belts as I descend the stair a second time. My father waits impatiently on the front step; he always hands my mother and I into the carriage. He rakes me over with his gaze but doesn't comment, and a moment later we are on our way.

Our parents' favorite, my brother Marco always told me that he would shield me from the worst of society. He wanted me able to live comfortably, to explore my interests and abilities without the same pressure that he faced, be it my disappointing spark of magic, or my rudimentary skill with swordplay that a parade of tutors have been able to elevate only so far. When he could, he would practice my lessons with me, run through my dueling drills with me. He was always a better, or more patient, instructor than the ones in our parents' employ. Though not a star duelist, not an in-demand bachelor, Marco had the distinction of being the friend of many. He got along with nearly everybody in our social circles, he got along with the members of the theater companies; I think he even had some friends in the City guard.

Then one evening, Marco didn't come home. Not unusual; the curfew does not apply to our class. Not even the first time. But when he did finally return the next afternoon, he was disheveled and withdrawn, and would give me no explanation. And three days later he was gone. He isn't in our city anymore, isn't within reasonable bounds of pursuit. I say pursuit because he didn't leave alone, he left with indentured members of two different theater companies. It's been quite the scandal and not something that I even fully understand, because I *did* let him shield me, perhaps too much. Had he not, I might have been in the streets with him of an evening, and know the people he knew and drank with and fought with, friendly and un. I wouldn't have been so surprised to be brotherless.

That's the only promise anybody has ever made to me, and with its breaking, I don't know how I am supposed to proceed.

I can't look at my mother anymore. Her spark hasn't grown so strong that I must avert my eyes, though that day will come soon enough if my own spark isn't successfully stoked. But to be divested of her only son, her favorite child, she is a burning brand even so, icy and in flames all at the same time, unbearable to spend any time with. I don't know how to speak to her at length, and haven't had to, between Marco and my tutors. When we must attend events together, or as a family, and there are many events, our conversation is frequently limited to her reminding me to stand up straight, to look at people when they speak to me. Sideways glances to see if I'm using the proper utensils at a dinner. When I make a mistake, because I often have, she'd look to Marco or my father to correct me.

My father is more distant, though less cold, somehow. He seems baffled by my presence, as though he doesn't remember having had a daughter, and his attention has tended towards indulgence rather than severity. When my swordsmanship has been lacking, he's gotten me better weapons and auditioned another tutor, rather than punishments I'm sure my mother would rather exact. I don't know if they were different when Marco was a child, and if this is a facet of their own gain in power, or if this is simply how the family has always been.

The city doesn't have rulers, exactly, or a council, exactly. The city has powerful families, and a magical academy, the theater companies, and the guard, though the working of the guard in absence of a distinct ruler eludes me. My lack of understanding just means that it isn't my place to understand; I am a part of a powerful family, and expected, indeed directed, to gain in my own personal power. Without Marco here, I now will have to partake of these social circles and these honor duels in a way that I've been able to escape for all this time. Now I am the face of my family, at this social level, and I am expected to find my seat at these tables.

It isn't as though all of these families are strangers to me, and my family is close with several of them. When we were all much younger, many of us children played together, but the weight of magic and responsibility grew ever stronger as our short years have added up, and while I still correspond with twin girls, Allegra and Andante, from one family and a boy from another, I am still now at a disadvantage. Marco once said that there was a certain bond you form with a person, when you've made each other bleed, or when you've fought back to back in a rarer larger skirmish. I have no such bonds, I've never fought a real duel, just practice ones, just lesson ones. I've worn my swords whenever leaving the house for years now, as we all have and all do, and have never once needed to draw one. When I think it's a matter of time, I simply mean that it's the next time that I go out. I'm resigned to it,and maybe I'm frightened as well. It's hard to make sense of it all.

Duels are as serious as you make them. They can be to lightest touch, or first blood, they can be for a perceived insult or for a bet or something greater. There are longstanding grudges, I know, some people who duel fiercely and often, and what of it? Terrible wounds can be healed quickly by an apothecary or witch woman or a companion with sufficient spark. To the death is both as near and as distant as those capabilities.

Duels are also not limited to class. Marco and others dueled with members of the stage companies almost as often as they dueled with each other. I met Marco's friend Katarina once, after we'd watched her perform from our family box in that theater. She was superficially friendly with me, because of their friendship, I think. I also thought that Marco might be in love with her, but it was hard to tell; I'd seen him look at only a few people with that sort of light in his eyes. I found no way to ask, and now I cannot ask.

Even when I try to send him a message, turning my letter into a bird to seek him out, I get no response. I assume the birds find him, but no birds find me in turn, and I'm left with no news of my brother, self-exiled but also now exiled in earnest.

Chapter Two

Lorenzo of House Valier

My temper has been a foul one for weeks, and though I'm sure plenty would prefer I stayed home from society dinners, I instead attend with a grim determination. I will not lose my standings due to a friend's foolishness, and people don't dare speak of Marco in my presence. We were like brothers, and to lose him so abruptly, and with no explanation or apology, is inexcusable. As mine is not the fault, I will not remain in my house, in my rooms, mourning his loss.

As my parents would also prefer I maintain my public face, they make no comment. My mother was the one who gave me the news, of the departure of Marco of House Galeazzo, from our fair city. There were letters sent about by the theater companies, wroth at losing their property, and they were inclined to accuse Marco of this theft, though so obliquely that I don't think either of his parents have yet taken one of the companies to the street for this perceived insult, which is both a surprise but clearly a calculation. I'm sure that will eventually come to a boil, and I should very much like to witness it. They did dearly love their son. They have said, publicly and private, to by all means send all the guard necessary, but should harm come to their son, there would be more than hell to pay.

House Galeazzo is late tonight, but what is late? There is no point in arriving early. The only people who do that are hosts, as it would be too ridiculous for them to leave their own home in order to arrive once guests have begun to mingle. I don't even look to the door when they arrive, in my cups already, though instead of suppressing my anger, the drink is stoking it. I could use my spark to remain sober, but see no point.

Dora sits to my left, chattering with Tristan about people's clothes, and Luca is on my right, also drinking but far more slowly than I. There are others here and others coming, though Marco's place at the table remains, accidentally or no. I should have a servant remove the chair, and I look around for one when something catches my eye. I'm halfway to my feet when I hear Dora say,

"Oh, it's the sister, of course." For what I saw, and recognized, was one of Marco's coats that he would wear to just such an occasion, and in my furious but wine-dulled state, I thought he had returned without fanfare. I thought to slap him, and then embrace him, and then duel him for the joy and the relief and what he had put us all through, before dragging him to the table to continue where we had left off. "I did wonder if we would see her tonight."

"Why?" I snap, and Dora narrows her eyes at me.

"House Galeazzo has but two children," she says, as though she needs to remind me. She should not have had to, I should have considered the sister, even if Serafina and I have spent little time together. Marco is older than I, and I older than her, just enough to make her utterly disinteresting to me. Further, because she took her dueling lessons out of duty and performed with neither charm nor vigor. She has always been a set piece who sometimes took Marco's attention with her childishness, which meant he took my time worrying about her future. Her spark was less even than his, and he squandered his. He said he saw what it did to his parents, our parents, and while I didn't understand him, I thought there was time for him to change his mind. He was not concerned that he would have to provide for Serafina; he was willing. He was concerned with her *happiness*, and I could not understand why.

She comes cringing in her mother's shadow, her hair dressed in a way that does not match the rest of her attire, even I can tell that at a glance. Her brother's overlarge coat, a shirt that is too plain, her throat bare. I hate the sight of her, I hate that it is she who remains, and takes up air in the room. Why couldn't it have been her? But she would have had to take interest in society beyond her walls in order for it to have been her. And so she is what we are left with.

"Her swords are well-appointed," Luca offers after a few moments of silence. He can sense my mood, but knows not what to do with it.

"It would embarrass her family if they weren't," Armand says. "All of that beautiful steel." His tone has a wandering note to it, and I wonder what he imbibed in before the party, or if it's his spark acting up. Armand does, infrequently, have visions past or present. Sometimes very clear, sometimes interpretable. His tutors have been little help with regards to informing control, and so in an effort to avoid dealing with it, he will sometimes visit an apothecary or witch woman for some tincture or other to, as he has put it, smear away the edges of things. Just as I can sober myself up, I can sober him with my spark, but I haven't yet done so without him asking.

Though control is very important to me, I'm not above also visiting an apothecary or witch woman for the same reason; there are times that there is no merit in being present in the world as it is. Maybe after tonight, I'll pay such a visit, for a tiny oblivion.

Dora gets up and straightens out her swords and her skirts. "You lot are impossible," she says.

"What are you doing?" I ask.

"I'm going to say hello. She isn't a *stranger*." She pauses a moment, perhaps gauging whether to request that I accompany her, and then goes off on her own rather than have to deal with the nuance of my refusal. Tristan shakes her head and sips from her glass.

"It's foolishness, but nothing will come of it," she says to me. "Look at the girl."

"I've seen her, yes."

"How now, Renzo, what has you so snappish?" Ottavia croons, returning to the table from I know not where. She and Sterling disappear regularly on such evenings, for indeterminate amounts of time. Sterling hasn't made it across the room, but rather has become ensnared in conversation with a member of theater management; I don't know, at a glance, the Company. Luca points, and Ottavia clasps her hands in delight. "Oh! Fresh blood."

"She isn't new or interesting," I say.

"Perhaps not, but she seems interesting enough to have you in quite the mood," she teases. "You obviously can't stand the sight of her now, how will you hide that?"

"I cannot imagine that I will have to," I say flatly. "She's already been introduced."

"I suppose," she says, flitting off again to Sterling and threading her arm through theirs. In a break in the conversation, they bend their head to her, look across the room, and then they excuse themselves.

"You know what will come of this," Luca says.

"Teodora is too kind for everybody's good," I growl because yes, I do. I don't need Armand's crooked spark to know.

"I guess you'll have an excuse to duel her then. It has been some time since you and *Teodora* crossed swords." Luca isn't serious, from his smirk. But I could use this an excuse, yes. I'm unlikely to, but any of us have dueled for smaller slights. In my silence, he refills my cup. I think to push it away, pick it up instead.

"Perhaps I will."

Luca laughs. "Perhaps you should. It would be eminently more interesting than your doldrums."

"So sorry that I've been boring you, my dear Luca, how might I make it up to you? Shall we go to your favorite bawdy house after this?" But my barb is not as sharp as it may have been.

"Perhaps we shall. Do you think Armand would accompany us?" Armand looks over at the mention of his name, but he has been focused elsewhere, on the silent play occurring across the room.

Lady Galeazzo receives Dora's greetings with her signature icy grace, inclining her head the proper amount in response to Dora's curtsey, and Lord Galeazzo kisses her hand, all proper for a known friend of their fugitive son, no stranger to their family. She then catches up both of Serafina's hands and after a moment embraces her; Dora's back is to me, but she must be speaking, because Serafina's eyes flick to me over her shoulder in that moment and she frowns fretfully. They part, Dora still holding one of Serafina's hands, and that's when Sterling and Ottavia add themselves to the group.

"She should have left well enough alone," I mutter.

Luca laughs. "She could not, of course. It's all a part of the *game*, dear Renzo. And look, here they come. Best arrange your demeanor now, while you've still got the time to."

"My demeanor needs no arrangement. I will not meet her with a false face."

"Honorable." Luca finishes his cup.

"Keep following this path, Luca, and it is you I will be crossing swords with before long," I say, and then they are upon us, Dora smiling serenely.

"You don't mind, do you, Lorenzo? I simply could not relegate her to such boring company as her parents' table for the evening, when we are right here, and all old friends."

"Hello, Lorenzo," Serafina says cautiously, quietly. Her eyes are searching my face, but I don't know what question she's asking, nor what answer she seeks.

Chapter Three

Serafina of House Galeazzo

Lorenzo is anything but happy to see me, and has no capacity to be welcoming, despite Teodora's velvet force. I'm sure I will be thankful for her once I get my footing, perhaps I'll even be thankful for her tonight, but I in fact wish she'd just ignored my presence and allowed me to dutifully and unobtrusively accompany my parents. But it would have been impossible, and though a childish part of me is inclined to be petulant, I know she has the right of it.

But Lorenzo is staring at me with bare-faced hatred, and his friends who had remained at the table, Armand and Luca, seem either bored or drunk or both. Marco always said that, while distinctly not alike in thoughts, or spark, or demeanor, neither are the firebrand that Lorenzo is. People all band together in little dueling circles like this, and Lorenzo is the clear leader, even if no discussion has ever been had. Maybe it is like how the city has no ruler. Just the Guard, the Houses and the Companies. Whoever holds the power has the power. I have never wanted such a thing.

Teodora's hand is on my arm so lightly as she continues to smile. Ottavia, on the other side of me, is practically thrumming with excitement, while Sterling, who I take to be her paramour, regards her indulgently. We are only all just of a marriageable age, or within a few years of, and from what Allegra and Andante tell me, there is fun to be had before any true vows are made. Marco would never, of course, relate any such tales to me. I can only imagine what went on amongst him and the theater company people, as he gave me no clues. Would Lorenzo know? Perhaps not, if he is as shocked and furious as he seems.

"We have quite the full table already," Lorenzo says, addressing Dora.

"She can have her brother's place," she says lightly, too lightly, as his face darkens further.

"She hasn't earned her brother's place." He looks to me again, dismissively. "And we know what company Marco preferred to keep, that rutting Canted Stage bitch instead of society where he belonged." Ottavia gasps with her whole chest, and I would guess from her name that she's from quite the large family, so our smaller-family styled squabbles entrance her. But I can't dwell on that, can't hesitate, not if I'm to be taking part in this society. Not if I must find my power amongst these people.

I drawn in a slow breath and call up a ghost of a smirk; I've seen enough of them to enable my ready mimicry, my one real talent, spark-driven or otherwise. "Did you love my brother?" I ask slowly, pointedly.

From the look on Dora's face, she was going to duel me tonight in order to get my first out of the way, but as soon as the words pass my lips, that's impossible, Lorenzo already is unbuttoning his coat, his face flushed in anger. Dora steps forward with her hands up peaceably. She dare not touch him, I think wildly, she won't give him the chance to throw her off and worsen the situation.

"Renzo she can't possibly have meant it that way. Look at her, she doesn't even have gloves with her." She's right, in my haste to change and be out to the carriage, I did not retrieve a pair of dueling gloves.

"She can borrow a pair."

"She could apologize," Armand says nonchalantly, and Lorenzo turns his bright eyes to me.

"Do you?"

I have no time at all to weigh my options. If I apologize, honor dictates he must accept. But he's looking for any reason to bare steel, and if not now, than when else might we repeat this same moment, again and again, teetering on the brink of disaster? I take another breath that is far more level than I feel, and raise my chin. "I do not."

Dora lets out a sigh like a laugh. "Oh you'll fit right in, if we all live through the night. Come over here. Luca, get him in order."

"We don't need to go anywhere," I say. I feel as though my resolve will only hold so long as Lorenzo and I are facing each other. If I turn away, I will run away home, and never be able to show my face again. I fumble in my, Marco's, pockets and come up with a handkerchief that I wrap around my right palm, as I've seen done by duelists far more sanguine than I. As I saw Marco's friend Katarina do, once. I think he must have loved her. Why am I thinking of that now? What else could I ever think of. "No amount of delay will change this outcome."

"Look at that courage, Renzo," Armand observes, and Lorenzo throws his shed coat at him with a silent snarl before turning to me as he clears his sword from its sheath.

"Draw your sword." He doesn't even bother with his main gauche, so neither do I, glad to be spared the complication. Once my sword is in my hand, though, he laughs. "I did not realize that I could have kept my coat on," he says, stepping to me.

I have a distant sense from the postures of those around us and still sitting at the table that Lorenzo should have waited for some signs from our seconds, some further formality, before crossing blades. Do I even have a second? Teodora, I suppose.

He doesn't disarm me with his first stroke, a surprise to both of us, and I do not know how he normally fights, but he keeps close, his breath on my cheek, sliding his blade down mine so that the cross guards clatter together, and that is when he gives a twist and there's a sharp pain in my wrist and my sword falls to the floor.

That should be that, I think, relieved, but he's still in motion and I have time to think that we did not set terms either and then he's hooked my ankle from beneath me and I'm flat on my back on the floor next to my sword and his swordpoint is in the hollow of my throat where my heart hammers frantically and even as somebody, Dora but maybe also Luca, says "Lorenzo, enough! That's enough!" he gives a little flick and cuts me just under the chin. Not a true wound; an insult. It doesn't feel like anything immediately, just the passage of steel, and then it itches and then it stings, tears coming unbidden to my eyes as hands help me to my feet, return my sword to me. I keep my face down, blinking away tears, but a rough hand seizes my chin and Lorenzo forces me to face him.

"You do not speak to me in that manner," he says slowly, deliberately, no less furious than before our duel, if it can be called that. "You do not ask me about your brother. You do not talk about your brother. Do you understand?" He squeezes harder for a moment, and I hate the small mewl of pain that comes out of me, but I can't help it.

"Has your honor been satisfied?" I ask, no other words will come to me, my fear rearing up as stupid courage, and he both lets me go and pushes me away in the same motion. I stumble back with the release and catch myself, shrugging away the hands that try to help. He stalks to Armand, retrieving his coat, shrugging back into it as he accepts an offered cup from Luca with still-bloody fingers. "My lord, your hand," I say, a tremble on the edge of my vision but my voice clear, and he cuts his eyes back to me. I unwrap the useless handkerchief from my hand, as though dueling gloves would have prevented my humiliation any more adroitly, and I hold it out to him.

There is a shift, in the immediate group, and in the spectators that I am now aware of. Of course nearby tables took notice, if not the entire hall. I feel ice in my stomach at what my mother might say to me in the carriage home. But I am still looking at Lorenzo, and he is still looking at me, blood running down my chin and now my neck, and my proffered handkerchief. He may have won the duel, but still I have stymied him in an unanticipated manner. To refuse would make him look like a petulant child.

It does nothing to soften his heart towards me, but changes the social balance ever so slightly in my favor, that I can take such a defeat with such immediate grace. I can see no face but his now, in this moment, but I can see him making these calculations. He sets his cup down, deliberately, looks at his hand as if he hadn't noticed my blood there. "You have my thanks," he says. He doesn't just take the handkerchief, he takes my hand and bows elaborately over it. "See how House Galeazzo comports itself," he says to those in immediate earshot, and I flush with embarrassment. He isn't proud of me, or acting out of admiration, it is simply part of the game. But it does prove that I somehow, despite everything, made the proper play.

He cleans his fingers with my handkerchief and casts it crumpled on the table. I accept a cup of wine that Dora presses upon me, allow her to guide me to the contentious empty chair. "He's a brute," she says conversationally. "He should never—"

"It was destined to happen sooner or later. Perhaps now that we've gotten it over with, things can progress more smoothly." I can't bring myself to laugh, and I'm not even certain I have proper footing at the moment, every emotion I might feel frozen away from me somewhere like in a fairy story.

Chapter Four

Lorenzo of House Valier

At the close of this evening, my mother makes it a point to come and retrieve me, and so I must see her to our family carriage on my arm. Often, I neither arrive to a dinner with my parents, nor go home with them either, instead spending the time before and after with Luca or Armand or sometimes Sterling, or a pack of us, at a tavern or a market. Or the theater, when it was Marco. My father does not ride home with us, and I do not ask after his business. If it was something I am privy to, I would be informed.

"I see you reconnected with Serafina tonight," she says in a mild tone, partway through our journey. Though her voice lacks reproach, the reminder renders me a sullen boy. I made sure I was sober before we left the dinner, at least I am not a drunken fool while carrying on this conversation.

"She thinks to take part in society at this late date. I gave her a suitable welcome."

"I do wonder." I look at her, but she's gazing out the carriage window. "I have not yet had to meddle in your affairs."

"Yes, Mother."

"Serafina's brother perhaps did her a disservice by shielding her in the first place."

"Perhaps." She knows Marco well, or did. So many of us thought that we did. I knew he was always dissatisfied with the clawing scrabble for power, and always maybe a little too soft hearted, and that is what led him to have so many friends in so many echelons of the city. It's what led him to leave the city. "She will have to learn swiftly, or she will fail just as fast."

"Which do you consider tonight to be, for her?"

"Pardon?"

"For Serafina. Did she fail tonight or did she learn tonight?" My mother looks at me now, wry amusement on her face. I have, at times, wished that I had the harsher-hewn warhawk that is Lady Galeazzo, as clearly she was wasted on Marco and now on Serafina, but my mother is no less steel-spined, just more pleasant of demeanor, which makes it far easier for her to take one off guard.

"She learned," I say grudgingly.

"Good. I trust you will remember the friendship between our houses, and allow that to inform your future dealings with her."

"Yes, Mother." I should not have been so quick to the swords tonight. I should have anticipated her presence, in the absence of her brother. As Dora said, House Galeazzo had but two children. I could not have anticipated the effect that seeing her would have on me, in Marco's clothes, her eyes so like his. Did you love my brother, she asked. Yes, damn you, damn him, I loved your brother. I loved your brother and it wasn't enough for him. I loved your brother and he loved Katarina, a plague on that bitch and her cousin, both of whom I knew more about than ever I asked, due to Marco's admiration. I saw more plays in the last three years than I had ever before in my entire life, because of him. Because of her.

"I should hope that she spends more time with her dueling master in the future, however, as she did not comport herself well in that regard."

I snort. "I'm sure Dora will have a hand in that as well. You know how fond she is of a project."

"She is indeed." My mother's tone, and face, are of restrained amusement, but something else is there. Other than giving me the news, she has never spoken to me again about Marco. Perhaps she's weighing whether to do so now. Instead, she reaches out and cups my cheek for a moment, something she hasn't done since I was small, before turning to look out the carriage window again.

Chapter Five

Serafina of House Galeazzo

Our carriage ride home is silent, for which I am thankful. At home, my father hands us out, and I hasten inside, thinking only that I want to flee to my rooms and remain there for perhaps the rest of my life. My hand is on the bannister, my boot on the first step, and my mother's cold voice rings out. "To the practice room, Serafina."

"Mother," I start, turning to her in appeal, but there is no swaying her from her intentions, and I swallow my heart and go to the practice room as I am bidden. She walks just too closely behind me, her heels ringing on the floors.

"It has cleary been too long since you've properly drilled," she says in clipped tones. "I shall be letting your fencing master go tomorrow, and take up your tutelage until we find suitable replacement. Where are your gloves?"

"There are some here," I say, hoping that is true. It feels like I can't raise my voice above a whisper. I go to one of the cabinets and pull it open; there are padded practice coats here, and masks, and yes, gloves. I pull on a pair, fumbling, hasty. I do not want to fight my mother. I do not want my mother to tutor me. I want to be anywhere but this room.

"Now. Come and show me a guard. Single sword, like when you faced Lorenzo." Her mouth twists just a bit when she says this last bit. I knew already that my showing was dreadful, this lesson will do nothing to change my skill, and will not change what happened at dinner.

I cross the practice floor to face my mother and draw my sword. She hasn't removed her cloak or coat, and so I don't either. There are mirrors hung along one wall, and there's a perfectly round bloodstain on my shirt front, like a misplaced flower. "I don't—"

"*Any* guard, Serafina. Any single blade guard."

My arms seem to have no strength in them, and I struggle to raise my sword, watching the copies of myself in the mirrors cock their elbows awkwardly, decide that isn't correct, try to adjust, blade wavering in the air, catching the light from the lanterns my mother lit with a gesture when we walked into the space. She gives an impatient huff and I don't even see how she disarms me, my sword clattering to the floor from my nerveless fingers. I look down at it; I cannot look at her.

"Pick it up," she says. I think I did not realize until tonight that my mother hates me. I don't know if she has always hated me, but tonight, at least, she hates me.

My breath hitching, I stoop to pick up my sword. I remember a different guard, low, that one is supposed to be able to readily attack, and guard, from. I arrange my foot forward, and make another attempt. Again, my sword falls to the floor, and this time she slaps me as well, her open, bare hand cracking on my cheek. I fall back a step, and she slaps me again when I raise my hand to my stinging face.

"Again."

"Mother, I—" My throat closes before she can cut me off.

"You will pick up your sword." Somehow, I do. Things do not improve.

I immediately lose any sense of how long it goes on. She slaps me only hard enough to hurt, not to bruise, not to bleed, except once when one of her rings catches my lip. It is either hours, or just enough time for my father to close out the last of the day's affairs, for he's the one who stops her.

"My lady, I should think that's enough for today," he says from a great distance. My mother is a marble statue; I am winded, flushed, too hot and icy cold all at the same time.

"We left her to weed for far too long."

"Maybe so. But that cannot be remedied tonight." The glance he spares me is neither warm nor cold, but dispassionate, as if I am an unfamiliar diversion, which I suppose is true. "To your rooms, daughter," he says, not unkindly

"Yes, my lord," I gasp out, as best as I am able, and stumble away from my mother, remembering to sheath my sword before taking flight from both their presence, lest I earn further immediate corrections.

So unsettled am I that I almost cannot find my rooms. I am not entirely in my head, choking on sobs so that the servants do not hear, my hand pressed to my bloody lip, my still stinging chin. How am I to do this? How? I thought that I would always have my brother, always be able to remain with my books and my daydreams.

When I finally do reach my chambers and fumble through the door, I close it with my back against it and slide to the floor with my face in my knees and cry until I cannot breathe, cannot think. What will become of me? Better that Lorenzo had killed me at dinner to spare everybody the misery of my continued failure. Instead, it will happen again. And again.

I don't know how sleep is able to find me, but it does so when I am still sitting miserably on the floor, still dressed, still tear-and-sweat sodden.

I'm awakened at dawn, or just before, when my maid Agnes tries to open my door and finds me still blocking it. "My lady!" she cries, dismayed. She's older than me, she may even be married, I've never asked. It's difficult, to know how to speak to servants, how much to ask them, when to leave things silent. "Your mother sent me, I am so sorry to disturb you."

"My mother?" I ask numbly, clambering awkwardly to my feet.

"She desires your presence in the practice room within an hour," she says, slipping in and closing the door and then, after a moment, resolutely barring it. "We shall see if you're in any state to do so, within an hour."

"I would not cross my mother in her mood," I say despondently, but I allow her to pull Marco's coat from my shoulders and down my arms, and then guide me to a chair, where she removes my boots.

"Whether or not you have intentionally does not alter your lady mother's perception of being crossed," she says carefully, going to stoke my little stove so she can warm water. Such was my misery last night that I paid it no mind, doing myself no favors. When have I ever done myself any favors. I shiver now in the morning chill.

Agnes washes my hands first and then my face and neck, the water in the basin turning pink. She is frowning but doesn't ask me any questions. My upset is plain, and there is little, or nothing, she can do in order to solve anything for me. All she can do is clean away the blood and see to my small hurts, frowning over my lip but exclaiming quietly over the wound on my chin.

"It's nothing," I say, shrugging her off with unwarranted impatience and getting up to shed my shirt, perhaps permanently stained now. Maybe I should have it washed, and then ply my needle and make the stain an actual flower, to remind me. As if I shall ever forget, for I shall certainly have a scar. But to embellish the shirt so, and then wear it to subsequent social events, is the kind of message my mother would approve of. Reclaiming my public embarrassment and turning it in to a lesson, hopefully one that isn't repeated. But then, that is why my mother would see me so early of a morning. For further lessons. "She said she was letting my fencing master go, has—"

"He has already departed, yes," Agnes says, at my wardrobe and selecting practice clothing. "Do you have any other hurts?" she asks carefully.

"I would say my pride, if I had any remaining to be hurt," I say in an attempt at levity, and am reward with a worried frown instead of a tolerant smile. "Agnes, there's nothing for it. My mother is to be obeyed. This is what my brother kept me from for all these years." We do not talk about Marco in this house, not anymore, and her eyes dart to the door as though his name will summon my wrathful mother. The door, and hall outside, remain undisturbed.

"You'll forgive me for saying," she says, her voice very quiet now, furtive. "But he should have taken you with him."

It's several shocked moments before I'm able to speak, and spare, hot tears fall as she helps me to dress. "Yes, he should have," I finally say, and she gives me a cold, damp handkerchief to prevent my red face from further antagonizing my mother.

Chapter Six

Lorenzo of House Valier

It is noon when Dora comes calling, and I am quietly impressed at her restraint; I expected her to darken my doorstep far earlier. I am in the library when the servant announces her, and she comes bulling in directly after. I give a short laugh at her presumptuousness, that I would agree to see her. But I have never refused her, or she has never accepted a refusal.

"Teodora, what a pleasant surprise," I say, schooling my tone into one of elaborate welcome.

"Don't play games with me, Renzo," she says, unusually snappish but once Dora has decided to protect somebody, this attitude and bearing is to be expected. "How could you?"

"I'm sure I don't know what you mean," I say, sitting in one of the armchairs by the window, gesturing her to the other. We ought to have bowed and curtsied and given actual greetings, but we know each other too well for such public niceties in private.

"You entirely know that I'm speaking of Marco's sister," she says, standing over me with her arms crossed. She's wearing her swords, of course, but she also has a fan in her right hand, and she taps it on her left elbow. It's a fan I haven't seen before, she must have visited the morning markets. "You didn't have to treat Serafina so."

I shrug slightly. "There would have been no benefit to her, had I coddled her."

"Don't act like you were doing her a *favor*." I shrug again. "Your best friend's *sister*."

"You would do well to stop speaking of him, or—" She clatters her fan at me, and I could almost laugh except my anger has already roused.

"Or what? You won't beat me so handily as you did her. Tell me, did you practice on infants that morning, to achieve the properly careless attitude?"

I reget having sat down so soon, but to stand would be giving her ground. "She is no infant, and she had the same opportunities we all did, plus the benefit of her supposedly doting brother. It is hardly my fault that she was so plainly unable to handle herself." I am not in the wrong, even though I knew this was the side Dora would take. It's almost interesting just how upset she is on Serafina's behalf. "Her inexperience will get her killed."

Dora closes her mouth on what she'd been about to say, and cocks her head, and says in a lower, slower voice, "Renzo, I swear to you now, if you—"

"I didn't say I was going to kill her, Dora, you are being entirely too dramatic. But she has entered society now, properly, when before she was a part in name only. There are risks, and not everybody will be so kind as I was. And yes I said kind, I had every opportunity to do worse."

"You're a brute who broke every rule of decency. You observed no rules, you set no terms, you just wanted to hurt her and humiliate her."

"Yes. But not kill her."

Dora stares at me a moment, then huffs out a frustrated breath and drops into the chair across from me. "What am I to do with you?"

"I thought we'd put that behind us," I say mildly, and she scowls.

"If you want to bring up things that we swore we'd never discuss again..." she says, and I hold up a surrendering hand.

"I'm sorry, my lady, forgive me. We've spent so much time together, as friends and otherwise, sometimes I don't take care with your feelings, and simply allow my displeasure to run roughshod. I did not mean to open anything between us that we had already put to bed." She looks mollified as I speak, then colors a little and raps my wrist with her fan when I say the last bit.

"Bedding you was a time of my life that I enjoyed while it lasted, I'd say we both did, but we will not be repeating," she says.

"I am well aware of that, my lady," I say, averting my eyes in false penance. We did, indeed, both enjoy that time of our lives, two summers ago. But we were not so well matched that a marriage could or should come of it, and thus we also amicably ceased those relations. But as she knows how to manipulate the vagaries of my moods, so I know hers, and it does well to remind her.

"Renzo, stop." Any further will be too far, and the playful fan tapping will turn into a more serious baring of steel. Had this discussion happened at dinner last night, we would have had to fight. With no witnesses, we can let the antagonism fade on its own. "We need to accept her. We would have anyway, should...other parties still be here. And now it is expected of us. Who else will she join? Our families are all too entwined, yours and hers especially, for her to have to find her way with casual acquaintances in other circles."

"You aren't incorrect," I say, grudgingly. Last night's dinner went late into the night, as those events are wont to do, and Dora must have been up early in order to have done her marketing this morning and be here now. "Perhaps I was too unprepared last night."

She raises an eyebrow. "Are you making excuses to *me*, rather than to the wounded party?"

"You must admit, that bit with the handkerchief was very clever on her part. Not a full recovery, but admirable." Which is not to say I personally admired the gesture, but it was an unexpected gesture, when I thought she was otherwise going to freeze and remain frozen.

"It was a small brilliance, and I am very proud of her for it. I am going to her house next, in fact, as I expect she spent much of the morning abed to lick her wounds, spiritual and physical."

"If she's able to lick that wound, then her spark has done something very unusual indeed." We laugh together, which I can admit to myself feels nice, in spite of my mood. I have not spent enough time laughing, of late. "You were right to come to me with this, Dora. I will make effort to bear myself better in the future, so that I do not disappoint you quite so deeply again."

"Thank you. It is all that I ask."

"But here, I am failing as a host now. Can I offer you anything? Have you eaten?"

"I have not, but I hope to take Serafina out to the tea shop by the fountain square." There are many fountain squares, but not many with tea shops by them, and I nod. "From there, perhaps to my tailor. We shall see her mood, and mine."

"Your tailor."

"Yes, she needs appropriate things of her own, she simply cannot keep coming out in her brother's clothing, and I imagine cannot yet fight well in her accustomed gowns. We shall work on that as well, in time, but she is already overwhelmed, I don't want to drive her into hiding."

I could happily never see her again, I think. "No, of course not," I say.

She smiles fondly. "You almost sounded like you mean it. You're such a good liar, my dear Renzo, it's so easy to forget with your angelic face."

"Come now, Dora," I say, moving my head away when she reaches to stroke my cheek. "I know how to behave."

"Mmm, and the best way to make me believe that is to behave as though you know how to behave. I will bid you good day, though, and see you at the next dinner. The night after tomorrow, I believe?"

"Yes. Though tomorrow, I will be going to the tavern with Sterling and Ottavia."

"And people will definitely think we are again an item, if I were to accompany you. But thank you, Tristan, Armand, and I are going to the theater, and I will be inviting Serafina along."

I nod shortly, rising with her to see her to the door. "The night after tomorrow, then."

"It was nice to hear you laugh again," she says, clacking her fan again before breezing off. She did not say which theater, but it's of no matter. I will not be visiting a theater any time soon, whether it is the Company of the Canted Stage or not.

Chapter Seven

Serafina of House Galeazzo

When the servant comes to the practice room with Teodora's calling card on a tray, I could have wept with relief. My mother frowns at the interruption, holding her hand out for the tray, and the servant pauses midstep. "It is for your daughter, my lady," they say carefully.

My mother inclines her head, visibly surprise. "Oh indeed?"

"Yes, my lady."

"Proceed, then."

They come to me, and I indelicately arm sweat from my forehead and take the card. This morning's practice has gone on for hours, with my mother calling positions to me that I must snap to without hesitation. This is not the first time I have done such drills, of course, but none of my tutors were so harsh as my mother. When Marco ran me through my paces like this, it was a game, and we laughed often. I have never laughed with my mother.

"Teodora of House Alvise," I read aloud for my mother's benefit, as I'm also thinking to myself how out of fashion my own calling cards are, and how I must have more made. Even as I'm thinking, who do you call upon, silly girl, but the presumption that I have renewed my joining of this society suggests that yes, I will need new calling cards.

A rare look of surprise crosses my mother's face. "She is a good friend to have," she says after an eternal moment, and even then I wait, still catching my breath. "Go and make yourself presentable. I will delay her until then."

"Thank you, Mother," I say, and also nod my thanks to the servant, who smiles sympathetically once my mother has turned her back. How is it I am so pitiable that even our servants feel their lot in life is better than mine? Or is it simply because I have tried always to be kind?

I don't know where my maid has got to, but I strip and give myself a hasty sponge bath, then stand in front of my wardrobe. It is early afternoon, a gown would be reasonable. Split skirts might suffice. I waver, and choose a gown, wear the jewelry that matches it best. My hair takes some powdering and brushing to return to its usual dark sheen, and then I sweep it up in an easy enough style that still looks very elegant. I look at myself in the mirror for a few moments. Thanks to my maid's ministrations, my lip did not swell from my mother's attention last night. The cut from Lorenzo, Dora would already know. I've done well enough, I think, and go to meet her.

They are standing just apart in the room, Dora chatting brightly. From my mother's posture, she invited that they sit and Dora declined, perhaps for this exact reason, to surprise her. "My dear Serafina," she exclaims when she sees me, as though we are the closest of friends, instead of near-strangers who only saw each other for the first time in months last night. She comes and takes my hand with her free one, and kisses me on the cheek, and says, "I was at the morning market and they had these darling fans and I got myself one and I got this one for you," pressing the fan into my hand. "And then I thought, oh, that little tea shop by the fountain square has the best cakes in the afternoon, I should go and see if Serafina has yet roused herself from last night's revels."

"I have," I say, because it is my turn to say something, and I examine the fan. "Thank you so much, it's lovely." It's dark-blue lacquered wood, and when opened, the picture is of fish swimming in a pond.

"I do hope you don't mind my stealing her away from you," Dora says to my mother in a tone of conspirators. "I'll have her home by supper."

"That won't be necessary," my mother says, and I have a momentary sinking heart, that she won't allow me to go. "Serafina may take as much time as she wishes today."

"My thanks, Mother," I say. I look at Dora, and thinking of my hastily-chosen clothing. "Will this be all right?" I ask, gesturing at my gown.

"Of course it is, you're lovely. Do you have sword belts to match?"

"I do, I must change them out, though." I hadn't put on my swords for this, technically allowable but perhaps a slip. But my mother's face doesn't change, doesn't reflect displeasure. "I'm so sorry to have you wait. Unless you'd like to see more of the house?"

"I hoped you'd ask," she says, twinkling a smile. I turn, and she loops arms with me as though we've been friends since girlhood, and leave my mother to her devices. I'm afraid that Dora will say something about her the moment we're out of the room, but she doen't, and I lead her through the halls to my room, as she exclaims over art that we have, and light coming through windows.

In my rooms, I fumble with my different sword belts, and she takes them. "I think this one, with the tooling," she says after a moment. Over her shoulder, I look at my bed that I did not sleep in, but of course Dora would not be able to tell that from my bed having been remade this morning. She does look at me a little more closely after a moment, though. "Oh dear, you do need to put something on your cut, though." Her eyes search my dressing table, for I'm not certain what. Some salve or unguent or other, but of course I have none of those things. "I have some here," she says, pulling a decorative tin from her little bag.

"Thank you," I say. "I'm not used to what supplies I must have on hand."

"You'll learn," she says with a little laugh. "Look up, so I can see." Her touch is light, and the substance feels cold, and smells a bit like violets. "It may not leave a mark; Lorenzo is a brute, but keeps everything clean and polished."

"I hope it does."

Dora laughs. "Oh, we're going to have ever so much fun. Put your swords on and get your purse, and we'll be off." I obey, both because I am accustomed to obeying and also because Dora has an infectious, enthusiastic energy about her that makes it very easy to go along with her, and also feel as though everything will be all right. I remember to put dueling gloves through my belt as well, as she has. This a lesson I am unlikely to forget so soon.

We don't see any other members of the house, family or servant, as we go out the front. It's a lovely day, in fact, mild temperature and sunny. I hadn't known, inside the practice room, which has no windows. Just the mirrors.

"I'm so glad you came," I say once we're in the carriage.

"I'm so glad to hear you say so! While I couldn't imagine you refusing my invitation, as I am so persuasive, I wasn't confident you would be entirely pleased."

"I am, though." I grasp for my words. "I'm pleased that you thought of me, and also I haven't been going out at all, these last few weeks."

"No, you've been in a sort of mourning, if you'll excuse me for saying so."

"How did you—" A foolish question. She was in my silent house not five minutes ago.

"As you said last night. Others loved your brother." She smiles, tinged with sadness. "But we must be able to make our own choices, right? Also, I didn't want to raise this question while we were still in the presence of your lady mother and risk upsetting her, but..." She trails off, meaning for me to lean in anticipatorily, and so I do.

"But what, Teodora?"

"But some of us are going to the theater tonight, and as you aren't expected back at any particular time, I thought to invite you. Not any of the Companies involved with the recent unpleasantness," she hastens to add, seeing my misgivings. "The Rose Garden Company."

"Oh I do love the theater," I say wistfully. She waits, hands hopefully clasped. "And as you say, my lady mother has said I am freed for the day and evening..."

"I hoped you would agree!" she says. "We can visit one of my favorite tailors after the tea shop, not because you aren't wearing a beautiful gown, you are, but because everybody needs some pieces to refresh their wardrobe on occasion. You are entering a new phase of your life and accordingly need some new clothing for it. Mine would be quite too big for you, or I'd just loan you some pieces that would need tailoring anyway."

"I give myself into your care, Dora," I say, feeling almost giddy with the release. Out of the house, away from my mother, and Dora has evidently decided that I am worth time and mentorship. I have much to be thankful for.

"It will all be much easier if you do so, yes," she says, eyeing me critically. "But, to the tea house first, because I'm not certain you've broken your fast today, and then everything after that. Oh, that small wound does bother me so. Lorenzo could have healed it himself, you know. I've already taken him to task this morning, though."

"Have you?" I did not know that Lorenzo could heal with his spark, but I barely know what I can do with mine. "I wish you hadn't."

"You fear him taking his anger out on you further, which I'm certain is his inclination, but I think I may have stymied him at least a little." She looks at my doubtful face and quirks her lips a little. "Renzo isn't so bad, this is just the only real loss he's ever suffered. He'll be used to your presence soon enough, and then won over, I'm certain."

"I wish I had your certainty," I sigh.

"He hates you because you are not your brother. It isn't anything to do with you." She's right, of course; I've known Lorenzo my entire life and before last night, he never directed a cross look or word towards me. But I am not my brother, nor will I ever be, and it is an impossible situation.

"Enough about Lorenzo," I say with a resolution I don't feel, but this has drawn a pall on the day already, and I should like to feel happy for once, I think. "Tell me, what are the best things to get at this teahouse? What is your tailor best at? I have so much catching up to do, and need to look to that, rather than dwelling in what I cannot change."

Dora brightens, and for a little while at least, I'm able to live in the bright moment instead of worrying about the past or the future.

Chapter Eight

Lorenzo of House Valier

This tavern is as it always is; performer just this side of acceptable on the tiny stage, getting less acceptable as the night goes on and the ale flows into and out of his mug. Ottavia chattering about more people than I can ever keep track of, her siblings included. I don't know how she has the time and inclination to get entwined with just so much gossip, and how Sterling stands it either. But they do, seem to be quite enchanted actually, and who am I to get in between a loving couple? They have been coupled off for quite some time now, and I can only assume a wedding announcement will be made within the year. It's about time, for some of us, though once one is married, the temperament of our society's late nights change, from the foot loose carousing and fighting in the streets that we do, to the more strictured meetings in houses, and political back and forth, sending letters like daggers before ever exchanging a cross word out loud.

But, the more we drink, the better the performer sounds, despite us knowing better. As we play cards and get deeper in our cups, we toss him the occasional coin. Apparently he knows Ottavia's oldest sister, and so she breaks off to speak to him for a time between songs, and I watch Sterling watch her cross the room.

"Young love," I say.

"You'll feel it one day," Sterling says with a smile. They're probably the least hotheaded out of all of us, level Sterling to keep flighty Ottavia grounded. Not how Dora and I were sparks, always. Sterling really is above this all already, so far as their demeanor goes, and though their spark and skill aren't entirely masterful, they would do quite well in the next echelon. They have the patience for it.

"Presumably." I finish my cup and consider. The tavern will be calling time soon, and then the options are wandering home or wandering a night market. I'm feeling too restless for home, I think. A pity that Armand stayed in tonight, and Luca; I think I shall be alone once the tavern closes. Maybe that's best for my mood, and hours spent at a night market can feel like minutes. It's no matter.

But Luca does present himself before the night is through, though, dragging a chair crookedly to join the table, picking up my cup and scowling to find it empty.

"Must I do everything?" He asks nobody in particular and goes to the bar, returning with a pitcher, and a cup for himself as well.

"How now, Luca?" I ask, watching him pour all our cups full.

"As you know, I've been seeing that painter," he says with a sigh.

"Indeed." I don't know how they met; either at a gallery or market.

"Well tonight she asked if I might become her patron, so she needn't concern herself with what little other work she's been doing."

I shrug. "Bold perhaps, but not unreasonable."

He drains his cup and pours again. "It's certainly done. But it's not her paintings that I see beauty in."

"Oh, I see " I watch him drink again. "Is that what you told her?"

"Damn it, yes, after much pressing! I can't have my name associated with what she daubs on a canvas, it would be an embarrassment." He sets his ringing cup down, and Ottavia laughs.

"Oh *no*, Luca. You told her exactly that?"

"Once she harried me to distraction, yes I did. It was not my choice! I preferred things how they were "

"I'm sure you did," I say. "Did she pelt you with your belongings as you made your exit to the street?"

"Here is where I was wise, I didn't keep anything there," Luca says, laughing. "Though she did bean me with a paint pot from her window, did it leave a mark?" He turns his head and I can just see a bright yellow streak in his dark hair.

"Like a ray of sunshine," I say, touching the spot and showing him the still-wet paint on my fingers.

"I just love artists," he says, partly lampooning himself and partly still genuine. "So passionate."

"Oh quite," I say dryly and Ottavia laughs.

"That's right, Luca, you saw the violinist before this, and the playwright before that..."

"We don't need to trot out all of my conquests here and now, I don't think," he says dolefully.

"Maybe see somebody of your own class, and you'll have fewer injuries as a result," Sterling says reasonably.

"I'm not entirely sure that is true. Given all of the swords, you see," Luca says, his grin resurfacing. "Fewer surprise attacks, perhaps. Unless it's Renzo I'm facing."

"Dora already took me to task for that, and if you continue down this path, I'll see you in the street," I say.

"I wouldn't dream of it," Luca says. "Though also, perhaps that's somebody who I should call upon..."

"Teodora?" I ask, entirely off guard.

"No, you dullard, Serafina." He watches me warily a moment, perhaps expecting another thread, but I shrug.

"If you'd like. I wish you well with her mother, though."

Luca regards me with raised eyebrows. "I was certain that would get more of a rise out of you."

"I've already said she is of little consequence to me." I dump the dregs of my cup on the table in front of me, trace some patterns in it so that my spark burns away the alcohol. I am no longer deriving pleasure, or even numbness, from it.

"So you say." Luca, and the entire table, is still watching me, but I give them no sign that I am not telling the truth.

"You'll be less excited by her soon enough," I say with a sardonic smile. "She's known but unfamiliar."

"Oh, to be so worldly as Lorenzo," Ottavia says. "We haven't added a new member to our circle in *years*, and this is the interest you can muster?"

"We have known Serafina her entire life," I say. My parents and Serafina's share a friendship that they do not with Ottavia's, or Luca's, though. Perhaps that's the difference.

"Mmm, yes, of course." Ottavia is perhaps about to say more, but she breaks off and looks at Sterling, and then the tavernkeeper rings a bell and calls,

"Time, please!"

"Let's get you home," Sterling says to Ottavia. "We shall see you tomorrow?" they ask me, and Luca.

"Yes, tomorrow night," I say, and Luca nods but looks dubious. He did just drink quite a lot in no time at all. "Yes, Luca."

"Yes," he says, blinking.

"To home, Luca, or to market?" I ask as we file out into the street.

"Market," he says. "I've wasted the evening."

"You could get Serafina some gloves!" Ottavia twitters, as they walk away.

"That isn't a bad idea, actually," Luca mutters. He looks at me. "I've been a fool, could you do your trick for me as well?"

"Of course." It isn't as easy without wine, but I can still do it. It just draws on me some, instead of what I give it to burn. "How's that?"

"Better, thank you. And thank you for allowing me to be a fool instead of rising to the bait."

"We are friends who understand each other," I say. We walk towards the night market, cobbles of the street damp even though it has not rained. Luca makes us stop at one of the fountains, fumbling in his pockets for a coin.

"This one is my favorite," he says. I'm not certain I've ever paid it much mind; though I think it is the way of things that we all have our favorite fountains. Mine is near the Company of the Canted Stage, which nearly guarantees I will not see it soon. This one has rose bushes planted around it, also dewey in the evening air, the leaves shimmering under the city's lamplight.

"It is pretty enough," I say.

"There's the real Renzo, I knew you weren't so hard hearted as you've been behaving," Luca says. I look at him, frowning. "We all feel Marco's leaving as a betrayal," he says carefully. "But maybe do keep in mind that the rest of us have not betrayed you, and hold your happiness as important."

I don't answer at first; I breathe in the damp evening air, the perfume of roses. I listen to the happy shushed babbling of the fountain. "Thank you, my friend," I say, clapping him on the shoulder. "I would do well to bear that in mind."

Chapter Nine

Serafina of House Galeazzo

Dora keeps me out later than I have ever been, even when Marco has chaperoned me. After the tea house, and then the tailor, who fits me with this season's split skirts and shirts that both lace and button, and gold-braid-edged capes, we go to the theater, and then after the theater to a tiny wine bar, and then after that we go to a pantomime at a different theater, and by the end of it, I am quite exhausted, and have no idea of the hour. We see so many people, both that I know and that are strangers to me, and it is all just a blur. I make conversation, somehow, and hope I do not make a fool of myself, but I remember none of it.

Teodora handles each situation masterfully, though I am acutely aware of my inexperience, and of her protectiveness. It's different from Marco's protectiveness; Dora is showing me so much I cannot possibly keep track of it all, but deliberately, calculatedly overwhelming me, I assume so that I am not such a wide-eyed lamb at everything that confronts me.

I try to fret about the cost of things, and she challenges me even on that. "You hardly spend money ever," she says. "No, don't contradict, I know you don't. And if it is a problem, then all of this will be a gift, which is too much for you to accept. And so you are stuck."

"You know every argument before I can even make it," I say, still just slightly tipsy from the wine.

"I do, so keep that in mind. Now tomorrow, or maybe the day after, I think that would be better since there is a dinner tomorrow night, I'll be by to examine your shoes and boots, and we will practice fighting."

"I can do nothing but accept," I say, helplessly, and she smiles.

"You *are* a fast learner." Then she kisses me, and I think it's a joke, or a mistake, and startle, and pull back

"Dora…"

"Fina, what's the matter?" She asks softly. No mistake.

"I never—"

"Shh," she says, and kisses me again, soft and firm at once. She tastes sweet, like candied rose petals, violets, and I don't know what to do. Do I do anything? Where are my hands? She pulls back and gives me a stern look. "You're thinking too much."

"I'm sorry," I say, breathless though we're still just sitting in her carriage, moving slowly through the city.

"It's to be expected, I suppose," she says, reaching out and brushing my hair back, stroking my cheek. "You don't have to do anything that you don't want to do."

I can't help but laugh, sudden and hurt-edged. "That is hardly the case," I say, despairing, in answer to her confusion.

"You're just starting out, and you will gain in strength very soon I'm sure," she says, misunderstanding or ignoring the ever-present specter of my mother and her anger, her driving expectations.

"As you say."

She smiles again. "There, that's much better." She reaches across me and opens the carriage door. I hadn't noticed us stopping. "Now to bed with you, it's nearly dawn. I shall see you at dinner tonight, and hopefully it will go far better than the last."

"Hopefully," I repeat, climbing out of the carriage with care. I am not normally tipsy, I don't quite know how to handle myself. The house gate opens at my touch, and the front door, the doorman blinking at me in surprise but without comment.

I expect my mother to appear from nowhere, towering, furious, but the house is silent. I feel relieved, and with the success of the day, and Dora's kiss. Dora is, indeed, a good friend to have. I should not assume she will be more, a kiss is not necessarily a significant gesture. Much as I'd like to think that I am significant for somebody, but perhaps not so quickly.

And I'd been so content, to stay in my house and wait for the world to come to me, or not. I was safe, it was quiet. Except for my mother. But the city has so much. The city is so full of entertainments and diversions, even more than Marco ever took me to. There is even a perfumier who makes personal scents, but they were not in when we tried to call, and Dora left our cards and promised to bring me another day.

I take off my shoes and creep carefully through the halls in my stocking feet, though also I know that if my mother wants to know that I am home, she will know that I am home. I make it to my room uninterrupted, sighing as I close the door behind me. All is as I left it, or slightly more orderly, as Agnes visited again before retiring for the night. I undress and pull on a nightgown, humming to myself as I brush out my hair. This is the happiest I've felt since Marco left, perhaps even before. He was so distracted, before he left, and would not answer my concerns about his well-being.

I slide between the sheets and fall asleep almost immediately, barely having the time to think that yes, that is dawn outside of my window and think, oh, I should have closed the curtains.

I am awakened by my mother's voice, just outside my door, speaking to my maid. I am confused, and grasp for meaning, and realize that my mother doesn't sound angry or impatient. It has been so long since I have heard my mother have a tone other than anger or impatience, I almost thought that I was dreaming. But then she knocks on my door, actually knocks. And waits.

"Come in," I say, sitting up and pushing my hair back from my face. It's late morning, from the light on the floor.

"Did you enjoy your time out with Teodora?" my mother asks from the doorway. She regards me with something like curiosity. Perhaps, due to Dora's interest, she's realized that I am somebody who might make decisions and take her own actions, in addition to being a pawn of our house in the city's political games.

"Yes, I did, thank you! And she said that tomorrow she was going to come and practice fight with me, but today she wanted me to save my strength for tonight's dinner."

My mother nods. "Very well."

She doesn't *leave* though, and I do not know what she wants. "I'm sorry, Mother," I say on impulse, for my existence is so often one of apology.

"You will not embarrass us like that again," she says, though not sharply. Inevitably. I feel an entirely warranted chill, and force myself to push my blankets back and get out of bed.

"Yes, Mother. I-I want to make you proud." Tears start in my eyes, and I hate that after everything, I crave her approval so strongly. It's because craving her love is to wish the impossible. I know that.

"See about making it happen, then," she says, and then withdraws. I blink my tears away and take a shaky breath. That could have been so much worse. Other times, that has been so much worse.

My maid gives me a few moments, and then comes in cautiously. "Did you enjoy your evening, my lady?" she asks.

I muster a smile. There are some things my mother cannot take from me. "I did, thank you. And I have new clothes coming, so we should go through my old."

Chapter Ten

Lorenzo of House Valier

As I make my way to the assigned table at dinner, I pause here and there to greet friends and rivals alike, shaking hands and kissing cheeks. Do I have hopes for tonight's gathering? What hopes might I have, I wonder. But the night is young and so full of possibility. I have taken a page from Armand's book, and left the house in advance of my parents, visiting an apothecary for an additional diversion that I have taken on the host's doorstep.

"Will we see another performance tonight, Renzo?" a girl in another dueling circle asks me. Venette, of House Massimo. I look at her coolly and she smiles coyly, unsnapping her fan. "You are masterful with the sword, what can I say?"

"I shall take the compliment then, my lady," I say, bowing. "If you're lucky, perhaps you will indeed see me bare steel again." She takes my meaning, one or all, and inclines her head, still fanning herself slowly.

Tristan falls into step with me, placing her hand in my elbow. "Did you bring a handkerchief?" she asks archly.

"Are you in need of one?" I ask, and she laughs.

"I was just thinking what an interesting gesture it would be if you'd gotten the little Galeazzo bitch a new one."

"Oh, I see." It would have, actually; far too interesting, in fact. "Why is everybody so obsessed with her?"

A slight surprised intake of breath, and then she smiles again. "Because she's *new*, but not new. I don't know that anybody else has done what she's done, been introduced and then stayed home for what, three years? While allowing her brother to take the public attention." A quick look up at me when she says 'brother' but I keep my expression impassive. "And now here she is again. Of *course* everybody is obsessed with her, Renzo, and you're the odd one out for claiming not to be."

"Claiming," I repeat.

"Well you can't expect us to think you're serious," she says, and then Ottavia swoops in out of nowhere and plucks her off of my arm, and they giggle off to a different area of the house. There are so many alcoves and powder rooms and nooks in nearly every house, it's a wonder any of us make it back to the table at all at any of these gatherings.

I sit at the table and pour my first cup of wine. Yes I come to nearly all of these social gatherings, no I do not wish to flit around from table to table for the entire time. Armand saunters in before long, looking fairly clearheaded. One of his good days, then. Perhaps we have traded our fortunes for the evening. I pour a cup for him, hold it out when he arrives. "Good evening."

"Is it a good evening, Renzo? Are you in good spirits?" He scrutinizes me, then takes the cup, and his seat.

"Should I not be? Shall I second guess the entire evening?"

"Not if nothing's happened yet," he says, and I wonder if he knows how cryptic he is.

"And are you well, Armand?"

"I am, Renzo." He smiles, and then looks to the door. "Oh, the evening's entertainment, perhaps."

I follow his gaze, and have time to frown, as the door is still empty, and then the Lord of House Galeazzo walks through with his lady on his arm. Serafina follows behind, her demeanor much changed from two nights ago. Her posture is more befitting of her house, and she looks around with bright interest. She's wearing proper clothing this time as well, not her brother's slightly-oversized castoffs. Venette waylays her as well, and I watch them laugh together, Serafina giving no outward sign of discomfort, holding a fan the way I'd seen Dora do just yesterday. Interesting that a single dinner at the grown ups table and a single day with Dora could effect such change. *How* could it effect such change? Perhaps her mother dosed her with something.

I don't expect Luca to drop in the chair next to me but, buffered by my apothecary's dose, I only part turn my head to him. "Coming in the back way?"

"I didn't want to ruin my surprise," he says, setting a paperboard parcel on the table.

"You must be joking." I smirk, then think of the way Serafina smirked the other night, just briefly. That damnable girl.

"I am not."

"Well. Do as you will." I finish my wine, pour another cup, but I pause before drinking more. Perhaps I shouldn't drink too much, after what I took. The lights are softening already, to my eyes. I shrug to a question no other asked of me and raise the cup to my lips.

Dora arrives, causing the little stir that she always does, and Serafina takes that opportunity to disentangle herself. I ignore Venette's pointed look in my direction, rather than try and interpret it. She is of no consequence to me.

"Teodora is coddling her so," Tristan observes through a fixed smile.

"She's a far more interesting project than a stray kitten, I imagine," I say, rather than defend Dora, whose judgment I do trust. She has a big heart but a level head, and coddling would not serve Serafina well, she knows that. If Serafina is to be part of our circle, she must rise to the task.

"Is she, though?" Tristan asks.

"Jealousy doesn't become you, Tristan," Armand observes, and she shoots him a glare.

"I am hardly—"

"Mmm, just so." Armand waves a hand. "It reflects well on us to take in the girl, it would have been an embarrassment if we did not. This bickering bores me."

"We've already taken her in," I say. Two nights ago, the night Serafina first came out again, I might have tried to fight Armand for this perceived slight. Tonight, my heart and my ego have more of a cushion around them, and I am able to be far more magnanimous. "And see Luca, with a gift."

"We shall hope she does not take it as insult," Luca says, smiling but watchful.

I laugh, perhaps a bit too loudly. "She's less thorny than I, dear friend, I'm sure she will be absolutely smitten. Perhaps once the bloom is off that rose, we'll all be a lot more comfortable with one another."

"Renzo, those are not my intentions," Luca says carefully.

"It it no matter to me if they are." I smile to show him how unbothered I am, and clink my cup against his. I should think it was clear already that I feel no protective instinct towards Serafina, nor instinct beyond making sure that she is not a detriment, and Dora is handling that particular situation. Otherwise, I would have nothing to do with her.

"And here they are," Tristan says, in her own thorny tone, as the little group makes its way to the table at last.

"Good evening, everybody," Serafina says with a desperate sweetness, emboldened by Dora's hand on her elbow.

Luca and Armand both stand to greet her; I remain seated, but pour her a cup. There, my show of goodwill. Dora bestows the smallest of smiles upon me, taking my measure at a glance.

"And how is Renzo this evening?" she asks, arranging herself in the seat on my other side and resting her fan on my wrist. "Festive? Jovial?"

"Benevolent," I say, laughing.

"I am happy to hear it," she says, giving me the very slightest of taps before removing the fan and leaning over to hear a question from Ottavia. I catch a glimpse of Lady Galeazzo, marking Serafina with her eyes as she engages in conversation at her table across the room. She sees me notice her, and arches her lips in a cold smile, and I tip my cup to her just a bit, to which she nods and turns her attention elsewhere.

Serafina has watched this exchange anxiously, but makes pretense otherwise when it seems my attention has returned to our table, taking an experimental sip of her wine. She can hardly be unaccustomed to it, but perhaps it isn't her favored vintage.

"I must excuse myself a moment," she says presently, slipping out of her seat and away. Luca allows a few moments to pass and then goes as well, taking his paperboard box with him and pointedly ignoring my look.

"What's that then?" Dora asks, interested but not on her wares.

I shrug, and Armand answers. "He bought her gloves, I think."

"Scandalous," Dora says with a little laugh. "People will talk."

"At least that would be *interesting*," Tristan says.

Chapter Eleven

Serafina of House Galeazzo

I am feeling emboldened by Dora's support when we arrive at the dinner, but it is a hard mood for me to maintain under the watchful eye of my mother, sitting at a table with Lorenzo. The others are all right, so far; interested, maybe a little bit impersonal. We have known each other for so long, but I was always Marco's younger sister. I was never a part of their group, properly, because I didn't need to be.

But then I see Lorenzo raise his cup to my mother, and I am confused, and even more unsure of myself. I cannot think if I've ever seen them speak to each other. I cannot think what he might mean by it, other than she has likely instructed him to be as harsh towards me as possible, all in the name of ensuring that I learn and learn quickly. That I never embarrass my house like that again.

I sip my wine, try to compose myself. They would not have conspired against me, that is ridiculous, if only because my mother is unlikely to have sought out any communication with Lorenzo. Though if she was to House Valier for an afternoon tea, with the lady there, who is her dear friend...

My thoughts continue to spiral and eventually, or perhaps very soon, I push my chair back and make some excuse that I forget as soon as I've said it. Crossing the room takes an eternity, and even though I very carefully do not look toward my mother's table, I can feel her burning gaze on me the entire time until I am away down a dim hallway, trying to find a place to catch my breath and regain my composure. I can feel her disappointment; I should have been made of sterner stuff, and that I am not is confounding even to me. I would rather be anywhere, right now, than this party. It is no wonder that Marco was so often at some theater or other, and making friends amongst the Companies; this is suffocating. But I must make conversation, and dance if asked, and duel if necessary, and at some indeterminate point, my spark will burn brighter, and I will advance in standing. By what mechanism our individual sparks do this, nobody has ever been able to explain to me. It is not because of the city; people in other cities also have sparks or do not, partake in this echelon of society or do not, or are born in the lower classes.

But what do I think would have happened, had Marco stayed and I not had to truly re-enter the dueling society? Who would have found me marriageable? Or might I have been permitted to be a spinster and just hide in his shadow for my whole life, staying in his house even after he married, somehow evading my mother's ire? Almost certainly not, that latter notion.

I find a quiet side room that feels as though it is outdoors but isn't, quite. The ceiling is open and there is a tiny fountain on a wide marble table in the center, night-blooming flowers surrounding it. I sit gratefully on one of the very inviting benches, and listen to the water, catching my breath. I hadn't realized I was so near to tears, and I carefully wipe my eyes, not wanting to redden my face. It is impossible to continue like this. I must do better than this.

The scuff of a boot nearby has me on my feet immediately. It is possible I shouldn't be in this part of the house and the hosts are here to gently and humiliatingly inform me that I am intruding. It is possible that somebody followed me to challenge me and advance their own standing. Witnesses don't matter; the city keeps the score.

It's Luca who comes around the corner, though, and I am perplexed but inclined to be relieved. He has never been cruel to me, that I can remember. I'm not certain that we've exchanged many words at all. When he sees me standing, he stops. "I'm sorry to intrude," he says. He has a white paperboard box in his hands.

"You aren't," I say. "I just needed a moment, I'm woefully disused to these gatherings and…"

"You don't need to make excuses," he says. "So often it's a big to-do and then nothing happens the entire evening. A whole lot of bored tension, and silly fights all over the place because of it, but nothing of substance. You'll be bored of it soon, along with the rest of us."

"I do hope so." I sit down again on the bench. "I forget how everybody's houses have all of these twists and turns. Nooks and crannies for conversations and conspiring. Mine as well, of course." One of these torturous nights upcoming, my own home will be the host, but I cannot keep them straight in my head.

"They do, yes," he agrees. "It makes you wonder how the underclasses live, and if it's simpler. Perhaps just less dusty." I'm meant to laugh, I think, and I manage it. He sits on the bench also, not too close, and sets the box between us. "I hope this isn't too forward of me," he says. "To have brought you a gift."

"What is it?" I ask, looking down at the box. The light in here has a reddish cast to it, which could feel lurid but instead is somewhat calming. I couldn't say where the light is coming from.

"You didn't have gloves the other night, and," he seems somewhat abashed, which is interesting. I am not one to have that effect on men. "Well I thought it might be a nice welcoming gesture, if I got you a pair."

He leaves a pause between us now, and I glance up at his face; he is partly turned away from me, to the fountain, but tilts his head just enough to look at me as well. "It is a nice welcoming gesture," I say carefully. I don't want to rebuff him, though I am still confused. I reach between us and remove the lid from the box. They are largely unadorned, though obviously well made, and I pick them up to admire the soft leather, the tiny stitching. The buttons at the cuffs, carved like roses. "Oh, they're lovely," I say, forgetting myself. "You have my thanks, Luca."

"I'm very relieved you like them, I didn't ask anybody's advice."

"Certainly Teodora would have given it, she's a master of this realm" I say with a little laugh. I hesitate, and then draw them on. "They are an exact fit! How did you know?"

"I have an eye for these things," he says. "Or my spark does, which amounts to the same thing."

"That must be very useful," I say. "It must allow you to avoid tiresome fittings."

He laughs, softy. "It does. And it lets me know where my blade is best placed. Or my hands." He reaches out and takes my hands as he talks, gently; he isn't trapping me, but he doesn't fumble even in this low light. Intrigued, I don't pull away, even as he leans in closer, just enough. "I always know where I am, and where the people around me are," he says, breath on my cheek, and then he kisses me, also gently, the taste of wine on both our lips. Another kiss, in as many days. I don't know what to do and when I don't pull away, or otherwise flee, he lets go of one of my hands and cups my cheek, lightly, and then strokes his fingers down my neck to my collarbone. Is this a joke? Will others soon burst in to ridicule me, that I'd think I could dally with Luca? I don't hear anybody. I don't know how people breathe while they're kissing and try to just do it through my nose, unobtrusively, and his fingers, dip lower, brushing my collar bone, the top edge of my bodice, then further. Nobody's ever touched me like this and I'm melting into him, hot all over, and he puts his other arm around me as we lean in together.

Then he breaks the kiss and sits up again, steadying me. "Why are you stopping?" I murmur, confused. He looks pained.

"You deserve better than this," he says, and I hear people in the hall, talking, then passing us by. "You haven't..."

"No, I haven't," I say, defiant. "What if I want to? What if I don't want you to stop?"

"I'm sorry, Serafina, this wasn't my plan. And I don't want to rush you into anything." He takes my hands again as he's talking, taking the gloves off, smoothing them, then putting them into my hands, closing his hands around mine. "And I don't want to rush myself into anything. I had not planned this. I don't want to take advantage of—"

"You *aren't*," I say, and then stop myself. I sound petulant. "I want you to," I say, lower, more urgently. I haven't given much thought to my virginity, other than that depending on one's match, it might be considered valuable. Not here, though. Marco wouldn't talk to me about it, but I know everybody has their dalliances, and I don't know why I'm seizing up on this now, but maybe it will be a way for me to take control. Be unburdened. Steer my own vessel. "Please continue," I say, in a spark-driven tone much like my mother's most imperious one, as though the mood had not already departed and I could *order* him to respectfully deflower me.

He isn't compelled, though he does have a bemused smile on his face, and he kisses me some more, but without his hands wandering this time.

I'm thinking too much about it, and trying to stay out of my own way, trying not to knock my teeth against his, not sure what my tongue should do, but he's gentle, and patient, and then he strokes my cheek again and says "Don't look like that, it's all right. Though you should have Dora take you to an apothecary, so that you can take what the girls take."

"This isn't fair."

"No, but it is right," he says. "Tomorrow night, I promise. You deserve a room with a door, at least. A bed."

"What if I find somebody else?" I ask, petulant, pouting. Seeking a pressure point, where he will do what I want, and relieve me of this sudden concern.

He grimaces and says, "If you must." More footsteps in the hall, illustrating his point once again, and this time, I am pulled back to myself, and realize what a brat I'm being. A child, who should not make such demands, he is right to refuse me, even as he started this.

"Tomorrow," I say, a question, a plea, a demand, and then I get up from the bench and all but flee the room. I can't stay here, I can't stand it tonight, even without Luca and his gift and his kisses that surprised us both. Tomorrow, of course there's another dinner tomorrow. The only way I know out is back through the room where everybody is sitting and so I go that way, but I don't return to the table. I don't look at my mother. I just keep my head up and walk briskly for the exit, tucking my new dueling gloves in my pocket. It wouldn't do to drop one and spoil the gift.

I still feel so warm, I'm hot all over, and I walk down the steps past the carriages that are waiting for their families to return, and out into the square in front of the house and straight into the fountain there. Steam rises up around me, and I realize that this feeling is more than just from kissing, it's my spark, my spark is burning brighter, growing. Is this advancement? I couldn't say what I've done to warrant it.

"Fina, come out of there," Teodora says from behind me, laughing. She thinks that I'm tipsy or drunk, I think. Maybe I should allow her to think that.

"I'm going to walk home," I say, floundering back to her, my skirts sodden, dragging. I'd walked out there so easily. I can feel how cold the water is now, feel coins and charms and trinkets shifting beneath my feet. My fingertips tingle, and the top of my head still feels flushed.

"You just got here, why are you walking home?"

"I don't want to stay." Not a lie, but not the entire truth, and she peers into my face as she helps me out of the fountain.

"Then you don't have to stay. I'll walk with you, but let me arrange my carriage back, wait here. Do not move."

I *do* feel somewhat drunk, I think, though rarely have I been so. I feel giddy with this feeling that my power has expanded, even though I could not say what my limits were to begin with, other than myself. I feel greater possibilities, prospects. I feel free of my mother's shackles.

Chapter Twelve

Lorenzo of House Valier

Luca returns to the table not long after Serafina makes her hasty exit, Dora chasing after her. He loosens his collar and drains the wine he'd left.

"Oh, already?" I ask mildly, pouring him a new cup.

"No, actually," he says, drinking again. "But on my honor, I will not disclose further."

"That's unusual, Luca, you're usually quite good about disclosures," Tristan says in a silken tone, and he smirks at her.

"If I recall, it is you who let the cat out of the bag midwinter. In...both senses of the word."

She gives a theatric gasp and we all laugh. "I'm certain Dora will tell me," she says when we've recovered.

"I'm certain she won't," I say, watching Lady Galeazzo across the room. She noted her daughter's exit, of course, and very, very occasionally glances to our table. I'm certain she is absolutely livid, but it would do more damage should she excuse herself now, and she has her own echelon to concern herself with. "Teodora's discretion is well known."

"Hmm, yes, but it's also so rare for this group to present a united front," Tristan says thoughtfully, eyeing me. "Is there a reason you're protecting her now, Renzo?"

I make a dismissive gesture. "Maybe you're thinking too hard, Tristan. You'll give yourself a headache."

"We all know that—"

"That I can embarrass you just as easily as I embarrassed her the other night. I'm giving you the courtesy of a warning." I sharpen my tone but not my posture. For a moment, I think maybe she will bare steel after all, but the nearby noise of a sword clearing its sheathe is not one of Tristan's pretty toys, or even at our table. A different duel has broken out, from a different argument, outside our circle.

Coats have already been flung to seconds or at chairs, and somebody is hastily righting a candlestick that was overturned in the scuffle, as two men circle each other, puffed up like cockerels. Do we always look so foolish when we duel in anger, I wonder. Perhaps it's just a price we pay.

I recognize one of them, Baltasar, if only because I recall he and Armand shared a tutor two summers ago. The other is taller, slower, angrier, and after a moment his name comes to me as well, Patricio. They aren't in the same circle, and while I do not know what Baltasar did to start this fight, my guess is that Patricio will finish it. I hope he does so quickly; I tire of the noise.

"What is it about?" I ask Sterling and Ottavia , who are watching with a calculating eye.

"Patricio's sister," Ottavia says.

"Why isn't she fighting then?" Having somebody fight for you is both acceptable and also unusual.

She blinks at me. "She's a child, Renzo." There are many implications there, none of them good.

"I don't see why they have to settle this here and now, and not in the street. Some of us are trying to have a nice evening," Tristan says.

"Oh? Who is that then?" I ask, and she huffs a sigh.

"I've half a mind to cross swords with *you* tonight, Renzo, you keep baiting me."

"We could, if you'd like," I say. "Perhaps after they've done."

"Perhaps. *Somebody* should get something out of the evening after all, and why not us?"

Luca ignores her barbs and I laugh. "Why Tristan, I didn't know you fancied a pairing."

"It doesn't have to mean anything, Renzo," she scoffs, snapping open her fan. Those come in and out of style so swiftly, I can't be bothered to keep track of when the girls like them or not.

"I didn't say it did."

"Then we understand each other." Patricio lands a solid blow, Baltasar crying out and dropping his sword, his right shoulder blooming red. Somebody from the household is already on hand to deal with it, though, and both seconds are drawing Patricio off to speak with him. He mops his face with a handkerchief, still scowling, but he nods, wipes off his sword, and sheathes it. "A child, you said?" I ask, turning to Ottavia.

"Fifteen and precocious, you remember what it was like. But it's still shameful of Baltasar to have not controlled himself." We're none of us older than twenty five, but also none younger than eighteen, even counting Serafina.

"And you knew all this before tonight?"

She shrugs. "Before Patricio, it would seem. It's been a somewhat open scandal."

"How sordid."

Tristan moves chairs to sit next to me, taking Dora's place. "Did you want to have a go or not?"

"Let them clean the blood off the floor at least," I say. "Or would we prefer to go out front?"

She folds her fan, lines it up on the table in front of her. "Oh that's a consideration. Which footing do you prefer?"

"It's no matter to me, but the wine is in here."

"So it is." She looks into my face, really looks, and a smile spreads across her face. "Though I'd say you've imbibed further this evening."

"And what if I have."

"It's no matter to me," she says, winking.

"Everybody's just so agreeable," Sterling says. "It's quite refreshing."

"Isn't it though?" Ottavia all but twitters, clearly very pleased. "Do we think Dora will be returning?"

"I'd guess she will," I say. "But that remains to be seen."

"What *was* that all about, Luca?" Ottavia leans around Sterling to look at him.

"Unlike some, I do have discretion," he says, clearing his throat.

"It is a rare quality," I say. The other table has been righted, and Baltasar has been removed, protesting, though not loudly. "Well then, who is your second? Luca, will you be mine?"

"Of course, Renzo."

"Oh I suppose I shall," Ottavia says.

"Thank you."

We stand, and I shed my coat. Tristan has some lacey wrap on over her dress that she takes the time to unwind. It didn't seem to restrict her movements much, but it does seem fragile, she probably doesn't want it to snag.

"One blade or two?" she asks with a sly smile.

"You know why I did that, the other night," I say, neither abashed nor chagrined. I clear both my blades.

"Of course I do. But variation can be diverting." Our slow deliberations haven't drawn much attention. Certainly not what Patricio and Baltasar did. But there are those at surrounding tables who are observing us intently, and isn't this part of the aim of these gatherings? Though the question here isn't whether my swordsmanship is better than Tristan's, which it is, or if her spark can make her quicker than me, which it can. It's a much more nebulous thing that we are grasping for, night after night. "I don't fancy any blood tonight, might we be satisfied with light touches? Say three?"

"What a silly girl you are," I say, and she sharpens her smile. "Yes, I will agree to that and abide by it." Ottavia and Luca nod, very serious, and I think of the last duel I fought with my proper second, Marco, before he left. I can't remember now, the perceived slight that the girl outside our circle challenged me for, and it doesn't matter. She also wanted lightest touch, three, and it was all so ridiculous that I wasn't even sporting about it. I toyed with her, tripped her up, made her foolish and frustrated; the final touch was a swat across her rear with the flat of my blade, and I half thought that she would demand we fight again, for real. Donnalee of house Verde, and a better man than I would apologize. I haven't.

With Tristan, though, it is as fine a way to pass the time as any. She surprises me by getting in the first touch, but I think I remember her having mentioned a new tutor. Not Serafina's recently departed one, I wouldn't think. I let her see my surprise, and she smiles, and then I feint, trap her blades when she responds, and kiss her.

"That isn't a touch," she says when we part again.

"Is it not?" I look to Ottavia who laughs, and Luca who shakes his head.

"Perhaps you should visit the apothecary more often, Renzo," Armand says, not properly raising his voice, but it carries all the same. "It has put you in quite the mood."

"Perhaps I shall," I say, and then parry Tristan's next advance, twist her main gauche to the floor, and touch her ankle with my sword rather than tripping her. She notes the touch, but I don't relent, advancing on her now, touching her left wrist and then tapping the side of her neck, no heavier than a whisper. "Did all of those count?" We're standing very close, breathing hard with the sudden, if brief, exertion. No, I do not think I will bed Tristan tonight.

"They did," she says, and I break away, give a short bow.

"Then your honor and mine are satisfied."

She curtsies at me in return, and there's a light scatter of applause from our spectators.

"Neatly done," Sterling says. "A pleasure to watch."

"Oh, have I missed everything?" Dora asks, appearing at my elbow.

"Only two fights," I say. "The night is young."

Chapter Thirteen

Serafina of House Galeazzo

I think my mother is sure to be furious with me for leaving the event early. So certain, in fact, that while all I wish to do is crawl into bed and wait for tomorrow, I instead change into practice clothes and do drills myself, and when my parents return from the evening, that's where she finds me

My flush of expanded spark has faded by then, and I am relieved; I was more than a little mortified to consider she might demand explanation, and I simply did not want to render it. But we regard each other across the practice space and then she nods and withdraws. This is what she expects, then. I wonder if she was trying to force my advancement, with the drills and training. Get me to an acceptable level through sheer focus and force of will. Of course, it is not predictable in that manner, as my mother well knows. As we all well know. And I can understand some of her frustration, anger, and not being able to change the unchangeable, even as it is unknowable. I cannot forgive her that anger, though. I can never forgive her treatment of me. I miss Marco as well, and mourn his loss though he is almost certainly still living. But my mother's mourning, and rage, fill up every space that she enters.

I don't remember much of my walk home with Dora last night. I suppose there isn't much to remember, other than my heat, my exhilaration, the feel of the night air on my skin. I didn't speak much, and neither did she, but I was glad of the company. I have never walked entirely across the city at night before; a time or two with Marco, during the day, but in the daylight there are other diversions. People from the companies hawking shows, merchants hawking wares, street performers, pickpockets, knife sharpeners, shoe shiners.

The city gets very quiet at night, especially as curfew approaches for the other classes, and the sharp sound of our heels on the streets echoed off the surrounding buildings, most of the windows dark, but the occasional one lit. I wonder, sometimes, at the people who live in the rowhouses, the hotels, the apartments that are above bakeries and tucked beside shops. What are their lives like, what are their struggles? Indentures and survival, some of them. That it was drove Katarina and her cousin.

Teodora's carriage waited for her at my house's gate, and before she left me, she dropped a kiss on my cheek and pressed a small vial in my hand. "That's almost used up, but before you let anybody bed you, three drops on your tongue and there will be no child."

"Thank you," I say, flushing again, but with embarrassment this time, not my spark catching.

"We must all watch out for each other," she says.

When I finally allow myself to retire for the night, I find myself wondering about my mother, and Lady Valier, when they were girls and entering this society. Not all of their dueling circle stayed in this city, but married and moved to other cities, to other high-ceilinged gated mansions in other cities, different from this one and yet very much the same. One has canals instead of fountains. Another is built into the side of an old, old mountain, the houses nigh castles, built of stone that's greened with ancient moss. I cannot imagine my mother as anything less than her harsh self; Lady Valier, though, has a rigidity to her but also a humor and kindness.

It's funny, though, that I don't wonder about our fathers like this, but it's the sons who spend more time with the men. Not daughters. Or, that is true of my family; the Valiers have no daughter, and so a complete comparison cannot be made. Have I wished, on occasion, for my mother to have been any other but the one I have? Yes, even before our latest time spent overmuch together in my brother's sudden shocking absence.

What would my father do, I wonder, if suddenly confronted with the need to spend time in each other's presence. We could carry on some manner of conversation, we are both trained and practiced in such things, but it seems overly formal for family. Or I am a fool.

I cannot identify the scent in the vial that Dora has given me. Floral but alkaline, not unpleasant but clearly medicinal. Not to be mistaken for perfume, or wine. I tuck in into my jewelry box, away from my mother's sharp eye. Or, she would praise me for having it, for taking part in society as expected and using precautions. I am always off my balance with her, and she is never satisfied with me. But she must also rest sometimes, and the household breathes easier when she does. It's almost a shame to waste the respite in slumber, but I am tired, so tired, that once I see my bed I drop onto it, all the strength running from my limbs, and I sleep until dawn without dreaming.

It is odd to awaken and think that yes, today I will lose my maidenhood. There is an excitement to it as well, both to finally know one of life's mysteries and also to have made a decision separate from my mother's influence. While I'm sure Luca isn't an unsuitable match, should it come to that, a lasting match isn't my goal. Not yet, not at my experience and tier. I have experienced so little of the world and of myself.

I'm surprised to receive an invitation from Tristan, inviting me to her home to prepare for the evening with herself and Teodora and Ottavia. I have never done such a thing, and I consider only a moment before deciding yes, I will. I write my reply, and then dither over whether I ought to use my spark to send it as a bird, or seal it with wax and send it with a servant.

Tristan sent it via servant and I'm sure that she means something by it. I finish my coffee and fold the bird, just a few quick little tucks, a tiny amount of spark flowing into it, and then it regards me with inkblot eyes, quivers its wings until I carry it to the window and release it.

My mother comes in just after, of course. Before she can start on the faults she's found with me today already, I say, "I do hope you don't mind, Mother, I've accepted an invitation to prepare for tonight's event with the other girls in the circle."

She regards me first with irritation and then an expression I almost don't recognize. Approval. "They invited you? Very good."

"Tristan did, yes." I don't want to, but I hold out the note, her boisterous script dashing down the page in deep blue ink. My mother glances at it, but doesn't take it from me to read.

"Have the smaller carriage take you," she says. "Your father and I are going to a different event. I trust you will not embarrass your house."

"No Mother," I say. Then, emboldened, I ask "Where are you—"

"It's for people of our echelon," she says dismissively. "You younger people have many years before you're of a level to attend, even that dreamy one, Armand." If *you* ever get to that level, she does not say, but so fleeting is my mother's approval.

"Is his spark the strongest in the group?" I ask, even if my every instinct is telling me not to pursue conversation with my mother. "I might have thought it was Lorenzo."

"Lorenzo has more control of his spark, anyway, though not his impulses." She looks at me narrowly. "There are ways of telling."

"Of course," I murmur. I should know how. I should read how, it must be in a book somewhere, maybe even a book I already own. I will not ask my mother how.

"When are you expected? It's best not to keep your new friends waiting "

"Around tea," I say. Hours yet, after luncheon and afternoon nap, waiting in my too-empty home, though some of that will be spent packing what I will wear.

My mother withdraws without further comment, which means, clearly, that I should be making those preparations now. I ring for my Agnes, who was waiting for my mother to be gone, I'd guess.

"I wasn't trying to eavesdrop, Lady Serafina, please forgive me but—"

"There's nothing to forgive," I say, perplexed.

"I just want to say that I'm excited for you."

"Thank you." It is embarrassing, for my maid to feel so sorry for me, but I'm gratified that she understands how valuable it is to get out from under my mother's watchful gaze and suffocating influence, however briefly.

Chapter Fourteen

Lorenzo of House Valier

I am unprepared for Luca to arrive at my doorstep as I'm making my preparations for the evening. "How now, Luca?" I ask when he appears, looking unfamiliarly nervous.

"I left Serafina wanting last night, but promised tonight that I would not." He looks at my face, frowning. "I know you hate the sight of her, and hate that she is not her brother, but she is the Galeazzo who is here. We must continue the game."

I allow the silence to hang a moment and go back to buttoning my shirt. "If you don't want to bed the bitch then don't. I've never known you to shrink from that particular task."

"And I haven't, before." He falls silent again, and I do not understand what he is wrestling with. "This feels like a responsibility that I do not want to fail at," he finally says.

"Strange, coming from the man whose previous lover was a painter of insufficient skill. Who told her as much."

He groans, collapsing into one of my arm chairs. "That's the thing, I do not intend to take Serafina for a lover. Nor does she want me to, I don't think."

"Then what are you playing at?" I ask impatiently. He isn't lovelorn. "This is most maddening."

"I shouldn't have come to you, Renzo, I am sorry for this. But Sterling isn't one to go to for such things, and Armand is Armand, and so there is only you."

"We should all keep better counsel," I say ruefully. Though Marco would hardly have been better counsel with regards to his sister's virtue.

"Indeed we should, and yet here we are."

I look my coats over, one by one. "What are you asking of me? Permission? Denial? Neither is mine to give."

"I know, I know " He stands now, helps me buckle on my swords, settles the shoulders of my coat. "I'm unused to feeling unsure. As though I am taking another's place, though I couldn't say whose."

"See? You should have talked to Armand after all." We laugh.

"You are in a better mood than I expected to find," he says.

"I tire of everybody commenting on my mood. My mood is my mood, we all know what has happened of late."

"We do." Luca holds up his hands. "I shall never speak of it again "

"You have my thanks." My manservant comes, to help me with my boots, and Luca stands off, availing himself of the wine decanter on my dresser. "Maybe not too much," I say, teasing, and he gives me a harried glance as he finishes his cup.

"For my nerves, Renzo, that is all, as I just stay my course."

"His nerves," I say to my manservant, Georgei, who smiles politely, not understanding the joke. "If only the young lady could know how much care you were taking."

"Maybe I'll tell her, and it will make her fall in love with me, and I can take us both away from all this." He grins at me, courage resurfacing.

"You love all this."

"Maybe I do, and what's not to love? Wine, women, and song."

"You're forgetting the fights."

"What are duels but duets?"

"How much did you drink before your arrival at my gate?" I ask.

He pulls a dramatic face. "You wound me, Lorenzo."

"Best we end on a high note." I finish my own half-drunk cup. "The hour is late already, and it wouldn't do for you to keep her waiting."

"Absolutely not." I gesture him out first and pull my door shut behind us. We descend the stairs, and my mother looks up from the front door at our clomping boots. My father has already gone to their carriage.

"Two of you," she says, bemused.

"Good evening, Lady Valier," Luca says smoothly, capturing her hand to kiss as he bows.

"Really, Luca," she says, but she smiles.

"The lady of the house is owed her due," he says, and maybe he did drink more before coming here. He's steady enough while also behaving, well, like this.

"We've seen fewer of you here of late," she says thoughtfully. "Perhaps plan to make a day of it, or several, ahead of the next tournament."

"Yes, Mother," I say. "But we must take your leave, Luca has—" and he elbows me in the ribs, not hard, but enough to interrupt me, and we both laugh, far more than the moment warrants.

"Good evening, boys," she says, still smiling. "I trust you'll behave even out from under our watchful gaze." And she goes out to the waiting carriage. Mine is just behind, with room enough for Luca to ride as well.

"Oh, I forgot there were other events tonight," Luca says. "My parents just barely qualified, I think."

"Your father is still recovering from that hunting injury, is he not?"

"He is, but you know how fathers are."

Distant, stubborn. "Your mother, though..."

"Has spent less time training due to caring for him. It's disgusting, how they dote on each other. Like they're our age, newly in love."

"What a scandal," I say dryly.

"There's just nothing to be done."

The ride is not long, and we don't speak any more of the task in front of Luca, and what it might mean. If anything. It doesn't have to mean anything; losing one's virginity is simply part of the game, another moving piece of the ever shifting board. Some silly girls, and boys, get overly attached because of it, which, if asked, is what I would have expected of Serafina. Instead Luca indicates she seeks to be unburdened. Wouldn't it be interesting if she were to become a valued member of the circle after all.

The girls are not yet there when we arrive, not even Ottavia, though Sterling is here, and Armand. "Have they all conspired against us, Armand?" I ask. "Tell it to me plain."

"I would tell it to you no other way, Renzo," he says with a slow smile. "No conspiracy in our ranks, unless they are able to hide it even from me "

"Well then," I say. Luca is watching the door. "Let us make merry then. The tournament will be announced tonight, will it not?"

"Will it?" Luca asks.

"I believe so, yes." Sterling seems unhappy with the wine, and they signal to a servant. "It is nearly the same every year."

"People like their traditions," I say, and more arrivals draw our attention to the door, but it is not the other members of our circle.

With most of the upper echelon at the other event, tonight's gathering has a looser, more festive air. Our parents' disapproving gazes are elsewhere and we are free to do as we will, within reason. Within expectation. A fight breaks out in the furthest corner, one of the pair shouting slurred oaths, and so not everybody is so rarified as to turn down the initially offered table wines.

Luca stands to see better, and so he does not mark Serafina's entrance with Dora, Tristan and Ottavia just behind them. They represent us well, in appearance; their clothing has had much care taken with it, and their hair. Dora's is pinned up, with some manner of trailing, dangling artifice. Tristan's is a number of complicated coils, and Ottavia's is nearly loose and full of flowers.

I don't look very closely at Serafina, but the red flower on her shirt catches my eye. It's a very plain shirt, and I realize it must be the one she wore the other night, though something else has been done to it to make it appropriate with the skirts she is wearing. I've never known her to be one for fashion, so most of this is Teodora's doing I'd wager. But that flower...

Somebody calls to Tristan and she breaks off, touching their elbow and looking towards the fight with an expression of disdainful interest. Nobody to trouble ourselves over, then. Sterling meets Ottavia partway across the room; I hadn't even noticed them getting up. I look at Luca, who's seen the girls now.

He glaces at me. "She's embroidered that blood stain into a flower," he says.

"Interesting symbolism, given your arrangement," I say dryly.

"I agree," he says with something like relief. "And an interesting show of courage, either way."

"Oh indeed?" Courage is not a quality I've yet ascribed to Serafina.

"She could hardly assume that you would be pleased to see her yet again. So to flaunt the outcome of your first reunion, on a night such as this..."

I wave a hand. "Thank you, yes, I follow."

"And how will Lorenzo react?" Armand asks slyly.

"He will not react," I say.

"Which is itself a reaction."

"Just so." They've reached the table now, and I stand to pull out Dora's chair for her, and Luca moves to do the same for Serafina. She smiles up at him through her lashes, bashfully playing at being bold.

"How does this evening find us?" Teodora asks, and then the shouting in the corner reaches a further pitch, the men engaged in a duel are now being pulled apart.

"Better than them," I smirk, reaching to pour her wine.

"So solicitous, Renzo," she purrs. "Has the secret all along been removing the upper echelon so that we are closer to the top?"

"Perhaps it has." We both know it has not, but as a group we've returned to a certain bantering comfort, at least for the evening. Serafina has kept silent, which is only a help. I also think that she isn't sure if she should leave the table first or Luca, and I watch the comedy of her indecision and inaction with a certain cruel amusement.

Luca takes the lead, of course, after that raucous fight is broken up, and two young ladies near us have a much more appropriate duel, and then Tristan finally sits. More wine is brought, and a cheese course, and then Luca stands and says, "I've heard that they had the frescos in the east wing restored. Would anybody like to accompany me?"

"Absolutely not," Tristan says, fanning herself, but of course Luca is looking at Serafina.

"Thank you, I haven't seen them," she says, rising and taking his outstretched hand, carefully not looking at any of the rest of us. They make their way across the room and out ostensibly towards the east wing.

I look at Dora, watching them go. "We all know, of course, but she doesn't know we do," she says. "Do be decent about it."

"I don't know but I can guess," Tristan says.

"I am simply not interested," I say.

"Perhaps you aren't. But I've said what I'll say."

"Are you warning me, Teodora?"

"I am, Renzo. Take heed." And we laugh and pour more wine.

Chapter Fifteen

Serafina of House Galeazzo

The frescos are very nice, vividly colored and shockingly large, encompassing many walls. We are not the only ones admiring them, and though Luca seems to know a great deal about them, I cannot hear a single word he says. I hear him speaking, of course, but what he's saying flies out of my head almost at once.

He has my hand in the crook of his elbow as we walk, and I have never spent so much time touching another person, I think. I'm aware of the smooth weave of his coat sleeve, and the quiet creak of his boot leather, the faint scent of wine, and of whatever his cologne is, something both woody and herbal, subtle and pleasant. I'm intoxicated on my own anticipation, in addition to the wine I had at Tristan's and here. I am both in control of myself and also teetering on the edge of disaster.

We leave the frescos presently, and we do not go back to the dining hall. We take a different turn, through less ornate hallways though still well appointed, framed with carved and gilded molding, hung with ancestral portraits, as all our homes are. We go up one sweeping staircase and then a smaller, charmingly crooked one, and then Luca lets us into a room with a pale blue-painted door that he locks behind us.

It contains a marble tub, and towels. The walls are curtained and mirrored, bright rugs on the floor. There is a canopied bed as well, and the sight of it brings me up short, and relieves me of some of my giddiness.

There is also a table with pitchers on it, of wine and water and I'm not certain what else, and a pair of cups.

"Would you like anything?" Luca asks, going to pour.

I catch my breath a moment. "Only if it's nice," I say, unable to tell if I sound flirtatious or beseeching. He doesn't give indication of scorn, though, but investigates the drinks.

"This seems to be something floral," he says, sniffing it and then pouring a bit.

"Thank you" I accept the cup and sip from it by rote. I think it may be rose or violet, though whether it is an alcohol or even some other drug, I cannot say. I already had my dropperful from Dora's vial, in the carriage to the event. We all did, giggling and jostling together, as though it is the nightly ritual, and perhaps it is.

Then I don't know what to do with my cup, and stand as a statue, smiling and holding it. Luca relieves me of it, setting it back on the table. All of my training at conversation has left me, and I am fumbling for words to say when he reaches out and tips my chin up so that he can kiss me.

It is more urgent than last night, less of a salutation. He kisses me deeply and I feel dizzied by it, or by what I drank, and even as I grasp at these thoughts, we together melt towards and then onto the bed, him guiding and supporting me so that we do not stumble. He breaks away a moment, to slide out of his jacket, to kick off his boots, and I try to consider just how much undressing I have ahead of me but then his mouth returns to mine, chasing away thoughts. And then his mouth drifts from my lips to the curve of my jaw, in that soft place where it meets my neck, and then down my neck, and I'm panting, a little moan escaping when his fingers stroke down my neck and reach my shirt collar, then find the first buttons, deftly undoing them even as he lays me back on the bed and I'm in such a pleasant haze that I cannot take the time to be shy about this thing that is happening, that this man is undressing me as we kiss, and that I want him to.

I start to reach for his shirt buttons, but his mouth has followed his fingers and where my skin is exposed as the shirt is pulled back, he kisses there, and there, and then he is unlacing my stays, and pulling my chemise away as well, and nobody has ever touched me like this and I am breathless but moaning, and his mouth and tongue are too much, overwhelming, but also I don't want him to stop.

He does, though, long enough to take my boots off, to remove articles of his clothing, but I'm in such a pleasurable haze that the pause is brief. When he comes back, he is on top of me, kissing me again, stroking my face, my hair. "If at any point you feel discomfort, tell me to stop. We'll go more slowly. Do you understand? I can always stop."

"Yes," I say. I understand that much, that he can stop, and he nods, satisfied, and returns to his ministrations. My skirts are rucked up around my waist now, and his fingers on my thighs, and then between my thighs, and if I thought the fire I felt last night was a release, I was so unprepared, so off guard, for this. This isn't my spark, it's me, it's pleasure, or it's both and I give a sobbing cry against his mouth, utterly helpless, wanton, willing.

I reach for him again but I don't know what to do other than cling to him as he kisses and fondles and strokes, and then finally adjusts himself between us and I can feel his heat too, and there's a pressure that replaces his fingers, a brief pinching tear, and then he's sheathed himself in me, I have no other way to think of it, the way our lives are, and his weight is on me, but pleasurable, not suffocating, and he pauses and looks into my face, questioning, and I breathe out, "Yes," and he begins to move over me, in me.

I get the rhythm of it, I understand it, without thinking, rocking my hips up to meet him, crying out again, and again, as though he is the ocean and I am the beach that waves beat upon and there is a building feeling, a pitch we are reaching together, in addition to all the smaller crashing waves I've felt, we reach a crescendo together and he strains against me, also crying out, before we are both still, breathing raggedly together, cradled in this comfortable bed in this quiet room. My fingertips tingle, like last night, and my toes, and the top of my head. Have I accomplished so little in life, that my spark kindles and expands at such minor events? I am not certain how long it will last; I'd prefer not to walk into a fountain again tonight. That is not the sort of thing I wish to be known for, though perhaps it's better to be known for walking into fountains than to be known for having a fugitive brother who ran away with two indentured actors.

After too short a time, Luca sighs and leaves my side, gets off the bed and stands a moment, stretching. "We'll be missed," he says.

"I won't," I say, perhaps too hastily, and he turns to me.

"Are you so certain Teodora will not come after you, if too much time passes?" he asks in a warm, teasing tone.

"I...am not." Dora has proven herself to be a very good friend, perhaps even a mentor, though if confronted with such a notion I'm not sure she would necessarily agree. "And I am certain that everybody else knows how long these things are expected to take."

"There are certain expectations in place, yes," Luca says with an amount of humor that I don't entirely understand, but I smile anyway and also slide off the bed, settling my skirts and my underthings and then picking up my stays. "Here, I can help with that."

"Can you?" I ask. Perhaps it is not such a shocking thing, that a young man of certain experience undressing women is also experienced in dressing them back up again. I had simply never considered it.

"Of course." He takes a similar amount of care with my lacings, with my waistband, with my buttons. Then his fingers graze the embroidered red flower on my shirt. "This is a nice touch," he says.

"I couldn't see letting the shirt be ruined," I say, prepared to be defensive, though also there are many known ways to get bloodstains out of clothing. There's an entire industry of it, in this city, and probably the others like it.

"No, of course not. And Lorenzo almost certainly noticed."

"I don't want to talk about Lorenzo," I say resolutely. Not now. Not after what we've done.

"Of course not," he says again, and turns to his boots, leaving me to confront my hair in the mirror. It isn't *so* bad, just some places need smoothing and repinning. I'm certain, when Dora put it up for me, she did so with this event in mind. I've trusted her with so much without even thinking about it, and without her asking, just as naturally as breathing. I'm not certain I trust any of my other friends or acquaintances so, not Andante and Allegra, nor any of my other letter writing friends who are not in the game. Though I was not either, for a very long time. Too long, my mother has clearly thought. Would that she would have married me off before now, perhaps into a House that lives in another city entirely.

When we are again presentable, Luca offers me his elbow and we depart from that little room, descending the charming crooked stair and then the larger one, and passing by the wing of frescos, where he pauses. "I'm a fool, I should have asked if you need…"

"I want for nothing," I say, because I cannot think of what I would require in this specific moment.

"Just so," he answers, and we return to the dining hall.

Chapter Sixteen

Lorenzo of House Valier

When Luca and Serafina appear once again at our table, Dora is on her feet immediately and whisking Serafina away. Tristan watches them go, eyebrows raised, and then looks back to Ottavia who shrugs, either not knowing or not caring. I pour Luca a fresh cup of wine and slide it to him. "How now, Luca?" I ask slyly.

"You know better than to assume I will discuss such matters at the table," he says, taking up the cup, draining half of it in one go.

"At the pub later, then."

"She is not my painter, nor my playwright. I shall not."

"As you say." Tristan listens, bright-eyed.

"This is not an ongoing arrangement then, Luca?" she asks, silky-toned.

"What did I just say, Tristan?"

"Surely you could, without divulging anything *too* sensitive."

"Perhaps I could, but I will not. Ask again, and you'll be choosing a second."

"It's Ottavia," she says airily. "These things aren't *secrets*, Luca."

"No, but the notion of respect evidently is," he says, and looks at me. "Renzo, will you..."

"Of course."

"Honestly, Luca?" Tristan hasn't stood up yet. I help Luca off with his coat; the shortest hairs on the back of his neck are still dark with sweat.

"Honestly, Tristan. I made myself plain and you continued." He pulls out his dueling gloves, flexes his hands into one, then the other.

Tristan rolls her eyes and flounces to her feet. "We're all so *sensitive* these days," she huffs and Ottavia laughs.

"We haven't had a new person in so long, nobody knows how to act," she says soothingly, but her eyes are twinkling when she looks at me over Tristan's shoulder. "Lightest touches again?"

"No, clearly that did nothing to improve her demeanor last night," Luca says. "First blood, though nothing vital. Civility is the aim here."

"Oh of course," Tristan snaps, turning to him and drawing. "No joking, no familiarity amongst friends and companions. Just civility and wounded feelings and secrets."

"As you've already said, there has been no secret." Luca draws as well, and bows, and Tristan curtseys, then from her crouch moves in rapidly. Luca stands aside, and her blade does not find purchase, though, curiously, he does not immediately strike. They square up again, and again she makes a pass that he does not meet. Now she's flushed high across the cheekbones, angry.

"Why would you start a duel with me that you will not fight?" she spits, and when she rushes him again, he steps to the side and gives the slightest little flick across the nape of her neck, opening a red line no wider than a papercut.

"First blood," Ottavia announces. "Duel to Luca." She presses a handkerchief to Tristan's neck, even as Tristan shoves her swords back in their sheathes and waves her off.

"Can we go back to normal now?" she asks. "Please?"

We can never go back to normal I think, helping Luca with his coat again. Unnecessary, but from his nod he welcomes the gesture. "We should all follow your good example," I say.

"When you say it like that, it makes it sound like I'll get a better result wishing in every fountain I passed on my way here." I am surprised to see tears in her eyes, and I bring myself into check, soften my tone. I pull her over to me, finish my cup of wine, and then reach out to her spark with mine, rubbing my thumb across the wound Luca gave her, to erase it. It leaves behind a scar, it always does, lightly golden as though somebody trailed a thin paintbrush across her skin. A less ugly scar than healing all of these wounds naturally, night after night.

"Tristan, it only makes sense for Serafina to join our circle. And it only makes sense that she needs to find her relationship with each of us. It does not make sense that you are privy to each detail of that, though, and while you are correct that we have all been so very sensitive..." I pause, as I notice a flash of red across the room, Serafina's damnable embroidered flower as she and Dora return to us. I release Tristan, so she can find her seat. "Well we need to master ourselves and consider the broader implications of the game," I say.

"Are you including yourself in these admonitions?" Tristan asks, but she does sound soothed.

"I ought to," I say ruefully. "And truth be told, I'd just as soon never see the girl again. But here she is and here we are, and that is our situation."

"Perhaps she'll have a bad duel," Tristan says, mustering a more cheerful tone, taking up her cup of wine again. Luca shoots her a dagger-filled look, but does not say anything, as Serafina sits again, next to him, and then Dora next to me.

"I do hope they bring desserts soon," Dora says, filling the silence before really taking its measure, though from the look she gives me, she knows which way the wind blows. "I desperately want something sweet."

"Sweets for the sweet," Ottavia says, giggling.

"Dora is the best of us," I say, and I am sincere. The steadiest and most generous of heart.

"You flatter me," she says, flicking open her fan to wave at herself, either through artifice or because the hall is very warm tonight.

"I only speak the truth," I say.

"I'm sure we all agree with Lorenzo," Serafina says carefully. I manage to keep my smile from fading entirely, but feel it tighten.

"Of course we do," Armand says. "There is no question Teodora is our golden heart."

"Oh Armand as well, things are truly in a state," Dora says, laughing. "Now let's talk about something else, before my head grows too large to fit through the doorways again and I'll be stuck here for the rest of my days."

Chapter Seventeen

Serafina of House Galeazzo

"Dora, I am fine," I protest as she brings me to one of the dressing rooms.

"I'm certain you think that you are, but it doesn't hurt to take a moment and make sure." She doesn't seem overly worried, to be fair, simply practical. "Sometimes there are certain pains, with a first—"

"Luca is very kind," I interrupt carefully. I don't have the vocabulary to discuss what occurred, and even divulging that tiny amount makes my face flush in embarrassment, or in greater knowledge. Two days ago, I didn't know anything could feel like that. I'd never received such care and consideration, physically. I'm at a loss, and in something of a pleasant daze.

"I'm certain he is. I've heard no ill rumors of him." She sits me down on one of the plush lounges, takes a perch on another nearby. "Still and all, this is hard enough for you in the first place without new considerations."

"You are also very kind," I say, and from the way she smiles, I know she knows how I meant it, and how also it could be taken, and I flush harder.

"Now then, let's not get ahead of ourselves. Here, drink this." She produce another vial from her pockets, hands it to me.

"What is it?" I ask, after I've drained it down. I should not be so trusting, I think, but if I cannot trust Dora then I am even more lost.

"It helps, when one's spark kindles and grows, to make you feel less off-balance. I should have offered it to you last night, I didn't realize, but now..."

"Am I so obvious?" I ask, abashed for no good reason. This aspect of our lives is out of our hands, it happens to everybody, as regular and mysterious as breathing.

"To me, yes, but again, only because I saw you last night. I'm sure not a single other one of them realizes, not even Luca, and by the time we're back at the table, all will be settled again."

"Thank you for being such a friend," I say suddenly and firmly.

She smiles. "You're welcome. You are not to blame for your brother's absence. You are only yourself."

"I am." It's such a simple thing, but to have it acknowledged gives me such relief. My mother places such expectation and responsibility on me, especially after Marco's accomplishments; he was not the most talented of the circle, sparkwise or swordwise, but he was also not the least. To my knowledge, Ottavia is in that ranking, other than myself. But we aren't actually sure of my ranking, are we? The thought surprises me; just last week, it would not have occurred to me.

"How do you feel? Don't tell me you're fine, sit with it a moment. I'll know if you're lying." She's smiling, but I believe her.

I do sit with it a moment. I feel pleasantly on the edge of intoxicated, by combination of what I've drunk tonight and the physical after effects of my encounter with Luca. I feel somewhat exhilarated, honestly, the second night in a row that my spark has kindled. The sort of combination that might make me do foolish, impulsive things, and Dora was right to pull me aside in this manner. "I feel very nice," I say finally, also smiling.

"That's better. They're announcing the tournament tonight, so we'd best get back to the table."

"The tournament?" I feel a thrill of both terror and excitement. I have never participated in a tournament before, just smaller matches amongst friends, or if I had lessons in a group with a fencing master that was employed by a neighboring house. I do not know what to think, how to expect I will measure up to members of other dueling circles.

"You'll be fine. The first one is always the most terrifying, but it's impossible to do as poorly as you fear you might."

"I don't believe you worry about doing poorly," I say, as she holds the door to the room for me.

"You're very sweet," she says, kissing me on the cheek. "We'll hope that you stay that way."

There's a bit of spark in the air when we return to the table, but everybody is still seated or seated again, and before I can wonder after it too much a woman I don't recognize stands and rings a knife against her glass. The effect is immediate, the entire room falls deathly still and silent. There is some effect in place, I think. We want to be quiet and listen, naturally, but I think that woman's spark has also quieted the room so that her voice will carry.

"In a fortnight's time, the next tournament will be held," she says clearly. I fumble for her name, or her house, my thoughts abuzz. House Massimo, that's Venette's mother. She is not the lady of this house, we are at House Linhares tonight, who have a twin son and daughter who have only just grown old enough to have entered society. "The schedules will be sent to all of your houses. You are expected to be at the appointed times of your duels and carry them out as per tournament rules, which will be two swords, first blood. You are all responsible for choosing your own seconds. The appointed houses will be sure to have prepared the dueling areas appropriately for hosting the event. If these appointments are not fulfilled, proportional punishments will be meted out." She gives a slight bow, and ambient noise returns to the room.

Immediately, Ottavia is leaning across Sterling to say something to Tristan, and Dora also has her head tilted to listen. She sees me watching and says "Nobody's had to be punished for any of that in a very long time. Not in our lifetimes, though there was quite the scandal when our parents were young."

"Was there?" I ask. I feel as though I am blinking a lot. What punishment could possibly be proportional to not preparing the dueling areas, and what could inadequately prepared dueling areas even mean? The actual dueling area at my house is separate from the practice rooms, but I know that it is maintained near-daily. My parents practice there, in fact, though I haven't watched them since Marco and I were small.

"Yes, somebody refused their duel. They went to the appointed time and place and all that, but they refused to draw. They turned their back on their opponent, who of course wouldn't strike somebody with their back turned, but then it counted as *both* of them refusing, which was utterly ridiculous and very confusing."

There is a bit of a pause; everybody but me knows this story, clearly. I wonder if Marco also knows this story. "Well then what happened?"

Dora hesitates. "They were both flogged by the guard."

Proportional punishment, I think. "I see," I say, through numb lips, and she pats my hand.

"It was a good many years ago," she says, as though that changes what happened. She hasn't said any names, I wonder who it was. If they are still here.

"My mother has said that she desires the circle to practice at our house," Lorenzo says, after a pause, as we are all standing to leave for the evening. I shoot a look at him; I've spent quite a lot of time avoiding looking at him, as he looks ever so displeased every time our gazes accidentally happen across one another. "She mentioned it tonight, as Luca came over before we made our way here."

"We can hardly disappoint your mother," Sterling says. They look as though they are picturing the passage of time in their head. "It has been some months, hasn't it. Perhaps even not since last year."

"Something like that," Lorenzo says, pointedly not looking at me. We are in dangerous waters again, the invocation of my brother's name so close. The last time they were all at House Valier to practice was when Marco was still among us, and Marco attended. They are all thinking it, I am very certain.

"Let us know the times, then," Tristan says. She has been less sharp for the latter half of the evening, and I am not sure who she dueled with or what the quarrel was, but the smear of recent blood is on the nape of her neck and a new golden scar gleams there. I do not know who she fought. I do not know who healed her. It's been mentioned that Lorenzo is spark-inclined to healing, which seems at odds with his general demeanor. Even when we knew each other better, in happier days, I was not aware of his spark's proclivities.

"I'll send to your houses," he says, turned enough towards me, towards the group, that I do feel included in his statement, however grudgingly. He hates me, but it serves the circle well for me to be prepared as well. He hates me, but Dora will protect me. Perhaps Luca as well, and that thought gives me a warm feeling. I am not *smitten* with Luca, even in my naivete I am able to be more pragmatic than that but I am already fond of him, inclined to trust him. And honestly, Lorenzo's hate is an embarrassment to himself; he should treat me better, his best friend's sister. "Is tomorrow too soon?"

"We hardly have anything else more pressing," Ottavia says, rolling her eyes, and so I can't tell if she is serious or jesting.

"I didn't think you did," Lorenzo says.

Luca falls into step with me, as the room empties. "You are well?" he asks, and I feel myself flushing from his attention, and from the mortification, that he will ask after my physical well-being in any way. It was one thing when Teodora did, but I will simply not be able to stand it if he questions me along these lines.

"I feel quite well," I say lightly, smiling and touching his arm. "Thank you for asking, you are quite the gentleman."

He nods, taking my meaning, to my relief. "Do you have a carriage here?" he asks.

"I ought to, yes." I rode over with the girls after going to Tristan's, but made the driver aware of the house and the event times. I don't mean to say it, but the next words fly from my lips unbidden, "My mother will demand an accounting of the evening." My euphoria is now quite past.

"And what shall you tell her?" he asks lightly, and then he sees my face and pulls me aside, out of the way of the people behind us. "How may I help?"

"There isn't any help," I say. "My mother is my mother, and what has happened has happened and it...it's mine, and not for her to be told." I am of course nowhere approaching ready to display such desperate defiance to her face but here, now, with him, I can in this small way. "I shall tell her about the duels, and tell her about the tournament, and about the circle practices at House Valier, and that will be enough for her."

"Surely she will notice you have advanced," he says after a few moments' consideration. I flush again, as I hadn't realized he had noticed. Perhaps it is another thing that everybody certainly knows.

"Then perhaps that also will be enough. Though she'll ask if I fought anybody, and I have not."

"Do you want to?" he asks.

"What cause could we give?"

"No one but your mother will ask." He is smiling, and I can't help but smile back at him.

"Yes, but where? We don't have seconds." Everybody else has gone, both from our circle and from the dining hall.

"Just outside, and we don't need seconds. This is just a friendly crossing of the blades, I want to get an estimation of who you can best practice with. You can tell your mother that."

"All right." We hasten outside, and while the girls have left, Lorenzo is still there, beside his carriage, mine the next in line.

"Luca, are you coming?" he calls impatiently.

"A few moments, we have something to attend to."

"What are you playing at?"

"Just a brief exercise, you needn't concern yourself." Luca winks at me and shrugs out of his jacket, laying it on a nearby railing. "Both swords?"

"That is my preference, yes," I say. I draw on my gloves, the gloves he gave me, and I see him note that as I button the cuffs before drawing my blades. I have a sense of Lorenzo coming to watch, but I take a breath and resolve to ignore him, as he has ignored me. I have trained at the blades for years, we all have. I have had excellent tutors, in addition to my mother, and Marco. Luca is a little older than me, more experienced, more practiced, but I again am trusting him to not hurt me.

We both draw, and he bows and I curtsey, and I wait. He takes a sidling step in and tries a testing strike with his off hand, that I block as I go into a high guard. He takes that as invitation to strike low, and I pass behind him and give him a touch on the shoulder. We didn't discuss terms but I'm not worried. He nods, acknowledging the strike, and now he waits, holding his sword casually, mid level. I move in first this time, low with my off hand, higher with my longer blade, and he parries both and laughs in surprise when I riposte with my off hand and touch him again.

"I'm going too easy, I see," he says.

"Perhaps you are." We haven't started to breathe hard yet, this is such a friendly duel, almost a game. I either need one more touch, or he needs all three, and I am prepared, mentally, for him to do so and make me look foolish, especially under the weight of Lorenzo's judgemental gaze.

"Fina," Luca says, and my attention snaps back to him. "Focus."

"Forgive me," I say. Is this flirtation? Perhaps. Is it necessary? Who is to say.

"Of course." I wait again, for his advancement, and use my mother's favorite trick, which is to forgo guards entirely and strike from a direction entirely opposite from the one you have been using. Leading with a different hand, coming in low instead of from high, any of it. Is there a direction he will expect from me? Perhaps not, though also it's my longer blade that he pays more attention to and not my off hand, and I almost get the final touch in but he recovers at the very last moment, catching that blade with his crossguard and disarming me, landing his own first touch.

Lorenzo sighs, loudly enough to distract Luca, and instead of withdrawing, I step further inside of his guard, my shoulder against his chest, and tap him on the forearm with the crossguard of my longer blade. I start to call the duel and Lorenzo says, "Third touch" in too loud a voice.

"Just so, Renzo." Luca lets out a laugh like a sigh, and then drops a kiss on the top of my head. "I have your measure now," he says as we part.

"Perhaps," I say archly, though I remember well what he said about his spark. "Thank you," I say more quietly, as he hands me my fallen blade.

"Of course. Now let us away to our carriages before Lorenzo punishes us." We laugh, and Lorenzo does not, already turned away down the walk.

Chapter Eighteen

Lorenzo of House Valier

As I've just given Tristan a small lecture on her behavior with regards to Serafina, I can hardly eat my own words as my carriage goes to Luca's house. He has done this by design, I am sure, for though Luca is the one among us with the least sense of spite, he is not without guile. "And what was that, then?" I finally ask, partway through the trip.

"The duel? So that she would have accounting to give her mother when she goes home. We do not consider how Lady Galeazzo is dispositioned, I think."

"We certainly do not." She was less harsh on Marco, the favorite, who gave the proper things correct attention, even as his attentions strayed elsewhere. Who among us has not had an affair with members of the Companies or others of classes outside our own. The issue was that Marco gave their concerns equivalent weight, or greater, and we did not know until it was too late.

"Say you aren't angry with me over that, Renzo? As you said..." but he stops himself, doesn't give me time to cut him off. "Anyway, as *I* said, I did want a sense of her abilities, for our practices. It will help us know what to drill."

"As you've said, you do not consider how Lady Galeazzo is dispositioned. She has already been doing all of the drills."

"Perhaps, but against just one person. Now she has the benefit of the circle." He looks at me. "As we all do."

"Yes, as we all do," I repeat, for what else can I do but agree? We cannot have a weaker link than Ottavia, our standings would be abysmal were that to be the case, and I can grudgingly admit that Serafina is more skilled than that. Woefully unblooded, but that comes of time and group practices of the sort we are planning. "Perhaps she'll become less of a shrinking violet, as time moves forward," I say, making an effort, for Luca's sake if nothing else. I do not think Luca is smitten with her, she is not, as he said, his painter or his playwright, but there is already a certain fondness and to go against that would only strengthen his resolve.

"Yes, I do hope that she'll gain confidence. You can see glimmers of it, when she isn't thinking of her mother." He glances at me, but then does not continue. I can guess his thoughts though. When she isn't thinking of her mother, or of my anger. It isn't as though I was ever another brother to her, but I think she expected more tenderness of heart, or at least less blame. Perhaps she was right to. But still, I see her face and think of her brother's, and I cannot change that. "All our mothers aren't as delightful as yours," he says.

"She is easy to get on with," I say. "Mostly."

"But even when it isn't easy, she's typically correct."

"Yes, also that, I can grudgingly admit it."

"Remind me, what is her favorite flower?"

"Luca, are you going to seduce my mother as well?" The carriage stops in front of his house, and he gives me a rakish smile.

"Absolutely not, as I should not like to fight your father. Goodnight, Renzo."

"Goodnight, Luca." Still he waits with his hand on the carriage door. "Those white lilies with the red centers, you damnable rogue."

"Thank you, Renzo." He closes the door and sketches an elaborate bow before going through his gate.

It is interesting for Luca to be both so shrewd and so lackadaisical at once, though he has always been this way. It causes people to misjudge him, often, and thus he often catches them unawares when crossing swords, because they do not expect him to be so serious and precise as he is. We are nearly an even match, with myself ahead.

He went easy on Serafina, perhaps also to boost her confidence, but she displayed an adroitness that I also had not expected. I would do well to keep an eye on her skill, for the sake of our circle. I have not had to worry about such things before; Sterling does their best in Ottavia's tutelage and she gets along well enough. Armand is all or nothing, either he knows where his opponent's blades will be before they do, or he is undone immediately. Teodora is next after myself and Luca, in my reckoning, and Tristan after her.

My parents are not in evidence when I enter the house, and I go up the stairs and through the silent halls to my rooms, loosening my collar and taking off my coat as I go. Sometimes this is how I like the house best, quiet and half-lit in the small hours. I am unlikely to happen into any servants at this time, and occasionally have a small quiet conversation with one of my parents, and that is it. I am left to my own devices, and I am able to be alone with my thoughts and not troubled by the expectations of those who surround me.

It is only by happenstance that I dueled no one tonight. I do not fight every day or at every dinner, but I do often enough that I almost feel on edge for having not done it. But instead Luca drove a not-quite-argument to bared steel, taking a page from my book. And there were the other fights throughout the hall and nothing else raised my blood enough to warrant it.

In my room, I hang my coat and then my swords and consider. Do I want to start the practice schedule so soon as tomorrow? Perhaps late afternoon, and then we can have a small evening meal before everybody disperses. But Serafina must be included, and imagining her face at the gathering stays my hand even as I reach for my pen to sketch out a plan. Tomorrow, I will consider it all when I wake tomorrow. She cannot be avoided and I am done with her for the night, I have had quite enough. Even though this lateness is my favorite time, I will retire to my bed now, that I might face those preparations fresh. That damnable girl and her damnable brother.

At the breakfast table, when I arrive, my parents are softly bickering about whether my father ought to have wounded his opponent in quite the manner that he did. "It isn't as though he were in any real mortal danger," my father says, in a tone that expresses pride in his prowess and perhaps also disappointment in the impermanent nature of the conflicts that we engage in. If my father meant to kill a man, he certainly would have, but almost nobody duels to the death, and certainly nobody sets those terms in a duel of the moment. Fights to the death do occasionally happen, by accident or design, but not at societal events. That is not the purpose of our duels, which are so much social jockeying, for an unknown golden ring to grab.

"You were *very* close to have putting him in mortal danger," my mother says firmly, but in a way that says she also is proud of his prowess but is concerned with his restraint. They are still wearing the clothing that they went out in last night, and are drinking jewel colored juice that certainly sparkles with wine.

"Close counts for nothing," I say, slouching into my chair. "If my lord father wanted a person dead, then that would indeed be a grave man."

"Our son supports me even if my lady wife does not," my father says with elaborate dignity, and my mother sighs and turns to me.

"And what tales do you have for us, from last evening?" she asks.

"Luca dueled Tristan," I say, almost without thinking, and hastily add, "There were other similarly inconsequential fights."

"He dueled Tristan? Whatever for?"

"She simply does not know how to leave a topic lie," I say, though seeing the gleam in my mother's eye, I know this will not be enough. "She is keen on knowing everybody's secrets, and he was not divulging them to her satisfaction, as he is possessed of greater integrity than that."

"A young man to be proud of," my mother says fondly. "And what of my brawling boy, no duels to report on your ledger last evening?"

"None whatever, my lady mother. Though I was Luca's second both times." I see her gaze sharpen, and curse myself for being too comfortable as to loosen my tongue.

"*Both* times?" She glances at my father, who raises his eyebrows as he sips his drink, and turns back to me. "And who was the other?"

I have no choice but to answer her. "Serafina. Not a serious duel, he was taking her measure in advance of our practice sessions. Now if you'll excuse me, I need to write to—"

"Sit, Lorenzo," my mother says, still lightly but with steel in her tone, and I sink back into my seat. "It has not gone unnoticed that you despise her so, and I was going to let matters lie, as I am not your foolish friend Tristan, but when you make it so apparent even in our conversation, you must lay the matter at my feet."

"Yes, my lady." I say, and yet my jaw remains locked.

She sighs and looks to my father again. He sets down his glass. "Lorenzo, we know that you feel your friend Marco's departure as a grievous betrayal. If you hate his blameless sister simply for existing, you must hide it better publicly, because otherwise you will be the fertile ground for petty gossip and that will be an embarrassment to us all."

"Yes, my lord," I say. I cannot find fault with any of what he says. Had Marco confessed to me, I would not have gone with him, I would have tried to stop him. Perhaps he should have brought his sister with him; I wonder for the first time if she is shocked that he did not. Betrayed, to be left to their mother.

My mother reaches across the table and lays her hand on mine, her face growing more serious, but softening. She wants me to know that she is not laughing at me. "You are allowed to have your space to grieve this loss. But do not allow it to cause actions you will regret later."

"No, my lady." I allow her to grasp my hand for that moment, and then gently withdraw it. "Now, if you'll excuse me, I retired early that I might get up and create our practice schedule in advance of the tournament. Some of the circle lack experience, and we can only make up for it in so many ways."

"You're honoring my request!" my mother says, taking up her drink again. "Somebody in this house keeps my counsel."

"Your counsel?" my father asks.

"I suggested that it had been some time since his dueling circle practiced in our home, and that perhaps our son should make arrangements."

"And so I am," I say.

"We'll have breakfast brought to you."

"My thanks."

There is only so much scheduling to actually be done, other than making it so that our practices end in enough time to prepare for the evening's event, if there is an evening event. Tonight, there is not. In three days' time, there is. I write my letters, noting the dates, and send them off one by one, paper birds rustling their wings on my windowsill as they take flight. I send Serafina's last; I have never sent her a note before. I write all of the notes exactly the same, each one no more or less than the last. This way, Dora can't compare any of them and take me to task.

I spend a lot of the morning reading, and picking at the breakfast that I am brought, as paper birds come back to me in turn. Sterling and Ottavia send one, of course, even though I did send them separate notes. Probably a waste to have done so, but they are neither engaged nor married yet. Dora will know if they intend to announce soon; I cannot imagine the benefit in waiting, but then I am not privy to everybody's private details, nor do I want to be.

Tristan's note includes a brusque apology for her demeanor last night, and I am darkly amused. Especially last night, she wasn't all that bad. Many of us have been worse, on differing occasions. I also have not been my best, and have been trying to find my equilibrium. Do I regret what I did to Serafina, her first night out again? No. I think something of that measure was necessary, and she ended up surprising us both that night, with the handkerchief, and then last night, wearing that shirt again with the flower embroidered over the bloodstain. Perhaps I will ask Luca if they discussed it. Perhaps I will put it out of my mind, though it is impossible to put her out of my mind as she will not go away. But as my parents have said, I am capable of putting up a better front than I have been. Public face is very important, and I cannot have a sensitive spot like this that is so apparent, or people from other circles will come to me and lean on it, and it's tiresome enough already without that much meddling.

Chapter Nineteen

Serafina of House Galeazzo

I have not been to House Valier since months before Marco left. It's only for a few hours, it's for practice and a meal. It's a familiar place and just the dueling circle; I'm not sure whether we will also see the lord and lady of the house. I expect not, if they are invited to the same function as my parents tonight, which they often are.

Lorenzo did not say to bring anything, and yet it seems ungrateful to be hosted and not bring a gift, and I descend to our wine cellars to find something appropriate enough without trying to be too personal about it. I recall him liking dry white wines, and I carefully smooth dust off of bottles until I find the right type.

I both dress carefully and also try not to take too much care while dressing. I don't want to seem like I don't know what is expected of me, though just now I am guessing. I dress in newer, slightly nicer practice clothes. I wear some light perfume; nothing with too much throw, nothing with too heavy a scent, but practice space can grow hot and close and unpleasant with enough people in them, and it is the custom to be scent-adorned in this way. I try not to take too much time with that either, and the scent is of honeysuckles and cut grass.

I am not sneaking, exactly, but I would prefer not to engage with my mother before leaving, but of course that is impossible. She stops me as I come down the stairs from my rooms once I am dressed. "Where are you going?"

"Lorenzo has invited the circle to his house for practice in advance of the tournament," I say.

"The tournament is in a fortnight."

"And we will drill as often as we are able up to that point, according to his note." I draw it from my pocket and hand it to her. I do not want to, but it seems the easiest means of escape. It is not a particularly personal note, nor would I have expected a personal note from him. I am grateful to be included in the circle, and then ashamed about just how grateful I feel. It would have been a dreadful thing, to try and include myself in another circle; it is a dreadful thing to try and include myself in my brother's circle, but at least I am familiar with their faces. At least I have received some welcome.

My mother reads it, frowning, and finally hands the paper back to me. "And you're bringing that?" she asks, looking now at the bottle of wine tucked under my arm.

I show her the label. "I know it to be to Lorenzo's taste."

"Very well, then." She is perhaps as surprised as I am, that she cannot find fault with these choices.

"They are expecting me, Mother," I say as gently and meekly as I might, because she is so unpredictable as to find fault with me simply for the possibility that such an occasion will arise.

"Of course. Make us proud."

Impossible, I think, but I bob a curtsey and slip out the door. Nothing I can do will be sufficient to evoke pride in my mother. Perhaps in my father, but he always seemed to have regarded us, his children, as curiosities to be indulged. I'd sent Agnes to make sure I had a carriage, and I'm able to step into the one waiting without looking back over my shoulder to see if my mother has pursued me for one last strike.

The carriage ride to House Valier is fairly brief, though long enough for me to fret over the things my mother will surely find fault with, and the things that Lorenzo will find fault with, though my very presences is what Lorenzo finds fault with, and as I do not care to simply cease existing, there is nothing for it but to ingratiate myself with the rest of the circle and assume that Lorenzo will extend his good graces to them at least.

In my avid desire to not be late and raise Lorenzo' ire, I am instead the first arrival. I see the flash of irritation in his eyes, when I am announced and shown in, though his expression has been schooled to appropriate blankness. We are as strangers, meeting for the first time.

"I thought that I ought not come empty handed," I say, careful with my tone so that it is honed politeness rather than cringing appeal, or careless challenge. We do not want to be alone in a room together. We should be able to cope with the situation until the other members arrive. I do hope that it's Teodora, as I like her best, or Luca, but I am not choosy with who I would consider to be my savior in this moment.

"Thank you," he says dubiously, but when he takes the bottle from me and looks at the label, his eyebrows quirk slightly in surprise, and I think I've done well in my selection.

Of course, the saying goes to be careful what one wishes for, as Lady Valier comes into the room. "I thought I heard a carriage," she says, smiling. Her smile reaches her eyes, lights them up. This is not always the case, in our society. "So nice to see you, Serafina."

"Thank you very much, Lady Valier, you are very generous to open your house to us," I say, curtseying to what I've been schooled is the correct degree.

She laughs and takes both my hands. "Of course, how could I do otherwise? We want to see you all do well in the tournament. Am I given to understand that your mother dismissed your tutor, and you've been going without?"

"Yes, that is true," I say, my lips numb. But even though this news has traveled at least as far as House Valier, the lady here cannot possibly know that said tutor was let go because her son caused me to look so foolish at that first dinner. I glance up at her, at the twinkle in her eyes. Yes, she very definitely knows, or at the very least inferred. "I'd outgrown him, and my lady mother has generously been taking the responsibility onto herself. I'm certain that I am not nearly dynamic enough to serve her own practices, but my own training has certainly benefited."

"Her mother!" Lady Valier says in delight, turning to Lorenzo. "Shall I tutor you myself?"

"If that is your wish," he says, smiling tightly. "It might be an amusing diversion for you."

"Perhaps you as well, it has been some time since we've crossed swords."

"Yes, it has." There are footsteps on approach, though, and he turns from his mother and looks past my shoulder to the door. Luca appears, seems surprised at the trio he has found.

"I was certain that I would be late," he says. "Instead, I am second?"

"You're just so adroit at being my second," Lorenzo says, with something approaching his former smile.

I watch his mother take note; then, to my mortification, she winks at me. "I will withdraw now and leave you to your exercise," she says. "Take care to stretch when you are done, lest you feel very sore tomorrow."

"Thank you, my lady," Luca says, and I also nod my thanks. "Have you been here long?" he asks me, once Lady Valier has sauntered out.

"No, only just long enough to give Lorenzo a bottle of wine and greet the lady of the house."

"It's a wonder Teodora isn't here yet," he says.

"Oh yes, I'm sure it is entirely by accident," Lorenzo says in a tone that suggests otherwise.

"Well she can't have delayed *everybody*, Renzo," Luca says, shedding his jacket and finding a hook for it.

"You underestimate Dora," I say shyly, and Luca laughs.

"It doesn't do well for anybody to underestimate Dora," he agrees.

"I hear my name, I hope you're only saying *nice* things." Teodora appears among us, smiling, carrying a covered basket on her arm that she hands to Lorenzo as she holds her cheek up for a kiss. He kisses her, bemused, and takes the basket, but when he tries to peek under the covering she says "Fie! That's for later."

"As you say." He sets it down on the same table with my bottle of wine, which she notes, and then looks at me and then Luca.

"Empty handed, Luca?" she asks with merry, false sharpness.

"Sometimes, it is all that I can do to bring myself," he says with equal false gravity.

"And whatever would we do if you failed to do that," she says, laughing, and I join in. "Such relief to have support, Fina," she says to me in a confidential tone, though everybody obviously can hear. And also I hear more footsteps approaching, Tristan and Ottavia and Sterling arriving together.

Coats are shed and bright weapons brandished, and we fall into our drills as though we have always done them together, and perhaps they have been doing them together for quite a long time, but I also have been drilling for a long time, and manage to match them despite my other inexperience.

I don't know what to expect from the others, when I face them in drills, especially not Armand or Sterling, who I have hardly spoken to, but everybody is very correct. Precise. These are practice drills to learn form, these are not swords drawn in the heat of the moment over petty squabbles or even for the heady rush of the high sound of steel on steel. This is hours of examining and correcting each others' footwork, and what our wrists and elbows and shoulders are doing, and how our hips rotate when we step. It is hot, and it is grueling, and I'm surprised to find, when Dora calls for a break, that I've been enjoying myself.

"Now, Lorenzo, open the basket I've brought," she says, delicately blotting at her face with a lace edged handkerchief.

He does, laughing once he's looked inside. "Are they back, then?"

"They are! In the same stations, glaring daggers at each other's patrons."

"Whatever are you—" Ottavia starts to ask, and then Lorenzo hands her a pink paper parcel and she all but squeals with delight. "The *noses.*"

"The what?" I ask, before I can stop myself, but nobody gives me a withering look.

Sterling plucks one from the basket and hands it to me. "There are a pair of confectioners who set up in a particular market, each only selling this one item, each claiming that theirs is the superior product." The paper on mine is lavender, and I unwrap it cautiously. The candy is about the size of my thumb, or perhaps of a nose, and conical. "The convention is to bite the top off, cautiously, as there is syrup within."

"What did Lorenzo mean, they're back?"

"They keep *fighting,*" Tristan says. "Each thinks the other stole the recipe, or steals customers, or is sabotaging the other, all manner of drama. I cannot decide it they are actually in conspiracy to boost their popularity, or if they genuinely are in a blood feud."

"Oh, they'll take that secret to the grave, I'm certain," Dora says lighty. "And there's no spark involved whatsoever, that I can tell. Just sugar and flavorings. The same molds, the same sizes. I'm not certain I'd be able to tell the two apart, were I blindfolded. This is just from one, I alternate who I buy from. They only fight each other, not customers."

"What a relief," I say, watching as others manage the sweet before I give my own a try, so that I have a sense of what they are like, but it indeed seems no more complicated than what Sterling described. The outer sugar is sturdy enough to be handled, but breaks easily when bitten, and the syrup is just thick enough to be manageable. It doesn't run everywhere, but it is also surprisingly light and refreshing, not so sweet as I might have imagined. The colors do seem to indicate the flavors, as mine is lavender. I'd guess Ottavia's pink one is rose, and the yellow one Luca has is honeysuckle. "Are they all flowers?"

"These are the ones they sell in the daytime," Dora says, in something of a conspiratorial tone. "If you buy them at night, they are filled with liqueurs and other intoxicants."

"Oh, indeed," I say, as though I am widely aware of other intoxicants. Perhaps I am, or rather I do know that one might get all manner of things at the apothecaries. "When do they find the time to sleep, between day markets and night markets and fighting?"

"Well perhaps they have products that help with that."

"They do," Armand says.

"Yes, you would know," Tristan says. and I don't know why the rest of the circle finds it funny, but I laugh along so as not to be left out. It isn't mean laughter, there's just an in-joke about Armand that I haven't learned yet, though I suppose that I can infer that it must be to do with products more heady than liqueurs or lavender syrup.

"Those they sell only at the witching hour, and they only taste of black licorice, though aren't to be confused with the absinthe ones, which are a particular shade of green that is *also* different from the rosemary ones." Armand pauses, perhaps to make sure what he said was straight before continuing on this path. "Those ones may give you sleep, yes, but they might also give you visions."

"And what if you already have visions?" Lorenzo asks him, in a gentleness of tone that is unfamiliar to me. Armand blinks at him.

"It lends them a clarity that might otherwise be difficult to attain."

"Does it also lend a truth to them?"

Armand gives the slightest of shrugs. "As true as they already otherwise would have been."

So that is it. Marco was very circumspect, always, when he talked about the circle's abilities, perhaps out of a sense of privacy. I was not in the game and thus it was not my business what Armand could do, or Sterling, or Lorenzo. Now that I am, nobody has explained anything to me, perhaps assuming that Marco had already told me. I can ask Dora, I'm sure, and she would tell me. It's possible I could ask them now as a group, but I'd prefer not to disrupt the comfortable rhythm we've attained today, and we eat our noses and drink some wine, both what I brought and what the servants bring out when summoned, and then we return to practice.

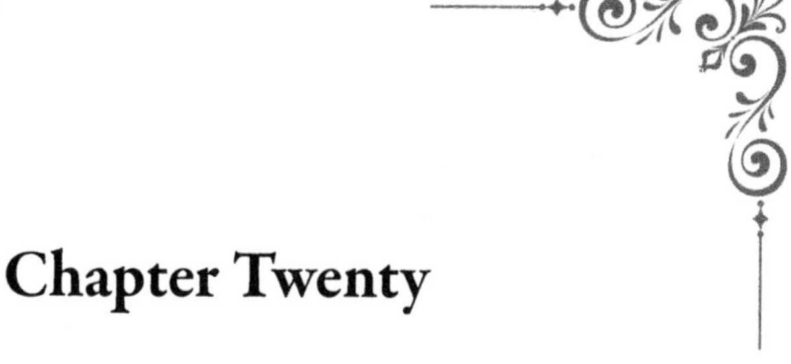

Chapter Twenty

Lorenzo of House Valier

I am relieved that Serafina does not seem as though she will drag down our standards in the tournament. She is timid, but has a surprisingly strong handle on many technicalities, and is able to best Ottavia and also Armand readily. Sterling and also Tristan are tougher for her, and I've already seen her fight Luca, even if he was doing it for the joy of it. Or to give her an excuse for her mother. I suppose I can sympathize with that; I was ever Marco's alibi, when necessary. He would have been mine, should I have required it, but our mothers are not the same.

It is my mother who comes to us in the evening, when she estimates we should stop. We probably should, before we are too tired and start to practice making mistakes. I can say that I am proud of our time spent, and think that probably we will do as well this tournament as we did in the last one, which was fairly distinguished though not winning. I do not think that we will win, but not being embarrassed is also important. I do not think we will be embarrassed.

"If my son has driven you quite to exhaustion, I should like to invite you all to a small meal. You might take the time to wash up, if you'd like." Thanks are murmured throughout the room, and my mother smiles and withdraws.

"I think everybody knows where to go for that," I say, not looking at Serafina, and we disperse, the girls taking her in hand.

"I had not thought your lady mother would dine with us," Luca says.

"I had not either, but it is no matter."

Just as every house has many rooms and nooks and crannies to go to, every house also has many washrooms. I go to my own rooms, of course, but the members of my dueling circle have many places to disperse to, and fully bathe or just wash up, whichever is their choice. Luca comes to knock once he is done, just as I've finished getting changed. "All our parents are here," he says.

"Oh indeed? What an interesting choice for my mother to have made."

"It is, isn't it? I can't help but think that it's because of Serafina, but I think that's because she's simply what we can't stop talking about lately."

"Said as though you aren't part of the problem." He grins and shrugs, and I shake my head. "Maybe it's to announce Ottavia and Sterling," I say.

"Finally. I can't see either of them making a better match, so their parents might as well give their blessing."

I hadn't considered that. "Did you think they might not?"

"I suppose it's always possible, right? We are in the game but so are our parents, and their decisions might supercede ours."

Another knock at the door, and I open it to Armand. "I knew you'd be here," he says either cryptically or to make the joke, smiling crookedly.

"We have to give the girls time for all of their ablutions," I say. "I trust Dora will let us know when it is time."

"I haven't spent much time with Teodora's family, is her mother also like this?" Luca asks.

"She is." Lady Alvise is a combination of being even more lenient than my own mother, and also in some ways as strict as Lady Galeazzo, and Dora's iron fist in a velvet glove is clearly a direct result of that upbringing. I'm not certain what she would think of that assessment of her character, and her mother's, if I was ever so foolish as to broach the subject. "And Ottavia's mother is an utter fool, so it's in spite of that she has reached the level she has. Her father is all right, I guess."

"This is quite the primer," Armand observes dryly. "My parents are entirely normal, before you ask. My condition is not directly due to either of them, that any master or witch or apothecary has been able to tell, but rather some anomaly of my own spark."

"I would never have asked you such a thing, my dear friend," Luca says. "Armand is Armand."

We have all met each others parents, of course. It is the nature of the city that we have met everybody in our society, but to know everybody in our society is entirely a different matter, and though our parents are also their own dueling circle, the time they spend together is not the time that they spend with their children. We have had tutors and nursemaids and governors and governesses, while our parent see to their standing, and that is what we will also do when we are all paired off and have begun to have children.

Eventually, Dora knocks, and we all go to the breakfast room, which my parents had made up for this small event. The doors to the terrace are open, letting in the fresh night air, welcomely cool after our exertions. Everybody is spread about the table, with the implication being that we will each sit with our parents, and even I sense Serafina's brief hesitation before she takes the seat between her mother and father.

"We know it is unusual for us to gather like this," Ottavia's mother, Lady Portela, starts, smiling happily. "But we thought it best that the group be made aware all at once, before a broader announcement. Our daughter, Ottavia of House Portela, will be marrying Sterling, of House Bonaro. The wedding will be after the tournament, of course, it is far too soon to have it now. You will all be invited, of course."

My mother raises her glass. "Congratulations to the happy couple." We all follow suit, and drink. Ottavia is nearly glowing, and Sterling looks doting and pleased, which is what we can expect of them. Weddings are for women anyway.

Dora is immediately talking to Ottavia about tailors, and Tristan is drawn into that conversation as well. Luca looks a little bewildered, and pours his next glass of wine; Armand looks distant, as though he is listening to music that none of the rest of us can hear. I somehow cannot hear what Lady Galeazzo is saying to my mother, but by pure accident, I catch Serafina's gaze for a moment and I can almost pity her. She is gaining something like real confidence when outside of her mother's immediate sphere, but that all goes away again so quickly, once they are in proximity. I find myself smirking, just slightly, and hide it with another sip of wine before Dora calls me to task, for I have no doubt that she would, even in such company.

"What are your feelings on the tournament?" my lady mother asks me a little while later, and much of the remaining other conversation hushes.

"It is hard to say after one day of drills and practice, but I should think we will do at least as well as last year," I say. "As we continue, perhaps my estimate will only grow."

"At least as well as last year is still heartening," my mother says. I suppose it is impossible for everybody to have not noticed Serafina's discomfiture, and my mother would like me to say something nice about her in particular, I am very certain.

"Yes, it's nice to have not lost ground," I say. It will have to be enough. I am not lauding our newcomer, but I haven't made any backhanded comments either, and I think that there are many around the table who are aware that is the direction in which this might have gone. It would be interesting, to see if Lady Galeazzo would take exception over a petty insult to her daughter, and demand honor's price. Or if she'd make Serafina try to fight me again herself. But I don't need to tarnish the wedding announcement with my own idle curiosities. My mother arches her eyebrow just slightly, though, and I reach farther. "We managed to keep practice bloodless today as well, which has not always been possible."

"Oh indeed?" Lady Galeazzo asks, in a tone that is both casually detached and also exceedingly focused. "Is that something you prefer?"

I answer carefully, but also take care not to pause too long to consider my words. "While I am able to stem the flow of blade-loosed blood, I do still prefer for it to not be shed so casually amongst practice partners, yes. Though as the tournament nears, it may become sparingly necessary; that remains to be seen."

"A measured response," Lady Galeazzo says, but she seems satisfied. Lord Galeazzo has been speaking to my father, and neither of them seem to have noticed this particular exchange. Luca's father indeed looks well on his recovery from the accident; if I hadn't known he'd suffered an injury, he would seem perfectly well. I do not look at Serafina again, though I can feel her gaze occasionally. I cannot imagine what she wants.

Chapter Twenty-One

Serafina of House Galeazzo

Despite Lady Valier's advice, I do not, indeed, remember to stretch after practice or even after I get home. I'm so bone weary that I change into a nightgown and crawl into bed, falling asleep almost immediately. It isn't until I've woken up the next morning, late, too late, from where the sun is on my walls, that I realize my mistake.

I *can* move; I'm not incapacitated. But it is very unpleasant, and it's worse than I'd previously experienced from drills with my tutors, or even drills with my mother. We practiced for hours and hours yesterday, in varying poses and guards and leads and angles, and speeds.

I roll over slowly onto my side, breath hissing through my teeth, and that's the moment that Agnes comes in.

"My lady!" she says. "I know you are still in bed, but Lady Teodora—" and before I can gather my thoughts, Agnes is making a noise of protest and Dora is in my room.

"I knew it!" she says, laughing, but fondly. "The dinner quite derailed us all, we didn't get to have a proper cooldown."

"It's okay, Agnes," I say after a shocked moment. "You can go, just close the door please. I'll ring when I need you."

"Yes, my lady," she says dubiously, but she withdraws.

"You must feel really awful," Dora says, once Agnes has gone.

"It's shockingly bad, yes."

"Here, roll onto your belly."

"What are you—" but she's climbed onto my bed and is knelt next to me, her hands on my neck first, fingers finding the knots there and kneading them into relaxation. Then she moves to my shoulders, and at first that hurts more and I squeak in spite of myself.

"I'm sorry, I know it's dreadful, but trust me."

"Of course I trust you."

She works down my arm closest to her, to my hand and fingers, and then back up to that shoulder again. Then she moves to the other shoulder and pauses a moment when she can't reach anymore. "Okay, stay still."

"What—" and then she straddles me so that she can reach, and from her new vantage, massages my shoulders again, leveraging her weight, and then down my back, and I groan but this time because she is very good at this and the pain and soreness is just running like water from my limbs. I can't even tell if she's doing this naturally or calling upon her spark to do so, I'm just so thankful that she is.

By the time she's done, I'm nearly asleep again, I'm so relaxed and comfortable. She rolls off of me and lays her head on my pillow, our noses almost touching. "Does anything still hurt?" she asks. I have nowhere to look but into her eyes and normally that would make me feel cornered, and instead I feel quite outside of myself.

"If I say yes, will you keep going?" I ask, unable to believe my own audacity.

She laughs, though, softly. "Oh, I could. I didn't do your legs, I know my calves cramp like the devil." Her words are businesslike, but her tone is not, and she pulls back the sheets and blankets as I try to recant and protest, and she starts at my hips and works down my thighs before pausing. "Turn on your back," she says, and I can only obey. I look at the canopy over my bed as Dora's strong, sure fingers work down my calves, which felt like too-taut instrument strings. She reaches my feet and kneads the arches before I can protest and I relax even further.

Then she moves back up my legs but she isn't relieving my sore muscles anymore, she's trailing kisses and I keep trying to form a thought or reaction and I'm letting out breathy little moans instead. She nips the inside of my thigh, sharp but gentle, and I giggle, but even that feels good, but I am unprepared for her to reach even further up and touch the lace edges of my underclothes. "Dora," I say, but I don't want her to stop and I don't know what will happen if she doesn't stop and I already said that I trust her. She ignores me, as I assumed she would. As I hoped she would.

She starts with her fingers, as Luca had, but then uses her tongue and I am gasping, panting, trying not to cry out because the last thing I need is or Agnes to rush back in, or or my *mother* to interrupt this this this

When she is done, when I am done, she again stretches out on the bed next to me, her head propped on her hand this time, and she strokes my cheek, my neck, with her other hand. "Better now?" she asks brightly, smiling

"Better, yes. Thank you." I am shy and I am too polite, after that, and I should reciprocate, I think, but I don't know how, where to start, and I start to roll towards her and she kisses my cheek and gets up off the bed before I can touch her. I stand up cautiously, but she did her job well. Both jobs. "It seems embarrassingly late, is it?"

"Not too late for mimosas, but too early for a proper lunch, so take that as you will." She smiles at me, and I don't have the heart to tell her that this is not a mimosas household. It never has been. "It was kind of Lorenzo to give us today off but also I know that you won't really benefit from the time alone and thus here I am."

"Oh I don't know," I say shyly. We are apparently not going to discuss what just transpired. "You don't need to—"

"No, I want to. We're going to go through your clothes and talk about what to do with your pieces, and you're going to show me all of your lovely swords, and sword grip ornaments, and then we are going to go to a tea house and the perfumer that I like best, and we will wish in fountains and maybe duel a stranger and just have a nice day. No don't look like that, this is how you are living now, and it's best to find it out with me than alone."

"I am grateful to you," I say, and she laughs.

"And I thank you, but also perhaps consider that this is what friends do for each other."

I blink, surprised; I had not realized that Dora would consider us friends. Consider herself as a mentor, yes. Consider me as a colleague. Friends, though, is more than I had hoped for and I cannot decide if that's because this has all happened so abruptly or if it's another thing that I should blame my mother for. Also, I am probably simply a fool. "I will consider that," I say, before too much time has passed. "But also consider that one is permitted to be grateful to their friends."

"Just so," she says, throwing open my wardrobe.

I'd thought, or hoped, that she was joking when Dora listed dueling a stranger as one of the day's goals, but once we've been through yet another market I had never visited before, she says, "Well, perhaps it's best to get it over with, and then we can pick out perfumes."

"Oh, Dora, I don't know if—"

"This is what we *do*," she says firmly. "It is expected, and besides, it's an excellent way to learn. You don't want to simply become accustomed to practice partners and not be able to handle a real situation."

I flush, as it is clear that is exactly what happened to me; I am adroit at fighting people who I have practiced fighting. I lack grace in fighting a fresh partner. I don't want to fight anybody, actually, but there are no alternatives to that which are attractive to me. "As you say," I murmur eventually.

"You'll be fine, see the young men like peacocks clustered in the corners of the squares. They come here daily spoiling for fights."

"They will not want to fight me."

"They will, because if nothing else, the reputation of your house precedes you." Still I hesitate; I know well the reputation of my house. "And it will be a mark against their honor should they refuse you. I am your second, and you can set any terms you'd like. First touch, even, you needn't go through the agony of three. Perhaps it will help you with speed on your initial strike."

"Did Lorenzo tell you to do this?" I ask.

"As if Lorenzo could tell me to do anything," she says with a toss of her head. "Now go. Just one. First touch. That's all." She doesn't physically give me a push, but she is I think approaching that level of necessity. I bite back any further argument and clear my mind as we approach one of those groups of young men.

I am trained in etiquette in all manner of situations, though somehow picking a stranger to duel was in none of those lessons. I give the boys a look up and down; I recognize none of their faces. I don't know if that is a relief to me or not, though Dora did specify a stranger, so it would be disingenuous of me to pick a face I know. One of them is taller than the rest, perhaps a little older, and he is the one I pick; I do not want to duel a child, though no children go into the streets strapped with swords. They all watch me watching them, of course, and I'm sure they look at Dora as well. We are not being subtle, and that works in my favor, as the tallest one bows and says, "Pardon, might one of you ladies fancy a fast duel?"

"My friend would, thank you," Dora says. "How kind of you to offer."

"Of course," he says, shedding his coat and handing it to one of his compatriots. He looks at me. "Terms?"

"Two swords, first touch," I say, thankful that the convention is one of brevity. He nods, showing neither excitement nor disappointment, just familiarity.

"Agreed."

We square off and draw our swords, and I take the briefest of moments to look at the guard stance that he has chosen before he is moving forward, and I double block, twist away, return with my main gauche, tapping him on the wrist with the flat of the blade as he begins to raise his longer blade.

"First touch," Dora calls, and the young man's second nods his agreement. We part, and he bows to me while I curtsey.

"Thank you," I say. He did not let me win, but I am still caught off guard by my success.

"My pleasure," he says, shrugging back into his coat.

Once we're out of earshot, Dora laughs and hugs me about the shoulders. "See, that was so simple!"

"I'm certain they would not all be so simple."

"No, but I'm certain you must start giving yourself credit when credit is due, or I shall be very cross."

"I wouldn't want to make you cross."

"Thank you, you're very sweet. Now, what sort of perfume *don't* you have, it's always nice to get something entirely new, and very easy to fall into the same patterns."

"I don't have a perfume that makes all of this seem so easy," I say, and she laughs.

"There, you can joke about it. It will come easier, I promise."

 JENNIFER R. DONOHUE

"You can't promise impossible things, Teodora," I say, but we are both still laughing. "Perfumes, though. Everything I have is very light."

"Okay, that's a start. Maybe something herbal, so the difference isn't a terrible shock to you."

"Or the choice should be deliberately jarring," I say. "To aid me in acclimating to my new role."

"There's the spirit now," she says.

Chapter Twenty-Two

Lorenzo of House Valier

It is to my minor irritation that Sterling and Ottavia are often caught up with and distracted by the niceties of wedding planning, and sometimes miss practices, or come late, or leave early. Ottavia is already our weakest link, so while it isn't a surprise that her focus is anywhere but her blades, it is a disappointment that she isn't trying harder. Weddings are commonplace, and not a typical advancement in the way tournaments are, no matter how joyful people make the occasion. The city does not put much weight to weddings. It is to my honor that they ask for me to be involved, but my role is very minor, and will not take time away from practices. As is sometimes the case, when a girl is married and falls pregnant, she stops being as active in the dueling culture, and the presumption is that Ottavia will indeed do this. I just need her efforts and attentions through one last tournament, and we will consider our circle's lack at a later date.

Conversely, Dora has taken Serafina in hand, and that has been much relief to me. I still think that she is a silly girl, too shy by half, too timid, too not her brother, but to watch a person gain in knowledge and skill is remarkable, even I can admit that she is doing well. Doing better than expected. I was familiar with the sort of tutoring and training that Marco had received, I should not be surprised that Serafina has received similar, though I am surprised she hasn't taken to it better before now. But that is more thought than I am used to giving her, and I am happy to turn my attentions elsewhere.

Though I am the best duelist in the group, I am not the best in the city, and thus must also keep striving. I fight my father some mornings, not long after we have both awakened. He enjoys the warmup, and while I could never claim to enjoy the humbling exercise that it so often proves to be, I enjoy the sense of ambiently absorbing techniques that will improve me, even if all of it has not come together yet. I have advanced often enough to feel that it is within my grasp, but I have not yet reached that crucial tipping point, and so my father and I continue to duel before breakfast.

"I regret that we have not spent so much time together in recent years," he says stiffly, when we have done for the morning.

"You had your own concerns, and I needed to come into my own," I say, surprised. I had not considered my father to be neglectful of me, or particularly absent. Indeed, more scrutiny would have been suffocating. I had not considered my father might have regrets about me.

"A measured answer from a well trained boy," he says with a short laugh. "No, you will always be my boy, I am not insulting you. And what if I were? We know the degree to which we are mismatched."

"I would not think to take insult from my lord father," I say, even if 'boy' did rankle a bit.

"A father can insult just as cruelly as anybody else," he says, catching me in a one-armed embrace as he holds his cup away from us to prevent spilling. "But I like to keep the air clear with you. How else will you know how to comport yourself, without a steady example."

"Not all parents give their actions such thought," I say, thinking of House Galeazzo across from me at the table last night.

"I know." He releases me, finishes his cup. "Go now, though. I'm sure we both want to get on with our day."

I return to my rooms; the smell of burned candles still hangs in the air. I fell asleep with a candle lit last night, which is not my usual habit, and it reduced itself to a stub before snuffing out right at dawn, the sudden fragrant smoke rousing me from my sleep briefly to look at the holders and see the one offender shorter than its fellows, before dreams pulled me under again.

I never remembered my dreams, just that I had dreamed. I suppose it's just as well; I've never been given much to make believe or flights of fancy. The plays that I prefer seeing, when I go to to the theater, are the bloody ones about wars and coups and things. Of course thinking of the theater sours my mood, and I fortify myself with black coffee before going to Sterling's for wedding suit measurements. Why the tailor cannot visit me, or why I cannot visit the tailor's shop, I do not know, but if ever there is a time to acquiesce to a friend's requests it is when they are getting married, and so I acquiesce.

Armand is there as well, at least, and perhaps he knew that I was coming because he was facing the door before I entered through it. "Good morrow, Renzo," he says.

"Good morrow. And how is Sterling?"

"They are getting worked up about the wedding of course. Not the relationship, but the pageantry of it all."

"They should just elope and be done with it. House Bonaro can host a more regular party without any of the wedding pieces."

Armand smiles. "I'm certain Ottavia would not want that."

"Mmm, perhaps not." The day is uncommonly gloomy, and even though the long curtains on the tall windows are thrown wide, there are candles burning in this room as well. Strange of me to note it, as candles burn everywhere always; perhaps some shreds of dream remain in my mind like cobwebs. "We could make a whole farce of it, pretend to kidnap the two of them and spirit them away to a private wedding just for them and the circle."

Armand is quiet long enough that I think maybe he will not answer me, but eventually he says, "Maybe Ottavia would agree to that."

"We would only be helping them." Sterling comes in, trailed by a manservant and a man who is dripping with pins and measuring tapes and can only be the tailor. "Sterling, we have a proposal for you."

"I am already betrothed, having made my own proposal," Sterling says with a tight smile, blinking in bewilderment.

"Yes, it is regarding that. What about elopement? I was just telling Armand that should you like, we can kidnap you and Ottavia and you can have a wedding much less public, perhaps more to your tastes."

Sterling laughs, and it is nice to see some of the tension leave them. "Oh, my friends, I knew I could rely on you. I do not think I'll be taking you up on that offer, but that you have even thought of it pleases me greatly."

"What are friends for, after all, if not to save you from yourself?" I ask with as roguish a grin as I can produce.

The tailor listens to this all with a fussy frown, but takes care not to interrupt. When he is sure we've at least paused in our foolishness, he says, "Very sorry to keep you waiting, gentlemen. Who should I measure next?"

"Take Armand," I say. "He's been waiting longer, and I'll pass the time with Sterling."

"As you say." The tailor bows to me, and then to Armand, who follows him back the way he came. I'm sure each of our houses has a room that tends to be the fitting and tailoring room, even if every house does not have its own tailor.

"Is that your house tailor?" I ask Sterling, because I do not know.

"It is, yes. Ottavia just loves him." Sterling pauses. "Well, I am fond of him as well, I should say."

"He is doing both of your wedding costumes?"

"He and apprentices, yes. The amount of embroidery and embellishment Ottavia intends to have on her train, I told her it is a good thing that we do not live by water, or else she would have to be kept from the edge lest the weight of it drag her in the moment she got close."

"Keep her from fountains as well, I guess," I say, and they laugh.

"Nobody's ever drowned in a fountain," they say. "I don't know why I feel so nervous. Our weddings are much like the other events that we attend, perhaps less bloody."

"Well there's no guarantee of that."

"No, I suppose there isn't." There's the tap of an insistent beak at the window, and we both turn as one to look. A paper bird pecks there, and Sterling goes to open it.

"Your bride just can't stand to be away from you," I say in a joking tone, but when there is enough of a gap to admit the bird, it flutters to me. "Oh, I was mistaken." It goes from bird to note once in my grasp, and I smooth out the slight wrinkles.

I'm sorry to have left in the manner that I did, and I'm sorry to write to you only now. We have had such pursuit, it was not safe before. It may not be safe now. I love K, and we have married. If we have a son, I shall name him after you, if she allows me to. Please do not fret over us; perhaps one day soon we will see each other again.

No salutation and no signature but of course, with all of that, any fool would know who wrote it. I recognize Marco's hand. I stand a moment, just taking in what he said. Of course that is the explanation; we always thought that was the explanation. There is no code here, no secret sign we agreed upon previous. I hold it in one of the candles and the paper catches but slowly, flame yellow and merry to mock us.

I realize Sterling is saying my name, and I turn to them. "Lorenzo, what was that?"

"Something I do not care to speak of," I say. "I know it is unfair of me, to receive a note in your house and not at least tell you the sender, but perhaps by that merit you can guess." They consider, and nod.

"I can guess. I will tell nobody."

"Thank you," I say.

"I just wonder why now..." they trail off, looking at me. "No matter, we shall never speak of it again. I should offer you lunch, for your troubles. Would you accept?"

"I do not think I will, today. I think I would prefer to get the fresh air of the street, and go to a pub."

"And fight a stranger?"

"Maybe."

"I will fetch Armand and we will go together." They hold up a hand. "You will not keep facing this alone, at least not today."

"There is practice later, so I will have to see you then. Please leave me to be alone for now. Give my regrets to your tailor, I will visit him on the morrow."

"As you say." They incline their head slightly, not a full bow. "I will be at your house for practice, then, and hope that Lorenzo will take care of himself."

"As much as I am able."

Chapter Twenty-Three

Serafina of House Galeazzo

Andante and Allegra have me over for tea, and I've been regretfully putting them off for oh so long, that even though there is practice later I simply cannot keep telling them no. Even if our friendship will allow it, my conscience will not. I slip out of the house early enough to buy them flowers on the way, and so that I don't have to explain to my mother where I am going, though thanks to Lorenzo's practices and my prior habits, she seems to currently assume that when I leave the house, it is to that purpose. Today, both will be true, there is no lie that I have to maintain when speaking to my lady mother later.

The day is gloomy, but it makes the flowers all the more important. The flower-sellers are almost all either old women or girls my age, and they seem to be fond of each other, even as they are understood to be rivals. There is no shortage of people wanting flowers, and thus they must all sell in good time. I do wonder what they do with the flowers that do not sell and that wilt beyond use; do people keep animals that eat flowers, so that they can be sold even for that, as the stale bread at the end of the day must? Or is that when they get boiled into syrups for the confectioners?

I look for the candies that are noses, thinking it would be amusing to share those with the twins, but those sellers are not at this market. I buy a ridiculous amount of flowers instead, not more than I can carry, or fit in the carriage, but more than I would normally buy. It is poor exchange, for friends I have hardly seen or written to in weeks or months, but they will graciously accept and we will get on as though there hasn't been such a lapse.

They greet me at the door, and we flutter over each other wish kisses and hugs and exclamations on hair and dresses, though I can tell that they are a little taken aback by my swords, as though they have never seen me wear them before. I am not fully in as formal a dress as I could be either, but in one of the more cunning split skirts that Dora cajoled me into buying, that seem like full regular skirts until I move a certain way, with a ruffle-necked shirt and a short buttoned jacket over that. I am not *incorrectly* dressed for their occasion, but I am also dressed such that I can go from here to House Valier without having to go home to change clothes, or have brought a change of clothing with me.

They are engaging in studies at the musical academy; their parents are formerly stage actors who bought out their indenture, and their daughters are gifted but do not have the gift of spark, and as new money in this manner there are only so many avenues open to them. It is somewhat politically interesting that we have this friendship, but my mother never discouraged it, which is perhaps a curiosity in and of itself.

"You're such a darling to bring all these flowers," Allegra exclaims, burying her face in the roses, which are her favorites.

"They're so lovely this year, aren't they?" Andante asks, as though any of us can remember a year when the flowers were not lovely. Perhaps there was such a year, and they've read about that at their academy. I could ask, and I do not.

"There are always so many, at every market," I say instead. "I always wonder what happens to the remainders, at the end of the night."

"Perhaps the flower sellers just keep them fresh using their spark," Andante says, with all the confidence of somebody who doesn't have it and thus thinks anything is possible. Or perhaps she has the right of it and anything *is* possible, with the right person and the right spark.

"Perhaps!" I say cheerfully, and we go to sit for tea. They always have a different variety, when we meet like this, and today is no different, rosehip and something else, with bowls of cream, and sliced lemon, and large-crystaled, amber colored sugar. There are spiced, snappy cookies that have flowers cooked into them and a cake that is covered in berries, and it is very hard to resist all of it, and I have small bites of everything. It doesn't do to fight on an empty stomach but also being too full works even less.

We talk about this and that and partway through the afternoon, after a moment of laughter, Allegra looks at me in sudden seriousness and says, "Serafina, what is that on your chin?"

"Oh this?" I almost unconsciously touch the scar Lorenzo gave me. If I knew an apothecary, I could have gone and had it healed. My mother could have. Teodora's salve helped, some, but there is a pale white line, slightly raised, rather than the golden marks that I've seen Lorenzo's healing leave. "This is a souvenir of my first dinner back in society," I say, in a voice that's meant to be funny rather than bitter, but they both are frowning now.

"You poor dear! It's all so barbaric," Andante says, quite wide-eyed. Allegra nods her support, opening her fan and fluttering it.

"No, it's—" I stop myself, confused; I don't know what, exactly I was going to say. How I was going to make them understand that this was a very, very minor wound and that this sort of thing is expected. That it was a fight I willfully picked, knowing full well what the outcome would be. That I would rather be cut by a sword in public than slapped by my mother in private in a practice that is meant to punish rather than teach. They are still waiting for me to finish, though. "It's a badge of honor," I say finally. "A point of pride."

"We have left you to them for far too long," Allegra says with sincere regret. "If you're believing all that."

"There's nothing for it," I say lightly. "My house had but two children, and one of them has gone, so I must take up my role. It was kind of Marco that I had freedom from it for so long." Time wasted, my mother's angry voice insists, and my friends' worried expressions do not abate. "Please. Don't let it ruin our time together." The time, though. What is the time.

"It hasn't ruined our time, we are simply worried about you," Andante says, but I am looking at the clock.

"I know it will seem that I'm fleeing your questions," I say, standing, "But we are to meet at House Valier for practice ahead of the tournament."

"So soon?" Allegra asks with real disappointment. "Please, can't you stay longer? We have hardly seen you since the winter."

I look at the clock again. It isn't the agreed time yet for practice. There's always chatting at the beginning, much as Lorenzo wants us to get right to it. Surely I can be late once; I have been punctual every other time, and stayed as late as I was expected. Surely he cannot fault me for wanting to minimize my time with him; he clearly feels the same way. "I suppose I can stay a little longer," I say slowly, sitting again. "I have really missed you very much."

Chapter Twenty-Four

Lorenzo of House Valier

When I leave from Sterling's house, I do not go straight home, but rather wander from fountain to fountain, market to market, until it is time for the circle to gather for practice. I buy the occasional drink during that time, and a swift meal standing up from a street vendor, but my thoughts are disordered, and none of it satiates me.

Marco loves Katarina; I'd always thought that. He brought her to parties sometimes, the sort that our parents didn't come to, so that he could evade his mother's questions. He went to the opening night of every show she was in, though she was never lead. He bought her drinks and included her in some of our nightly outings, or included her until curfew made it so that she must retire back to the gutter where she belonged. She was a woman of shrewd talent, sharp of tongue and swift with her sword, but she did not belong in our society. And now he's married her, the fool. I do wonder who his mother had in mind to pair him with; perhaps Tristan, perhaps somebody from another circle. I cannot imagine she would have left it up to his decision, and see where his decision has gotten us.

But who Marco loves and has married is not my burden. I do not have to pretend that Katarina belongs at our table; they are gone from us. I should be thankful for that, perhaps. Or perhaps his love realized would make her less abrasive to me, make me more generous with my good graces, were she to be in our presence of an evening. Another chair at the table. It would remove Serafina from my concerns again.

I return home and change clothes, for no real reason other than the ritual of it. I drink a glass of water, and then I drink a glass of wine. I feel nerved up, which is to be expected, but due to the secrecy of its source, I have no avenue for it to take. It is the same reason I have been upset of late, and so I can take comfort in the notion that my demeanor will perhaps not be all that different from normal.

Serafina is clearly not concerned with keeping herself in our good graces, though, as the agreed-upon time for practice comes and goes without her arrival. The rest of the circle arrives, and we greet each other, and stretch, and have some wine. Teodora sees me look stormily towards the door and says, "We may as well start, Renzo. You know that she is considerate, and would not keep us waiting without reason."

"We will start," I say, and leave the rest. *Do* I know that she is considerate? She has been absent for quite a long while before this, after all. Or perhaps that absence was the consideration, though Dora enjoys her presence and would not mean it like that.

And so we start, Sterling pairing off with me first, understanding my nervous energy and stretching to the utmost of their abilities to keep the fight engaging enough for me. They surprise me by getting touches in swiftly, coming through my guards where I do not expect from them, and when I recover, my touches are hard-won. We laugh when we are done, and I say "See, this practice has done well for you, my friend."

"This practice has nearly done me in," Sterling says, still laughing but fairly drenched in sweat. "But thank you for the recognition, Renzo."

"You're welcome. I say what I mean." I clap them on the back and offer them a fresh cup of wine, which they accept gratefully.

I watch Tristan and Ottavia fight. Tristan outmatches her but is holding herself back, trying to coax more boldness from Ottavia, leaving herself open in ways that would be careless if they were not so calculated. Ottavia is both unable to take this seriously enough and also takes it too seriously, deathly afraid of wounding anybody, as though those things have lasting meaning. Perhaps she simply hates the sight of *any* blood, and so has a special horror of producing it herself. Sterling would know, I should think to ask when next we are in private. Eventually Tristan ends it out of pity, but it was also the right decision, with Ottavia's stamina flagging.

Luca and I are going to face each other next when Serafina walks in. Her stride is confident, but the look on her face is very plain, that she knows she is late, she decided to be late, and that she hopes it won't matter.

"You'll excuse me," I say to Luca, who nods, and I intercept Serafina before she can reach Dora, who is making comforting noises at Ottavia, take her by the upper arm and march her straight out of the room and down the nearest hall, almost to the door that lets out into the side garden, which will also lead to the front gate. She stumbles to be pulled along so, but does not try to break my grasp and does not voice any protest. "You are very late," I say, releasing her once we are alone and at that remove.

She stumbles, recovers, straightens the fabric of her coat, not looking at me. "I am sorry for that, I had another engagement and I came once it was over."

"Is this something that your mother was aware of?"

"My mother does not trouble herself with my social calendar," she says, a properly evasive answer, and a tone that is, for her, strangely defiant.

"Your mother troubles herself with your standings, and in turn with the standings of this dueling circle. You are a member at my pleasure; we did not need to take you in."

"I am grateful that you took me in," she says promptly, woodenly. "I am making every effort to not be a detriment to the circle. I am sorry for being late."

"And yet you are so late."

"I'm sorry for that," she says again.

"I'm not certain that you are. I think that you've not taken the correct lesson from the freedoms that you are afforded, being in our society, and instead you have gained some measure of false bravado. You thought to tell me you had some manner of *social engagement* though I will guarantee you it was not with somebody of our echelon." She doesn't say anything, just looks at me, tight lipped. "You aren't taking this very seriously, if you will forgo practice for people who will not help with your advancement."

She is silent still, and this time I wait for her response, and eventually she breaks, saying "Please don't be angry with me, Renzo, I didn't—" but her calling me that is like waving a red flag in front of a bull and in a white hot fury I grab her arm again, slinging her into the wall, where she catches herself and tries to push off and face me, but I put my forearm across the back of her neck and shoulders, pressing her there.

"You don't call me that," I say into her ear. The scent of rosemary wafts up to me from the nape of her neck. "You and I are not friends. You are here riding the coattails of your brother's frayed good graces, and you are not your brother. You cannot think that you are taking his place, your inclusion is far more tenuous than that." I press more firmly against her and she squeaks softly in protest, lower my voice further. "You will adjust your behavior accordingly. I will not allow this a second time. Do you understand?" She nods jerkily, her face pressed against the plaster. I step back, leaving her facing the wall, and straighten my own coat. She stands there a moment, shocked into stillness, it would seem, and when she turns it is very sudden and swift, and her open palm cracks against my cheek, surprising both of us.

"You and I both know that my honor will not allow you to continue to speak to me like that," she says, pale but with color in her cheeks. She has committed to the motion, I can say that much. "You may not speak to me like that, you may not treat me like this. I demand satisfaction for this insult."

My anger gives way to great amusement, and I laugh, loudly. "I will not give you satisfaction, no. You are not the aggrieved party here."

She visibly takes a breath, resolves herself, and draws both swords. "You want me to take this seriously. I cannot, if you do not treat me as a peer. Fight me, Lorenzo."

We stand like that for longer than she deserves. I do not draw, and perhaps that also is a surprise. She blinks, and a tear drops down her cheek, followed swiftly by a second. "You are not my peer. Get yourself together. You can come to practice or you can leave out that door." I draw the folded handkerchief from my coat pocket and cast it in her direction, present her with my back, and return to the practice room.

Dora gives me a questioning glance when I come in alone, but she and Luca are fighting now in my absence, and she does not have the proper vantage to see what I am sure is my reddened cheek. It will fade soon enough. Sterling gives me a cup of wine, many questions written plainly on their face, but they do not ask. Armand does not either, though he is examining his blade with much concentration. Tristan is showing Ottavia footwork, and Ottavia keeps turning them into dance steps, and their laughter is distant to me as the stars.

After a time, Armand says, "I think—" and then Serafina walks into the practice room.

"I do apologize for being late," she says to the room in general in a measured, very correct tone. "The time just got away from me."

"Oh I'm sure it's fine," Dora says, and Luca gets the final touch on her. "Oh damn."

"All's fair in love and war," he says, grinning.

"And which was this?" she asks, pouting.

Chapter Twenty-Five

Serafina of House Galeazzo

When Lorenzo takes me by the arm and drags me down the hall, I'm not certain what to expect. He cannot hurt me worse than my mother ever has, I think. Every miserable thing she has done to me has been such a betrayal, for a girl should be able to trust her own mother and feel safe with her, and not be always concerned about the outside forces by which her mother has taken part of for power and standing. If I can apologize appropriately enough, he will have to let it go, because what alternative does he have? We are all of an age. We make choices.

Even as I agreed to stay longer at Allegra and Andante's, the mood was ruined for me, and once I was to my carriage and en route to House Valier, I anxiously wondered if I had been missed and if it had mattered. I had been missed, but not out of concern, but annoyance. And then I called him Renzo by accident, it slipping out as natural as if that is what I always call him.

I am not prepared for him to fling me into the wall, even if I do keep my face from connecting with the surface, my reflexes a testament to all of our practices, perhaps. I am not prepared for him to hold me there, his sword pommels pressing into my back. I am not prepared for his terrible, vicious hatred. I almost cannot hear what he is saying, even though it is right in my ear, for the wild hammering of my heart, for my sudden panic that he is going to hurt me here, where there is nobody to see, even though they are so close by. I nod when it seems like he requires an answer; I am my mother's daughter, pliant when receiving correction from somebody stronger than me. He releases me.

I am my mother's daughter, and I will not be treated like that.

I step back from the wall, pivoting on the foot closest to him and striking with my other hand, the motion traveling up from the rotation of my hips, my open palm cracking against his cheek, sounding as loud as a carriage whip in this small space. I have never slapped anybody before, and I am surprised, and he is surprised, his cheek first pale and then the red outlines of my fingers standing out. My palm stings.

I take a breath. "You and I both know that my honor will not allow you to continue to speak to me like that," I say, shocked at how steady my voice is. I have never stood up for myself like this. "You may not speak to me like that, you may not treat me like this. I demand satisfaction for this insult." He certainly dueled me for less, that first night. Me asking if he loved my brother. I still feel his sword pommels in my back, his furious grasp. Yes. Of course he loved my brother.

He laughs, loud and sudden, as if I am the most ridiculous thing he's ever seen, ever heard. "I will not give you satisfaction, no. You are not the aggrieved party here."

He has no idea how aggrieved I have become, though it is my suspicion that he would not be a sympathetic ear. I steel myself; I have started on this challenge, I must see it through. I draw my blades. "You want me to take this seriously. I cannot, if you do not treat me as a peer. Fight me, Lorenzo." He has to. He cannot refuse me. I'm astounded that he would.

But we remain in this standoff for seconds, and then minutes, and he does not draw, just regards me as an unwanted curiosity. I feel the tears welling up and I hate that they are, that I cannot control them, that he won't respect this obvious question of honor, and finally one runs hotly down my cheek. I expect him to laugh again, and he does not do that, at least.

"You are not my peer. Get yourself together," he says in obvious disgust, reaching into his pocket. "You can come to practice or you can leave out that door." He flings a handkerchief on the floor between us and turns his back on me. I briefly hear laughter echo down the hall, when he opens the door to enter the practice room. Perhaps they're laughing at the handprint on his cheek. Perhaps they're laughing at me.

I crouch to pick up the handkerchief almost by reflex; I cannot see leaving such a thing on the ground. A sob escapes my lips before I know it will happen, and my swords clatter to the ground as I press the handkerchief to my mouth so that nobody hears me crying. Dora would come to comfort me, and then she would fight Lorenzo. He would respect her challenge. Lorenzo would not have the decency to fight me, he hates me, he does not want me here. Why am I doing this?

I have to calm down. I cannot act like this. Through sheer will, I slow my sobs, blot at my eyes, not rubbing, I don't want to be red-faced, I don't want there to be questions that I cannot explain. I pick up my swords and sheathe them. The door is right there. I could walk out, get back into my carriage and—

And what, foolish girl? Go home and tell your mother why you aren't at practice? Perhaps this time she will go out to the stable and get a horse whip, as slapping me was not apparently sufficient. My hand is actually on the door handle while I stand and have these thoughts. No. I can only stay.

I straighten my clothes. I pat at my hair, then employ Dora's trick of using my main gauche as a narrow mirror to check my appearance. My tears have been sufficiently dried, and my complexion is ruddy from rubbing at my face. I lightly hold the chill metal against my face, check again, and now I am presentable. I stuff the damp handkerchief into my jacket pocket, and make sure that my swords are appropriately settled, and then I return to the practice room.

"I do apologize for being late," I somewhat announce to the room, not addressing anybody in particular. My tone is calculated, apologetic but my voice does not shake. Not too loud, I don't want to *command* attention, just be appropriately heard. "The time just got away from me."

"Oh I'm sure it's fine," Dora says, turning just slightly to me, and Luca takes her distraction as opportunity to get a touch in on her. "Oh damn."

He grins at her, and at me. "All's fair in love and war."

"And which was this?" she asks, with a pout but in a similarly light tone.

"I suppose that remains to be seen." He puts his swords away and catches up her hand, sword and all, and kisses it in apology. Then he comes over to me. "And what was more important than this practice, surely the most important one before the tournament?"

"The tournament is in three days, and we have two more practices before then," I say, making effort to meet his energy. From the corner of my eye, I can see Lorenzo's exasperated posture. "After this."

"Yes but *this* one is the third practice from the tournament," Luca says.

"Yes?" I am very certain he is being funny, but I am unsure of the joke. I think perhaps he also is unsure of the joke, but he's committed to it, and is hoping that more inspiration comes to him.

"Armand, can you believe she doesn't know?" he says, in a disbelieving, conspiratorial tone.

"I suppose we simply hadn't thought to tell her," Armand says obliquely.

"Don't listen to them," Dora says, rescuing me. "They're ill-equipped for these sorts of jokes. Were you someplace fun? Oh, we are wicked people who have forgotten that you had friendships outside of the game. Were you visiting friends? They must miss you terribly."

"I was visiting friends, yes. For tea. They're enrolled in the musical academy," I say cautiously. "But we don't need to focus on me, I've disrupted things quite enough."

"Nonsense, a break is good for us. Here, have a drink. Oh or perhaps not, if you've just come from tea." I see Lorenzo give an irritated twitch, and Dora flicks him a questioning glance.

"I *did* overstay," I say, forcing what I think is a correct smile. "But please, no, we don't need to focus on that. I'm sure Lorenzo would rather—"

"I'm certain he would, yes, but he isn't an *ogre*, and he mayn't dictate every moment of our lives."

"N-no, I wouldn't have said—"

"You know, Teodora is right. Why don't we hear about Serafina's afternoon?" Lorenzo says loudly, abruptly, in a tone that makes me want to flee the room.

"I really don't care," Tristan says, heaving an irritated sigh, but Ottavia is happy for the distraction.

"Tea? What types of cookies did you have?"

I've forgotten already, in my turmoil. "They had flowers baked into them," I say finally. "So that the whole top of the cookie is the flower."

"Oh those sound lovely! Who are your friends?"

"They're twins, their names are Allegra and Andante." Such a short answer will not be sufficient. I blink back tears again, as Lorenzo raises his eyebrows at me expectantly, his arms crossed. You wanted to have a taste of that other life again, his posture says. Now explain it to us. "Their parents were part of theater companies and bought out their indentures and now they teach at the musical academy and their daughters attend." We sing together sometimes, I want to say, but my throat feels very tight.

"Oh indeed? And what are their specialties?" Lorenzo asks.

"They both sing, but can play many instruments," I say after another pause that Tristan sighs heavily in. "Allegra prefers the strings, so violin and harp, and Andante is very fond of the piano, and often they accompany one another, and at least once, Andante filled with piano accompaniment in at the company one night when the typical performer was ill."

"That is so very interesting," Dora says, sounding genuine. "Does neither have any spark?"

"None to speak of. They're such peaceful little doves, both of them, they are somehow always shocked at the sight of swords."

"They must think we are quite barbaric," Lorenzo says laconically.

"They would never say such things..." I look to Dora again in silent plea.

"Of course we'll move on, that's good enough. I've made you so dreadfully uncomfortable, I'm so sorry. She catches me up in a brief, lavender scented hug. "Lorenzo, who is everybody fighting?" She turns to him and he raises his hands in defeat.

"Whoever you think is best, since I'm not to dictate every moment of your lives."

"Am I incorrect? This is *practice* for a *tournament*, it is not life or death. Honestly, Lorenzo, you are being very tiresome. Here, Armand, you fight Serafina. I will fight Ottavia while Lorenzo corrects us. You will win at least one of your matches, Ottavia," she says.

"I haven't yet, I'm simply hopeless," Ottavia says cheerfully.

I pull my dueling gloves from my pocket and there is a flutter of white from the corner of my eye; Lorenzo's handkerchief. I bend for it, but Armand is quicker. He picks it up, cocks his head slightly, and then seems to truly look at me for the first time as he hands it back. "Thank you," I say.

"It's nothing," he says. "Now, if you're ready?"

Chapter Twenty-Six

Lorenzo of House Valier

The morning of the tournament, I am up at dawn. Not by design; I went to bed earlier than usual perhaps, but in order to get extra rest, not to herald the sunrise. I try to recapture slumber for a time, rolling over, turning my pillow, and then throwing my blankets off in disgust when none of it works.

My tournament clothes are already cleaned, pressed, and hung. I bathed before I slept, and did not drink into the night, and these accustomed virtues have surely robbed me of rest, though I cannot say what I should have done otherwise. I am not nervous for my own prospects, I can say that much with confidence. I feel that I have a readily accurate assessment of the rest of the dueling circle. The only thing that remains is to get through it. Perhaps the weaker members will surprise me, I would not object to such a turn of events.

In general, the household make it as unobtrusive as possible, and I do not see a single servant as I make my way to the breakfast room. My parents do make it a habit to rise early, and even if they will not be there yet, coffee will be, and food on the buffet. I can avail myself of what catches my fancy, make my final physical preparations, and then dress and go to the first tournament location.

It is hard to not dwell on the fact that we had Marco with us for the previous tournament. That our chances had been very good to do very well, and that we'd been very pleased with our standings by the end of us, even with Ottavia's persistent foolishness, and Armand's wild inconsistencies. Nobody received much injury to speak of, just the slight bloodings and nicks and scratches that come with such an event. It's to be expected that somebody makes a mistake on occasion, accidents do happen, and some of the best healers in the city are always on hand at each fight, so that nobody's mistakes become permanent. There has only been one tournament death in my memory, surely others before that, but just the one, at my first tournament. One of the duelists slipped on sweat that had dripped upon the floor, and the tip of his blade went through his opponent's eye. His death was instantaneous, there was nothing to be done.

Which isn't to say there aren't people about who have lost their eyes to duels; there are, and they seem to get on well enough. Still fighting, many of them, though if ever there was an excuse to give it up, it's certainly that. But if your spark gets strong enough, you don't exactly grow back what you have lost, but there are other senses you can avail yourself of. People of strong enough spark, in my parents' echelon, have their own tournaments. They cannot be allowed to compete with circles closer to my level, they are far too out of balance for any measure of fairness. There are people of strong enough spark that it can be sensed even by those who have no spark.

My ruminations on that finish as my coffee cup empties and I pace through the house, return to my rooms. I've seen traveling exhibitions where they have great cats in tremendous cages, and their pent up energy, sleek dangerous muscle, is what I think of as I wait for a time to be able to *do* something. Those animals, with their sheathed claws and flashing eyes, had nothing to do, until they did, at the behest of their masters. No. Their captors.

Luca and Armand turn up around lunch time, and we eat, but not too much. My parents aren't here, I'm not sure when they left, and if it is related to the tournament or not. Perhaps they are judges.

"I always feel so nerved up before these events," Luca says with an embarrassed grin. "Once we're there and have had a few fights I'm fine, you know I'm not worried about fights, but I hate waiting."

"It's the anticipation," I agree. "The readiness to duel but it isn't time yet. It's very frustrating."

"I don't suppose you know how we'll do, Armand?" Luca asks.

"I don't, no," he says after a moment's consideration. "Though somebody's duel today will be very bloody. I cannot tell whose, if it's in our circle or not."

"Oh, okay, well now I'm worried about the fighting specifically, thank you Armand," Luca laughs, and Armand frowns.

"I never know when I should say anything. I never know if saying anything changes what I've seen or felt, but it doesn't seem to."

"No, no, I'm not blaming you for anything, my friend. It's honestly a surprise that these events aren't more bloody, is it not, Renzo?"

"It is indeed," I say. How strangely in line with my earlier thoughts this is. Or not strange; we know the nature of Armand's spark. I do think that we hope, every time he advances, that he will gain some clarity, some further control. It is typically how these things work, but then, the spark does what it will in each individual and there is nothing that anybody can do to change that. "Besides the fact that the rules for this set are first blood."

"So much room for creativity there," Luca says. "Do you try for a little slice on an extremity, or to give a more insulting souvenir? Though I suppose we know Lorenzo's preference on that..."

"Really, Luca?" I ask, but with no real force behind it.

"Really, yes, but it's also my nerves, forgive me. You know I am a fool in such situations, but right now we are only amongst ourselves, so allow my tongue its looseness."

"I will allow," I say, and he bows dramatically.

"You have my sincerest thanks, my dear friend. Armand, now you say something dreadfully stupid, please, so I am not the only one." Armand blinks at him, and Luca flaps his hand. "Never mind, forget I said anything."

I laugh. "Luca, you really are in a state."

"I am how I am," he says, with mustered false dignity.

"I wonder if it is not yourself you are all nerved up about," Armand says, and Luca eyes him narrowly.

"No, I said for you to say something stupid, not something incisive, please just let things lie. We cannot open a bottle of wine so close to the event. Maybe we should just walk there and get it over with."

"As you say," Armand agrees. "Shall we?"

"We may as well," I say. "It isn't so far that the walk will harm our stamina for the duels. Even so, we will likely still be early, but always better to be early than late."

"Yes, we all learned that lesson the other day," Armand says.

"Please, I am beset upon from all sides," I say stiffly, and Armand raises his hands.

"If a man cannot hear the truth from his friends, then he is due to be lonely soon."

I take a deeper breath, let it out through my nose, slowly. "True enough. I hope to thank you for that soon, but I cannot today."

"Just so." Armand's expression is unchanged; I will either duel him over such a statement, or I will not. It is the way of things. Today, I will not.

Luca claps his hands together once. "It's settled then, a walk will be good for all of us."

"We're like caged lions," I finally say.

"In more ways than one," Armand says cryptically.

It's a lovely day for it, and the first fights are scheduled for an outdoor venue, so the streets are full of spectators and vendors, even if they would not normally otherwise be. When the actual dueling starts, the spectators are moved back so as not to be dangerously distracting, and if they crowd proves too unruly, the guard summarily disperses them. Almost none of them are wearing swords, but I do spot a few, undoubtedly from the theater companies. No faces I recognize, which is lucky for them, probably. But I can't let that distract me right now.

I see Serafina, anxiously biting her lower lip and looking at the crowd, before I see Dora and Tristan, who look cool and collected. "We're all early, isn't that funny?" Sterling says right at my elbow.

"Almost as if we planned it," I say. "I'm pleased to see we've all been so eager, though."

"We've made the best preparations we can," they say with a slight shrug. "And there's only so long we can wait at home, as I'm sure you are well aware."

"True of so many things," Tristan says, angling over to us. "There are too many spectators already, I hope the guard moves them along soon."

"The people have so little to look forward to," Luca says. "Let them watch."

Tristan cocks her head a moment thoughtfully, then laughs. "Oh, I see, Luca. You're just on the lookout for your latest torrid conquest."

He lowers his voice to a conspiratorial tone. "Well how else am I supposed to find them?"

"*Certainly* not in the dueling halls," she says, matching his tone with a sly smile.

"Never, that just isn't my style. The dueling halls are to find somebody to settle down with, if my parents don't make that selection for me."

"Do you anticipate that they will?" Tristan asks, eyes sharpening; Luca must never have said such a thing in her presence.

But he laughs and shrugs. "There's never any telling what parents will decide to do. There's no sense in wasting time worrying about it."

Chapter Twenty-Seven

Serafina of House Galeazzo

None of the judges will allow the duels to start until all of the participants have arrived and been counted. I am not eager to duel, but I am eager for the day to be over. I haven't seen my parents since we arrived here and then Dora appeared at my side and took me away in a blur. She took my hair down and redid it for me, her touch so swift and light I hardly know when she's working at it and when she's done.

"I wish I could help you," I say. "I feel very helpless."

"Nonsense," she says. "It's good luck to have somebody do your hair for your first tournament."

"You're making that up."

"Am I?" she twinkles, and I can't help but laugh. "You'll never know."

"I'm certain I won't know, you're right." I also can't help but sigh. "But my luck has never been the best."

"Which is why I'm helping you, and you'll either return the favor in kind or pass it along one day, when we've got a new member in the circle and you're the experienced and confident one."

"You'll have to devise a way to lend me confidence as well as luck then," I say, chewing at my lower lip. It isn't a usual one of my affectations, but this scene is edging ever closer to overwhelming me.

This is when Lorenzo arrives, of course, Luca and Armand with him. The tournament has me in such knots that I don't even have my usual lurch of dread when I see Lorenzo, though I to try to manage a tight smile for Luca, who touches my elbow lightly, though he's listening to whatever Lorenzo and Tristan are saying, which I can't quite catch over a sudden argument on the other side of me, just the slightest scuffle about I'm not sure what, since all of it is just noise rushing to my ears, an ocean of sound, like listening to a seashell.

Then, just like that, everybody stops talking. I'd closed my eyes, I realize, and when I open them, one of the judges is standing in the dueling area and has raised his hand. That was enough to silence the crowd, so attenuated we are to the power structures and struggles.

"The tournament will start," they say. "You will all receive a schedule. If your duels are not at this location, you may proceed to the correct location. Do not be late to any of your appointed duels, this will count as a refusal. There is no spark usage permitted during the first round, other than to be healed after each duel is called."

I feel like not enough information has been given out, either verbally or by letter, but the schedules ripple through the crowd and I stare at the one in my hands without seeing for a moment until Luca leans over and places his finger on the page next to my name. I'm scheduled to duel Callum of House Orssino, who I recall speaking with in passing not all that long ago. The location is here, and it isn't the first duel, it's sixth.

People begin to filter out of the square, quietly chatting, nothing like the dull anticipatory roar that happened earlier, and the dueling floor clears for the first match. I look for the other names of the circle; we're all to fight here first, for the first bracket at least. If any of us will progress, the next location is at the Company of the Grounded Mermaid. I'm very certain that Lorenzo at least will, probably also Luca and Dora. The only tournament progressions that would surprise me, actually, would be Ottavia's and my own. Of course, as a circle, we will spectate all of our fellows; to do otherwise would be less than honorable.

Lorenzo fights first, and his opponent is Arnaldo of House Silva, who I have never met. Arnaldo is not so tall as Lorenzo, though he is broader in the shoulder, and I try to make myself watch, and analyze. Broader shoulders might mean longer arms which might mean further reach, how a person is built can work for or against them, in addition to whatever training they've had. They would not have been paired for a duel if they were poorly matched, and thinking that actually make me take heart, just slightly. If Callum has been matched with me, it must mean that my standings are not so abysmal as they might otherwise have been, with my late start in society. She has a few years of experience ahead of me, at the very least.

There are many parries, many attempts at ripostes, and then Lorenzo disarms Arnaldo of his main gauche and gets first blood, a cut on his upper bicep, blood immediately blooming on his white shirt sleeve. The duel is called, and the judge steps in to heal Arnaldo, and Lorenzo receives his first laurel wreath of the day. It is presumptuous of me to assume he will receive more, perhaps; he is the best of *us*, certainly. I am relieved that he has won, I realize, relieved and pleased and proud, as if I have had any hand in his success.

Luca fights next and his opponent is either overmatched or having a bad morning, as there is not nearly as much back and forth as Lorenzo had. It is not so showy a duel to watch, but it is clean and efficient, and the young man overextends on a too-open thrust, and Luca steps inside his reach, deflects his main gauche, and gives him a slight cut just above the knee.

Most people don't cut faces, I think with relief. I feel very calm but also on the verge of panic. Sterling's fight is very brief, it's almost as though they go to the floor to face Venette of House Massimo as a formality. Venette comports herself very well, and Sterling seems to want to be anywhere than here, which surprises me. In practices they had been serious and tried hard, and they seem no less serious on the dueling floor, but they exchange only a few parries before Venette catches the inside of their elbow.

Tristan is fighting next, and her opponent looks very capable from his posture but is also very nerved up, from the way he is pacing with his second beforehand, his second speaking to him in a low voice that doesn't carry, him nodding without looking at her.

"He's been ill for a time, and so wasn't in the last tournament," Dora says to me in a low voice that also doesn't carry. I'm surprised that Dora isn't her second, but Lorenzo is. "Martim of House Paola.

"Is he concerned that he's overmatched?"

"I'm not really certain, but his confidence has been damaged somehow. He wasn't like this before." The young man, Martim, is looking past his second now, at Tristan, and still nodding. Tristan has her back to us, but I can imagine the impatience in her face from her absolutely correct posture, the way she is holding herself very still. She has not drawn yet, and is just standing there waiting. Finally, Martim steps onto the dueling floor, and they both draw, and salute each other.

Tristan does not blood him immediately, he is too agile for that. I think she would not have felt satisfied anyway, if she had; not after her wait. They meet, clash, separate. His face reddens, and I don't know if Tristan said something to him, or if it is the situation. They match crossguards again, spin apart, and next to me, on the other side, I feel Armand's posture change, or maybe his breathing. I glance at him, and he is looking at the duel, but his eyes have a strange look to them that I have not seen before, and because I am looking at Armand, I don't see what happens next, just hear Dora's short exclamation, which is in turn swallowed by the crowd reaction.

I turn back, and there is blood on the dueling floor, too much blood, and Tristan is on one knee, one hand on the ground, wavering, and Martim is crouched next to her, his second hovering close by, and all of their swords are on the floor and in the blood and the judge is crossing the dueling floor, which I have not seen before, and Lorenzo is at Tristan's side in the next moment, and I think, is that correct, can he be there right now? But first blood happened, it more than happened, he can be there without having broken any rules. Dora has taken my hand, she's saying something, but I can't hear her at first. I have never seen so much blood. They must have called the duel but I didn't hear it. They *had* to have.

Tristan wavers and Lorenzo crouches on her other side, holding her up, and then I have a sense, sharply and suddenly, of spark being spent. I have never felt that before, though I'd known in theory that we had a sense of such things, when they occurred.

"She'll be all right, Lorenzo is right there," Dora says firmly. That must have been what she has been saying, either to comfort me, or herself, or whoever else is listening. Armand knew, I think. He knew just a moment or so before, that disaster was about to strike. He looks at her and I catch a glimpse of his pained face.

"I could have—" he starts, and Dora reaches past me and touches his shoulder.

"No, you couldn't have. You've tried before. She's fine, see, she's standing again already."

Martim is still standing there, stricken, his second speaking in his ear but he doesn't react. When Tristan stands, the judge and Lorenzo on either side of her, the judge then turns to Martim and says something to him that breaks the spell. He nods, shakily, and retrieves his swords,wiping them off before putting them away. He then looks at Tristan and bends to pick up her swords as well. She still has her back to me, I still cannot see her face, just the way she clings to Lorenzo's arm, the inward curve of her shoulders, so unlike her, but she turns her head a little to Martim and nods, takes a moment, then lets go of Lorenzo's arm and stands up straighter. Then she nods again and takes her swords from Martim, and the crowd starts clapping and cheering as she sheathes the blades and walks off the dueling floor without Lorenzo's help, but gingerly.

"What happened?" I asked. I couldn't see enough, I don't even know how to guess where she was struck.

"I couldn't see, I don't know," Dora says, though the frown is clearing from her face as she watches Tristan walk. "She'll be all right, though."

Sterling, who was a bit closer and had a better vantage, takes a few steps back to us. "It was clearly an accident," they say. "Martim's sword dipped a bit too low, and when Tristan deflected his thrust, the blade entered her thigh above the knee, and must have gone through the artery there."

"There's so much blood," I say, a silly and empty thing for me to say. We are fighting with swords, of course there is blood. Tristan's artery was likely cut, of course there is so much blood.

"Do you feel faint?" Dora asks. "Do you need to sit down?"

Yes, I think. I say, "No, no, please don't fawn over me, I'm fine. I'm not the one injured."

"Well neither is she, anymore," Luca says cheerfully. "Lorenzo is very good."

"Is there anything he isn't good at?" I ask, trying to make my tone light, joking, and I'm not certain it came off properly. I don't mean to sound envious; genuinely, Lorenzo is a man of many talents.

"Yeah, changing his mind once he's made a decision about something," Luca says cryptically, and then Tristan and Lorenzo have reached us, and Dora catches her up in a hug. Now I can see her face, paler than usual, both resentful of and grateful for the hug.

"Teodora, really," she says, but without much force.

"I know, I know, it's just hard to see, no matter how many times it happens," Dora says, producing a handkerchief from I'm not sure where and wiping a smear of blood off of Tristan's cheek.

"What happens next?" I ask, as servants come onto the dueling floor with mops, and buckets, and start to clean up.

"Well we wait for the dueling floor to be clean and dry again, and then the next fight happens," Luca says. He's looking at Lorenzo, who seems his usual calm and unbothered self, and then looks at me. "Oh, you haven't seen this before. It's unpleasant, but expected. The hope is always for little nicks and scrapes like we get in practice but sometimes..."

"Sometimes a man has weak wrists," Tristan says sourly. She's inspecting her blood-sodden skirts now. "I suppose this is ruined, and I should go up the row for a change of costume and hope it doesn't take too long."

"You likely won't want the momento, even without the blood," Dora says. "Come, let's see about what we can find." She glances at me. "Do you want to come?"

"I think I will stay," I say. I think Tristan needs her space and I might say something foolish to irritate her. "Be back soon, though, you are after Armand."

"It won't be but a few minutes, there are vendors set up for just such an eventuality." She kisses Armand on the cheek. "Please try to focus," she says.

"Since you asked." He tries to affect a carefree, joking tone, but I can see he is also shaken. I wonder if he has seen the possibility of his duel, or if there is just darkness ahead of him. Interesting, that he would get an inkling of what was to come in Tristan's, but from what I've gleaned, there is no rhyme or reason to the visionary glimpses that Armand receives through his spark.

Luca and Lorenzo briefly go off to a beer stand that is nearby. Lorenzo drinks one mug and then the next in rapid succession, to Luca's one, though when they return, his gait is steady and unwavering. It seems warm for how early it is in the morning, or I am flushed from the unpleasant excitement, and I do not comment on it to anybody, for what would I say? It is the sort of conversation to have with Andante and Allegra, but not here. We do not talk about the weather, here.

Soon, perhaps too soon, the dueling floor is clean, and then it is sanded, and I watch the judge walk across it, testing its fastness. The first time he does this, he is unsatisfied, and still we wait. Some of the crowd goes to other places, where the duels have not been halted by such a bloodletting, and that is a relief to me. I am not keen on having so many spectators, when I have my first tournament duel.

The second time the judge paces the floor, though, he nods and calls for the next duel. Armand takes his coat off and drops it into my arms without looking at me, as I have been standing closest to him. I am surprised, but more, I feel almost flattered. It is a compliment, an acceptance of me in the circle, that Armand so casually handed off his coat to me before going to duel. I smooth it, put it over one arm so that it hangs nicely.

Lorenzo is Armand's second, and I think that he would be nearly everybody's, except probably Sterling and Ottavia. And me. We haven't discussed it, but my presumption is that Dora will be mine. But in this tournament setting, doing what he can do, Lorenzo has already demonstrated just why it makes sense for him to be the second to the members of our circle. Tristan would have surely died had he not been so fast, or perhaps the judge would have been fast enough, but either way, she would not have been so swiftly in the condition to be put out about her dress, and picking out her opponent's faults.

Armand's opponent is about his height and built, and they seem an even match, to my eye. They bow slightly too long to one another, and then salute with their swords, not quite the usual affectation, but I have not seen Armand duel in a tournament before. Or ever outside of practice, actually. I mark it, but don't know it's unusual, necessarily, until Dora leans in to whisper to me.

"They were lovers, once," she says. "They haven't spoken in *years*."

"Oh," I say and then, "Oh!" again, more fully comprehending. "Did the judges know that? Did they put Armand against him on purpose?"

"Perhaps they did," she says. "Or perhaps they didn't. It's of no matter, it's mostly of note because Armand both fights and loves so sparingly. Their falling out was quite the shakeup for him, and for us, for some time."

Marco never mentioned it. But why would he? I knew none of the players involved, other than having met the members of the circle before. He also never spoke to me about anybody's romantic encounters, certainly not his own, and thus another reason I would not now know to recognize Armand's former lover, Iulio of House Vellera.

The duel has begun but neither Armand nor his opponent have moved. The spectators around us are shuffling and muttering, but at first they are curious, they want to know how this will play out. Then it drags on and somebody calls out something that I can't quite hear, in a jeering tone. A moment later, there's a scuffle there as the guard pulls them away, but not before a new horror had been seeded in my mind, of members of the crowd heckling the duels. Obviously, it is not permitted. Obviously, somebody did it anyway.

Abruptly, they are in motion. Armand steps to the right first, something that apparently he never does, for even in my slight association with him and his dueling habits, it looks strange to my eye, and Iulio is also baffled by this, but not in time to recover, and Armand bloods him on the left side of his chest. Over the heart, if I think he's being poignant, and I do. The duel is called, and they stand there for a moment just next to each other, as if engaged in a dance, then they put their swords away, bow again, and leave the floor.

I return Armand's coat to him, and he nods to me in thanks.

Chapter Twenty-Eight

Lorenzo of House Valier

There are ways other than alcohol to fuel my spark, when I'm burning it to heal people, but it's faster and easier than eating sweets, or anything else for that matter. Taking care of Tristan's wound took a lot out of me, but I knew that it was temporary, that the fix was just a few steps away, and was able to put up a false front. Luca saw through it, of course, but we've been through this before.

"I wonder why Armand seemed so bothered," Luca remarks, halfway through his mug of beer while I am picking up my second.

"Perhaps he had an indication of what would transpire," I say.

"Though also, you saw who he's scheduled to fight?"

"I did. I'm not sure he looked at the schedule."

"Typical Armand," Luca says with a laugh. "Can imperfectly glimpse the future but also won't look at a schedule for definitive plans."

I laugh too. "Perhaps he prefers the uncertainty, given the imperfect glimpses."

"Perhaps." He finishes his beer. "They'll have cleaned up by now, I think."

"Near enough that we should go back." I take a handful of salted nuts from a metal bowl on the bar, and wash them down with the last of my beer. "Maybe we'll get through everything today, wouldn't that be something."

"It would be something. We'll get through all of the first round today, anyway," he says and I make some noise of agreement. "Perhaps also seconds." Teodora is walking back up the street with Tristan, who has found a new dress and is adjusting her sword belts over it.

"Honestly it's astounding that he got you in the leg," Dora is saying in a light, jesting tone. "Most of the time, people go for all of the exposed flesh we have above our bodices.

"Some of us have more exposed flesh than others," Tristan says, casting a brief, comedic glance at Dora's ample bosom.

"Don't be crass, Tristan, we none of us can help how we're built. Isn't that right, Lorenzo?"

"Both of you have more exposed flesh than I ever shall," I say, matching her tone. "And I simply haven't the hips for either of your skirts."

"Oh I remember that ball," Dora says. "You were all so darling in your pretty dresses."

"I remember it too and hope it's never repeated," Luca says. "It was so humiliating, trying to stuff my top."

"You should've just used Sterling's tailor, they could've sewn ruffles in your bodice to fill it out properly." Tristan finishes her buckling to her satisfaction and smooths her hands over her hips. "Though also they guard their tailor fiercely, and it's a wonder he's getting shared enough for the wedding preparations."

"Isn't it, though?" Dora snaps out her fan. "What a rare pleasure."

We make it back to the rest of the group, Sterling and Ottavia standing with their arms linked, Armand now looking at the dueling floor with something like concentration. He glances at me, and then sheds his coat and presses it into Serafina's surprised arms without a word. She doesn't protest, though, or make any noise. She simply straightens out and folds it over her arm as we make our way down to the duel.

I nod to Iulio, who I also haven't seen in quite some time, but he and Armand have already locked eyes. I am unfamiliar both with the circumstances of their meeting, and also what separated them; they were together for a torrid summer and then one day it was Armand alone again, and he has never spoken of it. Unlike Luca, we have spared him the banter, the inquisitive prodding. Looking at his face now, I'm not sure if he is entirely clear on what separated them either.

They look at each other for an excruciatingly long time after their initial bows, and then their salutes, which are not done enough to be usual, but not rare enough to be remarkable either. The judge looks to me and I give a slight nod that I intend for him to take as reassurance that nothing is amiss, and that the duel will progress. I had been confident, until this point, that the duel would indeed progress; Armand has his oddities, but does not typically revolt against the rules. He knows the certain punishment he faces, should he now not duel this man.

And then they are in motion, banishing my doubts. I've fought Iulio, he is not to be dismissed as a serious swordsman. Armand is uneven, as everybody who knows him knows, through no fault of his own. When we were all younger, and practicing with wooden swords, he himself was far sharper, but it was before all of our sparks had kindled and advanced to be of any note, much less where we all are now. This is a truth that we don't often speak, the way that our sparks change us, even as our sparks *are* us.

Armand, who never steps to the right first, does so now. Iulio is quick of mind, and feet, and sword, but even that disarms him so that he is blooded just over the heart even before he knows it, and they pause in that moment, side by side. I hear Armand speak, but not what he says, and Iulio briefly closes his eyes. Then they spin apart again, bow into the open space between them, and Armand wipes off his blade before sheathing it. He never drew his off hand blade.

Armand turns to me and raises his eyebrows, and we walk back to our circle, with Iulio still standing on the dueling floor for a moment, Venette, his second, talking in his ear, before he also returns to his circle.

"Armand, that was just *masterful*," Ottavia is saying, and he ignores her, taking his coat back from Serafina, who is being quiet at least.

"It was quite the show," Dora says, a bit less effusively, shooting a glance at Ottavia. "Would that all of our duels are quite so flashy, it's a lot to live up to. Indeed, *how* am I supposed to follow that act?"

"You'll have to cat and mouse her a bit, I imagine," Tristan says, looking at the program.

"Or shall I cut her early? Stacci *is* so fond of being fancy, I wonder if she still does that cape nonsense? I haven't seen her all morning."

I clear my throat. "That cape nonsense is—"

Dora waves her fan impatiently, cutting me off. "Oh yes, yes, quite the style in a city *hundreds* of miles from here and thus of no consequence to us, it just makes her look like a lunatic. Honestly, Renzo, I'm surprised at you." From the corner of my eye, I see Serafina flinch slightly, and I smirk.

"Yes, my apologies Teodora, what was I thinking. Plus, it is so crass of me to get you worked up right before your duel." I bow deeply, reaching for her hand. "Can you ever forgive me?"

She puts her fan in my outstretched hand, laughing. "You are forgiven, now take me to my fight."

"It would be my honor." I offer her my arm, and she takes it.

Chapter Twenty Nine

Serafina of House Galeazzo

Though Dora ridiculed Stacci of House Belos for her dueling style, which is sword and cape, Stacci was able to get first blood on her. I held my breath nearly the entire time, not on purpose, but after Tristan was so grievously wounded, it has made every duel seem that much more potentially deadly. They have always been that way, of course, but the reality of it has never been so strongly in my mind. And my duel is next after Dora's. It's actually a wonder that she is so late in this roster, but I think it was randomly chosen, and not really by ranking. The new schedules will rank us, I think I hear Tristan say to Armand, who does not reply.

Early in the duel, Dora uses her long blade to trap up Stacci's cape, and nearly ends the duel there with her main gauche, but Stacci manages to elude the blade by being far more flexible than any of us had anticipated, and she forgoes the cape, rather than struggling for it. Dora shakes it from her sword with a swift motion, in time to parry Stacci's next thrust, and they both spin away from each other, but when they close next, Stacci grazes her on the back of the wrist and the duel is called as the blood wells up and drips on the floor.

Dora picks up Stacci's cape and hands it to her, and they're both smiling as they curtsey to one another and put their swords away. I shouldn't make Dora walk all the way over here, just to return and be my second, I think, but I am rooted to the spot. Lorenzo takes her hand and looks at her wrist, then rubs his thumb across it and no more drips fall on the floor. As soon as they step away, servants come and clean the floor, though it's far less of a production than it was with Tristan's mishap.

My opponent is Callum of House Orssino, and when I see her walking down to the dueling floor with Venette as her second, I recognize her from events, but we have never properly met. What an odd way to meet the people in our society this is, I think, and somehow keep myself from laughing nervously. Ottavia gives me a little pat on the shoulder, which surprises me, but I'm able to move from where I stand after that, and go meet Dora. Lorenzo brushes past without even looking at me, and she watches him for a fraction of a second before smiling at me.

"Here, let me look at you. You look all right, how do you feel?"

"A bit like I'm floating," I say.

"Your feet are firmly on the ground. You will be okay. This is only first blood, and I know Callum to be a cautious duelist. She's left handed, so that will be unusual for you, but try not to think too much, just rely on your training. You're so good with the technicalities, just remember that."

"Thank you." I manage to smile back at her, even though I do feel fluttery, and like I'm not quite connecting with the ground, and with the things around us. I touch my swords, either to adjust them or make sure they're still there. They are still there. "I hope to not embarrass myself."

"I don't think that you will," Dora says. "Perhaps you'll surprise yourself."

"Perhaps I will." I don't think so, but I don't want to disappoint her. We are at the dueling floor now and I can sense the spark in the air, maybe from all the little healings that have been done, or the big one. Maybe from something else, maybe the judge does something with his spark. I cannot tell, nor do I have the time or words to ask. I step onto the dueling floor, and Callum does as well. We curtsey to each other, and she is smiling. She seems almost friendly, but her gaze is intense. Cautious, Dora says, but I won't know until I know.

We draw, and almost as though we've planned it, we both sidestep, circling each other. Cautious, she's looking for what she thinks might be a break in my guard. I wonder. I waver my main gauche just slightly, as though it's lost my attention, and she darts in for a cross strike. I parry, but she is away before my riposte lands. I have never fought with so many people looking at me, other than when Lorenzo humiliated me that night, no, stop thinking about that.

We have a few failed thrusts, our swords kissing off of each other, and then almost by chance I flick her main gauche away, and she shoulders into me, trying to press her advantage against my inexperience, and I allow my-self to be knocked back and flick the tip of my long blade just across her col-larbone, carefully, so careful not to make too broad a gesture, or too deep one, but it's where my arm ended up and she stops immediately when she feels the scratch, as the judge says "First blood. Duel!"

"Well done," she says, surprised but genuine, and I feel my face flush hot and I curtsey. She returns the gesture, and we leave the floor, Venette retrieving her sword from where it skittered away.

Dora catches me up in a lilac-scented hug. "There, no embarrassment to be found. Was not thinking the correct advice?"

"I couldn't stop myself from thinking," I admit, smiling at my success, panting a little from the exertion.

"That first bit with your main gauche was very smart, I thought you would have her just like that, with a little wounded bird gambit."

"You said she was cautious, so I did wonder if I could draw her in."

"And it worked! I'm not certain it would work again, but nicely done."

Ottavia comes to meet us, laughing, Sterling just behind her. "Serafina, you won your first tournament duel! Congratulations, what a wonderful day!"

"A wonderful day," I echo, surprised at her delight.

"Now I go to lose, hopefully they are cautious with where they mark me."

"Oh I'm sorry, I should have put in a word," Dora says, winking at me.

"No matter! I'll be done soon and then we can go have supper."

Dora lowers her voice. "She just drives Lorenzo absolutely mad."

"With that attitude, yes, I've noticed," I say. "But his anger has no effect on her."

"None at all, it simply cannot touch her." Lorenzo hears this last bit, and Dora meets his questioning gaze. "Tell Serafina she did well."

He blinks at her, and then looks to me. "You did well," he says flatly, and I don't know if that makes me feel better or worse than him ignoring her request. He would prefer not to have to acknowledge me at all, and yet I continue to inconvenience him by existing.

"Thank you," I say. "I hope to not be a detriment." My mother would spit fire, to hear me speak to anybody but her in such a way, with such words of appeasement.

He looks past me, towards Ottavia's duel, and I turn around in time to see her receive a cut on her upper arm. "She did want it to be fast," he remarks.

"She didn't *not* try," Luca says, but dubiously. "She did try an attack."

"Well she has to, it's part of the rules" Tristan says. I wonder if she's thinking about her fight, or if she's forgotten it already. It perhaps isn't best to dwell on things, for any of us.

Lorenzo turns away from me, to Armand, and Luca sidles over. "You did very well," he says. "And I assume you didn't see, but your mother paused on her way past, long enough to see your victory."

"I didn't see, no." It's a wonder that I didn't feel a fell chill at her passing. I think I would fall apart if I needed to speak to my mother right now, or today. "Did she seem pleased?"

"Yes, actually, if ever Lady Galeazzo can said to be seemingly pleased." He hesitates, then reaches over and tucks a lock of hair behind my ear. "Now we go to dine, and find out if the next round is later today or not. I think it might be, an evening bracket, perhaps after we disperse to nap."

"To nap?" I ask, laughing, flattered by his attentions, giddy from my success.

"Well yes, we'll need to sleep off lunch. We can't compete on full stomachs and all that wine, it isn't sporting."

"I shall have to take your word for it."

"What nonsense are you filling her head with, Luca?" Tristan asks a little snappishly.

"Explaining the necessity of a nap after the meal that I anticipate being provided for us. Not nonsense at all "

"You're *hungry*?" she asks, her disbelief elaborate.

"Of course I am, and you should be as well. You have to replace that blood."

"I have made it through nearly an entire bottle of wine, I shall be more than fortified," Tristan says with great dignity. I had not noticed the wine until she mentioned, but there is indeed a bottle now apparent.

"Well you definitely need a meal then," Luca says, laughing. "Come now, before you are horizontal prior to nap time. Lorenzo, I cannot believe you did not keep an eye on her."

"Who do you think got the wine?" he asks, but he offers Tristan his arm and she takes it.

"Lorenzo takes his responsibilities seriously," she says, and Luca plucks the bottle from her fingers and drains the remainder.

"He does, he does, I'm being unkind to our captain."

"You're all ridiculous," Dora says, but with a deep-seated happiness. "They have tents set up, where we can go eat. Afterwards, my house is closest, and it would please me if you would be my guests for your after meal naps."

"Well if it pleases you," I say shyly, and nobody contradicts me, and she claps her hands.

"Good, then, that's settled."

Chapter Thirty

Lorenzo of House Valier

The meal tent is more raucous than our usual dinner events, everybody nervy and bloody and riding on triumphs or defeats or disappointments or near misses. I lose Armand in the shuffle very early on, which is unusual, but he knows the way to Dora's, and he knows how to follow a schedule should they post or announce the next matches, be they this evening or tomorrow. I'd like to do at least one more round today, I fought too early and have stood around for much of the day, even with the sudden excitement of Tristan's terrible wounding.

She has remained a bit needier than her usual, which is to be expected, and a bit thornier, which is also to be expected. Luca is being a clown and Dora smoothing and jollying everybody along in turns. She is disappointed to be out so early, I know, but such is her grace that she will never say so, at least not in this public venue.

Sterling and Ottavia are perfectly happy to both be out, but also they'll of course attend all the remaining fights to support the circle. It is simply how things are done.

At one point, I hear Serafina say to Dora, "It doesn't seem right that I am somehow still in and you are out."

Dora laughs, though I feel her glance at me. "It is simply how it turned out. I am proud of you, you did well."

"Whether I continue to do well..."

"You don't give yourself nearly enough credit, and consider yourself defeated before you even walk into the dueling floor. Do yourself, and us, a service and give credit where credit is due. You've worked as hard as any of us. Perhaps harder, in some notable instances." They both laugh, and I go on pretending that I was not listening. It is an unusual portion of us moving to the next round; myself, Luca, Armand, and Serafina. I had very much expected Dora and Tristan to also be in the next round, though for the moment, I am satisfied with Tristan walking among the living, seeming physically none the worse for the wear, perhaps emotionally as well, but that remains to be seen. A near miss is a near miss.

People break off from the meal, in pairs and trios, and some of us walk to Dora's house; myself, Tristan, Luca, Dora, and Serafina. Sterling and Ottavia took a carriage elsewhere, and Armand sent me a bird that he was fine and that he would see us later, if the matches reconvened tonight. I wonder if he is brooding someplace or if he has reconnected with Iulio, and I trust him to tell me which in good time.

I am not typically the napping type, which Dora well knows, even as she shows me to a guest bedchamber. "This one also has the most books in it," she says. "You know where to find me, should you need anything."

"I'm sure I will not. Thank you for your hospitality."

"So *formal*," she says, smiling indulgently, withdrawing, bringing the door softly shut behind her.

I take off my boots and I peruse the books, but despite my usual proclivities, I have spent much spark today, and have not eaten nor drunk nearly enough to offset it. I further undress and climb into the bed. I don't expect sleep to come as easily as it does, but it draws over me swiftly and I know nothing until I feel the weight of another on the bed with me, have a confused moment where I think Dora might have decided to have a bit of fun, but it isn't lavender I smell, it's lemongrass.

"Tristan," I say, or ask, and she comes up the bed and straddles me, presses her mouth to mine, both of us still sweetly wine-breathed. I don't know how much time has passed, the light has changed but I have never been in this room for any length of time. Why am I thinking of the light when I have a girl on top of me. "Tristan, we have never—"

"No, we have never," she agrees, sitting back. Her skirts are rucked up to allow her posture astride me, and her stays loosened, her hair in sleepy disarray. "See my scar?" She draws her skirts back on that side even further, so I can see the golden mark, almost star-shaped, where Martim's blade entered her flesh, and where I healed it.

I brush my fingertips along it, watch her eyes soften at my touch in the dim light. "I see your scar," I say, gently, as if I hadn't seen it when I healed her whole again. As whole as I can make a person, which just means the wound.

"Where do they go, Renzo?" I blink up at her, not understanding. "Where do the wounds go?" I've never heard such a plaintive tone from her.

"Away," I say, and I move my hand up her thigh, because I don't want to talk about it. There isn't anything to talk about, the way we fight, the way our sparks save us, the way ambition drives us. I hadn't planned on bedding Tristan but here she is, in my bed, soft and sharp and smelling good and she leans down over me, her hair curtaining us both, and her mouth finds mine again. She moans and softens against me, as I harden between us, and we adjust our hips, businesslike, magnetized, and sink into each other.

After, she curls against me, her head on my shoulder, and falls promptly to sleep. Tristan is not known to be sentimental, but still I absently stroke her hair. She has never been so badly wounded; it was a shock that even she needed comfort from. We do reckless things, sometimes, when reconciling just how often we stare mortality in the face, and how easily we come back from it, as though it was a noonday nightmare instead of a real bodily threat.

I fall asleep again as well, after a time. When I wake, Tristan is gone from my bed, which is to be expected. I have a dull headache, and I drink a glass of water, and then another, slowly making myself presentable in between gulps. There are times that water tastes better and more vital than others, and this is one of them. I poke my head into the hallway just as Dora is coming down it, in a fresh dress, looking bright-eyed and alert. "Oh good, I hoped I wouldn't have to wake you. They've sent word of the evening fights."

"Good, it'll be nice to get it over with."

"Did you rest well?" she asks, and I cannot tell from her expression if she knows Tristan came to me or not.

"I did, thank you. I hope you also did."

"Oh yes, slept like a baby, though Serafina has surprisingly sharp elbows." She laughs at my frown. "I will at the very least reacclimate you to her existence."

"As you will."

"As you know I will. Now go to the parlor, there's a light meal there, I'm gathering the others."

I pause in front of a mirror, scratching my head, and then look at what my hair has done. I spend a few minutes arranging it into something more presentable, and then straighten my coat and go to the parlor. Where, of course, Serafina is. She freezes like a startled deer when she sees me, a coffee cup and saucer in hand. There are little finger foods on the table, and a pot of coffee, but no wine.

"Good evening," she says after a moment. "I didn't say earlier, but your duel was—"

"That isn't necessary," I say brusquely, and she blinks at me in dismay. I move to the table and pour myself a cup of coffee. Perhaps that will help with the ache in my head.

Tristan and Luca come in, and she is laughing at some jest he is making, I could hear them talking in the hall but not make out the words. "I hoped there would be these little cakes," Luca says. "I'm just wild for them and this house guards the recipe far too fiercely." He addresses this last at Serafina and she murmurs some reply. "Here, you haven't tried one, you'll see what I mean." He presses it upon her and she must take it or drop it, and steals away her cup.

She takes a cautious bite, and then smiles up at him. "I do see what you mean," she says, as he finishes her coffee.

"I knew you would. Now we must lobby House Alvise's kitchen staff to share with ours, it simply cannot stand."

"Oh, I don't know, it might turn into a tiny war, like the vendors with the noses." A brief pause, as he stares at her, and then realizes she means the candy vendors and laughs.

"It would serve them right!"

"What trouble are you starting?" Dora asks.

"I've enlisted Fina to my cause, we *must* have the recipe for these cakes."

"I would have nothing to lure you here if the cakes recipe got out," Dora says. "The secret stays with my house, and that's final."

"What do you mean, you would have nothing. You have everybody's favor," Luca says, catching up her hand and kissing it with a dramatic bow. She laughs and swats at him.

"You're such a flatterer."

"I am known for it far and wide," he agrees.

"The girls in the markets all warn each other against him," Dora says to Serafina, in a lowered voice that isn't really meant to obscure her words.

"Little do they know, my attentions aren't limited to the girls."

"Is anybody's?" Tristan asks. She's had the cakes before but sampled one as though it might be something unexpected, frowning a bit.

"Everybody makes their own choices," Luca says. "Now let us go to our evening duels."

Chapter Thirty-One

Serafina of House Galeazzo

I hadn't intended to nap with Dora; I did not want to make myself a bother. She showed everybody else to rooms first and then looked at me and gently asked, "You don't want to be alone, do you?" and I shook my head miserably because no, I didn't want to be alone, but also didn't know that I was allowed to ask for that.

And she took me to her room and helped me undress enough to be comfortable laying down for a nap, kissed me on the cheek, and fell soundly asleep. I lay awake smelling her perfume and whatever it is that she uses in her hair, and in her pillow, and spent some time asleep but dreaming I was awake, I think.

I awaken when there is a knock at her bedchamber door and she gets up to answer it. Rarely have I slept not in my own bed, and I have a few moments of remembering clearly that this is Dora's bedchamber, but my self remembering only my bed, only my bedchamber, only my house, and I then have a half-waking panic that it is my mother at the door that Dora has gotten up to answer and I sit bolt upright as if that would help matters in any way if it *was* my mother at the door. It is not. I do not presume to know where my mother passed her day and is passing her evening, but she has not come to House Alvise to terrorize me.

I slip out of bed and start putting myself to rights as Dora talks to the servant who knocked, and then closes the door, a piece of paper in hand. "We've been sent the evening schedule," she says. "Another round of duels tonight, and then we'll all have a proper rest before convening again in the morning. Which is about what I expected, though why they could not be bothered to just announce it all ahead of time is anybody's guess."

"The judges do as they will, just like the city," I say.

"Just so," she says. "Here, turn around, I'll lace you. Your hair has remained immaculate though, how did that happen?"

I laugh. "I really couldn't say. I must not have moved a muscle once in bed."

"You really must not have, or I should have known. I didn't either, I don't think. These tournaments take so much out of us, even if most of our time is spent standing around watching."

"And fretting over what our duels will bring," I can't help but saying.

"You did *very* well this morning, and I have every hope you will also do well tonight."

I laugh again, trying to keep my expression light as I turn to face her. "I almost don't, isn't that strange? I am so uncomfortable with everybody looking at me."

"Not so strange, maybe. You were not always in the spotlight." She means to say more, perhaps, but stops; the group has stopped talking about Marco so completely, perhaps she's afraid of my feelings as well.

"I was not. Now let me help you." She does, even though I think that Dora is probably well able to dress herself.

"Put on your laurel wreath. Yes, good. Now I'll leave you off at the parlor and wake everybody. We have time, they are always generous about that, but some of us take longer to wake than others. Though I suppose the crucial ones are who's still fighting, though we don't know where Armand ended up."

"He won't miss his tournament duel, though," I say, unwilling to be questioning, feeling that same little thrill of horror at the idea of what happens when you refuse a tournament duel.

"No, I would be very surprised were he to do that. He has never yet done that." She looks at my worried face. "I can find him, if I need to. I can always find people."

I stare at her, shocked. "You...what? You can find people?"

She presses a finger to my lips, frowning. "Yes. I don't tell everybody, though."

"But—" But Marco. She knows, there can be nothing else that I would ask right in that moment, and she kisses me instead, either to fluster me into silence, or from the tangled-up passions of the tournament, and I find myself kissing her back for the same reasons. What I have lost cannot or will not be found, and we are here and now, and I am discovering who I am and what I will be. She is soft and confident and smells like lavender and coffee and I am dizzied by our kiss, by her fingertips trailing down my neck, and then her hands on my waist, and then we separate.

"Have some coffee. I'll be back." She winks and is gone, and I touch my lips, and wonder how many girls, and boys, she's kissed. I wonder how many boys, and girls, I will kiss. It has been so few, but also each of them have taken such care, so far. It is hard to take things with such care when we treat our everyday dangers with such inconsequence.

The door opens soon enough that I think Dora must have forgotten something, and I turn, but it is Lorenzo who comes in.

I startle, probably visibly, and take a deep breath to steady myself. "Good evening. I didn't say earlier, but your duel was—"

"This isn't necessary," he says, going to the table and pouring himself coffee without sparing me much of a glance. I drop my gaze, look at the dark surface of my coffee, all the while thinking that he must not know that Dora can find people. It is impossible for him to know. I'm both concerned that my face will show some guilt, some panic that I know something that must be kept from Lorenzo, and also confident that he will consider my expression with no more interest than an insect he might flick from his arm.

Tristan and Luca come in then and save me from further awful tension at being in the room with somebody who hates me so clearly, though Tristan is really still not a friend to me. If she ever will be. Dora is, though. And Luca. Every time Luca calls me 'Fina,' I feel a little thrill, a flutter in my stomach. I am not in love with him, I don't think, I am somehow more pragmatic than that. But his easy acceptance of me into the group is something that I am giddy, grateful for. His acceptance of *me*, who he doesn't need for social or political jockeying.

We go out into the night, to go to our next dueling location. I am buoyed by my morning success, though I cannot begin to hope that I will repeat it. While nobody was permitted to use their spark for speed in the preliminary duels, it is allowed now, and while that is within my ability, I have still only used it sparingly, other than when my mother or a tutor would make me use it to exhaustion, again and again, to ensure that I could react with it by reflex. It was a life-saving necessity, they said, and I remember feeling as though they were killing me in order to train me in how to save my own life, and I remember Marco *agreed* with them and I cried bitterly, weakly, into my pillow at this complete and utter betrayal.

Armand is there already, and Tristan and Ottavia, and I am so relieved to see them all that I almost *tell* them so, but I catch myself. To be so demonstrative would not be rewarded, and I can feel Lorenzo's imagined scorn just as deeply as if those events actually played themselves out.

Armand seems almost relaxed, while also more alert than I can ever recall seeing him. He's wearing his laurel wreath indifferently, cocked on his dark curls, which are in a curious disarray. "They haven't given the next schedules yet," he says. "But presently, once everybody fighting is here."

"I should think we'd have the same numbers this evening," I say, then bite my lip, hoping I'm not speaking out of turn.

"People come to support their circles. If they're all out, they sometimes don't come back," Dora says.

"Sour grapes," Tristan says, and Dora laughs.

"Some years we only had Lorenzo still in, even now. We've done well for ourselves! You're allowed to say it too, Renzo, you're supposed to be leading us."

"We have done unusually well," he says slowly, but with a deeper thought, not reluctance. "All of that practice paying off, perhaps."

"Yes, practice," Tristan sniffs.

"I know I felt better for it," Luca says, picking up the conversational threads before we go too far astray. "I almost felt bad for my opponent, he seemed quite overwhelmed."

"You were actually paying attention for once," Lorenzo says.

"And I'll take that as a compliment Renzo, thank you." He grins and Dora laughs, and Lorenzo grudgingly smiles after a moment.

"I'm not in dull spirits, I'm just trying to keep sober for my next match."

Luca claps him on the back. "Well it's your way, and there's nothing to change about it. You never lose your focus."

The schedules get passed out, and even though it is nighttime, there are lanterns everywhere, lighting this square brightly and casting some shadows very deep. The dueling floor is a bright white spot in the night, and a judge is inspecting it. Soon enough, they step into the center of the dueling floor and raise their hand, and we all fall immediately silent, all eyes on the judge.

"The second round of the tournament will start," they say. "You will have all received a schedule. If your duels are not at this location, you may proceed to the correct location. Do not be late to any of your appointed duels, this will count as a refusal. Spark usage is permitted in this round, insofar as to increase one's speed, and to heal after a duel has been called."

This time, we are among the crowd who filters off to the other dueling floors, to the Company of the Grounded Mermaid. It will be quicker, I think as we walk, with our sparks speeding us on our way to our bloodings. Hopefully there will be no further accidents, I think; I hadn't really known to hope against it in the first place. I thought I knew, but it wasn't real, until Tristan's blood was all over the dueling floor.

We enter the sprawling theater company building, welcomed by members of that Company, and the seats and boxes are full of spectators, others waiting for their duels, and members of the upper echelons, who are not part of our tournament. I know I will regret it, but I look until I find my mother and father in the crowd, sitting in a box with the Lord and Lady Valier. Once I've seen them, I cannot shake the weight of my mother's gaze; it was better that I hadn't known. It was impossible for me to not know.

We are made to walk down the central aisle, to the stage, where the dueling floor is set up. We are then filtered to either side of the stage, in the wings, where we can watch from just a few steps away, and be right at hand when each of our fights come up.

Lorenzo is first again, of course. I wonder if he is supposed to have kept his laurel wreath on, but his opponent does too, so the answer seems to be yes. They stand at either end of the dueling floor, bow, and then they are in motion. I almost need my spark to see how they move, spark-fast, swords grating off each other, Lorenzo's opponent's style very aggressively strike-heavy, with straightforward footwork.

"First blood," the judge calls, and they are still again immediately. Lorenzo shakes off his blade, a fine mist of blood on the floor and sheathes it. They bow to one another again, his opponent's shoulder bleeding.

This morning felt festive and leisurely. Now, the duels feel sharper-edged, and the theater is dark beyond the stage, though I have a sense of all of the people there, of their eyes, their breath. I both dread my duel and cannot countenance stepping onto the dueling floor.

Armand is next, and he is blooded almost before he can move. Unlike his earlier turmoil, with Tristan's injury, with fighting Iulio, he both seems to know this will happen and also be accepting of it.

"It's because you didn't kiss Serafina for luck, Armand," Luca says, and then to my horror, he tips my chin up and kisses me right there in front of everybody before going to the dueling floor.

"I'll keep that in mind," Armand says, bemused.

I know I flush scarlet, thinking that my mother will have seen that. My mother will have noted it, and I will hear about it when we are all back to our own houses again, when the tournament festival has ended and we are back to practices, and near-nightly events, and hoping for our advancements, whenever those befall us.

Dora is laughing, though, delighted, and Tristan has deigned to smile. Lorenzo only watches Luca and ignores me. I decide to watch Luca and ignore everybody else, though perhaps that will continue to give my mother the wrong impression.

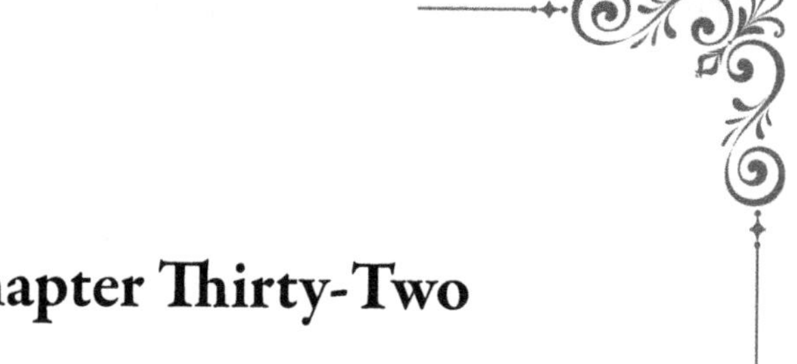

Chapter Thirty-Two

Lorenzo of House Valier

Luca may be a clown, but some of his carefree nature seems to also be where his combat prowess comes from. The less socially serious he behaves, the keener he is with his blades. I cannot explain his motives in kissing Serafina like that, in front of a third of our society, other than simply to clown on Armand, but when he draws his blades, he spins his wrists to flourish them, and his opponent takes the wrong message from that. His opponent thinks that Luca's earlier win was a fluke, and that this will be as easy as whatever just happened with Armand.

I saw Armand's face; what was happening on the dueling floor was not what his eyes were seeing, and more's the pity, because his fight this morning was very good, and if I had to guess, his afternoon with Iulio was also very good. If that's where he was; I will not ask, and he will not tell.

I am irritated to be in a theater company for this, and on a stage, though these things are not unusual. My complaints, should I care to voice them, would be viewed as petty and inconsequential, and so I keep them to myself. Those who know me, know already; Dora pats me lightly as I step forward to be Luca's second, though the way the stage and floor have been set, it is hardly necessary. We are all very close.

The duel starts, and Luca's opponent is surprised to find his first thrust has missed. He overextended, so sure was he that Luca would not have the good sense to move out of the way, and Luca, instead of having the good sense to just blood him immediately, has instead moved behind him, flourishing his blades again, grinning at the crowd, to scattered laughter and applause. The judge frowns, which Luca seems to catch from the corner of his eye, and he winks at me.

His opponent has turned now, tries again for a strike, but is too slow again. This time, Luca does the decency of parrying his blade, but then ripostes, his posture as correct as a statue, and he cuts him in the exact center of the chest.

The duel is called, and Luca accepts his second laurel. The judge remonstrates him lightly, his voice not carrying to the audience, but the rest of the circle can hear. "You would do well to take this more seriously."

"You have my apologies," Luca says seriously, bowing to him. "Thank you for your patience with me, a young fool." Some of the audience claps at that too, and Luca returns to us. "See, Armand?" he asks.

"I did see," Armand says evenly, amused. "Though Lorenzo won his duel handily without such purported luck. And what is Serafina supposed to do? She cannot kiss herself."

"In a mirror she could," Tristan offers. Serafina is quietly, and anxiously, listening as this exchange plays out.

"Hmm, that is an issue," Luca says, glancing around. "Perhaps she should kiss Lorenzo."

"Absolutely not," I say, before not even a heartbeat has passed. "She can get by on her own luck, or she can't."

"Oh honestly, Renzo, you used to engage in fun once in a while," Dora says, before anybody else can. "I'll kiss Serafina for luck, perhaps she'll find mine, that I lost this morning."

"Oh, I'm no longer fun?" I ask.

"Yes, you heard me." Dora shakes her head and clicks her tongue, turning to Serafina, who had been blushing but who is now very pale. "Here, now, Fina, before they call you."

"No, I shouldn't like to think you believe I can never be fun again," I say. Dora may have missed the edge in my voice before, and though she catches it now, it's too late. "Of course I shall kiss Serafina for luck."

"Oh, I don't need to impose further on your—" Serafina says, and I hold up a hand, because I don't want to hear whatever empty words she's desperately grasping for to appease me.

"Nonsense. Everybody has been ever so patient with me and my petulance. Come here." I hold out my hand, and though the audience could not have heard all of this exchange, they see that motion, and if Serafina refuses me, it will not reflect well upon her, and I see her making these calculations, standing very still. Then she arranges her features in a practiced, docile smile that does not reach her eyes and steps forward, taking my hand. I pull her close and look into her eyes and softly say, "Don't lose," before pressing my lips to hers firmly, kissing her deeply, even as I can feel her trying not to stiffen and pull away from me too soon. Appearances, appearances.

There is more applause when we part, and tears in her eyes. "I shall not waste your luck," she says shakily, meeting my gaze for once, and then the judge calls her for the duel. So she didn't tell anybody about our conversation the day she was late to practice. I would have heard of it before now, from Dora, and Luca would never have pressed these antics so far. That is interesting, I think.

Serafina and her opponent curtsey to one another and draw their blades. I have fought her opponent before; she's a lanky girl with some new-foal awkwardness, even after these few years in the game. Like Martim this morning, she has trouble keeping her sword tips up, and she seems more comfortable striking with her shorter blade than her long one, which is unusual, but a clever way to make up for her discomfort with the longer blade.

Serafina moves first, which is unlike her. After watching her practice with us these weeks, I can objectively say that her footwork can be very good, she moves lightly and quickly, and her opponent clumsily blocks, just, forced to use her long blade and striking out with her short, which Serafina blocks before spinning away in a way oddly close to the way Luca just maneuvered, but she isn't showboating, she isn't spinning her blades and looking at the crowd, she is looking only at her opponent's face, and when the girl tries her short bladed attack that nobody ever expects, Serafina cross blocks with her long blade and then grazes her on the inside of the arm with her short blade, and the duel is called.

"I was making an ass of myself, but maybe your kiss did just bring her luck," Luca remarks. "I'm not sure we've ever seen her fight so well. What did you say to her?"

"I told her not to lose." I am unwilling to praise her, but he isn't incorrect.

"Well if it was as easy as that, why didn't you say that to Armand?" He laughs, and Armand smiles, bemused, when Luca claps him on the back. "All in good fun, my friend."

"Of course."

Serafina returns to the group with her second laurel wreath, looking as though she suspects she is dreaming. "What a good fight that was!" Dora says, effusive as ever. Tristan is nodding, so it would seem as though her support in my dismissal of Serafina is weakening. It's just as well; I'm more than capable of stoking my own moods and misgivings.

"I need a drink after all this," Luca says. "I can't believe they didn't provide refreshments here of all places."

"It's on account of this judge," Sterling says. "They are very strict about drinking before duels, and so it's just easier for fools like us to be deprived for the duration, so that there are no unfortunate disqualifications."

"Would being disqualified for drinking…" I cut a glance at her, and Serafina trails off. Of course that would count as refusing a duel, whether you knew this judge's proclivities or not.

"Well that's neither here nor there, we're done for the evening, we can go out for drinking, and then retire to rest up and do it all again tomorrow," Dora says cheerfully. "Handily, there is at least one acceptable bar just down the street, and we shall all go, like a proper circle."

Her tone would brook no argument, and we make our way off the stage, and then we are directed through the overly complicated backstage area, leaving the audience to filter out the front, as though we had been a proper stage show. The road behind the theater is little more than an alley, and we wander between buildings until we are back on the street again, Ottavia and Sterling arm in arm, Serafina walking between Luca and Dora, Tristan walking with me.

"I suppose it's just how it is," Tristan says, looking up at me.

"That would seem to be the case," I say.

"It's just as well." I shrug. "This afternoon…"

"We both needed it," I say. I am not interested in longer dalliances with Tristan, nor has she ever been with me, to my knowledge.

"Yes, we did."

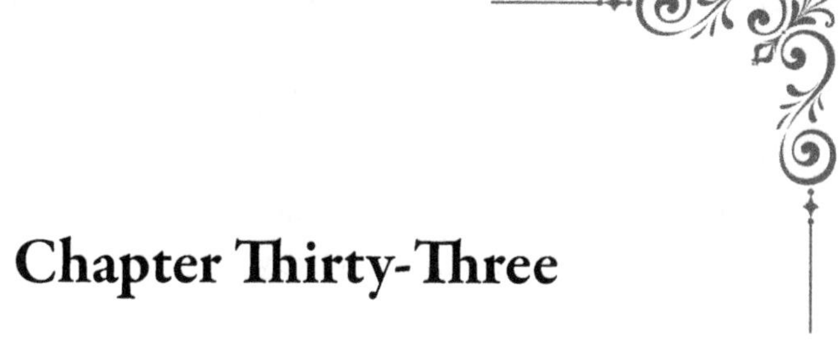

Chapter Thirty-Three

Serafina of House Galeazzo

We are a little down the street from the theater, on the way to the bar, when my mother says my name and freezes me in my tracks. "Yes, Mother?" I recover as quickly as I can, turning to the carriage, which is stopped just near us.

"Don't be too late," she says. From her face, she wants to say far more. She wants me in the carriage, now. But she won't take me away from the circle on the street like this. She knows I'll be at the house for her soon enough.

"I won't, Mother."

"That was a good fight, Serafina," my father says, leaning past her a bit, his tone jovial.

"Thank you," I say, surprised, pleased. So rarely do I have his regard, and so rarely has he praised me. "Good evening, my lord father and lady mother."

"Good evening, daughter," my father says, and they drive on.

"I'm surprised they're letting you come at all," Tristan says, that little nasty note in her voice. It isn't always there.

"This is part of it all. They have to, if they want me to be taking part in society." There is a a mixture of defiance and despair in my tone that I can't quite master in time, and Dora blinks at me. I must take more care. "Let us go now, lest they change their minds," I say lightly, laughing, catching Luca's arm.

"I must excuse myself..." Armand says, and Luca holds up his hand.

"Just one drink, all of us together, and then we can scatter. I can tell Ottavia and Sterling are one foot out the door on us already," he says, and

Ottavia blushes prettily. I wonder how she does that, because it does seem purposeful. I cannot say why I think so.

"We *lost*," she says. "We hardly have anything to celebrate, Sterling and I."

"You can celebrate those of us who won," he says.

"We will of course celebrate those who won," Sterling says. "Though also we won't want to stay out *too* late, as Lady Galeazzo pointed out, we will need to do this all again in the morning. Well not all; the rounds are shorter now." They smile as Ottavia huffs a little, and we continue to the bar.

The minutes pass and the drinks go down, and almost as a group, we laugh and joke together. We reimagine each of our duels, not drawing swords, no that would get us removed by the guard, but waving toothpicks about, or just imagining we brandish steel. Iulio joins us at some point, I do not notice when he arrives, but similarly, I did not notice when Sterling and Ottavia left us.

The barkeep calls "Time," and I have a moment of near panic, because time is indeed late, and I was not supposed to be nearly so late.

"Oh, I must go," I say, standing and then almost just falling over, and I giggle, unable to help myself.

Dora catches my arm, but then we *both* almost topple over, and she giggles too, as we cling to each other, swords tangling in our skirts, cheeks flushed. "Oh no, we've gotten ourselves in quite the state, haven't we?"

"How are we to get home?" I ask. I have never done this. I have not the faintest idea how to cope with this, my thoughts slippery as fish. Eels.

"My carriage will be outside, I can take you. But Renzo, can you help us?" she asks, turning to him. "I'm so sorry to task you further."

He sighs, but he takes her hand for a moment. "One of you, anyway." She starts to withdraw her hand, and I'm not entirely certain what she's even asked him for, but then it seems as though her drunkenness is gone, immediately. He lets go of her hand, smirking.

"Oh now that was a mean trick, we can't send her home like this." Dora looks at me, frowning.

"What did he do?" I ask.

"Lorenzo can take away a person's drunkenness," she says, even as he and Luca are herding us to the door. Armand and Iulio are gone, though Tristan is leading the way out into the street. "But he's sorely tapped his resources and couldn't get rid of it for both of us."

"Oh," I say as though I understand, and then "Oh!" When I do understand. That *was* a mean trick indeed. I am already late, and also drunk, and all of the day's ups and downs crash onto me at once and I burst into tears.

"Oh dear," Dora says, still laughing, perhaps still a bit tipsy, and Lorenzo makes a noise of disgust clear enough for me to hear.

"Fina, no, it's all right," Luca says, still a bit unsteady himself, his arm strong and comforting around my shoulders as the bar goes dark behind us. "Teodora and I will take you home and make your excuses to your lady mother and put you to bed, well I expect Dora will do that part of the job, and you'll be right as rain in the morning. This is expected, we've all done this, and your parents surely did this."

"They surely did not!" I don't want to be wailing but my wants are not a part of the considerations. My mother never got foolishly drunk, that is not something I can imagine or believe. "My mother—"

"Shhh," Luca says. "Shh, that won't help."

"There isn't any help," Lorenzo mutters.

"Not from you!" Dora says. "Honestly, Renzo…"

"It's a learning experience," he says. "And, as you said, I have already been sorely taxed today. It isn't as though I'm approaching sober at the moment either. You asked for help, I helped you."

"Renzo is very interested in the letter of the law versus the spirit of the law," Tristan says airily from someplace nearby, and I'm not certain why she is even still here other than to witness my mess. Perhaps that is reason enough.

"Tristan, will you be all right?" Dora asks sweetly.

"All right what?"

"In your carriage home when you leave? Or should Lorenzo go with you? That sounds like a good plan to me, I think. Lorenzo, see Tristan home."

There is a long pause and I've somehow progressed to sniffling against Luca's shirtfront, I'm not exactly sure how that happened, as the world is slowly tilting and spinning around me, and my hands are knotted in the fabric. No, I don't like drunkenness one bit. Oh, my laurels, where are they? I feel at my head suddenly, and they're both there, tangled now in my hair I think.

"We will see you in the morning," Lorenzo says from a great distance, and he and Tristan move away, Tristan laughing and I don't really know why.

Luca and Dora get me into her carriage, and I spend much of the trip holding my face in my hands because the rocking has me quite undone, while Dora works gently to get the wreathes out of my hair and Luca absently rubs my back, humming something just slightly off-key, either by design or he genuinely does not know the proper key, I cannot decide and cannot find the words to ask him.

We stumble into the front door of my house, only some of the lamps lit, as it our custom. "Will your maid still be here?" Dora asks. I think she thinks she is whispering but she seems very loud to me, or maybe it is just that the existence of anybody at all makes the house seem loud.

"I don't know, I hope not. Poor Agnes..." I have a *maid* and even though I have always had a maid, that thought sticks in my head, and I start to giggle.

"Shhh, you'll wake the whole house," Luca says, but he's laughing too, and we are definitely being very loud, and I am hanging on his neck as we go tripping up the stairs, my limbs all loose and not doing as I'd like and finally Luca just swings me up into his arms, even though we are on the stairs, and I worry that he will drop me, or fall, and say neither of these things because it is all very much effort but I keep laughing instead, but I am trying to be quiet. Luca's laurel wreaths are not tangled in his hair, but piled up at a rakish angle, he is so *nice* I'm lucky he is so nice to me.

Dora remembers where my room is, somehow, she takes the correct turn at the top of the stairs but we are only a few steps down the hall when my mother's voice echos to us. "Do you have any idea of the hour?"

Luca and Dora turn as one, which means I turn too, but I'm afraid to look at my mother's face. "Unfortunately we do, Lady Galeazzo, we didn't *mean* to stay in the bar until Time was called but we did and we kept Serafina much later than she meant to stay and we're so very sorry," Dora says, curtseying deeply.

"Can Serafina not answer for herself?" The ice in my mother's voice draws my eyes to her and she is...not as I expected. I thought she would be livid, just white-hot with fury, but she is regarding the three of us with something like curiosity. I want Luca to put me down but I don't want to *ask* him to put me down and draw my mother's attention, though obviously we already have her attention, and I wriggle a little and he almost drops me as a result and then sets me on my feet, and then my knees buckle and he has to hold me up anyway, and a giggle escapes me.

"I'm so sorry Mother," I say through my giggles, which are part the drink and part terror and part confusion and I just cannot stop myself. "I know I said I wouldn't be late but I simply *couldn't* leave earlier."

Luca is trying very hard not to laugh as well, shaking a little bit from the effort, and Dora is smiling as well, amused, but also hoping to cajole my mother into feelings of good will, and I could tell her that it won't work but I'm honestly not certain what to expect at the moment. Surely punishment will follow, perhaps she is waiting until my friends leave. Or until tomorrow. When nobody else is here, certainly. I need to stop laughing and I cannot, clinging to Luca's arms, one of my laurels slipping down over my eye rakishly.

"You'd best to bed, Serafina." Is my mother hiding the ghost of a smile? No, that is impossible, I just can't see properly. "Are you two quite able to get yourselves home? May I offer you our hospitality?"

"No, no, we cannot possibly impose. My carriage is just outside, we were just going to pop Serafina in bed and be on our way. We are dreadfully sorry at having woken you, Lady Galeazzo, and at having disturbed your household at this hour. We do apologize, again, for keeping her out so late."

My mother looks at Dora and now she does actually smile and the world slips further from beneath my feet. "It isn't anything that you need to worry about, Teodora. Thank you for taking care with my daughter." She regards Luca a bit more shrewdly, and he stands up straighter.

"We made sure no harm came to her, Lady Galeazzo," Luca says.

"I trust that you did." And then my mother withdraws and I sit fully on the floor in relief, and Luca picks me up again, and Dora leads him to my bedchamber.

I think it is perhaps unseemly for Luca to be in my bedchamber but also I gave him my virtue and thus, what more could I possibly have to keep from him? Also, after what Dora did to me here in this very bed...

Agnes is not in evidence, and I am glad for that, that she had the sense to retire for the evening when it seemed I would not be returning at a reasonable or decent hour. I don't know the hour but to learn it would only horrify me and Luca sets me down on the edge of my bed and looks at me, and then at Dora. "Tell me how I might help," he says, perhaps also realizing the tenuous nature of this arrangement.

"Swords and laurels first, I think," Dora says. "Then jewelry and then boots. Where do you keep your nightclothes?"

I gesture at my dresser, because where else would I keep my night clothes, and she goes to investigate while Luca unbuckles my sword belts and hangs them on the rack. It takes him some time, but he gently disentangles the laurels from my hair and places them on top of the dresser.

"Do we bring those tomorrow?" I ask.

"Bring what? No, no they'll have pins for everybody, to put on their collars, and give fresh ones for further won duels. You should dry those and save them, though. Two wins on your very first tournament day!" Dora draws a nightgown from a drawer and brings it over.

"Luca says I'm lucky," I murmur.

"Luca might not be wrong. Now stand her up, please, so I can unlace her."

"Are you certain you want me to..." Luca is perhaps rightly hesitant but also he must know that Dora knows what we did.

"Yes, you're a perfect gentleman, thank you." And Dora is a perfect lady, I don't say, just allow myself to be pliant, allow them to change my clothes without wilting or protesting. I feel cared for, not manipulated. They care, what happens to me, who I am. I start crying again but this time happily, and put my arms around Luca's neck to embrace him.

"Fina, are you—"

"I'm just *happy*," I blubber.

"Oh is that all?" I can hear the smile in his voice, but he isn't laughing at me. "Dora...?"

"Drink this water," she says, not unkindly, having found my pitcher and pouring a glass. "And now to bed with you, and if any of us were paying attention, we'll have to remember that your tolerance for drink is a bit less than what we ended up putting in you." She takes the glass and sets it down, then pulls my sheets back, and Luca guides me into the bed, pulling the pillow into position for me, and then they both cover me.

"You might feel like hell in the morning, but if you do..." Luca rummages in his pockets and drops a paper packet on my night table, next to my water pitcher. "Drink that down with a glass of water and it'll help you."

Dora leans over and examines it, and then nods. "Yes, exactly right. I can't believe I haven't introduced you to an apothecary yet, but there just hasn't been the time."

"Thank you both," I say muzzily, sleep overtaking me slowly but surely. "I can never thank you enough." They both lean over and kiss my cheeks but if they say anything else, I am asleep and do not hear them.

Chapter Thirty-Four

Lorenzo of House Valier

I am breakfasting with my parents when a servant announces that Luca of House Braggadin has come to call. "He is not normally an early riser," my mother says. "Show him in, and have a plate brought," she says to the servant.

"I'm not certain that he—" I start, and my mother smiles at me.

"He will sit at the table with us, and whatever he has come to see you about can wait until after." Her tone will accept no further argument, though her smile remains pleasant. My father clears his throat and drinks his coffee.

"Of course, Mother."

Luca strides in, indeed more alert than I typically see him at this hour, when I have seen him this hour. Perhaps he visited an apothecary on his way here. He does not falter when he sees my parents, but turns his energy into a vigorous bow. "Good morrow to House Valier," he says.

"Luca, welcome. Have a seat, please," my mother says.

"I couldn't possibly impose," he says.

"It's no imposition, I insist. You did well at your duels yesterday, how are you feeling now? Ready to continue your victories?"

Luca has now caught on, and sinks into the chair with the waiting place setting. A servant appears and pours him coffee. "Thank you, yes, I'm more than ready to continue my victories. I should be interested in seeing how far our circle gets this tournament; the last time, only Lorenzo went beyond the third round." Wisely, he does not say that it was Marco, Dora, and I in the second round with him. He glances at me, as though he knows I am thinking it. It is obvious that I would be.

"That is true. And what a surprise Serafina has been! Did your practices indicate that she would perform so well?" Here, my mother looks from Luca to myself.

"She takes instruction well," I say. "And has little real experience. So it was hard to know what we might expect from her outside of the practice room."

"A measured response from my son," she says to Luca. "Is your opinion the same?"

"I had more hopes for her than Renzo did, but I think I tend to have a sunnier outlook than he does." I snort, and Luca grins. "The poor girl was also inexperienced with drink, though, which we did not fully realize when we took her out for celebratory libations. My visit this morning was mostly to inform Lorenzo that Teodora and I got her home safely, and Lady Galeazzo was grateful."

"I see," my mother says slowly, though with suppressed amusement. I wonder if she already had some inkling of Serafina's homecoming last night, but I am not always privy to the niceties of my mother's communications with her friends. "Well that was very good of you two. Teodora has a good heart."

"She is always stalwart and true," Luca says, sitting back as a servant puts a plate of breakfast in front of him, meat and eggs and toasted bread. "And knows how to take charge of a situation."

"She has a good head on her shoulders," I say.

Another servant enters the room and stands at the head of the table, and we all look at him. "Teodora of House Alvise has come to call."

My mother raises her eyebrows and looks at me. I gaze back at her, keeping my expression schooled blank. My father reaches for the pot and pours himself another cup of coffee. "See her in, and have another setting brought," he says.

"Of course, my lord."

Dora sweeps in, assesses the room at a glance, and curtseys to my mother and father. "Good morrow, Lord and Lady Valier," she says.

"Good morrow, Teodora" my father says. "We were just going over the events of last evening. Please have a seat."

"Thank you, I will." She arranges herself, setting her fan next to her place setting, cutting me with a glance. "I hope I was given a good accounting."

"The best accounting," I say. "Much better than your duel went, at any rate." She shifts her jaw and then smiles again. Interesting, that they both came here to...what? Dress me down for allowing Serafina to remain drunk? Such an inconsequential decision. Sobering Dora was the best choice, for her grace in handling every situation she is in, and Luca was hardly tipsy by that point. They aren't remonstrating Tristan, who declined to even involve herself. I hadn't entirely been lying when I said my spark had already been taxed more than enough yesterday, but I don't need to justify my decisions to myself.

"Yesterday was not my best showing, that is true," she says evenly, stirring sugar into her coffee. "You are doing quite well, though, and I presume you will continue to."

"That is my hope, yes." Today, with how many people will have been weeded out already, there will likely be three rounds of duels instead of two, and then tomorrow the finishers.

"It is so very nice that your friends surprised you to give you well wishes this morning, Lorenzo," my mother says. She is smiling, amused. Curious.

"I agree, my lady mother, it is. We should all be so lucky as to have such stalwart friends and compatriots."

"I'm not certain luck has anything to do with it," my mother says. "Though I wonder, in our dueling circles, especially when we were younger, we used to do funny little things for luck. We'd get charms, of course, everybody does that sooner or later, and wish in fountains." She is looking at me as she embarks upon this speech, but then switches her gaze abruptly to pin Luca with it. "Tell me, is there anything your circle does like that? For luck?"

"Not generally," Luca says, after a single too-long beat of silence.

"Oh, Luca, you wouldn't lie to me, would you?"

"Of course not, Lady Valier." He cannot use his charms on my mother the way he can on the younger ladies, but his smooth confidence is part of that package.

"Now that's interesting, because it seemed as though you'd started a new tradition last evening." She remains gazing at him for a little too long, before looking again to me. "Lorenzo?"

"Luca decided on a whim that it was necessary to kiss Serafina for luck," I say.

"Mmm, interesting. And so how was it that you kissed Serafina, after you had already won?"

"It was that or make her kiss a mirror, and we did not have one on hand," Dora says, lightly, laughing, rescuing me. "And while I've often used my main gauche for a mirror in a pinch, it would not have been suitable in the moment, and so Lorenzo, who'd already won on his own luck, kissed Serafina so that she would not lose hers."

"I see." My mother smiles, and it is impossible to tell if she believes this answer, which is as true as any. I did not particularly want to kiss Serafina, but that I did exactly because she did not want me to. "And how do you find Serafina, now that you've spent more time with her in your circle? She seems to have adapted well."

"She is still in the tournament on the second day," my father adds.

"She is more serious than Ottavia," I say judiciously.

"Is that the best accounting you can give of the girl? Your best friend's sister?"

"It is a fair accounting of the girl." I do not waver from my mother's gaze. "If you press me further, you would be asking me to lie to you."

"I see," she says again, glancing at my father. I am unable to read the look they exchange. "Teodora? Luca? Do you agree?"

"She is loads more serious than Ottavia," Luca says. "And she is eager to please, which is more than I can say about any of the rest of us. It remains to see if that will stick, or get rubbed off by association." Dora nods along with him.

"She is very sweet," she adds. "But her softness belies a stronger core, I am sure of it."

"There, Lorenzo," my mother says. "At least your fellows are more descriptive." She pushes her chair back from the table, and we all stand and bow. "We will see you later, at the tournament. Your father is the judge to one of your rounds. Not the first, though, so there is still time to avoid it."

"I would never," I say, and my father laughs.

"Of course not."

They depart, and Dora drinks her coffee and Luca eats his bacon, and when my parents' footsteps fade into the hallways of the house, I look at them. "What do you want?"

"Now, Lorenzo, why greet us anew and so harshly, after we had such a nice time with your parents?" Luca asks, elaborately wounded.

"You know why, I expect." I look at Dora. "What do you have to say? You usually have ample opinions with regards to my behavior."

"And you mine," she says, setting her coffee cup down. "While I believe you that last night you were at your spark's end with exhaustion, and could truly only relieve one of our drunkenness, to leave Serafina impaired was a mean choice, such a casual cruelty."

"Was it? Or did she learn a valuable lesson about where her limits are?"

"I would not confidently say she learned anything, no," Dora says. "Other than that Luca and I, at least, are truly her friends."

"Friends," I repeat. "Is that how you feel about the girl, Luca? A deep and abiding friendship? That's what's driven you to my doorstop at this unusually early hour, to defend a *friend*?"

"If we didn't have a tournament today, I'd fight you for that," Luca says, picking up his toast, his elbows on the table. "Yes, damn you, friendship, nothing more and nothing less."

"And you relieved her of her virtue in the name of friendship as well, I suppose?" I ask, sitting back in my chair. "Started that nonsense about kissing her, for *friendship*?" We've fought for less. He's fought for far less.

"Renzo," Teodora says in a cautioning tone. "I thought we'd gotten past—"

"*You* had nothing to get past," I say. "I am the one who has to keep agreeing to things, and putting up with them, and acting counter to my nature."

"If this had been your nature all along, the circle never would have formed," she says. "And as it stands, I'm not certain it will stay together, if you continue along this road."

"What, will you break us up? Who do you think you could take with you?" Instead of raising my voice in anger, I lower it.

"Everyone," Dora says, matching my tone, her gaze level.

This surprises me; *could* she take everyone? Perhaps. Luca has not hastened to contradict her and is still angrily chewing his toast. Armand might remain with me. We are certain to lose Ottavia, once Sterling gets her with child; she's never been able to take this seriously, she will not return to the dueling floor once this prize has been achieved.

"That is quite the threat," I say finally, and her gaze softens.

"And it pains me to make it," she says.

"I am always myself." Not an apology, I don't think I've done anything wrong, even if Dora feels that a wronging has occurred.

"You're always like this, that's the truth," she says, with a wry laugh. "Luca, get your elbows off the table."

"My apologies," he mutters, but he complies.

"Accepted." She looks to me again. "Now what are we going to do with you, Renzo? We can't keep having these conversations."

"We can't," I agree.

"Oh is this not your first?" Luca asks. "I'll admit I didn't have a plan for when I got here but—"

"No, it is not our first," Dora says tiredly. "I'd like to say it isn't the last either but..."

"Who knows, perhaps one of us will have another bad duel," I say with a fake cheerfulness that makes her grimace.

"Perhaps you will," she says, "though perish the thought. But I must take my leave, I assume Serafina will be waking about now, if she hasn't already, and if last evening was one of unaccustomed drunkenness for her, which it indeed seemed to be, then this morrow's waking will not be kind for her, despite the powder Luca left her. You'll forgive me for saying that Lady Galeazzo seems as though she would be small comfort."

"I will forgive you, and never tell her that you said so," I say, raising my coffee cup to her as she goes.

Chapter Thirty-Five

Serafina of House Galeazzo

The morning light lances my skull like nothing I have ever felt before, and I press my face into the pillow and groan.

"My lady, are you ill?" Agnes asks from somewhere nearby, and though I know her voice is not truly too loud, it seems it. "It is far later than you have ever awakened."

"Suffering the ill effects of last night's well-meaning decisions," I mumble. "There is a packet on the table," I say a moment later, or maybe longer, I don't entirely know, dim memories of Luca leaving it there.

"Should I mix it with your water?"

"Yes, I think." I can't remember. It is probably just as well, in the water first or swallowed first. They would have written it down, if the difference was so dire. Or assumed that I knew anyway, because there are so many things that everybody knows that I do not.

I regret giving Agnes that instruction, though, as she also *stirs* the powder and the sound of the spoon against the glass makes me very aware of my eyes in particular and I have never felt this way before. I will myself to sit up, though, and manage to crawl from beneath my covers, my eyes slitted shut against the sunshine spilling through my windows, and shakily take the glass from Agnes. I prepare myself for a medicinal flavor, but it doesn't taste of anything, and after a moment, I'm able to breathe again without feeling as though it is too loud.

"My lady, are you well now?"

"I think that I might be Agnes, thank you." I blink and experimentally turn my head, and the pain has dissipated, and the sunshine is just sunshine again, and not sharp knives. I have much to thank Luca for, though perhaps also much to scold Luca for, and the two might cancel each other out. It was due to his foolishness that Lorenzo *kissed* me in front of everybody. He didn't want to, either, but it meant more to him that it made me uncomfortable.

There is a knock at my bedchamber door, and Agnes hastens to answer it. She has a whispered conversation with the servant there, and she is surprisingly vehement, and yet they are surprisingly insistent. "My lady?" she asks, and I manage to turn and look at her.

"Yes, Agnes?"

"Lady Teodora of House Alvise is here to see you. She insists she is aware of the state that you are in, and that is part of the reason for her visit."

I cannot face Teodora. Though Teodora can help me pick up the pieces of myself in order to get ready for today's tournament events. The thought of it fills me with such dread, and I prostrate myself again. "Yes, she may come up. Thank you," I say after a moment, realizing that my return to the pillow might have indicated a negative answer. How did she know I would be awake? Perhaps it is another part of her spark, in line with how she can find people. I am unable to reconcile my new knowledge. How could she not tell anybody? How could she let us miss Marco so, for this time?

But Marco left purposefully, under his own power. Of course Dora would respect that, no matter what the rest of us might want. Like Lorenzo, she also loved my brother, and for him to take such drastic action must have been in the name of love, must have been as true an action as any one of us can dream up. Dora would never go against such a thing, and so she keeps her secret. She must trust me very much, to have told me.

I think I must have fallen asleep again, because then Dora is by my bedside, shaking me gently. "Serafina, we have time, but it's best if you get up now."

"You're too kind, to have come to help me this morning after all you did for me last night." Facing my mother for me like that. Though my mother was...amused? No, I must have dreamed that. Strange that my mother hasn't visited my bedchamber already this morning. Very strange.

"I'd like to think you would do the same for me, Fina, you're all sweetness and light." She looks at me, smiling. "Luca's remedy did the trick, yes?"

"Yes, it did. I shall have to remember to thank him as well."

"I'm sure he won't even think of it. Now how shall we dress you? You must wear something with a collar, for your laurel pins."

"You have command of my wardrobe," I say, getting up to brush my hair. Agnes is still lingering by the door, uncertain. "You may take the day off," I say. "Unless you have other duties for my lady mother?"

"I don't, my lady. Thank you." Agnes bobs a curtsey, looks at Dora worriedly one last time, and then slips out of the room.

"She wants so badly to be able to defend you," Dora says in an idle tone, her back to me as she looks at my dresses. "She is also very sweet."

"She is invaluable," I say. "Sometimes, I feel as though I am closer to her now than—" I break off, because I was going to say 'than anyone else in the world' and that seems like such a bereft statement, I need to stop being so, so soft. "Than my friends the twins," I recover. "They really do not understand the duels, the tournaments. They were quite horrified, the day I visited, and told them. I didn't understand either, not so long ago, but now that I have plunged so recklessly into it all, I feel as though I am gaining ground."

Dora turns with a dress, dark sky-blue with white lace at the front, and elbow length sleeves that have more lace. "I'm pleased to hear it," she says. "I know you've received an...let's call it an uneven welcome. But I've tried, as has Luca, and—"

"Everybody's tried, it's all right. It was a tremendous shock to everybody and we are all coping as best we can," I say. Every day I think of Marco. I cannot talk about Marco, for what would I say? And it would change nothing.

"You are more generous of spirit than I am," she says thoughtfully. "Now, is this a dress you can fight in, or will these sleeves be a problem?"

"I don't think they will," I say, trying to think. "Because of their length."

"Good, then this is what I select. The laurels will look well against the lace, and this blue is good for your coloring. It's a wonder you don't have more that will set off your eyes, though now that I'm thinking about it, I'm not sure what that would be. Wearing gold would be too much, and wearing brown would be too drab."

"We shall have to return to your tailor and hold up swatches of cloth," I say, and we both laugh.

"I am happy to be your friend," she says after a moment. "I wish I had known you better, these years."

"Thank you." I feel a bit flustered, but not overmuch. "And I you. You've made, and continue to make, this easier for me than it otherwise would have been. Without being able to fill Marco's space in the dueling circle, I entirely don't know where I would be right now."

"You will always have a place in any dueling circle I have a say in." She kisses my cheek and says, "Now get dressed and we'll see about your hair."

"You are forever doing my hair."

"It's interesting to have a new person's hair to work on," Dora says, studying her canvas. "My hair is so straight, and Ottavia's hair is so fine, and Tristan doesn't like letting me do her hair, and you've got this nice thick hair with some curl to it, but not tight ringlets like Venette has, say."

"I just didn't want to take up too much of your time."

"I wouldn't offer if it was too much time." She sits me down and brushes my hair, and then twists some of it up, and braids other sections, and brings together a masterfully well-balanced style with all of it up, so that turning my head one way or the other isn't heavier, and it isn't distracting. "How does that feel?"

"Very nice, thank you."

"And how do *you* feel? You seem steadier than when I first arrived."

"The aftereffects of last night's celebrations were a little embarrassing," I say.

"Oh, it could have been worse. There doesn't seem to have been any vomiting."

"No," I say, feeling even more embarrassed. I hadn't considered that. "No, luckily not."

"There, count your blessings. Now let's go meet the others and get a sense of how the day feels. They haven't sent out any schedules yet, but I do think they expect to move rapidly through the rounds today."

"I am glad I have you to advise me, as I don't know what to expect." I've watched the tournaments before, with my parents, but all of that is a blur now that I am one of the people fighting.

"Will your lady mother want to see you, before we leave for the first round?"

"I don't know," I say carefully. "If you'd asked me last night, I would have been certain she would have already been to see me, or would have sent word to summon me, and she has done neither."

"What would you like to do?" Dora asks, and I have been asked that so rarely that both the situation and the question give me a full pause.

"I think I should like to leave for the tournament," I say slowly, carefully. "My lady mother left the decision up to me, and I have unfortunately already slept in. If she had a dire need to speak with me, she would have done so."

"Then we will go," Dora says brightly, looping her arm through mine as we leave my rooms and go down the hall. I hope I have made the right decision.

Chapter Thirty-Six

Lorenzo of House Valier

Luca and I leave soon after we finish breakfast; there isn't any sense lingering, especially as my parents have already left. We walk to the initial meeting place, close to my house.

"I wonder if you would mourn me so vigorously as you have Marco," Luca says unexpectedly.

"My dear friend, what?" I look at him, but he is still facing forward, his usually more cheerful mien serious.

"I don't mean to sound jealous, Renzo, that isn't my aim. But watching you mourn our living but departed friend, while the rest of us are still here, is difficult. I know there isn't any help for it, mourning is mourning. Perhaps our persistent cheer has been an affront to your sensibilities." He glances at me. "I mean no insult either. Or even think that voicing these questions might alter your course. As Teodora said, there are only so many times we can all say the same things."

"When you first spoke, I thought you had a dire portent about your duels today," I say, with an attempt at lightness in my tone, but Luca does not reward me with a smile. "Yes, Luca, I would mourn you. I would redouble my mourning. My heart seems so hard because it is shocked at having been hurt; I did not think myself so vulnerable, until now. That is the affront, that I could be so wounded."

"You are able to speak so reasonably, and yet your actions, when your vile humors take hold..."

"As you say, my vile humors. I have no more control over them than the sun or the moon." Is that a poor excuse? Am I luxuriating in my anger and betrayal? It is too much to ponder on a morning like today's, with duels ahead of us.

"If only we knew his mind," Luca says, surprising me. "We knew he had a friendship with Katarina, an affinity, but not that it had gone any further than that. Indeed, it seemed as though she was very carefully avoiding such entanglements, though I cannot say why. Surely Marco would have been able to buy her indenture?"

"There was a cousin," I say. "A pretty slip of a thing. Lady Galeazzo perhaps could have been convinced to buy one indenture for true love, and especially with as good of a swordswoman as Katarina, even without a hint of a spark. But not a second one that would not benefit her house."

"I heard the cousin died." Luca shrugs. "But it is neither here nor there. I tried sending him a bird and it returned, frayed and bedraggled, unread, unable to find its addressee."

"I also have tried," I say, surprised. Of course I tried, and received such bedraggled and lost birds back, but to find that Luca also did... "Why did you never mention it?"

"There was nothing to say," he says, shrugging again. "If the bird had reached him, or if I had gotten an answer, you would have been the first person I told. The only person, perhaps. But there was no need to bother you over something you'd surely also tried."

We are quiet for several moments, and I say "If he had died, the birds would never take wing."

"Truly. I've tried that as well."

"Have you?" I look at him, and he glances at me, and then away, abashed.

"As a child, when my grandmother died." I put my hand on his shoulder. "No, it was a foolish thing, and I am not so gutted now as I was then. But the bird would not take form, even. Just remained paper, until I forced too much spark into it, trying to perform the impossible, and it burned to ash in my hands."

"Luca, that is the most tragic thing you have ever said to me." I say, in all seriousness.

"As I said. It is how I know Marco is still in the land of the living. It is probably best for his safety that our missives cannot reach him, after all."

"I hadn't considered that."

"Nor I, until my bird came back." Now he puts his hand on my shoulder. "But let's clear our minds and think of where our sword points may land."

"You always know where your sword point is," I say.

"And yours, for that matter," he laughs. "And here are Teodora and Serafina." He leaves me to go meet them. I watch him go, and he bows elaborately and kisses them each on the hand, and then on the cheek. Neither of them seem to be suffering any ill effects from last night, and Dora smiles still when she sees me looking, waving her fan at me and calling out, so I also am forced to go and meet them, as there are observers all around us.

In a fit of wickedness, I also bow, and kiss each of them on the hand, and then on the cheek, Dora laughing, Serafina silent but a flush blooming in her cheeks, avoiding my gaze. "Good morrow," I say. "And are we ready for our duels?"

"I should think so," Dora says. "Especially after all you've put us through."

"Respectfully, Teodora, I wasn't asking you," I say, looking at Serafina. She is forced now to look at me, and where she looked at Luca happily and openly, she is far more reticent.

"I hope so," she says. "Though what additions will there be to today's duels?"

"What do you mean?"

She quirks her lips briefly, unhappily; she didn't think she would have to explain. Or realizes she should know already. "Our first duels were just plain, no spark. Our second duels allowed spark for speed. And now, today?"

"Oh, I see," Dora says. "And now, today, you may do as you will. Well. You mayn't use your spark on your opponent, but otherwise, you may use it to boost your swordsmanship and dueling ability however you see fit."

"I thought that might be the case," she says, and I frown.

"Do you even have further talent with your spark?" I ask. "If you do, you ought to have told me before now, so that I could have accounted for that with practices."

"No," she says. "None that I know of, none that I was taught further. I can't even do the little bit of healing that some of you can do, much less the heavier work."

"That surprises me, that your mother would have neglected you so." What a waste, I think. Lady Galeazzo was so focused on her son that she did not consider how much it would benefit her house to have also made use of her daughter. It should not be up to me, to her dueling circle, to make up for these inadequacies.

"Yes," Serafina says hesitantly, as though she expects her mother to appear at her mention, but we remain unblessed by that apparition. "I shall ask her about further tutoring. She will be pleased that I am taking that interest."

"Perhaps you should've taken that interest earlier," I say, and Dora frowns.

"Perhaps you could recommend a tutor," Serafina counters, surprising even herself, I think.

"Isn't that a fantastic idea," Dora interposes. "It's rare that we have the opportunity to work with such a blank slate, it is very exciting, wouldn't you say, Lorenzo?"

"Exciting," I repeat slowly, and then Armand wanders up, looking for all the world like he was out for a constitutional and has happened to run into us, from the bemused look on his face.

"Good morrow," he says, peering at each of our faces in turn. His eyes are those of a sleepwalker, and I wonder if he slept at all last night, if he is coming from his house, or if he just left Iulio.

"Are you quite well, Armand?" I ask.

"That remains to be seen," he says. "Which does nothing to allay your concern, I am aware. Nothing has happened."

"If that is what you have to say, I shall have to accept it," I say. "If you have any necessities, do not hesitate to make me aware."

"You can be a good friend, Renzo," he says, squeezing my arm. "I can always rely on you."

"Why do we all look so serious?" Tristan asks, Ottavia in tow and Sterling paused just before us, bidding their parents good day.

"We heard that your arrival was imminent," Luca says, straight-faced until she swats him on the arm with her gloves, then laughing.

"Very funny," she says. "Are the schedules out yet?"

"No, but soon," I say. While it isn't required that a full circle be present if not all the members are fighting, I am gladdened that everybody has decided to attend. I do wish that more of us were having a third duel, and beyond remains to be seen, but if wishes were horses then beggars might ride.

Chapter Thirty-Seven

Serafina of House Galeazzo

When they do hand out the schedules for the morning duels, I am horrified to see that mine is first. I will be fighting Bioncah of House Zanchi, somebody I saw Marco fight at a prior tournament, and he introduced me to her afterwards. She was a friendly enough girl, stocky and with her hair cropped unusually short, but with a dancer's poise and grace. She bested my brother but in a way that the duel was just delightful for both of them, and he even laughed when she got third blood, as those were the terms at that stage of that tournament. I am not afraid to face her, I don't think, but I cannot imagine why I have been placed first, other than perhaps as a curiosity. No, they choose the order randomly, Dora assured me. It is just poor luck.

Judges bring around the laurel pins for those who won yesterday, and Dora helps me affix mine on either side of my collar, while Lorenzo and Luca do the same for each other. They are lightweight so as not to be bothersome, green enamel and gold, pretty in their plainness, and for me, reinforcement that yes, I can belong here. I haven't lost so much time as it seems.

The duel isn't due to start yet, but I feel as though I must try and come up with an approach that I might take. I have seen Bioncah fight, she has not seen me fight. She moves like a dancer, I know how to dance. If only I had Luca's sense of distances, and dimensions, I feel as though I could put all of those things together. I have never yet tried to combine dancing with dueling; I know in my heart that it is the sort of notion that my mother would have slapped out of me had she known it to be a thought I was having, but I think that perhaps it could be successful. I cannot be the only one to have ever thought of it, there must be a style, as Dora's opponent yesterday had a style using a cape.

"Now who is kissing who for luck today?" Lorenzo says abruptly, right before they call the first duel.

"I thought that was a first day convention, not that it continued," I say lightly, even as my stomach turns to ice. "You'll forgive me for not realizing what all of our quirks and superstitions are just yet."

"Oh it's simple, Serafina kisses Luca and Luca kisses Lorenzo, and then everybody is covered," Tristan says.

"Or we both kiss Serafina," Luca says, catching me up in his arms and spinning us in a circle.

"Luca, I—" But then he is kissing me and I am kissing him and then he sets me down and then the judge calls my name and I have to go to the dueling floor and don't look at anybody's faces before I do so. I should feel flustered but instead I feel a strange exuberance. Perhaps that is how you should feel, when you are kissing people.

Bioncah smiles at me as we curtsey, and nods, and I return both. Yes, I remember you, we are each saying. Then we draw both our swords and then, spark fast, we both try and catch the other off guard. Our swords clash together and we break off, circling, and I think, if this were a dance, she would go left, and I would go right, from how our hips and shoulders are leading, and so I follow that instinct, coming in under her guard as she moves, grazing her knee with my long blade.

"First blood, duel," the judge calls, and we stop, breathing hard, and she is still smiling as we curtsey again. The judge gives me my fresh laurel wreath.

"Nicely done," she says.

"Thank you," I say, surprised, and we walk off the dueling floor in opposite directions.

"Fina what was that? It was brilliant!" Dora says.

"I saw her fight Marco once," I say, darting a look at Lorenzo when I say my brother's name. He is staring at me, but doesn't seem more angry than he usually does when staring at me. "I remember her moving like a dancer, and I wondered if treating the duel like a dance might be the key with her."

"Well you were right, my goodness. What a clever idea."

"I thought you were going to say it was my kiss," Luca said, his hands folded behind his head.

"I didn't want to cheapen it by lying about it," I say, not quite able to reach the same bantering tone and sounding more coy instead, I think, but he laughs, which is what I intended.

"Just so," he says. "Oh this round will go very fast, I'm next."

"Are you going to kiss her again? You're making such a festival of this, Luca," Tristan says.

"What, are you jealous? Should I kiss all the girls?" He purses his lips at her and she smacks him again with her fan, lightly.

"No thank you," Ottavia giggles, hiding her face against Sterling's shoulder.

"Teodora?"

"Oh, I thought we decided last night that I was *bad* luck," she says airily, and Luca turns to Lorenzo.

"Well, Armand doesn't seem in the kissing mood either, Renzo, and Sterling is taken, so…"

Lorenzo sighs, angry, amused. "You are a clown, Luca."

"A *successful* one," he retorts.

"Yes, I'll kiss you again," I say shyly.

"There is one true heart among us, at least." Luca bows low over my hand and then stands up, and I get up on my toes to reach his lips. Not so dizzying as when he kissed me, but also the first time I initiated a kiss. "You have my thanks, my lady."

"And you have my luck," I say, and we all ignore Lorenzo's snort as Luca goes to his duel. He is fighting Briani of House Massimo, who is Venette's sister and who I have seen at events but not otherwise. It is somewhat unusual that she is not in Venette's dueling circle, but not unheard of. She's slightly younger, and might simply have other acquaintances. She does not seem very confident when she takes to the dueling floor, which is quite a thing for me to be able to think. It makes me wonder if Venette denied her entry to the dueling circle.

She curtseys and he bows, and then she trips on her skirts when trying to close and rather than accidentally impale her on both his blades, Luca throws them on the ground. There's a slight gasp when he does that, perhaps the question of whether it would be interpreted as surrender, or refusal to duel, but as Briani catches herself on one knee, Luca relieves her of her short blade and bloods her, lightly, just above the cuff of her glove.

"Duel," the judge says in a sour voice, and Briani flushes scarlet. Luca helps her to her feet and returns her blade, and I think that he says something to her, when they are in close like that, for she frowns a bit and then nods. He retrieves his blades and sheathes them, and they face each other for the final bow and curtsey before he accepts his laurel wreath and returns to us.

"Well that was invigorating," Luca says. "I would have given her more of a chance to recover herself, just to make it more sporting, but I really couldn't see just leaving that opportunity."

"I thought that she was going to gut herself like a fish on your blades, that was fast thinking," Lorenzo says.

"Tell the truth, Lorenzo, you wouldn't have dropped your weapons," Tristan says.

"I don't know," he says, frowning. "Maybe I would have. Or I wouldn't have, but then would have had to heal her afterwards, because how could I act otherwise?"

Tristan nods. "Fair play."

"What would you have done, Tristan?" Luca asks. He actually seems slightly shaken by the possibility, though is putting on a brave face.

"I'm certain I would never have reacted in time and just gutted her like a fish, and then Lorenzo would have had to heal her." Tristan smiles sweetly and Lorenzo shakes his head.

"That's the kind of spark tutoring you all should be getting," he says.

"Oh who's getting a tutor?" Tristan looks around.

"Me, of course," I say, there's no sense leaving the silence to hang. "I am so dreadfully behind in so many things. Though as with everything, practice makes perfect, and at least I'm getting kissing practice." That gets a general laugh, and I am glad.

"Oh, right. My luck." Lorenzo sounds anything but enthusiastic but we've engaged in this silly social game and I have a sense that backing down now will not reflect well upon me.

"Your luck," I say. He does not move, making me come to him, and so I do. He is taller than me, slightly taller than Luca, and so I take his coat fronts in my hands and pull him to me as I reach up and kiss him firmly on the lips. I might be frightened but I am not a coward. He does not soften towards me, but I'm not sure that I want him to.

"My thanks," he says dryly, when we part, looking into my eyes. I back up from him, sweep into a curtsey, and he laughs and takes Luca by the shoulder and they go to the dueling floor.

"Well done," Dora murmurs, when he is out of earshot. "He is being terrible, but you are adapting, and I am proud of you."

"Thank you," I say. "I'm trying."

Chapter Thirty-Eight

Lorenzo of House Valier

For all our joking about gutting people like fish, Luca is a bit unsettled by his duel. We glance at each other, and he knows that I have a sense of his turmoil. "Sometimes, it seems as though we should not be doing this with real blades," he says lightly.

"Sometimes," I say. "Between what happened to Tristan, and what you averted today."

"It's just how it's done," he says. "Don't let me spoil your luck."

"Yes, my luck, damn you," I say, laughing about it finally. What a ridiculous situation. That damnable girl.

My opponent is Tiago of House Donato, whom I have fought before, both in tournaments and in group lessons. We shared the same dueling master for a time when we were all much younger and not in society yet.

He is still buttoning his gloves and talking to his second when I step onto the dueling floor, but then he turns to join me. "Renzo, it's been a while," he says.

"It has, Tiago," I say, despite the judge's frown. We bow to each other, and draw our swords. He was always strongest with his long blade and struggled with his main gauche, and whether that is still true remains to be seen, but when he steps forward, when we both step forward, spark quick, I relieve him of that long blade when he tries to strike and he continues his motion and punches me in the jaw even as our main gauches mirror each other and lock across our forearms, our breath on each others' cheeks, and I reverse grip on my long blade, closing the embrace to keep him there, and draw it lightly across the nape of his neck, blooding him even as a trickle runs from the corner of my mouth. I run my tongue along my teeth to see if any have loosened, but they are all sound.

"A draw," the judge says. "Continue to second blood."

We part and he kicks his long blade up to his hand and spins both, the flourish meant to confuse me, but my eye follows his hands and not his blades and while he tries to bait me into disarming him again, I go lower, trip him instead and open his forearm when he throws it up to block, forgetting his blades

"Second blood, duel," the judge calls. Tiago shakes his head, frustrated, but accepts my grip to help him up. There is applause all around us

"You've always been a clever one, Renzo," he says grinning, embarrassed.

"You had me worried," I say, clapping him on the back. "It's why I had to get your sword away from you."

"Buy you a drink later?"

"And I you."

Luca helps me on with my coat. "You make the disarm appear so easy, always."

"I've always had the knack of it."

When we are away from the dueling floor, Luca says "You and he never..."

"No, we never." By accident or design, we all have quite the catalog of each other's conquests.

We've barely regrouped before we are given the next schedule. Faster today indeed. We move to the dueling floor where my father will be judge, through the crowds of dueling circles already out but still here to watch, the food vendors, the carriages for hire. It's a wonder how full this city can be, and a wonder how empty it can be. All depending on the day, like most cities, I suppose.

Lord Galeazzo is there speaking to my father when we arrive, and I wonder if his lady wife and my mother are off someplace scheming together. I don't know why I should think that, other than it might suit their moods of late. He marks us in the crowd, sees that we three all have new laurel wreaths, and gives a slight nod. Serafina doesn't even notice, she is embroiled in some conversation with Dora and Ottavia. About dancing, I think.

I am fighting Martim of House Paolo, and I hope he has found his courage or at least gotten lighter swords, after yesterday. Luca will be first, though, fighting Hieronimo of House Tomaso. He is more or less our age, but also something of a newcomer, having moved here with a new wife in the last year or so from a city in the mountains. It's a wonder there are available dwellings anywhere, but each city manages its own population as it sees fit. Sometimes there is a mansion where there was not one. Sometimes they are gone. We have so many concerns of our own, masonry cannot always be one of them. Some of us live in our parents' house after we marry and some do not. Some stay in their home city and some do not. Hieronimo's wife is from here, I think, but I cannot be bothered to remember just now.

"Sorry to interrupt, ladies," Luca says, and Ottavia laughs and Serafina flushes pink across just her cheekbones, the way Ottavia typically does. Why I should notice that, I cannot say, and I set my jaw in irritation, looking at my father to make sure Luca isn't missing being called while he carries on with this luck-kissing foolishness. Dora puts her hand on my arm briefly, but when I look at her, she isn't irritated or warning me, just smiling gently.

Hieronimo is a very large man; broad of shoulder, muscled such that it seems like he'd be more at home in a blacksmith shop than wearing lace at his throat and sitting at a society dinner. His long blade looks comically skinny, like an oversized needle in his hand, and by contrast his main gauche is almost like a trowel. I watch Luca take this in and then shrug and hand me his coat.

"If he guts me it'll be quick, at least," he says with a grin.

"I'm inclined to think he'll be faster than he looks," I say. "Even with spark speed."

"Agreed."

"And if he isn't, then it's still fine to overcorrect. It's still only first blood."

"I think you are more nervous than I am, Renzo," Luca says, and I laugh.

"Maybe I am."

"You're a good friend," he says, and kisses my cheek before stepping onto the dueling floor. My father watches this exchange incuriously; I wonder how much of it he heard.

Luca and Hieronimo bow to each other and draw their swords. They both advance almost at once, spark-fast, and Hironimo's reach causes Luca to have to do a swift and improbable backbend almost at once to avoid being cut. I haven't seen him do a backflip recently, such acrobatics were something we played at when we were much younger, but he reaches a tipping point where that seems to be the only logical recovery. This stumps Hieronimo, who pauses to watch him move, his head tilted curiously, as the crowd applauds. I glance back at Dora, who is frowning in concentration, as though through sheer will she can bring Luca through to the next round, or at least unscathed.

It's only first blood. Presumably Hieronimo didn't maim his first two opponents, I cannot explain my foreboding now. Armand seems bothered as well, though, watching with complete calm, and I can't look away from the duel for too long, that would be irresponsible.

Hieronimo has advanced twice more, and Luca has evaded him both times, less desperately than with the backflip. From the look on his face, I'm certain he's calculating his own advance, the one with which he hopes to end the duel. They both try a few thrusts, and parries, and ripostes, as though they are running the handbook of two weaponed swordplay, and the audience is muttering, uneasy, perhaps growing bored. They expected this to be done faster, though I cannot say who they expected to have already been the victor. Hieronimo, I think, expected to have already been the victor by now, and it is with relief that he receives Luca's sudden charge, and then confusion when Luca tosses his main gauche in the air between them, feints in under Hieronimo's guard.

Coming in so close was a mistake, though, as Hieronimo closes his arms reflexively, as one might clap their hands while trying to catch a fly. He pins Luca in a rib-cracking embrace, I hear the muffled noise of at least one breaking, and Luca's pained grunt, but there is no blood and my father does not call the duel and Hieronimo squeezes again, perhaps hoping to wind Luca, and then drops him on his feet again and when Luca staggers back, opens a line across his front with that spade-like main gauche.

"Duel," My father calls, and the opponents salute and bow to one another before putting their weapons away.

"What a good showing," Luca says to Hieronimo, though he is pale, and breathless.

"I didn't hurt you too badly, did I?" Hieronimo asks, frowning.

"No no, it will be nothing soon enough."

"You're a slippery one."

"My thanks," Luca says, laughing and wincing.

"Come here, you idiot," I say quietly.

"I'm only being sporting, Renzo," he says, and walks stiffly off the dueling floor. I'm not certain anybody but we on the floor knew he'd broken something. He's flushed now as well, high on his cheeks, and what an interesting time it is for his spark to advance. The city keeps the score, and we have to simply go along with its reckoning.

"You can be sporting sitting down over here. Have the girls minister to you once I've healed you, Armand can be my second."

"Really I'll be all right."

"Yes, you will. Now shut up," I say, and put my hands on him. Some people particularly spark inclined to healing have told me that they feel the hurts that they heal, and I am daily thankful that this is not my experience of it. All the same, I have never healed broken ribs before, and it is an interesting feeling, this capriciously commanded magical force feeling its way through the living flesh to the bone within. After a moment, though, the more normal color returns to Luca's face, and he takes the draught that we use when our spark has advanced. "Better?"

"Better," he says, his smile returning.

"Armand, can you...?"

"Of course, Renzo," he says.

"Lorenzo," Luca calls as I turn away for my duel, starting to put my gloves on. "You must—"

"I will not. I tire of this game already, Luca, I will find my luck elsewhere." I turn my back firmly, but not before I see the relief plain on Serafina's face. It is no surprise, that she is relieved. I know how I have, deliberately, acted towards her. "I did not consider that I am facing Iulio when I asked you to be my second," I admit to Armand as we walk.

"Does that mean I should kiss you for luck?" he asks with a smirk, and I laugh.

"That is not what I meant."

"It is no matter; it is a tournament, there is no emotional weight to it. I do hope you beat him, for our sake. I expect you'll be the only one of us going to the next round."

"Are you guessing, or have you seen?"

"Guessing, actually. My spark has been quiet today." He offers me a flask, and I take a pull from it, watching Iulio talk to his second across the dueling floor.

"Any advice?"

Armand smiles. "You've never needed my advice for a duel."

"Need and want are different things, my friend."

"You flatter me, but you know all you need to know."

Chapter Thirty-Nine

Serafina of House Galeazzo

"It's because I kissed Renzo on the cheek before my duel," Luca says, seeing my face. "I gave the luck away."

"It's a silly game," I say, frowning.

"Some of the best games are silly," Luca says. "But please stop looking at me like that. It's like with Tristan, I'm fine again already. And I was in nowhere near the danger as Tristan."

"Sword *right* through my leg," she says sulkily. "Let the daylight through when he pulled it out. Let all the blood out too, he should've left it there until Renzo told him to take it out."

"I feel quite lucky to have gotten away from the tournament without so tragic a wound to recall," Dora says. "Best be careful, Fina, you're after this one."

"I'm always careful," I say. "Unlike the rest of you."

"You wound me," Luca says dramatically, clutching his heart and leaning back far enough on his bench that Tristan and Sterling catch him.

"You're all ridiculous," Ottavia says, fluttering her fan. "And it is impossible to take this all so seriously."

"It's possible when we're shedding real blood," Dora says. "But you're lucky you said that when Renzo was otherwise indisposed."

"I don't care anymore," she says boldly.

"Shh, it's starting," Luca says. "We'll see if Renzo stole my luck after all."

"Did he do that on purpose, take Armand as his second when he was facing Iulio?" I ask.

"Perhaps, but I don't think so," Dora says, as Iulio salutes Lorenzo, and they both bow.

"There's only so interesting it can be," Ottavia says. "Renzo isn't going to do a backflip."

"I assure you, I did not go into my fight assuming that I would be doing a backflip," Luca says.

"I was not aware you *could* do a backflip," I say, watching Lorenzo and Iulio circle each other, each with a different guard up. Iulio has still indeed only drawn one blade. We've all seen Lorenzo disarm people by this point, I'm interested in whether he will try that with Iulio or no. I am a little surprised when there is no rejoinder, and I turn right as my father puts his hand on my shoulder.

"I saw your first duel today, daughter," he says. "Very well handled."

"Thank you, my lord father," I say, caught desperately off guard, but wildly pleased to receive a compliment from him.

"I don't mean to interrupt you. But I wanted you to know that it hadn't escaped my notice." And he squeezes my shoulder and moves on through the crowd. I don't know where my mother is, I neither see her nor feel her fell presence, then realize I am entirely unaware of my facial expression but I am only smiling, it is acceptable.

"That was very sweet," Dora says after a moment.

"It was," I say, surprised, pleased. I am almost disappointed that he hasn't lingered to watch my duel next, but perhaps he realizes just how nervous such a thing would make me. "Oh, have I missed it?"

"No, they're having quite the stalemate," Tristan says as I turn my attention back to the dueling floor.

Lorenzo seems frustrated to me, as though he assumed he would be finished already as well. Iulio's expression is not open to me, other than one of concentration. I glance at Armand, whose expression is similarly focused; I wonder if he knows the outcome already, or is seeking it. He wasn't seeking it yesterday, when Tristan had her duel.

Then Lorenzo does something that surprises me; he lets his main gauche dip, as though it has lost his attention; the same thing that I did yesterday when I fought Callum. Did Iulio also watch her duel? It seems unlikely he would have missed that trick, but maybe he did. Maybe his circle didn't spend the evening all together, progressively deeper in drink, reenacting everybody's fights, because he *does* fall for it, or he starts to, and that is enough to undo him. He seems to realize, even as he is darting in for his strike, that Lorenzo played a false gambit, but it is too late and he has been blooded just across the shoulder.

"Duel," Lord Valier calls, and they both stop. This time, Lorenzo also salutes Iulio, and then they both bow, and then they leave the dueling floor.

"He did steal my luck," Luca says with something like admiration. "Damn him."

Dora laughs. "As though he ever needs anybody's luck but his own."

"Still." We watch him accept his laurel wreath from his father, who speaks to him for a moment further and then he leaves the floor with Armand.

"Ready, Fina?" Dora asks.

"I suppose I must be," I say with a wry smile. If nothing else, the tournament has made duels so much more commonplace for me, as it has been impossible to sustain anxiety about them for all this time, and it isn't even over yet.

I am fighting Lara of House Agustin, whose family's box was near ours at the Company of the Canted Stage, and so I used to gossip with her often over the actors, and people's theater dresses, and the little scandals that we learned about. She'd been going to the theater less in the last year, becoming more involved with society, and with Marco's departure I haven't seen her at all in months. I've never seen her fight, though by that turn she has never seen me fight, and so in that regard we are on even ground.

We are about the same height, and she seems slighter than I remember, which is a surprise. Perhaps she has been ill? I haven't heard word of that, but it isn't something I can dwell on now. We curtsey to one another and draw our swords, and she blinks at me across the dueling floor. She can't be confused about who I am; while we weren't friends, necessarily, we knew each other in passing. Perhaps she is simply thinking of my brother.

That thought unsettles me and further, irritates me. So many people think they have such stake in my brother's life, myself included, and he has left all of us, and for what? For love? We may never know.

I move before I realize it, but my sword meets empty air. Lara did not take the time to try to parry, or riposte, she wholly dodged, spinning away to face me, whatever thoughts she'd been having banished now by the immediacy of the duel. She recovers immediately, though; no sooner did she turn to face me then she is coming to meet me, pressing the issue, and our swords clash off each other once, twice, thrice, and then she tries clumsily to trip me and I try to blood her with my main gauche, but I catch my blade on the buckle of one of her sword belts and drop it rather than get tangled with her, and we step apart, circle again. I take a high, one-handed guard, breathing hard.

I make her come to me, and she tries to press her two weapon advantage and I relieve her of her main gauche instead, with a strong flick of the wrist as though I've been practicing disarms for these weeks, but I can't think about that now I can't *think* now, I must only act, and I parry, I block, and then she trips on our fallen weapons and, in swinging her hands out to save her balance, drives her sword tip through the top of my boot at an angle, and so it doesn't go *through* my foot but does slice my instep. I stop myself from crying out at the last moment; even Tristan didn't cry out, when she received her terrible wound.

"Duel," Lord Galeazzo calls, and Dora comes and takes my hands as I'm still standing there, stunned by the pain, and not entirely sure how to walk off. Oh, but I need my main gauche back.

I must make a motion towards it because Dora says, "Stop, stand still" and goes to get it for me.

"Thank you," I say, in as steady a voice as I can manage, and that makes her frown.

"Renzo should be here in a moment," she says, looking past me. "We need to get you off the dueling floor, though."

"Am I bleeding terribly?" I haven't looked down yet, and I have a sense that's a good idea, to not look down, and see whether there is quite a lot of blood or not.

"No, actually. Does it hurt very much?"

"I don't know yet," I say, and a jagged little laugh escapes me at the look on her face. "I haven't...I think from the fight I'm still..."

"It's okay. Here's Lorenzo." She's guided me to a bench without me really realizing, and Lorenzo saunters up and crouches down.

"Don't touch it," I say suddenly, and he frowns but puts his hand on my ankle instead. Looking past him, I see I've left a trail of blood from the dueling floor to here and the pain has a second to roar up my leg and then it feels warm all over instead, and then like nothing at all, just my foot, as it always feels. Maybe cold, even, but I have a hole in my boot now, that is perhaps to be expected.

"Wiggle your toes," he says, looking down clinically, and I do so. "Now stand." I do, and he gestures, and I take a few steps here and there. "Does that feel quite all right?"

"Yes, thank you," I say, feeling breathless, desperately grateful. My boot still has a hole in it, but a surprisingly narrow one.

"Of course," he says, with a shadow of a smile. I can almost fool myself into thinking that he cares about *me*, but he cares about the appearances. He hastened to heal each other member of our circle, and thus it would stick out were he to do otherwise for me.

"I'm sorry I lost," I say, and Dora frowns.

"That hardly matters," she says. "I lost the first day! My first duel!"

"I know," I say, but Lorenzo is still looking at me, actually looking. "But I wanted to win more."

He smiles, surprised, and she laughs. "Oh heaven help us. Well there's always next time. Let's get drinks before we've got to cheer Renzo at the next round."

Chapter Forty

Lorenzo of House Valier

I feel my father's gaze as I minister to Serafina, but he doesn't speak to me until Dora leads her off to one of the stands for wine. "She handled that well," he says.

"Teodora nearly always knows what to do in a situation," I say, watching them go. Luca has gotten up from his bench, and from his gait, somebody has brought him libations from said vendor while he waited. Tristan looks to me, and I gesture for her to go ahead, that they should go ahead.

"I meant Serafina," he says, and I look up at him. "This is her first tournament, and she got further than some of your most seasoned members."

"She did, yes," I say. "She knows many things by the book, it would seem. The technicalities, though not necessarily the practicalities."

"A very generous assessment," he says, and his posture and tone are correct and yet I still feel as though he is laughing at me.

"As plain an assessment as I can give," I say stiffly.

"Just so," he says. "And yet you admired at least one of her practicalities enough to imitate it."

"An approach that preys on the foibles of one's opponent should always be at hand," I say. It isn't as though I've never done that exact move before, in private duels but especially tournament fights.

"As you say." He does not embrace me, here on the street, though he would be within his rights as my father. He claps me on the shoulder. "I won't see your next duel, but you have my well wishes, of course."

"And you my thanks, my lord father." He squeezes my shoulder, and pats my face, and lets me go to meet the rest of the circle.

"And only Renzo is still in it," Armand says, handing me a cup when I reach the group. "As happened last time, and the time before."

"Are you suggesting I'm peerless, Armand?" I ask, teasing, smiling.

"I'm merely observing," he says.

"Perhaps it'll finish today," Ottavia says hopefully. "There can't be too many left now, can there?"

"Perhaps not," Sterling says. "After all, the finalists will need their rest."

"What about *our* rest?" she cries dramatically, and we laugh.

"We don't get rest," I say, finishing my drink. "I suppose, if you'd like, you can forgo watching the rest of my duels. Though of course, were you still in the tournament, I would be nearby to support you."

"I could never abandon you like that, Renzo," she says.

"And yet you are plotting your abandonment as we speak," I say.

She blinks at me. "It is a valid exit, Lorenzo."

"It is." When all is accounted for, do I really want to keep her? She is a detriment to the circle, her swordsmanship never improving, despite all of the drills, the practices. But it would be insulting were I to let her go without comment.

"And I have not made any sort of official decision," she says primly.

"No, of course not. You won't until after the wedding, I presume." She fans herself and smiles at me, and I know I'm right. Already, my influence on her has faded.

Luca pats me on the shoulder. "You're assuming she's decided, Renzo. Best not to worry about it now; you've got your next fight to worry about."

"I'm not worried," I say in reflex, but it is the truth of the matter. I will win, or I will not. I have already progressed furthest of the circle in the tournament.

"Are you ever?" Dora asks, smiling, and I shrug.

"I can't say never. Maybe rarely." I notice some children running up the street, and have such a strong, distinct memory of how Marco and I, and others, would roam about having our own citywide game during the tournaments, while the adults weren't paying attention to us and we were just old enough to not have governesses and nursemaids anymore, but tutors instead who didn't or couldn't watch us every moment.

We ran up streets and scaled gates and walls and fought in courtyards and squares abandoned by their usual folk, and while we got split knuckles and skinned knees and split lips instead of laurels and applause, and none of us knew how to heal, I think it was good for us. I look at Dora to see if she noticed the children, but she and Tristan are speaking quietly about something, and Serafina is listening but not adding anything, looking around as she does so. She accidentally meets my gaze and drops hers immediately, flushing slightly. If only she was the one who had a too-serious affair with a Company member and fled the city, instead of her brother. But no, such indiscretions are impossible for Serafina. I would have thought such indiscretions were impossible for Marco as well, but he is gone.

Serafina didn't play those games with us, she was too young, though Dora and Tristan did. Ottavia didn't want to, and we didn't make her, which is perhaps why she's so ready to give up the game at this point. I'm not sure any of our sparks advanced as a result of doing this, we were children playing at what we imagined the adults actually wanted to do, a city-wide free for all where anybody with a sword was fair game, rather than standing at each end of a marked off dueling floor and having all the pomp and ceremony of the tournament duels.

But the truth of it is, outside of tournament duels, nearly everybody in society is fair game at all times. It takes little pretense for a duel to start, and little structure is necessary; terms, a second. Which isn't to say people disregard even these spare rules all the time, but nobody honorable does. Nobody who remains in society does. They are subject to censure from the upper echelons, subject to detainment by the city guard. They might find themselves banished, though such measures are rare, as such breaches of the social contract are rare. Perhaps they used to be more common, and that is why we do what we do.

The new schedule comes around, and it is the last one that will be printed before the remaining duels are decided; there are so few of us left at this point that they'll gather us all in another one of the theater companies and we will finish today after all. And, damn them, the theater is the Company of the Canted Stage, the exact one I've been avoiding all this time, and I cannot help but think that Company's owners did so on purpose, in order to get the Galeazzos under their roof.

Dora reads over my shoulder, and then lays her cheek against mine. "I suppose it was just a matter of time, Renzo," she says, and I shrug her off.

"It has no meaning to me," I say.

"Of course not." I do not want to be angry with Dora and I step off to get another cup of wine before we walk to the theater. The tidal pull of the crowd is already pushing in that direction, and I watch them go without really seeing their faces. Anybody aware of Marco's betrayal will be talking about the theater's willingness to host the final duels of the tournament, and I'd say that everybody is aware of Marco's betrayal. Anybody who hasn't yet will be hoping desperately to catch a glimpse of his sister, if they haven't already, because isn't that also a bit of juicy gossip, that while House Galeazzo had a favored son who ran away with theater trash, they had a daughter in reserve, of age to enter society and fill her brother's place. They had a daughter who won three laurels in this very tournament before losing a fight. This all reflects very well on Serafina, actually, and in turn reflects well on my dueling circle, for accepting her in our ranks and training her up these short weeks, on such little notice.

I finish my wine, resist the urge to throw the cup down on the cobbles just to hear it clang around, just to see it dented. I feel wounded in a way that healing would not touch, and that I cannot articulate properly. I was only his best friend, after all, not blood. Not his lover. What right have I for public mourning, when his family is not publicly mourning, but rather seeing to their standings?

My opponent is Bridger of House Neto. It amuses me that I remember him as a boy, playing at practice sword tournaments with us. I have not seen him yet this season, but there was a time I knew him well. He married recently, I think, House Malvito though I can't remember her name. We do not still know each other well enough that I received an invitation to the wedding, which is just as well.

I see Dora watching me with knitted brows, and I salute her with my empty cup, set it back in the window of the wine vendor's, and rejoin the dueling circle. "Come, let us see how far I can ride this streak of luck," I say. "The most I have ever won before is five laurels, it would please me to exceed that."

Luca hugs me around the neck with one arm, boisterous, excited by my returned mood. "You have all the rest of our luck," he says. "We are hopeful you take it to the end."

"I am not *that* hopeful," I say, laughing. "There are far better swordsmen than I in our echelon. But two more laurels, I can humbly hope for that."

"Don't let your mother hear you talking about humble hopes," Armand says. "She will drill you severely."

"My mother has not run my sword drills in years" I say. "Though I would welcome her tutelage." Serafina's face drops in a way that I neither understand, nor can trouble myself to be too curious about, as we pass under a flowered arch into the courtyard of the Company of the Canted Stage and are welcomed by a section of their musicians, playing raucous battle music.

"Ridiculous," Tristan says, but she's smiling.

"You *love* this," Dora teases. "Even the music."

"Even the music," Tristan agrees, after a pause where she clearly considers denying it, wrestling with the pervasive air of good will. "I can only hope any man I marry feels the same way."

"Marriage, Tristan? Is love in the air?" Ottavia teases, suddenly interested.

"I would never tell you until I was *certain*," Tristan says, also smiling. "I know how you gossip."

"Oh how *I* gossip, Tristan? Forgive me, but I seem to remember—" And Tristan crowds in and hushes her, both of them giggling in a way that I have rarely heard from Tristan.

"I may just be hoping that my parents arrange something," Dora says. "It's so much to think about, *love*, when we have all of the rest of this going on."

"Very pragmatic, Dora," Armand says, his eyes sharpening.

"Perhaps." She shrugs. "Marriage for love is all well and good but marriage is also a social agreement and business arrangement and it's so troublesome to choose those things well."

"Teodora are you saying people should get married for marriages' sake and then...have affairs?" I ask in a falsely shocked voice.

"Maybe I am," she says, smiling at me. "It's the best way to make everybody happy."

"Until there are children."

"Said because you despise children or..."

"Well then the parentage would be called into question, would it not?"

The girls, other than Serafina, laugh, and I am caught off guard. "Oh, Renzo," Dora says. I look to Luca for support, and he also shrugs.

"There are things the girls go to the apothecary or the witch woman for," Armand says, waving his hand. "Preventing pregnancy among them."

"Well how was I to know?" I ask.

"Indeed, how would it ever be your concern," Teodora says, patting my cheek.

Chapter Forty-One

Serafina of House Galeazzo

We enter the theater, the others talking, and I take a deep breath. I have not been here in months. The last time was to see a show months before Marco ran off with Katarina, and he took me out to a tavern afterwards and she came along, one of the few times I met her. She'd played her role formidably, the general in a rebellion, supporting a claimant to a throne in a coup. It was an uncomfortably funny show, and an uncomfortably bloody show, and while I was glad to have seen it, I was also glad when it was over.

I look up, and my parents are in our family box; I wonder if it has stood empty for all of this time, or if the tickets for it are typically sold. It never occurred to me to want to come here, and it never occurred to me that it would be permissible, blameless though I am in my brother's actions.

Dora surprises me by squeezing my hand, and I smile at her by reflex. She must know the direction of my thoughts; my hurts are not private. The circles of the individuals still dueling have seats right up in front, temporary seating set up even in the orchestra pit, so that the space right in front of the stage isn't wasted. I glance at my parents again, expecting my mother to intercede, to beckon me to them, and while I don't want to sit with them, such a thing would be unavoidable if that is what she wants. But she doesn't give me any sign and I sigh with relief.

The air is just electric with excitement and I think again of that last show. What a bloodthirsty society we are, even if the wounds that we give and that we receive are as temporary as we can make them. I still feel the cold blade of my opponent's sword punching my boot, slicing my foot, though the only scar that will be left will be the flat golden scar from Lorenzo's healing, more like a smear of paint than flesh knitted together. Unlike the scar on my chin, a thin white line, but raised, easily felt and easily visible. I'd relaced that boot tighter, having no time to buy a new pair and change in between duels, even though this is not my duel.

One of the Company's managers or owners takes to the stage before the fights begin. They are well-appointed, their clothes, their hair, their adornments Their swords.. They command the stage with their presence, either through practice or through their spark; their spark is very apparent, though I'm poorly equipped to describe why I think that. Strange, that pains are not taken to give us better vocabularies, about our magical sparks. Maybe the city takes pains to keep us ignorant.

"You honor us by coming to this, The Company of the Canted Stage, for the finality of the dueling tournament. Everybody involved has fought valiantly over the last two days, and spilled their blood in this noble effort of self enrichment. You are an inspiration to us all, and I wish the final duelists the best of luck." They lead the theater full of us in applause, their gaze raking over those of us gathered, and it seems that they look at me for a little longer than necessary, but it's impossible to tell, when a person is on stage, what they are looking at actually. I am not a final duelist, after all.

The first three fights are not people that I know, other than having seen them at events, and then Lorenzo takes the stage for his fight. I am relieved that Luca dropped the joke of kissing me for luck; it was fine enough to be brief, though still uncomfortable. But I am comfortable with so little, and so much is always happening, that it was probably good for me. It was a joke I chose to play along with, not something that was forced upon me.

Lorenzo seems to know his opponent, they look at each other a moment and nod before they bow. Watching a duel like this, from this side of the stage, lends it an otherworldly quality. Or maybe it's simply because I've watched so many stage productions here. Watching duels from the wings of a different stage, last night, did not feel like this.

I've learned, in the past two days, that it's possible to use a little bit of spark in order to watch people who are moving spark fast, and it's necessary to do that while watching Lorenzo and his opponent. They are breathtakingly fast, and very evenly matched, swords clashing off one another, circling, passing, parrying. Lorenzo has perhaps the happiest expression on his face that I've seen of late; he pines for a good match, I think, for a reasonable challenge, and his opponent has given him that. His opponent has given him more than that, has made him push himself.

They go for far longer than expected, before Lorenzo draws the first blood. I'm not even sure how it happened, if Bridger dropped his guard or just misjudged, or if Lorenzo got even faster, but there is a moment when they are both a further blur and then they have both stopped, the tip of Lorenzo's blade dark, the shoulder of Bridger's shirt blooming red. They bow to each other, both of them grinning like fools, and sheathe their weapons. Then Lorenzo offers his hand, which Bridger accepts, to further applause, and then Lorenzo heals his wound, and they say something to each other, close, and turn to the audience and both bow.

The person from the Company comes back onstage with Lorenzo's laurel, and Lorenzo accepts it from them with another bow before leaving the stage. He is fighting again, but he gestures to Luca, who gives him a flask that he drains.

"That was quite a lot, Renzo," Luca observes.

"It was, but it was worth it. And you remember Bridger, do you not?"

"I do, and I went to his wedding a few months past. I had not known you would remember him so fondly."

"You went to a wedding? Who did you bring?" Tristan asks.

"My painter, of course." Luca grins and Tristan swats him, and I cannot tell if he's telling the truth, and I don't know who his painter is, though the rest of the circle seems to. It isn't my business, it isn't my concern, I think. I reassure myself. Luca and I are unlikely to have more dalliances of that sort; it would not do to become smitten with him.

"They won't pass out more schedules," Dora says to me. "They'll just call people onto the stage."

"There are only so many left," I say.

"Truly. Lorenzo could have a handful more fights, if he keeps winning. Or just one."

The next duel is over so very fast it makes my head spin, both duelists drawing and striking almost as one, and then the girl getting second blood immediately when the initial strikes are called a draw.

The duel after that is so drawn out that it is practically a technical demonstration, and by the time first blood is drawn, I have an overwhelming urge to get away from all of this. "I just need some air," I whisper to Dora, and slip out of my chair and up the aisle before she replies. I am not the only one who has left their seat and so I am not the only one fleeing the theater at this exact moment, and so I don't think I drew my mother's undue attention. Perhaps Lady Valier will distract her.

The street is lit but empty, a set stage on which the cast has not yet had their cues. The air is much cooler and is exactly the relief I sought. We have been inside for uncounted hours, fighting and sweating and cheering and gasping. Even though I have not had a duel for quite a long time, it's still exhausting. I find my handkerchief, somehow still starched and pressed after all these hours, and pat at my face and neck, breathing in the soothing clean scent.

A group of city guard pass by, looking at me long enough to see my swords, the laurel wreath still in my hair, and give me a nod as they continue on. I should go back in, though, it wouldn't do to miss Lorenzo's next duel.

I turn, and that theater Company manager who had announced the welcome is standing in the doorway, not rudely close to me, not inappropriate, but far closer than I expected, and I give a start.

"It was not my intent you frighten you," they say, not exactly an apology.

"I didn't expect to see you there," I answer, not exactly excusing them.

"You are of House Galeazzo, are you not?"

"Yes, I am Serafina of House Galeazzo." They incline their head, and I slightly bob a curtsey.

"I recall having seen you here, with your brother. Watching our productions."

"Yes, I very much enjoy the theater." This is a dangerous conversation to be having, I think. My mother would be furious to know they are speaking to me alone in this manner.

They regard me thoughtfully for an excruciating moment. "Your brother caused us quite the trouble. And our Katarina, of course. Only a fool would think her blameless."

"We miss my brother very much," I say carefully. I have the distinct feeling that I absolutely must not say anything that might be interpreted as an apology. I feel as though they are trying to trick me into that.

"One can't help but think their elopement was preventable," they say. Their gaze is uncomfortable to meet, eyes dark as embers but without the flame.

"I only wish it had been. It was quite the surprise," I say truthfully. Had I known Marco's plot, I am not certain I'd be able to be guileless in the face of such scrutiny, but as I was kept in the dark as everybody else, I am able to be genuine, and I can only hope they perceive me as such.

"We had been unaware that your brother and Katarina had such serious feelings for one another," they pressed.

"I can only agree. I met her just a handful of times and they seemed only to be friends." Cheers inside spill out the open door. "I will be missed," I say.

"I would be incorrect to keep you," they say, holding the door for me and bowing. "My thanks for your time, Serafina of House Galeazzo."

I curtsey again, and slip past them back into the theater. I cannot explain why I feel shaken by this conversation, nor can I tell anybody about it, I don't think, not even Dora. My mother would be furious were she to know, which is all the more reason to keep it from her.

Lorenzo has just gotten up to take the stage for his next duel when I find my seat again, and I keep my head bowed against his incurious glance, though does he pause for a fraction of a second, when Dora says "Are you well, Serafina?"

"I am, thank you," I say, managing a smile. No, Lorenzo did not pause, he has no interest in me.

Chapter Forty-Two

Lorenzo of House Valier

This is the furthest I have ever arrived in a tournament; it is a testament to my hard work and increase in skill and spark that I even take the stage once more.

My opponent is Radolfo, and I recognize him as well, from simpler times. We are of a height, and his build is similar to mine. The pause draws out between us, after we have saluted, both having lit our internal matches and both waiting for the other to make the first move, give some indication of motion, weakness. He breaks first, moving a bit to the left while his eyes flick to the right, and I meet him where he will be instead of falling for the ruse, ruining his opening gambit and immediately getting first blood. We break, salute, and begin again without the extended pause this time. He drives hard towards me, spark-fast and spark-strong, and I meet his strikes with crossed swords, directing his momentum about the stage, and his smile is flashing white in the stage lights, so confident is he that the duel will be his, when he gets his first blood on me finally, in the upper arm. His pause to gloat gains me second blood, though, across the chest.

We don't salute this time, as I call on my spark for more, sweat steaming off of us. I catch his main gauche with my own and spin it away onto the floor and then strike at him from a high stance, but he bloods me the third time, sword just slightly going into the top of my boot, and I stop myself just in time.

We step away from each other, bow, salute. We're both panting.

I am a mixture of disappointed and relieved to be out of the tournament. I am exhausted, exultant, worn utterly thin. I leave the stage with Luca nearby, doing his best to act casual and not hover solicitously. Armand hands me his flask; everybody else's is empty, and I smell the licorice even before I gulp down the contents, absinthe coating my tongue.

"My apologies for not having sugar to crunch down with it," Armand says.

"Don't concern yourself, Armand, for I'm certain I am sweet enough," I say, and he laughs, though looks at me appraisingly.

"Are you well, Renzo?"

"I am in shambles, but I will recover," I say, hugging him briefly around the neck with one arm.

"After all those drills you put us through, I should hope it improved your stamina," Tristan sniffs, but she is here to support me, the whole circle is, even Serafina who I have treated so poorly, though will I think of it as that in a few hours? In the morning? I am hardly looking at her with new eyes.

There are still more duels, though, and we must find our seats again. I am still very interested in the duels; it is important, to see the technicalities of those more skilled. Of those who win ten laurels at a tournament, or more, depending on how many fights there have been. But my mind wanders, as it has been doing of late. To other fights, other tournaments. To that childhood game. To Marco, of course. To the bedraggled birds that both Luca and I got back. He should be here with us; that he has chosen not to be is a hurt felt more keenly than any blooding I've received in a duel.

It is in the small hours when the final duelists come onto the stage, the candles all burnt low and newer ones lit in their place, a haze of all the combined smokes in the air. These two, after all the fights of the last days, are the strongest duelists in our echelon, Sadie of House Orazio and Bernardo of House Calogera. They're exhausted by this point, they must be, but it's easy to read their eagerness, their excitement, in their postures. The final duel is only ever to first blood.

The dueling floor has been cleaned and sanded in between each match, but it is not so bright white anymore as it had been at the start of the evening. Before our eyes, it has gone to the gray of a dove's downiest feathers, or the palest ash of a burned letter.

Sadie curtseys and Bernardo salutes and the judge gives them the sign and at first they don't move. Not unusual for a certain type of dueling style, or even for being the final fight of the night. The muscles in my arms are still occasionally fluttering, the muscles in my legs have both cramped and relaxed, as there is only so much room to stretch here, in the seats. There is some cruelty of purpose, in making us all compete so long and so physically and then also immediately after sit and observe those still fighting. But it is how we as a society do things, and so we discreetly pass our flasks and rub balled fists along knotted muscles, and attentively watch those who have made it so far.

Bernardo breaks first and advances. Sadie is wearing a long enough skirt to obscure her legs and feet, but not to hamper her movements, and the gathering swirl of all that rustling fabric distracts Bernardo and causes him to falter in his first thrust. Perhaps he's also afraid of stepping on her hem, though also it would be to his advantage, perhaps, to pin her into place. But she is not where his sword blade ends up, and he is unable to perform a back flip like Luca, apparently, and just like that, he is blooded, a shallow scrape across the belly, and the tournament is over.

"That was anticlimactic," Tristan says with a sigh and Dora shushes her. I catch a confusing glimpse of Serafina's face; she seems upset, but what difference would it be to her, whether this last duel is long or short, climactic or otherwise? But the judge calls the duel, and then the theater company owner returns to the stage to make a final monologue and send us off into the night, that I scarce hear. We have all been in this position before, we just want to leave.

We filter out of the theater and into the street, and it's a similar unreality to leaving a very good performance and returning to the world, or perhaps even more so. Perhaps this is how performers feel, once they step out of their roles and into the night air, vestiges of stage makeup still on their faces, whatever drugs or drink they'd taken still propelling them forward into some further revelry. I cannot tell if that its what I want, or if what I seek is my rooms and my bed and a sleeping draught to deaden my nerves and soothe my muscles until the midday tomorrow. I'm leaning towards the latter, as the reality of the end of the event settles around us.

I look around, and my dueling circle is around me. Dora is glancing at Serafina, frowning, and it's hard to say where Serafina is looking or what she's thinking. Ottavia and Sterling are hanging arm in arm, Ottavia laughing, and Luca nudges me. "What say, Renzo?"

"Home after all this, I think," I say slowly. What did we do after the last tournament? We went out. I didn't get so far, the final fights were not such a letdown.

"That surprises me, Renzo," Tristan says, and I cannot tell if she thinks that I should celebrate how far I got, or drink the disappointment away.

"I suppose it would," I say, and Dora squeezes my arm. "You all did very well. We will celebrate those accomplishments a different night, when we have all recovered from the events of the last few days."

"Thank you, Lorenzo, that means a lot to hear it. You worked us hard, and it paid off," Dora says.

"Except where it didn't," Ottavia says cheerfully, and I think, wearily, that I should like to slap her. I don't. "We just aren't *lucky*, we need luck charms for the next time."

"And what luck charms would you propose we all get?" Tristan asks.

Ottavia shrugs, I think confused by the question. "The usual sort, I suppose."

"Are you in the practice of having luck charms?" Serafina asks, as though the idea has never occurred to her, and even in my weariness I feel a dull irritation.

"I'll get you all sleep charms if you continue this, let us disperse," I say. Dora begins to tug on my arm, leading me gently away.

"Walk my to my carriage, Renzo," she says. "Goodnight lovelies." Everybody murmurs their goodnights.

"I don't need you to meter me, Teodora," I say.

"Perhaps you think you don't," she says amenably. "And perhaps you are right. But also, perhaps, I just wanted you alone for a few moments before we all go back to our big houses and don't see each other for a week."

"Are you so sentimental about me?"

"How can I not be, after what we've been through." We reach her carriage and I hand her up, and she offers her hand to me, which I bow over and kiss.

"You're quite right," I say, shutting the carriage door gently and going on my way.

Chapter Forty-Three

Serafina of House Galeazzo

After the tournament, and so many nights of dinners and afternoon teas and days of dueling practice and times Dora has scooped me up from home and taken me out for all hours, I'm happy to have an evening at home. And I *did* have dueling practice earlier in the day, with Ottavia and Dora, and had lunch after, and indeed haven't changed from my practice clothes.

I've been home less than an hour when my mother walks into my rooms and fixes me with her icy gaze. "What are you doing?" she asks, though I know she can tell from her vantage. What else would I be doing at my writing-desk?

"Reading letters from—" I say haltingly, and she interrupts anyway.

"Why are you home?"

"With the tournament, I've been so busy for the last weeks. I made no plans tonight," I say. "I only just got home, I was out with—" My mother waves an impatient hand.

"It is no wonder that you haven't progressed very much at all, you have no ambition. Go out."

"Where should I—"

"That is something that you should have already considered. Go. Put your swords on and go. Come back when you've *accomplished* something." She picks up one of my newer jackets from the rack where Agnes hung it and all but throws it in my face. It still bears my tournament laurels and is ill-matched for my plain practice clothes, which were also purchased under Dora's advisement, the new style of shirt, split skirts in a fabric I liked, but there is no arguing with my mother, or at least I cannot. I buckle on my swords and pull on my jacket and slink out the door, almost forgetting to stuff a purse and a pair of dueling gloves in my pocket.

There is no carriage for me at the front steps, and my mother has followed close behind, so I do not hesitate but continue across our drive and out the front gates, which close softly behind me of their own accord. It is very early, by most people's accounting, the time of night when the lamps are lit, and it is not yet curfew for the lower classes. While not crowded, the streets are not empty.

It is late enough that any stage production would have closed admission, curtains raising, but early enough that I can go to a tavern. I start with that, hoping that I may run into somebody that I know and divert myself that way, but there is not a single familiar face to be found, as though the city is amusing itself by keeping me among strangers. It's been known to do that, though I've never yet been subjected to its petty wiles. Until this night.

I drink a small glass of sherry, alone at a corner of the bar, watching the bright conversations around me, the dice games, listening to the raucous laughter. I have no place here, this establishment is not known to me, nor likely to be known to any of my acquaintances. Other than the barkeep, nobody takes notice of me, and when I've finished my glass I leave extra coins and slip out again. That spent some time, at any rate.

I suppose I could walk all the way across the city to knock at Allegra and Andante's door, but wouldn't it be embarrassing for me to arrive there and to find them hosting guests already, or out for the evening, especially in my odd mix of practice clothing and dining coat, my hair braided and tucked up for swordplay and not socializing. No, I now think it's best that I see not a single soul that I know, that I don't have to explain to them that my mother drove me out into the night. Surely I can find a fountain to sit by for a time, and go back home again, and that will be enough. Surely she won't bar my entry.

But no, I know that my mother says what she means. I am not to return until I've accomplished something, whatever that might be, however long it might take. Sitting by a fountain will not do, though I do indeed find a very beguiling one, all carven mermaids, raising shells like trumpets that the water issues forth from. Lilies float upon the surface, and I know before I look that this is not a fountain that you toss coins into. It is for flowers, or maybe charms, and I have neither, and so walk on, hurrying my steps a little as I hear voices ahead, slowing myself again as I fear recognition.

It's a night market, one that I haven't been to. I laugh at myself at that thought, as if I'm so versed in the city's night markets. The smaller night markets are ever-shifting and hard to recognize, and I have never been to the crooked square that it has nestled itself in. I do not know the songs that the performers are bandying about, sometimes falling into a harmony with each other even as they voice different rhythms and rhymes. That must be by design, I cannot see how it would be an accident, and I tuck myself away from the bustle to listen and sort it out by ear.

Marco used to joke that, had we been born to a lesser family, I might have been able to be the star of a stage. I'm good at mimicry, and I have an ear for music and tones. I can pick up dances easily, so heaven knows why the sword is such a struggle in my hands; I can see in my head what needs to be done, but have the utmost difficulty making the blades obey me. It's one reason for the mirrors in the practice room, that I might see myself, and my form. I did used to also have a dancing instructor, but my mother let them go years ago. She thought that it was distracting me from dueling, and while that might have been the case, I do think the two could be made to work together, with the right practice and attention. Were I more determined, I could do it with my self study. Perhaps if I bring it up to Dora.

I've just started to get the knack of it, the way the four songs are coming together, for it is four songs, when I am noticed. A man and his friend, young men but older than me, have stumbled out of a nearby building, one muttering angrily, the other placating. I recognize that they are of middling station, but don't know either of their faces or insignia. I am suddenly, painfully aware of how alone I am, even though I'd been able to forget for a short time. I'd almost been *enjoying* myself, what a fool I always am.

For whatever reason, I draw the attention of the angry mutterer of the pair, and his gaze rakes over me with an almost physical feeling that I struggle not to shrink from. His companion spares me a glance, every line of his being tense and apprehensive, as I'm sure mine is as well. For different reasons, initially, but perhaps we have some similarities in this moment. The angry man could decide to go on his way, not spare any more of his focus on me, but of course that is not the case.

"A lady of your station shouldn't be alone in a night market," he says with chilling, elaborate false sincerity. It must be the drink, I think. He's drunk too much and it has made him coarse and unpleasant, and his friend has seen this gone badly before. In a more genteel setting, he would never behave in such a way.

There's enough of a pause that I realize I am expected to answer, and I cast about for something I can say. "My business is my own," I finally come out with, in as steady a tone as I can manage. "A lady of my station owes no explanation."

"Oh indeed?" He swagger-staggers closer, his friend advancing at his elbow but getting waved off as being too close. "Most proper young ladies prefer chaperones. Or company. Do you require company this evening, my lady?" There's an insinuation in his tone that I'm not quite grasping, other than it is distinctly not nice, and my cheeks burn as I back away from him a step or two before steeling myself again.

"No, my lord, I do not. But I appreciate your willingness to offer." I throw a pleading glance to his friend, who seems less concerned with my plight and more concerned with his inability to keep his friend from mischief, which somehow are not the same thing, to him.

"Hmm, I wonder." He leans a hand on the wall next to us, and I realize that I've somewhat backed myself into a corner, as I'd been keeping out of the way of passers by while I listened to the music. "I think perhaps I have overestimated my lady, and she is quite at home, alone in the night market."

"I would agree that perhaps you haven't taken proper measure of me, sir," I say, trying to work out how and when I might maneuver around him. I look past his shoulder, hoping now again to see a familiar face in the sparse crowd, but the vagaries of my wishes are never things that have been answered. "And I'm afraid I must bid you—"

"Now, I have already been rebuffed far too much this evening," he says, his anger resurfacing. "And I will not be rebuffed by the likes of you."

Such comment cannot go without immediate answer, even I know that. I draw myself up further into even stiffer posture, and my voice is steady and clear, not quite my mother's voice I'm far too shaken for that, but an approximation. "I am Serafina of House Galeazzo, and I will not bear such insult from the likes of *you*. Now kindly remove your arm, I will be departing your company immediately." I walk towards him without waiting for a response, and he, startled, does remove his arm and step aside for me to move past. Even if *my* reputation is scant, despite the tournament laurels on my coat, that of my house is robust.

"Begging pardon, my lady," his friend says hurriedly as I remove myself from the corner and walk past both of them, and I can hardly hear him for the blood in my ears, but I incline my head in what my instinct tells me is an appropriate amount.

I think I don't breathe again until I am across the crooked little square. The music is still playing, but this market has soured for me now, and I look for a street to lead me out of this square again. There are other markets in the city that I might visit. There might even be a tea shop that is open so late, I remember Dora describing one, and the fountain it was by. There are fewer people here now still, and I find myself in the next street over with ease, where it's quiet again. Nothing happened, I say to myself. I need to be less nervous, I'm bound to speak to people on occasion, even people who are rude. It doesn't mean—

"House Galeazzo," a harsh voice calls, and I turn. Oh I am a fool to have thought it was over so easily. I should have stayed at the little market amongst other people until I was sure his friend had jollied him off.

What would Teodora do? She is always so confident. I deliberately rest my wrist loosely on my swords as I turn. My mouth is bone dry. "I would answer you in kind, but you did not deign to tell me your house," I say, trying for that tone of confident boredom, of danger at rest.

"Only because I think you are lying, and are using a name that is not yours to walk the streets of an evening. What would Galeazzo do, were I to take you there? Would the guard have to get involved, to punish such an imposter?" His tone is taunting, but he thinks that he has the right of it, and that I will be cowing, apologetic. That I will beg him for mercy.

"The guard would get involved, yes, for your harassment of me." Where *are* the guard, actually? I should dearly like to see some right now.

"Maybe if you tell the truth, I'd go easy on you." He looks me up and down again, eyes narrowed. "Did you steal those swords?"

"These are not insults that I can let pass," I say carefully. I look from him to his friend again. "As I have no second, I will allow you the chance to apologize." Slowly, I remove the dueling gloves from my pocket and pull on the left first, then the right. They both watch me, him sneering still, his friend with a face full of trepidation.

"I think that you should—" his friend starts, putting a hand on his shoulder, and he pushes him off with a scoff.

"She's bluffing. I will not apologize."

"Very well," I say, and I draw both of my swords. I cannot take the time to be terrified. I can be terrified later. I see his friend's face change further when I raise a guard; his friend knows I am telling the truth.

"Nunzio, you must apologize," the friend says, and is rebuffed again as he draws his swords in return, shaking his head like he can't really quite see. I can sense his spark, oddly, I don't know what he's doing though. I just know he is very angry and very determined to fight me.

"Nunzio, is it? We must set terms, and—" He steps to me, spark-fast, and I guard, just, reaching for my own spark to match his speed. He isn't as practiced as me, I think desperately, look at his wrists. But he's taller than me, and stronger, and keeps me on the retreat through one, two, three more attempted strikes. He's also winding himself, already red-faced and now dripping sweat, and I have been drilling strictly for weeks and my endurance has grown past my previous estimation.

On his fourth strike, I know his pattern, and meet his sword with my crossguard, then twist it away like Lorenzo did mine at that disastrous dinner before lunging to trip him. Unlike at the disastrous dinner, though, he has his main gauche and I remember that half a second later when he punches me in the stomach. No. No he's stabbed me and I can't breathe and I slash wildly with my own left hand, to ward him off, to get him away from me, and the tip of the blade slices neatly through his throat and his eyes open wide even as my vision is flooded with crimson, and we stagger sideways together, thumping into a pillar, and that's when he falls from me, and his sword pulls out of my flesh and I take a choking, whistling breath but it isn't enough and I try again and it isn't enough.

His friend has fled, the coward, and I waste precious seconds standing there looking at the empty street, looking at Nunzio on the ground. My swords in my hands are tremendous weights. Put your swords away, I think, put them away. I feel hot all over, hot, and shaky, and sticky, and I put my swords away and I look down at Nunzio who stares up at me but I don't think he's looking at me, I think his eyes just haven't closed. I've never seen anybody dead before. There is so much blood and I am burning up but I am alive, I was challenged, unfairly, and I won anyway and is that an accomplishment, Mother? Only if I live to tell her.

For the first time since I am very small, I want my mother. Not for comfort, she won't comfort me, but to say look what I've done, Mother, is it enough? I have done as you asked.

I press my hands to my stomach where it hurts or maybe it's my side I can't tell, so great is the hurt, and when I press my hands there, I can breathe a little deeper but it hurts more, and I force myself to take a step, and then another.

If I don't, I'll die in the street with Nunzio. Nunzio of house I don't know, who couldn't hold his drink. Whose friend lacks courage. Maybe his friend is getting the guard and I should wait.

But no, I have decided to walk and it is too much effort to decide to stop. I must get home or I must get help, and help will be at home but home might be too far. I don't know where I am. I take another step, and I reach for my spark in a way that I haven't before, that none of my tutors pushed me towards before, and I use it to dull myself, because if I keep thinking about what terrible thing that blade may have done I will not be able to help myself. And I use it to give me strength to keep walking. To find help.

I should know a witch or an apothecary but I do not. Or, Dora told me one, and I've forgotten. I look at the buildings around me but cannot see properly, as though the night has been smeared with drink, but I had only that one small glass. I don't have my friends, but my house knows many houses, somebody will help me, I must get to somebody's gate. Home is too far but is Dora near? No. Allegra and Andante? No. I don't know where I am and I stumble and nearly fall, shouldering into a statue that flanks a gate, our faces pressed close as though we are lovers sharing secrets.

The gate whispers open invitingly, I don't know how, and I stumble inside before I lose my nerve. I'm running out of energy, maybe I'm dying, it feels like I'm dying, but as the gate closes behind me I realize I know this house, it's House Valier, and Marco told me that he often climbs the walls and whistle for Renzo and they'd prowl about of an evening, or sit inside and play dice and drink together, and I'm too far outside of myself to be able to leave again. I cannot see Lorenzo like this. I must see Lorenzo like this, I haven't the means to get any further. I cast through my memory for Marco's stories, and purse my lips to whistle.

Chapter Forty-Four

Lorenzo of House Valier

I hear a whistled sign outside of my window, the one that Marco and I used, and I have a momentary lift and then think no, it's his damnable sister, he must have told her, and almost don't even look. It comes again, weaker, incomplete, and something about that rouses me from my seat. I open my shutter and look down; Serafina stands just inside the wall, shoulders rounded forward, head hanging down, swaying just slightly. She must have climbed the wall and then not known which window was mine. She's dressed in what looks like practice clothes, plain boots and unadorned split skirts, but then a double-buttoned coat with braid on the collar, her tournament laurels catching the light. "What do you want?" I ask, not bothering to control my impatience, my harsh tone, and she raises her eyes to me. Her hair has come half loose, draggling about her neck and shoulders, though it is a dry night.

"I'm sorry," she says in a thready, labored voice, a plea in her wide eyes that I can see even from here. I give no immediate reply, and she says "Please, Lorenzo, I didn't—" and wavers, catching herself on the wall, leaving dark smears on the stone.

"Stay there," I say, pulling the shutter closed again. Damn it all, what trouble could she even have gotten into? Why would she come *here*? Teodora would have been a much better choice, or even Tristan, when it came down to it. Why is she alone?

I pass through my dark house without lighting any lanterns, calling my spark to see clearly. It is possible that this is minor, and she is in a frivolous panic, overreacting, and I can swiftly handle it before sending her away again.

I go out the side door to where she is. In the time it took me to come out, she's put her back against the wall and slid down to a seated posture, leaving more blood, because it is blood, smeared on the stone. But she's still conscious, and still looks up when she hears me coming, bloody foam on her starkly pale lips. This is serious after all; I'll have to bring her inside. I take her elbow and pull her to her feet, and she immediately starts breathlessly babbling even as her knees buckle and she almost slips out of my grasp.

"I'm sorry, I didn't know where else to go. The city made me get lost." I shift my grip and pick her up, her swords sticking awkwardly out. I don't understand how there is just so much blood and how she is also still salient. There is too much blood. It hotly soaks into my shirt as I pull the door open and bring her inside; there's a utility room just off this entrance, with a table, and that will have to do. It clearly costs her a lot, but she somehow keeps talking. "D-Dora and I were at a night market, and she got into her carriage and was going to take me home, but it was just a short walk. I've walked before."

"You should have taken the carriage ride," I say, scowling. What was Dora thinking, letting her go alone? I sit her on the table and roughly pull the coat off even as she wilts over, crying out weakly when her hands are dragged away from her side with a noise that tells me some of that blood had started to dry; she's still wearing her gloves. "Was this a duel?" I ask as I unbuckle her swordbelts and set them aside. I wonder at the state of her swords in their sheathes, but there's no time now. Best try to get the information from her, though; if she dies, her family won't know who to call the guard after.

"Yes. Yes somebody followed me, a drunk man and he had a second, and he called an insult to me and I told him that as I had no second, I...would allow him the chance to apologize."

I snort, imagining her tremulous voice, her obviously false courage. "Am I to understand that he did not take that chance?" Her shirt is also somehow stays, buttoned down the front but laced up the back and on the sides at her waist, I can't figure it out, and from the rasping whistle in her labored breathing, I can't take the time. I reach over and draw her main gauche to cut the lacings, and with some difficulty loosen the stiffened, blood-soaked fabric of her shirt and then her chemise from her skin before pushing her on her back.

"We exchanged blows and he, and I..." her words choke off when I near the wound. She tries to cough but cannot, and more foam comes to her lips.

"Why didn't you go to an apothecary? A witch?" It's deep and it's messy, a short ugly thrust up under her ribs. I think my spark can handle it, just. If it cannot, there is no time to find somebody stronger. I don't know how she walked here.

"I don't know any," she says in a small, frightened voice, between reedy gasps. "I was lost and, and then found myself at your gate but I was too embarrassed to ring the bell and—"

"Too *embarrassed*?" Wound assessed, I now realize that I can sense her spark flaring up in a way I've never felt from her before. She must have killed that man, that must be why there is so much more blood than she could possibly have shed, even in this dire state. That must be why she is so gravely wounded but still conscious, her normally gold-hazel eyes black. She's so warm that I can still feel her across the space between us. There's only so long she can keep burning so bright before she faints. Or dies from her wound.

"I'm sorry, I'm so sorry." And she actually tries to get off the table, but whatever strength got her here, it's a guttering candle.

"You're an idiot," I say, holding her there with one hand flat on her belly where I know it hurts and she cries out in protest. "Stay there, I need materials." She catches at my hand as I withdraw, and I pause but don't turn to face her.

Making an effort she cannot afford, she carefully enunciates, "Lorenzo. Thank you."

"You won't be so hasty to thank me once the crisis has passed," I say sourly, and hasten to the pantry for a bottle of spirits and some herbs. My hands are sticky with her blood already and I wipe them on my pants. One of my tutors was particularly spark-inclined to healing, and I have some basic groundwork and some few advanced techniques that I picked up from him easily, thought the rest failed to stick.

Back in the utility room, she's still flat on her back staring at the ceiling, half-humming a melody I don't recognize. I've never heard her hum, or sing, and did not know before tonight that she could whistle. "You came back," she says in floating, quiet wonderment, and I frown harder.

"What else could I have done? You came for help. I've brought you into my home." But now she's weakly crying and I bite back my irritation and hastily combine the ingredients, pressing them on her wound and dousing them in spirits. She makes a torn, pained little noise and then faints away completely, and so now I don't have to listen to her anymore, just her troubled breathing. I take a pull from the bottle myself, and as the spirits soak into the herbs on her skin, I feel for her spark with mine, and allow the will to pass through me to mend her wound.

Even unconscious, she tries to grasp my hand for comfort, and, grimly, I let her have it, and drink more. I have never had to use so much of my spark and for so long. Too much time has passed for it to be an easy mending, like in the days of the tournament. I have never had to spend so much time with her, and in such close quarters. I may loathe her, but I could not be responsible for the dishonor it would have meant for my family had I turned her away, nor would I face the ridicule and shame for such cowardice, turning away a mortally wounded girl in the middle of the night. Even if she was a stranger, I would have been duty-bound to help, and here she is, my best friend's sister. I could not stand Marco's disappointment, should he return and hear the story. And no other in our group could do for her what I have done.

They have the same eyes, she and Marco. Surely I noticed before tonight?

It takes time enough that the bottle is empty between administration to her wound and to my lips; so bad is her hurt, that I must redouble my efforts periodically. When the thin, gray dawn lightens the window, she lets out a sigh, still unawares. She's in more like a sleep now than a swoon, her troubled brow smoothing, her skin cooler now to the touch. Color has returned to her face, though I notice now the pale line of a scar I gave her a few scant weeks ago. She no longer whistles with each breath. The room looks like an abattoir; I must change my clothing at the very least, and then finally I can give my mother charge of Serafina.

I see one of the morning servants immediately upon exiting the room. To her credit, her eyes widen briefly but her face remains nearly neutral.

"Please excuse my appearance," I say, feeling my unfamiliar exhaustion keenly. My spark was kept burning such that I couldn't even benefit from drinking that entire bottle of spirits. It kept me painfully aware of whose company I was in the entire time. "And have my mother made aware that we have a guest who needs tending."

"My lord," she says, with a slight curtsey, and moves off.

I've had time to wash up and change my shirt when my mother enters the room. "And here I thought you stayed in last night," she says, for she can sense so much spent spark hanging in the air around me.

"I did, dearest mother. It was Serafina of House Galeazzo who was out in the evening and small hours."

"And she came...here." My mother is visibly skeptical, and with good reason. I've in no way hidden my attitude towards the girl. It was not so long ago that I drew sword against her for nearly nothing, in front of our entire society. I wonder that she has a scar from that at all, but Marco gave me some indication of what their mother is like.

"The city itself deposited her here, it would seem." After Dora left her alone. Though thinking on it now, I'm not certain Dora would have done such a thing. I'm too tired to work it out to my satisfaction.

Curiosity lights my mother's eyes. "Very interesting indeed. And she's in the utility room? Your disdain for her is such that you don't even give her our least-appointed guest room?"

"It has a table and time was of the essence."

"I see." My mother is quite amused by this, I should say, and it does nothing for my demeanor. "I'm proud that you are able to set aside your feelings and offer the aid and hospitality that our friends are warranted."

"Of course, Mother."

"Now, shall we go to her?" I think to object, but my mother blinks mildly.

"Of course, Mother," I say again, through a firmly clenched jaw. No more fool than I, for thinking I would have done with her already.

My mother does not react to the sight of Serafina's bed of blood, her hair stiffly haloed around her head. She bends to examine the healed wound briefly, tracing the new golden scar there with her sensitive fingers. "You did good work," she says, proud, satisfied. She lifts Serafina's hands one, then the other, removing her ruined, gorey gloves every so gently, setting them aside. I wonder now if they are the ones Luca gifted her. "You saved her life. Carry her up to the guest chamber nearest my rooms, and I will make her mother aware that she is with us "

I again do not object, despite having just burnt my spark past exhaustion and exchanged my charnel clothes for fresh, and bend to pick Serafina up from the table. Again, the sound of blood's bond breaking, but she doesn't awaken or even stir, so deep is her sleep, her limbs relaxed and pliant, her breathing even. It is a slight task, carrying her to the guest chamber, and I can't help but think that my mother has assigned some significance to it, as though my obeying her orders is the same as feeling tenderness for this girl. It isn't, and I trust that my mother will see this to be the case.

I do not want to deposit her on our clean linens in this state, but it seems as though provisions have already been made, a blanket of lesser quality spread there to receive her. I leave her there without lingering; I am not fond of being covered in second and third hand blood, and desire to bathe before retiring to my rooms after having been kept awake the entire night.

Chapter Forty-Five

Serafina of House Galeazzo

I have indistinct dreams of darkness, and light, and burning. I dream that I'm on fire, burning without being consumed. I dream harsh voices, and steady ones, and I dream about the last time that I saw Marco without knowing it was the last time. In my dream, I still didn't know. He gave no indication. I dream about my mother's rage, and I wake with a start, sure I hear her voice.

"It's all right, Serafina, you're safe," a familiar but unfamiliar voice says, and I struggle a moment with how to open my eyes exactly. It feels as though it's been ever so long. But that is not my mother's voice, I have never heard such comfort in her tone, and it is not my maid. I open my eyes and look into Lady Valier's face. I'm so confused, why would she be in my rooms? But I am not in my rooms, my bed has a canopy, my ceiling is not painted with a garden, and I blink at her in astonishment while I try to reason out what circumstance may have brought me here. And then I remember what circumstance brought me here, and frantically feel at my belly. "Shh, now. My son was able to heal your wound with his spark."

"I can never thank you enough. Thank him enough," I say automatically, my voice rasping. I'm so thirsty. How much time has it been?

She smiles, though. She looks so kind, how can she be so powerful and so kind? "You would have done the same," she says. "Our houses have been friends for a very long time. There are no debts between us."

"My mother..." I say reluctantly, but am unable to form a thought, just feel dread, mixed with a stir of panic.

"She knows you are here, and she is pleased with your advancement."

"My advancement?" I repeat, but then I remember burning. I remember killing that man, and I'm struck by it anew, as though I'd been outside

229

of myself but now I am firmly seated once again. I killed that man, I think, I was covered in his blood and I left him there in the street, and I killed him and—

Lady Valier sits on the side of the bed and pulls me into a firm embrace, and I'm so surprised that my thoughts stop chasing themselves. I remain stiff for a moment, unsure how to react, and my emotions break free of my desperate, tenuous control and I burst into tears. There is no mastering myself for several moments, and I sob wretchedly against Lady Valier's shoulder. She strokes my hair gently, and hums a soft tune that my frenetic thoughts latch onto. My mother would never. My mother never.

She lets me weep until I am quiet, hollowed out, shaking just slightly. "She wanted to be sent for when you awakened, but I think that it might be best for your recovery if we don't move you so soon? Provided you agree, of course. I've no intention of making decisions for you."

"I can stay?" I ask, dumbfounded. I know it cannot be for long. But even just a day away from my mother would be such respite.

She laughs lightly. "Of course. We would hardly turn you out into the street." That's almost what Lorenzo said, only his hospitality was far more crisis driven, duty-bound. His mother is reaping the political benefits. Though she knows my mother, and has their entire lives. She knows.

"Thank you," I say. "It isn't enough, but thank you."

"I should say Lorenzo is the one to be thanked, but he's bound to sleep the day away, I'd think. Which you are welcome to do as well. At dinner, we'll see if everybody is in a state to sit together."

"Shall I...do you want me to write to my mother?"

"Nonsense, I'll take care of everything, you just rest. You've had quite the experience."

I try to think of some further protest, it feels very self-indulgent to have slept for however long I did and then rest further, but instead I find myself melting into sleep again. Perhaps LadyValier pushed me to that with her spark, I couldn't say.

When next I waken, it is again abrupt. I'm sitting up before I fully realize it, because that is my mother's voice I hear, sharp-edged, questioning. I'm still alone in the comfortable, light-filled guest room, and I look at the door mistrustfully. I do not know the Valier home well enough to gauge how far my mother is from this room, or even if Lady Valier will actually keep my mother from me or lead her here. They are conversing far enough away that I cannot hear who my mother is speaking to, nor really make out her words, only her tone.

There is a lull in the conversation, and then brisk footsteps, and I clutch at the blanket covering me but what will I do, fling it off and leap out the window? There is no escaping my mother. It is ridiculous to have such a thought, and impulse. The door opens, and Lorenzo comes in and closes it behind him before even looking towards me. He seems surprised, perhaps irritated, that I am awake, and advances nearly to the bedside before stopping, which is when I think to wonder at where my surely ruined clothes from last night are, and whose nightgown I am wearing. Where my swords are. My gloves.

"Do you wish to see your mother?" he asks in a low tone and I stare at him. What a question to ask me. I shake my head, and then grasp for the words, but he holds up his hand as I draw breath to speak, studying my face. "I shall tell them you are still sleeping." He turns and leaves again, the door whispering shut behind him.

I remain sitting up in bed, straining my ears towards my mother's voice as I listen to his receding footsteps. Down the main stairs and into the foyer, I think, and then I hear Lorenzo speak, and my mother answer. I can envision where I am in the house now. But why would he lie for me? Perhaps at his mother's instruction; I cannot imagine Lorenzo caring a fig whether I wish to see my mother or not, but he respects his own lady mother. My mother's voice raises slightly; not enough to be considered an insult, I'm sure she's carefully attuning herself to what she perceives concern for her child would be. Perhaps she's remembering how she felt when we lost Marco. Lady Valier is soothing her, I'm sure, perhaps even using her spark to do so, I think, remembering how sweetly I slept again after my first awakening.

After a very long time, those voices recede. I don't think my mother has left, but I think Lady Valier has persuaded her to a day room, where they might talk and have tea. My pounding heart slows, my breath comes more evenly, and I am able to unclench my fingers from the blanket. My mother will not burst into this room today, I don't think. Tomorrow, perhaps, but not today. It is not so normal, I don't think, for a girl to think her mother to be the opposite of comforting. After what happened to me last night, I think most girls would *want* their mother for comfort. I can only imagine the ways she will fault me for what happened and how it happened. Oh, I shall have to speak with the guard eventually, I think. I shall have to see my mother eventually.

But not today, I think. I do not remember lying down again, but my face is on the cool pillow, and I drift away again.

Chapter Forty-Six

Lorenzo of House Valier

My mother and Lady Galeazzo spend much time in my mother's day room and I hover nearby, expecting to be summoned and not wanting to have to traipse all about the house to accommodate them. It is hard for me to say what I think of Lady Galeazzo's behavior; it would seem that she thought she would arrive here and march Serafina right into their carriage and return home again, and while I do not know what exactly my mother put in her letter, I am certain she did not indicate that Serafina was in a state to do that.

At long last, my mother opens the dayroom door and beckons me in. Lady Galeazzo frowns over her teacup, and my mother gestures at the place settings for me to help myself. I pour a cup of tea, to give my mother the time to resettle herself and gather her thoughts.

"How did Serafina come to be here?" Lady Galeazzo asks after an appropriate measure of time.

"She walked," I say, which sounds flippant, I'm certain. "It was not her intent, she was disoriented from her injury, and said something about the city making her get lost."

"Oh indeed," she says, and my mother sips her tea. "And her arrival?"

"Though the gates were closed, I would place bets that she did not climb the fence. But, once within, she whistled the sign that her brother Marco used to use when he came for me. He must have taught it to her." Was it necessary to mention Marco? Perhaps not, but was it worth it to see the flicker in Lady Galeazzo's expression? Yes, it was.

"There's no accounting for what he told her," she says brusquely. "What else did she say? About what happened?"

"That a man had insulted her in the street, and that since she had no second, she gave him the opportunity to apologize." This surprises her too; is that a glimmer of pride on her face? I think it might be. "She did not otherwise detail the duel, other than to say that she killed him. She was utterly covered in blood, hers and his."

"She opened his throat," Lady Galeazzo says. "The guard gave me what they thought to be an accurate accounting. The dead man's friend told them that he had focused on her, and there was no redirecting him."

"Did he also tell them that he ran away like a coward and left her there wounded?" I am surprised at myself, that I would bother to insult this man that I had presumably never seen.

"He did, and though she almost certainly should have left a trail of gore, they were unable to trace her, so though the guard visited my house before your lady mother's letter, I was unaware of where my daughter might be." She seems irritated again, that Serafina is here. "Thank you, Lorenzo, for helping her."

"It was my duty," I say, by rote.

"Perhaps, but the burden of duty is lightened if it is not thankless." She smiles then, calculated but polite, and I return the smile.

"You, and she, are welcome."

"No more will come of it, then?" my mother asks.

"What more would come of it? Serafina was within her rights."

"What I don't understand is why Dora would have let her walk home alone," I say, almost entirely without thinking. What do I care, after all?

"What about Teodora?" Lady Galeazzo asks.

"The other thing that Serafina said was that she and Teodora were out and that, while Dora offered her a carriage ride home, she declined, and it was after that her duel took place." I believe I understand it to be a lie, what I don't understand is the purpose of the lie.

Lady Galeazzo makes a dismissive gesture. "She was out with Teodora earlier in the evening, but she'd been home in between."

A brief moment of silence and my mother asks, "She went out alone?"

"She did. I told her she wouldn't find advancement staying home reading letters."

"Which would explain, I suppose, why Serafina found advancement last night but Lorenzo didn't," my mother says lightly, looking at me.

"Quite so, my lady mother, though had I been out, I would not have been in a position to help her." I match my smile to her tone, but I have a confusing, troubling feeling about all of this.

"So right," my mother says.

"But, if I have satisfied your need of me, I must beg your leave," I say, standing and bowing.

"Yes, Lorenzo, thank you," Lady Galeazzo says.

"I shall see you at supper," my mother says, and I incline my head to her and depart. And so now my question: did Serafina lie because she thought that her mother would hide that she drove her daughter out into the night? Or did Serafina lie because she was embarrassed to have needed such goading? Perhaps she felt foolish for having gotten herself in that situation, but then, there is no accounting for the actions of a man who would insult a young lady and then duel her when she has no second. Knowing that Lady Galeazzo made her go out explains the dinner coat over the practice clothing.

I return to the utility room, curious as to its state. It has been cleaned within an inch of its existence, though Serafina's swords are on the table there, and on an impulse I cannot explain even to myself, I retrieve them and take them to our armory space, where I pull them from their sheathes and clean them, then polish them. It is some work getting the dried blood out of the sheath for the main gauche, but I take the time to do that. They are fine pieces of equipment, the sheathes included, and while it would also take a lot to ruin them, it wouldn't do to just leave them uncared-for while their owner is a guest in this house. Satisfied with my work, I sheathe the blades. Then, on second thought, I remove the sword-grip ornaments; more horror underneath there, of course. I wonder over the ornaments a moment, pretty birds like peacocks but also different; did she choose them, or was that how the swords were sold to her?

It is not Serafina's fault that her brother left the both of us. And it is not Serafina's fault that her mother would see fit to expel her daughter alone into the night because her advancement was not to her taste. Serafina has the laurels to prove that she is no helpless maiden, though still and all, she might have died last night for her mother's foolishness. She has advanced at least twice since retaking her place in society, and I am unclear what trajectory Lady Galeazzo would have preferred. Of course, it was Lady Galeazzo's right to do so, and yet it certainly caused me a modicum of trouble, and now my mother as well, indirectly.

I walk through the halls and narrowly avoid crossing paths with my mother as she sees Lady Galeazzo out. I return to the upstairs and stand outside the guest room where Serafina is for a few moments; earlier I had not expected her to be awake, and I listen now, to see if she is still. Were I to knock, it would awaken her. Returning her swords is a simple thing and requires no conversation; indeed, I would prefer to avoid it.

Her breathing is quiet and deep, and I slip into the room and confirm with a glance towards the bed that she is unawares. I also don't wish my mother to catch me in here and mistake me for being tender towards the girl, and I put her swords in the racks by the dresser without much clatter and leave again without Serafina stirring, or so much as her breath changing.

It is not my mother who catches me outside the room, but my father. I gesture for him to be quiet, and we continue down the hall. "This is quite a business," he says after a time. He is dressed to go out, I realize.

"Entirely unnecessary," I say. "Though over soon enough, I suppose."

"Yes, I suppose," he agrees. "Though I should think your mother will enjoy having such a houseguest, for a time. You know how she is."

"That I do." We are all perhaps a bit too independent, for my mother's taste. Being able to coddle Serafina a bit will satisfy her. And it would seem that the girl has actually received little coddling, other than from her now absent brother. I am not used to devoting so much thought to her; I would rather not.

"Our houses have been friends for a long time," he says as we reach the doors that lead out to our stables. "It is plain to me that you don't care for the girl, but you've still done our house proud, and I would expect nothing less of you."

"Thank you, my lord father."

He surprises me with a hearty embrace. "Take care that you rest yourself. I know well how much spark you spent."

"Yes, Father," I say, touched, perhaps gratified, that he felt the need to give me such counsel.

Chapter Forty-Seven

Serafina of House Galeazzo

My mother allows me to remain at House Valier for three days. In that time, Lady Valier sits with me, and entreats me to play cards with her, and I do not see Lorenzo.

Dora comes to visit on the second day, sweeping into my guest room with warmth and concern, sitting on the edge of the bed and taking my hands in hers. "Tell me everything," she says, and I do, immediately and without any guile. I tell her about reading letters and my mother telling me to go out because it was no wonder I had hardly advanced at all. The music in the square, and foolish angry Nunzio, and my nightmarish walk through the city until I staggered through the gates and whistled for Lorenzo. Then, my cheeks hot, my lie, saying that I had been out with her. I could not countenance, even with what might have been my dying breaths, telling the truth about my mother casting me out in that manner. I hardly remember what I said to him, but I remember that.

When I am done, we sit in silence for some time, and then she reaches out with a handkerchief and blots at my cheeks. "Thank you," I say, surprised. I had not noticed the tears passage.

"You poor thing," she says. "How your mother had children as delightful as you and Marco, I will never understand."

"You flatter me," I say, flushing again.

"I do not. I am not yet a mother, but treating my daughter with such carelessness is not something that I can understand."

"She wants our house to be in good standing," I say, coming to her defense by rote.

"She almost got you killed," Dora says brusquely. "I don't know how you can stand to go back there."

"I haven't got a choice," I say. "I'm surprised she is letting me stay here this long."

"Lady Valier favors you."

"At least one member of the house does." Not that I crave Lorenzo's attentions, or even necessarily his approval, but even reaching a place where he possessed neutral feelings about me would be an improvement.

She smiles ruefully. "Lorenzo does have his way, doesn't he."

"He saved me," I say, guilty at my complaints about him, however oblique. It is not my fault that I am not my brother, and it is not his fault that he would prefer my brother be here.

"That he did, and I'm sure you've already thanked him, and your mother has already thanked him, and he said he was just doing his duty."

"I don't remember," I say, truthfully. I do think I thanked him. I remember catching at his hand. I am embarrassed to remember catching at his hand, as though I thought he might comfort me. Lorenzo, who hates me so.

"You're polite to a fault, of course you thanked him, and if you thank him now further, he will only be irritated." It is a joke, but it is also true, and we laugh together. "Oh, Fina, I was so worried when I heard, but you do seem as though you are all right."

"I am starting to feel so," I say. "I have been so tired."

"Yes, nearly dying does weary one so," she says dryly, and laughs again to lighten the mood. "I'm sure it's a relief to sleep under a roof that does not also shelter your mother, I'm certain I would never be able to fully relax knowing that her presences is always imminent."

"Perhaps I also should elope, to get from under her thumb," I say, as lightly as I can manage.

"We shall have to pick somebody for you at the next dinner. It is a shame that Luca is so unserious."

"Luca is very kind," I say shyly. My mother would not approve of a match with Luca, I am certain of that. Though my mother has never yet uttered an opinion on what manner of match I might make, which is puzzling, now that I think of it.

"Luca is a joy, and I am unsure what his future will hold."

"He will be very happy with somebody, someday," I say, distracted now. Does my mother really have so little regard for me, that she has no thoughts on my eventual marriage? Or does she have a plan that, similarly, she has not thought to include me in?

"I've kept you for too long," Dora says, kissing me on the cheek and standing. I look up at her, frowning. "You've gone away from me, and need more rest."

"Thank you for coming to see me," I say. "Though I imagine we'll see each other again at dinners and practices soon enough."

"Oh yes, very soon," she says, with a theatrical little grimace. "The cycle never waits long to begin anew."

"I enjoy *some* of it," I confess.

"It really just catches us all up when we are working together and doing well, but it is also exhausting," she says. "All of the social jockeying and little games."

"Those are the parts I like less." Tristan's little snipey comments and the in jokes that I don't understand.

"You've come through a tournament with us, things can only get better," Dora says. "Rest now, I'll see you again soon."

She is not gone for very long when there is a knock on the door. "Yes?" I call, hesitantly.

The door opens and Lorenzo steps in. "My lady mother wanted me to invite you to dinner," he says stiffly.

"I will happily accept," I say. I have no desire to hide here from my gracious hosts, or even from Lorenzo, who even now clearly hates the sight of me but did save my life. "Oh, except..." and I trail off, for troubling him with such details would not be appropriate.

"Do you have a prior engagement?" he asks, smirking.

I drop my gaze, the words jamming together in my throat. "I have nothing to wear," I say eventually, with difficulty. "I'm sure the clothes I was wearing when—" I can still imagine the fabric of my shirt, soaked through with blood, clinging to my skin. Drying there. Not being able to breathe.

"My mother will take care of that," he interrupts, either to save me struggling or because he lacks the patience to wait for me to gather my thoughts and confront the reminder of what happened to me. He saved my life, he is not also responsible for my humors. "That shirt was too far gone for flowers to fix it." I give a surprised little laugh, not expecting the joke, but he does not laugh with me.

"Thank you," I say, trying to keep my voice steady. "I did expect as much." He looks at me unhappily for a moment longer and then walks out, closing the door behind him. I can only imagine it was unhappily; his face has a studied blankness at times that is absolutely impenetrable.

I notice, then, that there is a rack for swords by the door and that my swords are there. Have they been there all along? I do not remember. The scabbards and handles do not seem bloody; perhaps some servant cleaned and polished them. Another thing to give somebody thanks for.

I haven't much time to wonder more about that, or what to do with myself, before there is another knock at the door, and when I respond, Lady Valier comes in with a maid behind her who is carrying an armful of clothing. "Before we do anything, I want you to tell me true whether you feel well enough for dinner, and are not just saying so out of some sense of duty or propriety."

"I'm well enough," I say, dutiful yes, but also gratified that she wants to be sure. Relieved at the lack of expectation. "I thank you so much for your concern."

"You arrived here at death's door, and though I know your wound has been healed, I also know well what the healing of such a wound leaves one feeling like."

"I'm well enough," I say again, more firmly, a smile finding its way to my lips.

"Very well then," she says, studying my face. "Other than your coat, your other clothes were ruined, of course, but we have your measurements and I think some of my older things could do for you, if you don't mind being a bit out of fashion."

"I would hardly place any expectations upon your generosity, my lady," I say.

"You are too sweet by half, and I hope that you don't ever lose all of it," she says. "I shall have a bath brought in for you, and then Berthe will help you with your hair and dressing. I considered inviting your parents for dinner but did not; I think we shall all have luncheon together tomorrow before we send you home."

"Home," I say, almost without meaning to. I feel so very distant from that place, though I have known no other home. This is not even the longest I have ever slept away from it; as a child, Andante and Allegra and I used to have quite a lot of sleepaways at each others' houses. Lady Valier reaches out and touches my shoulder.

"This is probably one of the worst things that has ever happened to you," she says gently. "Even if your wound is healed, it isn't unusual to have feelings about it."

"But I'm no longer in danger from it," I say.

"Not physically, no," she says. "Such is our lot."

"My mother will say that I am malingering," I say. My mother, who sent me out into the night despite my advancing other times in the scant weeks since I entered society properly.

"Likely she will, yes. Your mother—" she pauses, glances at Berthe, and perhaps rethinks. "Your mother and I have different thoughts on that. We've all been through it, though, and so long as this is our society it is our burden to bear."

Something else that Marco has escaped, I think distractedly. "I suppose I will get used to it," I say.

"You're very brave," she says, helping me from under the covers and to stand.

"I'm not so certain," I say, but blushing under her kind regard.

"Nonsense. Now, let's pick what you'll wear."

Chapter Forty-Eight

Lorenzo of House Valier

My mother's delight in Serafina is almost enough to make dinner bearable. It isn't as though the girl is a stranger, but it has been quite some time since we all regularly shared a table, and she was quite young previously, and tended to be quiet under the weight of her mother's gaze. Marco had given me to understand what his mother was like, but I think that it was what his mother was like when her favored child was still present. In his absence, Serafina does not benefit from the protection of her mother's regard for Marco, the favored child.

I am irritated at having to consider her circumstances so closely, but she has left me no choice. She did also comport herself well in the tournament, it would be unfair for me to think or say otherwise. She simply is not her brother, which is not her fault, but also not a situation that can be set to rights. How may times must my thoughts turn in these circles?

I dress for dinner with more care than I usually would for a meal at home, to avoid my mother's disappointment, my father's frown. It is a small thing, to keep my parents happy. I drink a cup of wine in my rooms as I get ready, from habit and also to fortify me to the job I must set myself to, maintaining a congenial face for the duration of dinner with a person I would happily never see her again. I do not wish her ill, I simply wish her not.

We have been seated across from each other at the table, my parents at the head and foot. We all have wine in front of us, and that is some small relief, and I briefly catch the eye of the servant who waits in the wings holding the wine bottle; Magnus is very good at unobtrusively keeping glasses full. My mother keeps Serafina politely chatting about things like the tailors and tea houses that Dora has taken her to. And then, of course, my mother asks the question, "And how do you find your reception, now that you're taking an active role?"

Serafina's eyes flick to me briefly, and she says, "Renzo's dueling circle is hardly strangers to me. And we've just spent the last while talking about how Teodora has taken me under her wing!" She smiles in a way that is meant to elicit a return smile, which my mother does.

"You are right, how foolish I am!" Serafina is transparent, of course, but my mother has the grace not to press her further. My mother, instead, changes her angle of attack. "I'm so glad that you have found such well-deserving welcome. Your house's reputation has always been strong, and the laurels you won in the tournament prove that you are able to uphold it."

Serafina flushes a little, across the cheekbones, and does not raise her eyes. "You have my thanks, Lady Valier. I do my best."

"Your best is quite good. You've spent all this time in the shadows, and it's been to your own disservice."

"Yes, Lady Valier," she murmurs, her shoulders rounding a little.

"No, now don't look like that, I'm scolding you but it's all in good fun. It's hardly a surprise that you might have wanted to avoid all the little wounds—and larger ones—that come from taking part in society." She glances at my father, who clears his throat. Magnus comes in silently, filling our glasses.

"Quite right, there was no need to risk yourself like that for all these years," he says. "And you've made a very good first impression with your re-entry, and with this first tournament. I imagine you'll feel quite at home very soon, if you don't already."

"You both flatter me, truly," Serafina says. "I appreciate that, and your hospitality." She looks at each of them in turn as she says this, and then me briefly as well. For her fault of existence, she does have her manners well in hand. Her wine glass too, but I'm not sure that's truly intentional; in my experience, Serafina has a single glass, perhaps two, and prefers water otherwise. The way Magnus keeps the glasses, this is impossible for her to gauge, and anticipating this is the only enjoyment I am getting from this meal.

"Our houses have been friends time enough that we are practically one anyway," my mother says, still smiling, charmed by the girl's glances.

"My parents always speak very well and fondly of you," Serafina says.

"They had better," my mother says, and Serafina's smile wavers as she tries to gauge whether she should laugh. My mother laughs, giving the rest of us permission to join in. "We should have you for dinner more often, my dear, I'm not used to having such an attentive audience."

"That is a falsehood, my darling," my father says. "We dote on you always. Though Serafina is always welcome at our table."

I am drinking from my own wine at the moment, and the rest of the table waits on me, my mother holding her head tilted just slightly. "I have been keeping her all to myself with practice," I say finally. I know my expected role here, it would be foolish to deny it. "Though Teodora also has monopolized her time."

"Yes, everybody is fighting over me, it's quite the scene," Serafina says airily, and my mother laughs, delighted.

"And rightfully so. I'm shocked that no other dueling circles tried to cut in and poach you," she says.

"Your son is formidable," Serafina says, then blinks as though the words got away from her, frowns at her still-full wine glass.

"We've done our best with him," my mother says, and the specter of Marco hovers at the table as physically as though there was a place set for him. "Though I suppose it only makes sense that you would settle into this circle, you know everybody well already."

"Well enough." Serafina glances around. "I'm so sorry, may I have some water instead? I think I've had my fill of wine. It doesn't always agree with me." She is making great effort not to look at me too much.

"Of course," my mother says, and gestures. Water is brought out, and Serafina's wine glass is taken away, and I'm certain she is thinking of the first night of the tournament, when I sobered Dora but left Serafina intoxicated. Would she be mortified or pleased, if she knew both Dora and Luca came to dress me down for that little trick the next morning? Will it hasten her from my house sooner, if she were to think that I wanted to see her make a fool of herself with wine over dinner with my parents? "But you've been occupying yourself for all this time outside of dueling. What do you like, when you aren't wielding swords?"

"What do I like?" Serafina seems genuinely astonished to be asked this, and fumbles a moment. "The theater, I like going to the theater quite a lot.

And I like dancing, though I haven't had a dancing master for years now. Mother thought…well I've had tutors for the sword for all this time, you see, it isn't as though I haven't done anything."

"You needn't defend yourself at the dinner table," my mother says gently. "All of us are wearing swords, none of them drawn. Dancing, you say? Perhaps that's something we should all do more of." She smiles down the table at my father, who chuckles a bit.

"We do already," I say, wrestling with my irritation. "What is a duel if not a dance? You have a partner and must pay attention to where your feet are."

"Fighting and flirting are one and the same," my father says in his most serious tone, and when I shoot him a stormy glance, he winks at me. If my father does not already understand that I hate Serafina for not being her brother, then any protest that I make will only convince him otherwise. I should not fault him for assuming that I have a fondness for the girl, but my mother ought to have informed him. Unless she did, and this is still the result.

"I'm not certain that they are," Serafina says cautiously. None of us want to be misunderstood.

"Nonsense, Lady Valier and I used to fight like cats and dogs. We were not in the same dueling circle, but our parents were good friends, and so we were very often at each other's houses even when there was not an event." My mother is nodding in agreement. "She gave me a black eye once, and I had to explain to my lady mother that we were the bitterest of enemies and should never be required or expected to be anything other than exactly polite when we are forced together in public."

"But…you're married?" Serafina looks between them, and then to me, as though a dreadful trick is being played on her. I look back at her deadpan; to my knowledge, all of this is the truth. "And if you'll forgive me for saying, you have always seemed very fond of one another."

"I pray every day that we don't fall back into those old habits," my father says, and winks again.

"I don't understand," Serafina says.

"My mother used to tell me that her mother went to a witch woman for a love potion," I say, sighing. I don't know why we're entertaining this foolishness.

"I did used to tell you that, because it was true. And *his* mother went to an apothecary for the same, or at least a potion that would settle his blood. While I blacked his eye, he certainly returned the favor."

"And then they lived happily ever after," I say sourly, unable to maintain the facade.

"Until we had an ungrateful son who doesn't seem to be the slightest bit serious about finding a bride," my mother says. Were we sitting next to one another, she would stroke my cheek and tuck my hair behind my ear.

"My apologies, lady mother, have I been remiss? I don't recall being instructed to locate a bride, but rather focus on my advancement in society. Or was my showing at the tournament for naught?"

"Your showing at the tournament was the best you have done yet, and you know it did not go unnoticed, but with your friends getting married, I would have thought you would take your own initiative. No matter," my mother says, as the servants come and clear away our dishes. "We shall stop boring you with tales of our past. Lorenzo, show Serafina the library, and then you may occupy yourself as you will."

"My thanks, lady mother," I say, pushing back from the table, then finishing my wine after I stand. "Do you want to see the library?" I ask Serafina bluntly, not the expected tone at all. I do not like this game that my parents are playing, and tire already of their maneuverings. How could I not see what they were trying to imply? I shall place myself in exile before agreeing to such a thing. I will try again, to send a bird to Marco, after Serafina is gone from my presence. From my house.

"I do, thank you," she says, as though I had been far more gallant, standing, her eyes searching my face. Despite her constant cowing and hesitation, she plays this game well enough. "Teodora has said that you are quite fond of it."

"Has she?" I ask, more than a little archly, and when I see my mother actually glaring at me, I offer Serafina my arm like a gentleman would be expected to. "Teodora does enjoy being in everybody's business."

"She does," Serafina says, though without the note of displeasure that I had been striking. I guide her from the room without giving my parents the satisfaction of a backwards glance. I wonder if Serafina has sensed their mood and inclination, but my guess would be that she has not. I don't think that she is dull, exactly, mostly unsure of herself, but this would be much easier to navigate were she anybody but herself.

We walk silently through my house, and I know that she knows these halls from when she followed Marco here when we were all much younger. My mother always wanted a daughter, and so liked to see Serafina here. It is perhaps a shame that they did not retain that closeness as Serafina got older, but I think perhaps Lady Galeazzo was inclined to keep her separate from society, once she was shown to be such a shrinking violet and Marco was doing so well. Would she have preferred to have two children that excelled at the same time? Certainly yes, but did she want to spend the time on her daughter, when her son was here? No, it was not necessary.

I am not responsible for having collected all of the books in the library, though I have added some of my own, finding them in bookshops on crooked city streets, seeking them out both casually and with intent. It is impossible to know all the books that exist in the world, but on occasion I hear of one, or it is referenced in another's work, and I must track it down. There is a thrill in that hunt, an intellectual pursuit, and one of patience and stamina, rather than the physical contests to which I am accustomed. There is nobody to draw steel against, when I am seeking a book to buy.

But there are generations of books on the shelves, and though I think Serafina must have been in the library before, she gives a little start when I open the doors and she sees it. "I don't remember there being so many books," she says. "Perhaps I didn't care so much, when I was here last."

"Do you read much?" I ask. It feels very strange, to ask her a question. Do I even care to know the answer?

"I do, yes. Novels, when I can, though my mother detests them. She approves of poetry, and of history."

"An odd juxtaposition," I say.

"They don't quite allow you to escape in the same way," she says, dropping my arm and moving to the nearest shelves, trailing her finger wistfully across the bindings. Were I kinder, I would offer to lend her a book. But I see Marco's eyes in her face, and instead of softening my heart towards her, it does quite the opposite. I do not offer, and she does not ask.

"They are quite instructive, though. The histories."

"I think that people who like to read history are trying to avoid repeating mistakes," she says. "Though there is always room for new ones."

I laugh, surprised at her, surprised at myself. She gives me a startled glance, but turns her eyes back to the books, as though she hesitates to look at me for too long and invoke my ire. I have never laughed with her before, and I return to frowning immediately. That damn wine at dinner better not have been a love potion.

Chapter Forty-Nine

Serafina of House Galeazzo

Lorenzo is appropriate to the letter when he is forced to show me his library. No kindness, but none of his unwarranted cruelty either, and if neutrality is the best that I can hope for then I can accept that. After he shows me the library, he doesn't seem to know what to do with me. Perhaps that was his mother's design, to force some manner of cordial association, though why, I cannot say. It is enough, for me, that he's accepted me into the dueling circle. That he saved my life.

He needn't play at politeness any longer than necessary, and after I've looked at the books for long enough, almost certainly longer than he would have preferred, I pretend to stifle a yawn. With the amount of wine he smirkingly wanted to watch me drink, I'm certain that it is fairly believable. I'm quite capable of making a fool of myself on my own, I do not require that sort of help.

"Perhaps you could return me to your guest room? I'm not used to wearying so quickly." I almost referred to it as 'my' room, and could only imagine the reaction that would have provoked. I still remember what he did when I called him Renzo, the day I was late to practice. I never returned his handkerchief, but then, he didn't return mine either so I suppose it is fair.

"Of course," he says. He does not offer me his arm again, and I am relieved. It is an unnecessary farce; we both know who we are to each other. We walk through the halls; I don't know his gait well enough to tell if he is slowing himself to accommodate me, but I don't think so. I would not expect it of him.

"Before I forget, who must I thank for seeing to my swords?" I ask. "I know they must have been in a dreadful state, I just remember thinking that

I had to put them away. If I didn't I would drop them and they would be lost." I may have been about to say more but I stop myself, mortified. I did not mean to even say quite that much, to Lorenzo. He cannot possibly care.

But he shocks me into a brief standstill when he says, "I saw to your swords."

"Thank you," I say. "I didn't expect—"

"They're of very good quality and it would have been a shame to leave them for too long." He pauses too, so that he isn't just walking away from me, and turns slightly to look at me. "I know you did not mean to come here, and say that the city made you get lost, but had you gone anywhere else you certainly would have died."

"I am in your debt," I say, both in reflex and wholeheartedly.

"I know," he says. I don't know what to say in response to that, and he takes me to the guest room.

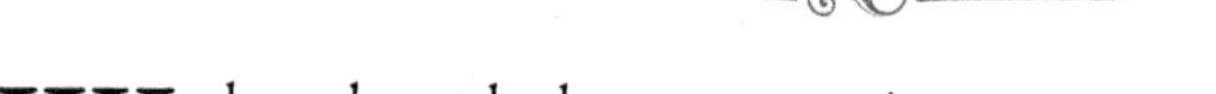

We have brunch the next morning, my parents, and Lorenzo's parents, and Lorenzo, and I. There are mimosas, and I have to keep myself from laughing, remembering how close I was to having to tell Dora, once, that mine was not a mimosas household. House Valier however, is.

My initial weariness after my injury has worn off, and I thought perhaps I would have trouble sleeping under this roof on my final night, but to the contrary, I slept better than I have since before Marco took his leave of us. What a curiosity, t find such rest there when I have such unease with at least one of the house's members.

We should have been able to find solace with one another, in our mutual love for my brother, but instead we have this divide between us, this hatred that Lorenzo has for me, and while I don't hate him precisely, I at this point could just as happily never cross paths with him again. Even after he's saved my life. Even after he's cleaned my swords.

We are seated next to each other for our meal, the sun streaming in through the doors and windows all around us. My father and Lord Valier seem to be organizing a hunt of some sort, continuing another conversation from who knows when. Our mothers are similarly engaged, and we seem to be expected to converse with one another. Lorenzo seems entirely willing to drink wine and stare off in stony silence, but I grow more uncomfortable by the minute, the weight of my mother's expectations ever on my shoulders like an unwanted but ever-reliable cape.

I am the one who breaks first, and I say "I have quite lost track of the days, I imagine there is a society dinner soon though?"

Lorenzo gives a slight sniff and cuts his eyes towards me, setting down his cup. "In three days," he says. "The expectation was that everybody was resting after the tournament and licking their wounds, or having their own private celebrations. But the lulls cannot be allowed to go for too long."

My mother moves her head slightly to the sounds of our voices, but otherwise does not turn. I see Lady Valier glance in our direction, smiling or still smiling. "I'll have quite the little tale for everybody, at least."

"They do already know," he says flatly.

I hadn't considered that, though of course they already know. Dora already knew. "Perhaps it will be good for some laughs then," I say, emboldened by my frustration. He knows how to be polite, he could at least pretend. "The ridiculous situation I got myself into, and then happening here and making a mess. Did I get blood on the statue outside? I seem to recall leaning on it for a moment, as the gate opened."

"I'm certain I don't know," he says, but he's looking at me now with something like curiosity. "As the gate opened?"

"Did you think I climbed the wall?" My tone is not quite a mimicry of his oft-derisive one, but I do put something of that note in, picking up my own cup. I don't know what's come over me, but if he can be awful, perhaps I can be too, despite my thankfulness.

"I did at first, and then did not think of it further. The gate opened on its own?"

"The city opened it, I expect." I have a sip of my wine, which is slightly sweet, slightly fruity. I look around for the servant who was in the dining room the other night, who poured with such a heavy hand and was always ready to return the cup to level, but he does not appear to be in attendance. "I didn't recognize where I was until your gate opened and I was looking at that statue." The statue and I, faces pressed together.

"Serafina, the dinner table is hardly the place to relate your recent experience," my mother says icily, and where normally I would wilt under her regard, I feel something inside me catch instead, like striking a match.

"My apologies, lady mother, and to my hosts. I should be well aware of what is and is not appropriate dinner conversation, I'm really not certain what's come over me," I say sharply, elaborately. "My recent experience, which we will not be discussing further at the table, must have clouded my judgment, and rendered me unfit for such company so soon. If I may take my leave?" I stand a little too abruptly, knocking the table and overturning my cup on the white tablecloth. I reach for it, but a servant is under my elbow already, clearing my dishes, applying a cleaning cloth to the violent bloom of red. It is, and is not, the color of blood, and there is so much of it. I hardly imbibed.

I do not know why my mother does not answer, or call out to stop me, as I turn on my heel and stride from the room, the heels on my boots ringing very loud in my ears. Perhaps she does, and I simply do not hear her, for that noise, and the roaring of my own blood. What's left of my own blood. I do and do not know where I am going, in House Valier, and walk through the halls until I find a door and let myself out into the garden. My cheeks feel both hot and cold, and when I put my hands to them, I realize that I've been crying. I fumble in my unfamiliar, borrowed pockets for a handkerchief as more tears fall, my breath hitching in a small sob that I muffle against the back of my hand, even outside, far from the dinner table.

"Here," a rough voice says from just behind me, and Lorenzo stands there, hand outstretched, white handkerchief in his fingers. I take it silently, not trusting myself to speak, and blot at my eyes. His mother must have sent him, there is no other explanation. There is some manner of flowering tree here, and a bench beneath it, that I sink down onto. I wish to be done with weeping, I do not want to continue to weep in front of Lorenzo, who regards me dispassionately. I wish to be far from here, but that isn't possible. Marco was able to run away, and I will never be able to seize that opportunity.

"My mother must be furious," I say eventually, when I think my voice will be calm and steady.

"Your mother is always furious," Lorenzo says, not exactly comforting, but kinder than I expected. "It is impossible to please her, and at least one of your attempts to do so is what brought you to this house."

"I'm sorry that I lied to you," I say, staring at my hands, the handkerchief crumpled through my fingers. It's hard to look at him. "Even in my state, I couldn't bear to tell the truth of it, that—"

"That she sent you out, I know." He sounds irritated, but not at me for once, and I look up. He isn't looking at me, but back towards the house. "I just don't know what use she thought it would be, sending you out alone late at night. You already represented your house well in the tournament, it just seems nonsensical to me."

"She told me to come back once I accomplished something," I say, and my voice feels brittle like glass. He laughs, and I flinch, and then he looks at me.

"You certainly accomplished something," he says, shaking his head.

"Don't." The word tears out of me unbidden. It is not something that I'm able to *laugh* about, and I was foolish to even try to speak to him. "Please don't, I—"

He holds up a hand. "Serafina, I am being sincere. I have never seen somebody so consumed with their spark as you were that night. You advanced, and in what seemed to be quite a large step."

I don't know what to say to that. I know that Lorenzo will never lie to make me feel better; my feelings are the least of his concerns. "I felt like a box of matches somebody accidentally set ablaze," I say. "It felt awful and frightening." He doesn't care, I tell myself, but he looks at me steadily. Actually looks at me.

"I imagine it must have. As I said, I've never—" and he breaks off, his head cocked.

"What is it?" I ask, but I hear it too, bells ringing through the city. The Guard ringing their bells through the city. They only do that to announce something, and Lorenzo crosses the garden to go to the front of the house, eschewing the paths, and I follow him, a hope starting in my heart. There is only one thing that I think about, when I consider what the guards may be announcing.

There is a little side gate, that opens into the front courtyard, and we reach the front gate at the same time our parents come out the front of the house. The street is nearly empty, as our dinners do tend to run late even when the smallest of parties like this one, nearly midnight. Not yet curfew for the lower classes, but if nothing of interest was happening until now...

The bells are nearing. It is a contingent of guard, with a messenger, and they reach the gates of House Valier and pause. "We were told that the Lord and Lady Galeazzo could be found here?" one of the guard says, stepping forward, and my mother moves to meet him, my father close behind.

"We are here, yes, what is it." My mother does not look around for me. My father does, briefly marking me with his eyes.

"We have located your son, Marco of House Galeazzo, and returned him to our city with his wife."

Chapter Fifty

Lorenzo of House Valier

When Serafina leaves the table, the fury on Lady Galeazzo's face is plain. She half rises, and my mother lightly puts a hand on her wrist. "How now, my lady, please remember your daughter is in quite a fragile state. She reached a threshold that not many come back from, and deserves your grace." My mother casts her glance at me. "Lorenzo, please see to our guest."

"Yes, my lady mother," I say, removing my napkin from my lap and setting it on the table, rising and going to follow Serafina. She has finally done something interesting, actually. It is interesting to watch such a soft dove changing into something more sharper-clawed.

I follow the echo of her heels; I would have expected her to flee to the guest rooms, but she's gone out to the garden instead. Her stride is tripping, stumbling, and I know she did not overimbibe so I'm briefly confused, until I've drawn close enough to hear her weeping. She seems to realize it at the same time, though without being aware of my presence and, head bent, is rummaging in her pockets for a handkerchief.

I sigh, withdraw mine. "Here," I say, holding it out. She turns to face me while also moving away a few steps, beseeching, apprehensive. As though she expects me to strike her. She takes the handkerchief hesitantly, blots her eyes with the practice of somebody who knows not to redden their face.

"My mother must be furious," she says presently, with the slightest tremble.

"Your mother is always furious," I say, for though I've been around the Lady Galeazzo only a little, most recently, she has been consumed with her grief and loss, and turned it outwardly to fury. "It is impossible to please her, and at least one of your attempts to do so is what brought you to this house."

She drops her gaze, working the handkerchief through her fingers. "I'm sorry that I lied to you. Even in my state, I couldn't bear to tell the truth of it, that—"

"That she send you out, I know." I look back towards the house, but see no one. Not even a servant appears to be observing us, at the moment. "It just seems nonsensical to me." She worked hard in advance of the tournament, and showed herself well. Her mother would do well to be forgiving of the child that she has left, even if she cannot find it in her heart to support her.

"She told me to come back once I accomplished something," she says, barely audible, and she flinches when a laugh escapes me.

I shake my head, thinking of the heat coming off her when I carried her inside. Her eyes. "You certainly accomplished something."

Her brows knit together anxiously, and she clenches her fists, rising from the bench beneath the oleander. "Please don't, I—"

I cut her off. I can give her this. She has proven herself enough for this, at least. "Serafina, I have never seen somebody so consumed with their spark as you were that night. You advanced, already, since rejoining society, and you advanced that night, in what seemed to be quite a large step all at once."

"I felt like a box of matches somebody accidentally set ablaze," she says, hesitantly, as though I might laugh again. She steals a glance up at me, and I hold her gaze. "It felt awful and frightening."

"I imagine it must have. As I said, I've never—"A sound in the distance, barely enough to hear, draws me away from our conversation. Bells, the city guards' bells. Drawing nearer. There is only one thing to do with the guard that is ever on my mind, and I walk away from the girl and walk to the front courtyard.

We all arrive there as one; our parents, myself, the guard.

"We were told that the Lord and Lady Galeazzo could be found here?"

Lord and Lady Galeazzo step forward, and Serafina starts to go to them but stops when her mother does not look to her. "Yes, what is it?"

"We have located your son, Marco of House Galeazzo, and returned him to our city with his wife."

Serafina and my mother both gasp. Lady Galeazzo appears to have been carved from stone. "You will bring them to my house, of course."

"There is the matter of—"

"We will move forward with legal proceedings, of course, but my son will be at my house. And his wife." Lady Galeazzo's voice brooks no argument, and as the guard bows and take their leave, she with a glance sends her husband for their carriage.

"Mother—" Serafina says, almost in spite of herself.

Lady Galeazzo, regards her daughter for a moment, as though reminding herself who this person might be. "We are joining our house with house Valier. It is hardly seemly for you to stay here, but the situation is unusual. Your engagement will be announced once we know what is to happen with your brother."

"My *what*?" Serafina exclaims, at the same I turn to my parents and ask, "Joining our houses?"

"Oh dear, we did not anticipate these circumstances," my mother says apologetically. My father grimaces, and it would be comical except that they are somehow serious.

"My lady mother, no," I say. Lady Galeazzo gives a sniff, and she and my mother exchange a glance.

"I don't see what you're so upset about," Lady Galeazzo says impatiently, carelessly, to some further plea Serafina made that I did not hear. "You need only bear some heirs, and you might stop troubling yourself with any effort with society, since it it so difficult for you."

"We will discuss it further," my mother says, as House Galeazzo sniffs and gets into their carriage, departing without their daughter, who stands like a statue in my courtyard.

After a few moments, my mother goes to Serafina, puts an arm around her shoulder, and guides her inside. She casts a glance at me, as though I should have done so, but I am similarly rooted to the spot, unable to reconcile that Marco is returned to us but also that my mother and father would have engaged in such an agreement as marriage without ever consulting me.

They could not possibly have decided this today, or even in the last week. These things take time.

I look at my father, who appears also to be wrestling with this development; wrestling with what to say to me, if nothing else. "You have my regrets, my boy. This was not how we meant to broach the topic to you, and I am shocked that it is how Lady Galeazzo felt it most appropriate."

"I'm shocked that any of you found the idea appropriate to begin with," I say. But I find I wish to hear none of it, and I take stock of my appearance, and the contents of my pockets, and go out through the front gates. My father does not call after me.

I lack Armand's foresight, but I have the distinct feeling that he will be at a particular tavern we frequent, and that is where I walk. I am not angry, though I ought to be. I'm certain I will *become* angry.

The streets are fairly empty; the citizenry wants to know why the guard was ringing their bells, and will be gathering at guardposts and where announcements are made. Perhaps even in front of House Galeazzo itself. I can feel the pull to go there, but it would be too soon. Tonight, after curfew. Perhaps Armand will try to stop me, or perhaps Armand will tell me why it is a fine idea.

He is sitting at the bar where I expect, and I also half expect Iulio to be there but he is not. There is a cup of wine waiting for me when I sit, and Armand casts a sidelong look at me. "I wasn't sure what it was that was wrong, exactly, until you walked in," he says.

"There are multiple things wrong," I say, frowning stormily into my ready cup.

"I know." Armand sets his cup down and turns to me, his elbow on the bar. "Which are you the most upset about?"

"Upset makes it sound like I am simply being petulant," I mutter, before taking a drink. He nods, waiting. Well, which is it? "The marriage arrangement. Mine, damn you, not Marco's."

"House Galeazzo has been plain at their discomfort at having a daughter."

I scoff. "*Discomfort.* Yes, it was very inconvenient for them to not have had two sons, but I'm not certain it would have made a difference in the lady's treatment of the younger."

"I'm not either," he agrees, affably. "So the problem is not that she is a girl, but simply that she is. Which is quite confusing, as there are obviously ways to have handled such matters."

"You've clearly spent more time considering this than I," I say. My cup is drained already, and I tap the bar for more. Of course, there are draughts that we take to keep from getting a child upon a woman, perhaps Lord Galeazzo was hoping for a second son and his lady was not. Or perhaps they just thought their next child would also naturally excel.

"Clearly." The barkeep pours our cups full, and Armand waits for him to move off before continuing. Perhaps Armand is already following multiple threads of the possibilities that this conversation might weave, and making his choices among them. His spark is the one we least understand. "What shall you do then? Your parents cannot force a marriage."

"They cannot. And yet, in the way of things, they can." While I don't expect my parents would disown me for refusing to marry Serafina, I do not think Serafina is in quite the same circumstance. If her mother is rid of her, where would she go? Though also, I cannot imagine why my own lady mother would expect the girl's plight to sway me. Though, damn her, the fact that I am having these thoughts at all is troublesome. Wouldn't that be a trick, if part of Serafina's spark made people sympathize with her, while making her mother hate her.

"And so what will you do?"

"I won't know, until I talk to Marco," I say. And his wife. I don't care to speak to her, but there is only so large our world is, which is how I'm in this mess with Serafina. Do I just need to get accustomed to the idea? This must be something that our mothers decided years ago and only just now deigned to tell us. What damnable timing. "Though I'd wager my stable is far more guarded than his used to be."

"His betrayal was so easy in that it was so unexpected," Armand says. "Both from him and because nobody had ever done that before, somehow."

"It does seem impossible, for him to have been the first." I've lost track of cups and refillings, in our silences and starts. Does it matter? Perhaps tonight it does not. Perhaps tonight, if we are drunk enough, I can get Armand to teach me some of his prescience, if he is able to teach his prescience. It seems unlikely. "You didn't know that—"

"No, I did not know that he was leaving," Armand says. I must have asked him this before. A thousand times over, in anger and in despair and begging for reason. He really did just love Katarina all along. "Nor did I know that he was returning. Nor do I know what will happen next. I know that there will be weddings, but there are always weddings. I know that there will be blood, but there will always be blood."

"Night after night," I say. I am certain that Serafina does not want to marry me either. "What will happen with Marco, do you think?"

"The Company of the Canted Stage will want satisfaction, for their indentured actress. But whether they will want that satisfaction in blood and spark or in coin, I cannot say."

"There was that other company too. The other actor. The guard only mentioned Marco and his wife."

"I wonder," Armand says, and every other time tonight I have believed him, heart and soul, but here, I think that he knows more. I do not care about any of the actors and will not press.

"I want to see Marco," I say, and stand from the barstool, stumbling.

"Not tonight," Armand says, steadying me.

"Yes tonight."

He pauses, perhaps weighing the options, perhaps seeing the different threads. "Do you want to call a carriage?"

"No, I will walk."

"Then I will walk with you."

Chapter Fifty-One

Serafina of House Galeazzo

My brother is returned to us, and I am not permitted to go to him. Not yet, anyway. My brother is returned to us, and I am abandoned at the house of my enemy. Or, even if Lorenzo is not my enemy, he is not my friend either. Unless all is forgotten, now that my beloved brother is returned to us, but I think that is foolish to hope for.

I do not think all of this immediately; I find myself too shocked to think much of anything, at first. Lady Valier guides me back into the house, back to the guest room. I am not insensate, I know what she is doing, I know what she is saying to me, but I no longer feel as though I can speak. I've had a shock, I think, of a different sort than a sword sheathing itself in my belly. A shock of the soul, and I wonder how many of these I am expected to endure.

My mother would slap me, I think eventually, stirring myself dully to look at my hostess. She's seated me in a plush little arm-chair, and seated herself in its twin. A tea service is on the table in between us, and glasses of sherry, and vials that I do not recognize, and a plate of cookies shaped like birds. My mother would not bring me tea and cookies, my mother would slap me until she thought whatever sense I had, had returned, and then set me to a task. Lady Valier's hands are in her lap, holding her fan. Everybody is affecting fans this season, I ought to get one, I think. No, Dora got me one. It must be in my room, at my house. I am still clutching Lorenzo's handkerchief, I realize, and relax my fingers on it, which I see Lady Valier note with her eyes.

"This is all very sudden," she says to me, gently. "A lot has happened in a very small amount of time."

"How long was this planned?" I ask. I could mean my brother's leaving, since I could not ask him myself, my birds always came back. But how could Lady Valier know this, and so she answers the question of the arranged marriage.

"Your family and mine have been friends for a very long time," she says. "Joining our houses is something we have discussed at length, over the years. Your mother and I, your father and my husband. I'd meant to have a daughter, after Lorenzo, but that was not to be." She pauses here, and I look at her. She is in control of herself, people in her echelon are nearly always in control of themselves. My mother is in control of herself, when she is treating me the way that she is. It is with full intent. This is an opportunity, I think, to escape her.

"I cannot marry your son," I say instead. "He will not have me."

Her lips tighten slightly, but her hands do not move. "That remains to be seen. Lorenzo knows his duties, though it may seem otherwise."

"Then I will not marry your son, until my brother is free."

She smiles at that. "Now that, my dear, is very clever. We can use that."

"You want me to marry your son, though."

"I do, yes. I have always wanted a daughter." She sets her fan aside, pours us both tea. "But I am foolish enough to also want people to be happy, which Lorenzo has not been in the time of your brother's absence. And which you never are, around Lorenzo."

"Then why—"

"Happiness cannot be the only motivator in these decisions, unfortunately." She holds the cup out to me and I take it, the thin porcelain warming my cold fingers. "Good political decisions require a cooler head and heart than happiness always allows for."

"I don't want to make political decisions," I say.

"And yet you must. We must." Lady Valier sips her own tea, and I look at the vials on the table again. They are still sealed, and full, the tea is just tea. I take my own sip, find it strong and sweet.

"What will happen?"

"I wish that I could say."

"I just want..." I trail off. I drink more tea. I *want*, but what I want is foolish, simple, safe girlish wants. I want things to be how they were. I want my brother back. I want to be freed of my mother's control. I know better than to want her to be anything resembling nice to me, that is not in my mother's makeup. Would it be so bad, to allow Lady Valier to be my mother? No. She is already nicer. She is waiting for me to finish, watching me with the slightest of smiles. "I want the impossible," I say finally.

"You are too hard on yourself, even as your mother is clearly too hard on you. Consider what your other wants might be. You are welcome in this house, as my guest, and we do not need to decide the future today, or even tomorrow."

"My thanks, Lady Valier," I say, tears stinging in my eyes. My hands with the cup and saucer are steady, though, and I am proud of that in a new way. They would not have been steady, a week ago. I would have been sobbing, a week ago. This is the way my spark is changing me, I think suddenly. Tempering me. I didn't know.

"Your mother will be distracted with your brother's affairs, and looming over you less. But she has made her decision, and you do need to keep that in mind."

"I know," I say. I finish my cup of tea, set it down softly on the table. "What are those for?" I ask about the vials, before I can allow myself to explain them away as something others know better about than me. Look at where my meekness has gotten me.

"If you wanted to seek some relief," Lady Valier says. "One will let you sleep, or if you didn't want that, the other would alter your senses."

I know the others indulge in such things, Armand especially, Lorenzo occasionally. Ottavia as well, I think, though she doesn't talk about it. But her persistently inattentive and flighty demeanor seems less than natural to me. "I've never…"

"There isn't any shame in it. And also, you don't *have* to. As you see, I brought an array of remedies." She picks up her own sherry to illustrate, and sips it. "We are only just getting ourselves acquainted as adults, I was not certain if you had any proclivities. When you were small, I know you liked flower-flavored confections, and thought that may have carried through."

"It has," I say. I gather my courage, take a deep breath. "I apologize, deeply, that I seem ungrateful to be engaged to your son, I don't mean to disrespect your house by—"

"Hush with that, for now," she says. "Your mother is very smart, and very skilled, and sometimes just as impetuous as when we were girls. Our intent was never to rush this; you needn't have a double wedding with Ottavia and Sterling. Indeed, you and Lorenzo may stay resolved that you are not suited for one another and cannot possibly be married. But nothing needs to be decided today, right now. We as parents can make plans, but ultimately, what you do is your choice."

"Thank you," I say. "Though I don't know what I will do, if we do not marry. My mother is already done with me." It feels so strange to be able to speak so plainly, and maybe I should not speak so plainly. But Lady Valier is so easy to talk to, it must be her spark, that compels my tongue to remain unguarded.

"She was never terribly warm, even when we were girls, though I know that is no comfort for you to hear. And as she advanced, she became more and more as she is now."

"I take some comfort in knowing," I say, blinking away tears again. "It means that she is not like this because of me."

Lady Valier reaches out and takes my hand. "My darling girl, why would it be because of you? No, she was our ice queen all along. Where she thaws is where your brother is concerned, he is the exception."

"He has always been the exception," I say. I am not jealous, I love Marco too. But I have never been enough, even when I was all they had left. Even when I won three laurels in my first tournament, even when my spark advanced so much in such a short amount of time. I look again at the vials on the table. "I think I will try one of these," I say. "If only to sleep."

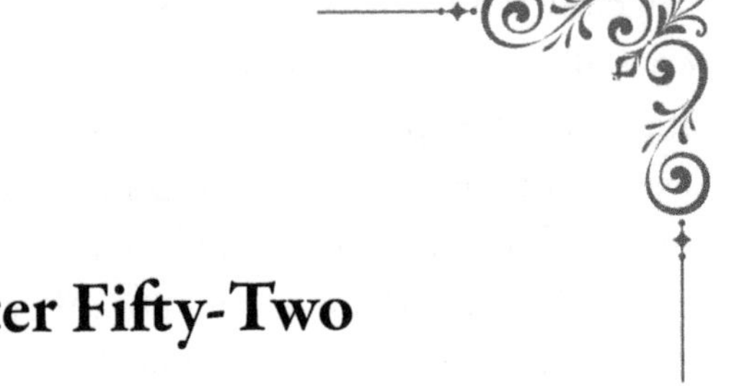

Chapter Fifty-Two

Lorenzo of House Valier

The gates don't whisper invitingly open for us when we reach House Galeazzo, in the small hours after time has been called and the street lights for the lower parts of the city have gone out. No matter, I've scaled this wall a thousand times, and Armand follows me without protest. Armand does not often try to *stop* me, but does follow along to bear witness as he sees fit. Granted, who knows how often he's borne witness without even being present? Not I.

It is a testament to how drunk I am that it has not occurred to me to burn it off with my spark, and even when I do think of it, I don't do it. I look at the windows of the house, dark and not, and then I whistle our signal. At first, I hear nothing, see nothing. Open the window, I think. Armand crosses his arms and leans against the wall behind me, reminding me of Serafina that night, after she'd mimicked the whistle to draw me out.

Open the window, I think, and I whistle again.

After a long time, so long, a shadow crosses Marco's dimly-lit window and then the curtain twitches and then it opens and there he is, leaning out on the window sill. "My mother will kill you where you stand," he says, laughing, worried, serious.

"I would face your fearsome mother to know my dearest friend again," I say with great dignity, swaying slightly where I stand.

"You are drunk."

"In celebration of your return. You and your *wife*." I don't mean to spit out the word wife, or do I?

He is willing to ignore such things, at our first reunion. "How is my sister?"

"Alive." Why must he ask of her immediately?

266

"I'd hoped you would look after her," Marco says, not chiding me, he cannot possibly be chiding me. But there is regret in his tone.

"Teodora readily took that role," Armand says behind me. "And you are well?"

"I am," Marco says, reticent. He looks well, I think. His hair is longer.

"Come down here and fight me, that we might get on with our lives," I say.

"Lorenzo, I can hardly—"

"You'll be within your walls. The guard cannot possibly find fault with that." I pull on my gloves. "Come down."

A voice within, indistinct. Marco turns and withdraws, but leaves the window open. I look over my shoulder at Armand, who smiles cryptically, and I face forward again. Marco will not leave me out here in the night, unsatisfied. He cannot. The time stretches on, surely not so long as it feels, and he returns to the window. "Will you catch my swords?"

"I will." He lowers his sword belt outside and gives it a toss, as we have done hundreds of times, and I catch it, as I have hundreds of times. I sober myself up, as Marco climbs down from his window. By the time he takes his sword belt from me, I'm steady enough, and I wait for him to buckle it on, and put on his gloves.

In that time, Katarina climbs down too, and I frown at her. At a glance, they are otherwise unchanged; I cannot imagine why they would return. Why they left to begin with. "He needs a second," she says, frowning back at me, as if I have come here specifically to get her husband into trouble. Perhaps I have. But her sternness surprises me, and I cannot help but laugh. Marco looks back at the house, but it is too late now, we will not be deterred.

"Exactly right. And Armand, are you my second?"

"I suppose I must be," he says. "What are your terms, Marco?"

"First touch, you lunatics," he says, shaking his head but smiling fondly. Katarina frowns still behind him. "Armand, I would have thought..."

"He's been impossible," Armand says with a shrug.

"Just so." Marco draws, and so do I, and we square off, my heart brimming with joy to be facing him again.

Neither of us even draws on our spark, at first, we just step to, and our swords clash off each other as we thrust, and block, and parry, in and away, laughing. We increase our speed after that, the spark burning off of us. Sometimes we would see just how fast we could go, and we do not push that limit now, but the courtyard blurs and it is only Marco, and I, and our swords. And then I slip past his guard, and give him a tap on the shoulder, and we stop, just like that, breathing hard, steam rising off of us in the evening air. I jam my swords back in their sheathes and embrace him, feel his heart thump against mine.

"Your absence wounded me," I say in his ear, grinning as we part. "It brings me much joy that you are returned to us."

"It brings me much joy to see you again," he says. "I fear that the rest of the city will not so readily embrace me, but it gives me courage that my dearest friend is willing."

"Whatever comes, we will face it."

"My mother says that as well," he says, with a short laugh.

"Yes, how *is* your lady mother? I saw her and your lord father at luncheon, but of course their visit was cut short."

"There will be a formal meeting with the guard and designeés from the two theater companies tomorrow," Marco says.

"Two?"

"That foolish boy," Katarina says, and Marco gives her what I imagine is his sternest warning glance. "But Marco's mother says that she will buy the rest of my indenture, as a wedding present." From the wry twist of her lips, I can see clearly how she feels to be indebted to Lady Galeazzo.

"As I tried to do years ago," he says soothingly, catching at her hand. She does look at him with something like fondness; her expression is so schooled, from all those years on the stage, it is hard to take her at face value.

"What does the other company have to do with you, then?" I ask. Perhaps I am still too drunk to grasp these implications. Marco does not answer me, though; he looks to Katarina.

"The boy was in love with my cousin, and dueled with Marco in the street one night just before curfew, wounding him terribly. He fled the city once the guard were after him, and once he left the guard banished him. My cousin killed herself in despair, and so I left in pursuit, to cut the dog down. Marco helped my escape." This anger does not seem as though it has been put to bed, but rather is still a fresh cut.

"And did you?" I ask.

"Did I what?"

"Cut him down?"

"I did," she says steadily. "And so we returned."

"I did hear that a girl died," Armand says. "My regards to you, for your loss."

Katarina blinks, the only time I have ever seen her off guard. "My thanks," she says after a moment. I think she is so used to speaking from the stage that normal diction is no longer quite within her grasp.

"Have you quite finished your foolishness?" Lady Galeazzo's icy tone strikes from across the courtyard, and she is standing in one of the side doors.

"My apologies for disturbing you, Lady Galeazzo, I simply could not keep away from my best friend in this life," I say, with a theatrical bow. I overbalance myself just slightly, by design, and Marco and Armand catch me, startled into laugher.

"I must say, Lorenzo, I did somewhat expect this." She looks at me, and then makes it a point to look around. "Though I am surprised that my daughter is not here with you."

"I am not certain why you would be," I say stiffly.

"Hmm. Just so." She turns and goes back inside, the door snapping shut behind her.

"How are you finding your mother in law?" Armand asks, in the most serious of tones, and I am unable to keep from shouting with laughter.

Katarina smiles tightly. "We will require time to become accustomed to one another," she says.

Marco embraces me once again, and we clap each other on the back. "I will see you again soon enough, Lorenzo," he says. He reaches to grasp Armand's hand, and Armand surprises him with an embrace as well.

"We will be back to our old habits soon enough," Armand says, and then pulls me away by the shoulder of my jacket.

I look back to Marco just before we go around the corner of the house to the front gate, and he raises a hand to me. I see his eyes in the night, and think again of Serafina and realize, suddenly, fully, the weight of how I've treated her.

Chapter Fifty-Three

Serafina of House Galeazzo

The room is totally dark when Lorenzo roughly shakes me awake, fingers too strongly grasping my shoulder. "Get up," he says in a matching tone.

"What's the matter?" He has *never* initiated contact with me, something must be terribly wrong.

But he's away from my bedside and grabbing my swords from the racks. I sit up, put my feet on the floor as he shoves them at my hands. "Get up and fight me."

"Lorenzo, *what*?" I have to take the swords, or else I will drop them, and I do not know what would happen if I dropped my sheathed swords, but even cobwebby from sleep, it becomes important to me that I not drop them. No, not just sleep; I remember now the sleeping-draught that I chose from Lady Valier's offerings. "Are you drunk?" I can smell the wine on him.

"I have seen your brother." He again paces across the room from me, and then sheds his jacket to the little stuffed arm-chair his mother so recently sat on, and turns to face me.

"I fail to see why that means I must duel you in the middle of the night." I stand now, though, obedient as always. "Perhaps we could revisit this in the morning."

"No, now," he says. He isn't angry with me, but I cannot understand his mood.

"I'm too tired, I took..." I gesture vaguely towards the table, where the vials had been, as though he will understand." He does seem to, though, he follows my gesture and then comes and takes me by the wrist and I try to pull away but he holds me, and I feel his spark and mine, and the remaining effects from the sleeping draught simply disappear, leaving me far too clear-headed.

"Select terms," he says too intensely, too close to me.

"Lorenzo, we don't have seconds," I say, feeling a tickle of panic; the last time I was challenged, and had no second…I give an involuntary, shuddering jerk and drop my swords on the floor at my feet. "No."

"Serafina, fight me." his face is flushed and his eyes are bright, too bright, and I step back away from him, crossing my arms, trying to keep from shaking. Feeling that cold blade enter my belly again.

"I will not. You are not acting reasonably." We stare at each other, unmoving. "Please leave." What will I do if he does not, if I am unwilling to fight him? This is ridiculous.

"No! I need—" he bites off whatever he was going to say next, struggling visibly. His eyes search my face a moment, and I remain silent, waiting. I can only imagine what he sees there. Apprehension, fear. I've finally stood up for myself; what will be the cost? He takes a deep breath, and when he lets it out, the frenetic energy seems to leave him as well. "I have treated you badly," he says finally. "And thought to somehow discharge that dishonor by getting you out of bed and forcing you to duel me. I would ask that you forgive what I have just done." Without waiting for my answer, he turns and retrieves his jacket from the chair. At the door he turns to me and bows, then leaves, closing it softly behind him.

I stand like a statue for I don't know how long, waiting for him to come back through the door, despite what he said. My brother has returned to us, which is what we all wanted, and it is only now that Lorenzo admits that he has treated me badly. I am glad that I refused his duel; he will not receive absolution so simply as that. There would have been no honor in that.

I think that I should take my swords up off the floor, and put them back in the rack, and when I crouch to pick them up, I find I cannot get up right away. I sink to my knees, and I cover my mouth with my hands as I burst into tears. I am a veteran, now, at the art of hiding my tears from any who might hear me. My tears have always only enraged my mother. How *could* he? How *dare* he?

But I do not wish to spend the night on the floor, and the storm of tears passes eventually. I pick up my swords, and then pick up myself, and set them in the racks next to the dresser. On the dresser, as though Lady Valier somehow knew something like this would happen, is another vial of the sleeping draught. I look at it for a long time, and then pick it up. Until Lorenzo interrupted, I was in a deep sleep, untroubled by visions of my mother and worries for my brother. I want to have that again, I think. I can face these things in the morning.

I have time enough to get back under the covers after drinking it, before the velvet darkness gently welcomes me again.

Chapter Fifty-Four

Lorenzo of House Valier

I awaken with the first light with a headache and an unaccustomed feeling of regret. Marco is returned to us, I am overjoyed. But Serafina...

No, the best I can do for her is to leave her alone. She does not want to marry me, nor I her, and we will work in concert on that front, at the very least. It is interesting to me, perhaps telling, that my fury did not transfer to Katarina the moment I saw her again. I have been such a petulant fool.

I am alone in the breakfast room when I drink my first cup of coffee, and then another, and then go to the practice room. My father will not have risen so early, but I can run through my exercises alone, or with a practice dummy. I do, until I am sweating and out of breath and need to have a bath drawn and the rest of the house has woken up.

My mother passes me in the hall, after I ascend the stairs. "Is my darling boy up so early, or going to bed so late?" she asks.

"Up so early," I say.

"And did you see our returned friend last night?"

"I did, yes, and fought him, and we are well with each other." Unless Serafina gives him an accurate accounting of my behavior, I think. Which would only be fair; she does not owe me her complicity.

"And fought him," my mother replies with a laugh. She steps to embrace me, disregarding my general dishevelment. "I should not be surprised."

"I am what you have made of me."

She gives me a further squeeze and kisses my sweaty hair and then releases me. "I suppose that is the case, yes."

"When will we—" Visit House Galeazzo, I am about to ask, of course.

"This afternoon, I expect," she says. "Or in the evening." She smiles at me, then gives me a little push. "You stink of practice, go bathe. Then sleep more, the bags beneath your eyes could carry a week's meals home from market."

"Yes, my lady mother." I bow elaborately and kiss her hand. She laughs and shoos me on my way. She does not go down the stairs, as I expect, but instead towards the guest rooms. Is Serafina an early riser? It has never occurred to me to wonder.

My mother was clearly already aware of my morning exertions, as a bath is waiting for me. I take my time, letting my muscles stiffen and then relax in the water, my head leaned back, a towel on my face. Then I take care shaving, knowing that the longer that I take with these preparations, the less time that I will have to wait for our visit to House Galeazzo. The impulse is so childish that I can't help but laugh at myself, but still, though I have seen Marco briefly, the joyous anticipation remains.

A tapping at my window, a bird, and I let it in for it to alight on my hand and return to paper form. I unfold it; a missive from Luca. "I can only assume you've heard the news," it reads. "Have you seen him yet?" He hasn't spoken to Armand yet, then. Armand, wiser than I, is likely still abed. But the whole city has to have heard the news, whether they cared about Marco and the sordid story of his absence or not. It is rare for the guard to be so involved in our affairs; the theater company owners are not part of our society, they don't travel in our circles, they don't participate in our tournaments, but they are adjacent, and some are of similar power. The Company of the Canted Stage owner, Katarina's former company, is at a formidable level.

I draw out paper and pen, uncap my ink. "Last night," I say. "And will again later today." Luca will want to know when we are all meeting. There will almost certainly be necessity for it, even outside of our usual habits. "Conditions permitting, we should all meet tomorrow, at his House." I wait for the ink to dry, and carry the paper to my window, folding it into a bird even as I cross my room, and it nearly strikes the window frame in its eagerness to leave from my hand. My mood is uplifted, energetic, and I am entirely unsure what to do with myself. I finish dressing, and walk to the library, if only for something to do. My lady mother told me to sleep more, but I cannot.

I see the glances that the servants give me; they too are well aware of the news, and of what Marco's disappearance had done for my demeanor. I wonder how much they care about our petty goings-on, if they think about it only in terms of the disruption to their lives, to the humors of their days. I don't trouble myself often, with what the servants think, no more than I do with what the flower-seller thinks, or what that damned actress thought, though now that she and Marco are wed, I suppose there must be room made in our circle for her. I recall Marco saying that she had no spark to speak of, but also I've seen her fight, both on the stage and in the street, and in that regard alone she is unbelievably more skilled than Ottavia as the least of us.

It is amazing that I can forgive her so easily for taking Marco away from us, when I have made his sister pay.

Chapter Fifty-Five

Serafina of House Galeazzo

"You haven't done your drills today," my mother says to me by way of greeting; I could not say how she knows. From long practice, I do not break her gaze, but in my periphery, I see Marco and Lorenzo exchange a glance.

"I encouraged her to save her energy to greet her lost but found brother," Lorenzo says before I can answer her, stepping forward to bow to her. "Please, forgive me Lady Galeazzo, if that was incorrect."

"Hmm," she says, folding her fan. But I am free now to embrace my brother, and I do, my thoughts and emotions both awhirl. I did not expect Lorenzo to come to my aid, to lie for me. We shared a carriage here, of course, and exchanged only the barest of greetings in front of his servants, as he handed me into the carriage.

"Marco," I say, and then have nothing else to say to him. All these months with him gone, after having been so close all of our lives, I thought that there would just be a fountain of words from my mouth, but everything I wanted to say has fled my mind, and I can only hug him again, squeezing tears from my eyes.

"Fina," he says, and hugs me firmly. "I'm sorry that I couldn't tell you."

"No, you were right to not, I would have tattled on you immediately," I say, stepping back and fumbling a handkerchief from my pocket to dab at my eyes with. He laughs, his hand on my shoulder.

"I would not have said that, exactly..."

"But it's what you *meant*," I say, laughing and crying. My mother gives a sort of huffing sigh, and we turn to her. I glance at Lorenzo, who is regarding us curiously, though I cannot read his expression further.

"Reunion merriment aside, we must discuss what is to be done," our mother says.

"Done about what?" I ask, but I do feel very stupid. Of course the matter isn't settled in any way; the guard brought him back in chains. I am to marry Lorenzo. The anxiety knits my brows once again.

"About the matter of your brother and his wife's debts and freedoms. But let us go inside for that, I will not discuss such things standing in the courtyard." My mother turns and sweeps inside, Lady Valier falling into step with her, our fathers walking with each other as well. Marco takes Katarina by the arm and she has such a practiced poise walking with him that it gladdens my heart. Of course he loves her, and she him. But now is not the time to get acquainted with my now-sister.

Lorenzo clears his throat, and I realize he's offered me his arm. "Thank you," I say, surprised, and accept.

"It is the correct thing to do," he says, stiff but not cold. "Whether we accept the parts we have been given or not." We do not, I think, but what a change this is, in him. I'm not watching for what cruel thing he might do next, he is different now, with Marco returned.

I catch sight of Agnes, on the balcony of the second floor, as we walk inside; I don't see her face long enough to begin to read her expression, but she seems very wide-eyed, if nothing else. I wonder what she has been told. I wonder what instruction my mother has given her.

We go to the larger sitting room, and the men all see us seated before taking their own chairs. Tea is brought, but that is all. We are meant to have dinner after this discussion, and I don't know what to expect from either.

"There isn't any sense in prevarication," my mother says, once we are settled. I have a cup of tea on the little table at my elbow, but cannot imagine wanting it at the moment. "The Company of the Canted Stage is willing to accept payment for the remainder of Katarina's indenture, and that check has already been written out to them. The Golden Company, however, wants recompense for their missing actor, who evidently dueled my son and fled the city immediately thereafter, ahead of a banishment." I turn to stare at Marco, thinking of the night that he didn't come back, and the state he was in that morning. He does not look at me, just our mother. "This actor was involved with Katarina's cousin, and the girl—" Katarina makes a small noise, as though she hates to show any emotion at all, but it gets away all the same.

"Mother, I think we all—" Marco starts, and I shock myself by interrupting him.

"I don't know all of this," I say. "I have not been told a single thing."

My mother looks at me a moment, and I think that she won't continue. To my surprise, she does. "The girl killed herself, and Katarina sought satisfaction in the life of the other actor. Having done so, she and Marco got married and gave themselves up to the guard to be returned."

"So then what could the Golden Company want?" I ask. "If there is nobody to be returned to them, what then?"

"Because Katarina is now of our House, they want satisfaction for their loss of property, and would not accept money for his indenture."

"I said I would face any one of them," Katarina says, sullen now. "They want more of a production than that, to draw a crowd and make sales and a spectacle over it."

"Another tournament, then? Something like a tournament?"

"I know Lorenzo cannot speak for his whole dueling circle, and thus nothing is decided in this room at this moment, but yes. The Company's ownership will not duel Katarina, but they want to set their best against what we consider our best."

"Of course we will," I say, half turning to Lorenzo. "We must, nobody will say no, they can't possibly."

"We will have to ask everybody," he says, looking steadily at my mother. "And if we win, that is the end of the matter?"

"It is," she says. There is too long a pause after her answer, and I cannot understand why nobody is speaking. Even Lady Valier's accustomed smile has faded.

"And if we don't?" I ask.

"We will," Marco says, and Katarina smiles at that, a glint in her eyes unlike any I've seen. I have met her, she is not unknown to me, but she herself has a bladelike sharpness.

"But—"

"Whatever the terms they set, the guard may enforce if we do not abide." My father is less demonstrative of his disgust in this than my mother is, but also no less firm.

"It's simple then," Lorenzo says, and we all turn to look at him. "We must not lose."

Katarina laughs, clapping her hands together once, and I see the corners of my mother's lips tighten. "I am glad of your support," she says. "And I think that...through some marriage math you will be my brother in law?"

Lorenzo clears his throat, glances at me. "Yes, that is the sum of it," he says.

"That will not happen until this matter is settled," I say. "I will not be wed until I am sure that we are all free."

My mother gives something of a start and opens her mouth to speak, and my father lays a hand on her arm. "That is your right, daughter," he says. "We will make no engagement announcement until such a time." My mother shifts in irritation but does not contradict him; she unfolds her fan with a clatter and waves it gently.

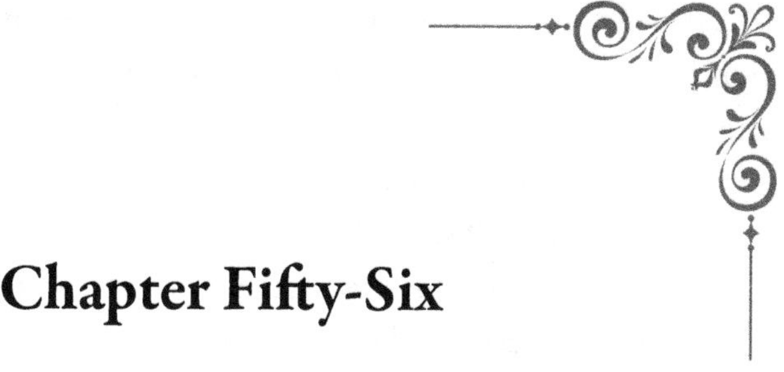

Chapter Fifty-Six

Lorenzo of House Valier

Though I am confident they will say yes, I do feel the jitter of nerves while waiting for the dueling circle to come to House Galeazzo the next day. We are in the practice room, as it is the best suited for all our nervous energy, though Katarina is looking around blinking owlishly, and I can only assume that she is not in the habit of seeing the world before midday. Dora arrives first, with a covered basket from the market, and I see her take note of Serafina's worried face before embracing Marco and curtseying to Katarina.

"I have brought wine, which is either a very poor wedding gift, or the best of wedding gifts, that is best enjoyed in the moment and then forgotten, and no troubling yourself with where you might display it to avoid snubbing anybody," she says, laughing.

"You are always so thoughtful," Marco says warmly.

"They're reds, which I thought I remembered you liking? Katarina, I do not know your preferences, I do apologize."

"Oh, there is nothing to fret about; I am still educating my palate," Katarina says, bowing in return. She has never been given to skirts, that one.

"What a delight! We shall be able to have such fun," Dora says, and then Tristan arrives with Luca.

"You're always having fun without me," Luca complains, but he's smiling, and he and Marco embrace hard enough that their chests thump together. "You were missed."

"I gather," Marco says. He is delighted, and abashed, to be such the center of attention.

Armand arrives with Ottavia and Sterling, and those greetings are slightly less demonstrative, Ottavia sizing up Katarina and eyeing her short hair with disapproval or envy, I cannot quite tell.

"Are you well?" Armand asks Serafina, aside but not in secret, and she seems perplexed, as if she's already forgotten her ordeal, somehow.

After a moment, she says, "Thank you, I am, thanks to Lorenzo. And now with Marco returned to us, I am much overjoyed." She smiles, embarrassed. "I forgot that everybody would know."

"Know what?" Marco asks.

"Oh! We needn't go into all the details now, but I had a bad fight the other night, which is how I happened to be at House Valier; Lorenzo helped me." She opens her fan when she's done speaking, waving it slightly, in a gesture uncannily like her mother's when Lady Galeazzo will not be speaking further on a topic.

"You will tell me all about it later," he says.

"Of course. There is simply so much to tell you."

"It would probably be best if we got to the matter at hand," I say, and Serafina shoots me a grateful look. Any port in a storm, they say, which is I suppose part of how we arrived here to begin with.

"Yes, what are we to do?" Tristan asks.

"The short of it is, we need to have a series of duels with members of the Golden Company, to satisfy them for their loss of indenture."

"Is that all?" Dora asks, when I'd hardly finished. "Of course we will." There are nods around the room, even Ottavia.

"Thank you," Marco says. Katarina looks utterly surprised.

"Just like that?" she asks. "You require no convincing?"

"Why would we?" Luca asks. "It isn't like we never get to fight with the Company folk but some of them have been out of reach for years, so maybe this will draw them out."

"Oh, I thought you were going to talk about the sort of woman—" Tristan starts, and even as Ottavia is pre-emptively laughing, Luca interrupts her.

"Now is that necessary? In front of a guest?"

"Mm, what was I thinking." But Tristan, smiling smugly, does not continue her line of thought, and Katarina watches all of this with keen interest. When Marco took up with her in the first place, we all expected her to be something like one of Luca's artistic types, and when instead it seemed that they became very close friends, it was a bit mystifying, but also made perfect sense. Marco has never made an enemy, that I can tell. I am careful not to look at Serafina too much; her refusal of my duel last night was well-founded, and I am ashamed of myself, both for that and for my actions before that. Her refusal of my duel has made me respect her, the way I ought to have all along.

"I owe you all so much," Marco says.

"Don't thank us yet," Ottavia says, giggling.

"Hush, we will drill you within an inch of your life and you will win at least one duel," Dora says. "Plus, we will have insider knowledge, for Katarina is sure to have fought at least some of them."

"And without spark!" Ottavia says, then claps her hand over her mouth, turning pink. Katarina laughs.

"And without spark," she says, somehow both agreeable and challenging at the same time. No wonder she is the only one to have ever held Marco's interest. "It makes me sneeze."

"Pardon?" Sterling has been quiet until now, but that draws them out. "People's spark makes you *sneeze*?"

"It does, which makes for exceedingly awkward sessions with the apothecary after a night of drinking and fighting." She laughs, and we with her. She might lack spark, but she's practiced to govern an audience, and when I remember that, I think that I would do well not to entirely trust her. I think that I may have had this thought before, it's hard to say.

"Well then perhaps we will give Ottavia over to your capable hands," Dora says thoughtfully, tapping her fan on her chin. "For we have done all we can with her." Ottavia's eyes widen; surely she didn't think her self-deprecation would result in being excused?

"I simply meant—"

"You have nothing to worry about, I'll be gentle," Katarina says, and the edge in her grin makes all of us laugh.

"You have everything to worry about, when she says she'll be gentle," Marco says. "Her idea of gentleness and—" Were she a lady of the city,

Katarina would have a fan to swat him with, and must make do with her open hand instead.

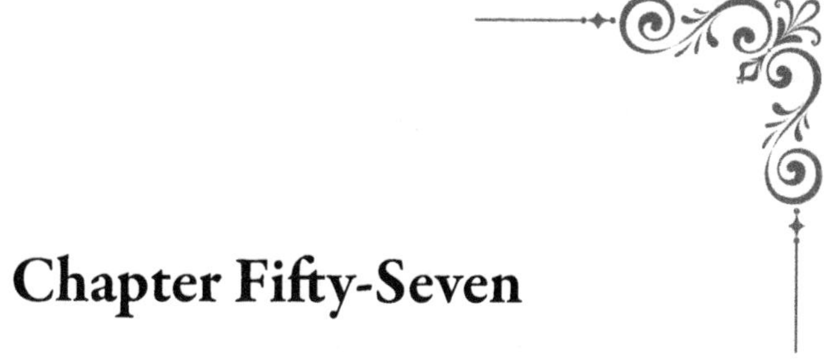

Chapter Fifty-Seven

Serafina of House Galeazzo

It is strange, being something like a guest in my own house. After we have met, we run through some practice, but nothing that requires too much exertion, and then adjourn to one of the sitting rooms. We're invited to refresh ourselves in various rooms before that; I slip off to my rooms, which feels surreptitious, like sneaking, but how can I be sneaking, in my own house? Except that, perhaps, it is my house no longer.

The apparition of my mother does not present herself, though, and I reach my rooms unchallenged. Agnes is there, as I hoped that she might be.

"My lady!" she says, and rushes across the room to me, stopping just short of embracing me and flushing pink when she remembers herself.

"Agnes, I have missed you," I say. What will become of her, I wonder? Will she be sent to House Valier with me? Will she seek employment at another house?

"We didn't know what became of you at first, I was so worried, and then—" here she stops herself again, hands knotted in her skirts. She is so desperately close to overstepping, though I would never think to punish her for such a thing, she fears my mother would know. My mother always seems to know. "I've been instructed to pack your belongings," she says finally.

"I won't be marrying until after my brother is free," I say. Which means if we lose, I will not marry. We cannot lose, for what would happen then? But we cannot win, for that means I am then duty bound to marry Lorenzo, and that is not something either of us wants. Oh. Oh dear. But I cannot say these things to Agnes; I'm not certain that I can say these things to *anybody*.

I sink into my little wooden chair and gather myself a moment. I am dry-eyed, I am not about to burst into tears, but I feel a certain teetering panic that is testing its teeth on me. I could simply run away. That would trouble my parents less than when Marco did, and now they have him back. I could ask Marco what it is like, outside the city. In other cities. But no, he would never let me go either.

"My lady?" Agnes ventures carefully.

"I am quite exhausted from everything going on," I say, managing a smile. "Thank you, for everything you have always done for me. I take it my mother is not sending you to House Valier as well?"

"No, my lady, I will be attending Lady Katarina."

More's the pity for both of you, I think, but maintain my smile. "She will benefit well from your care."

"Thank you, my lady," Agnes says. She seems dubious, but aren't we all. "I should tell you, Lord Marco retrieved his articles of clothing that you borrowed."

I give a surprised laugh; I'm not entirely sure why I find that comical, but I do. "I must remember to thank him for the loan," I say. It is sheer luck that it was my own jacket ruined by my misadventure, and that my mother had not thrown one of Marco's at me. Would that the laurels on my jacket have meant more protection for me from fools. "I will be missed," I say, standing again.

I glance in my mirror for the first time since my dreadful wounding, and perhaps for the last time. I look serene; cool and collected. There are items I've been doing without, like handkerchiefs and dueling gloves, and I slip a pair of gloves into one pocket and two handkerchiefs in the other. I haven't had any of my jewelry either, and I take a moment to select a necklace at least, just a small pearled pendant on a stiff golden collar, before leaving for the smaller dining room, where we hold intimate gatherings, not the large hall where we host societal affairs.

I am not the last to be seated, though my intended place is clearly next to Lorenzo. To take another's place would mean sitting near my mother, and I shy away from that option. Lorenzo surprises me by standing when I approach, and pulling my chair out, and I am practiced enough in my etiquette that I smile at him and take my seat, rather than embarrassing myself further by hesitating or acting startled. What is etiquette, after all, but drilling in how to act without too much thought, other than when thought is required.

There is wine and water in front of each of us, the reds that Dora brought perhaps, and I sip mine gratefully. It is sweet and dry, and perhaps goes down too easily, and I set my glass down firmly. Another manner in which I might make a fool of myself, if I am not careful.

"I trust everything went well," my mother says, once the first course of soup has been brought out.

"The circle has agreed to face the Golden Company," Lorenzo says.

"We are very grateful," Marco says, and Lorenzo waves a hand.

"You would do the same for any one of us, it would shame us to do otherwise." Ottavia looks very slightly dubious, but Sterling has their hand on her wrist, and no doubts are voiced.

"Very well. I will send word to the Golden Company, and a date will be set, and terms. There may be negotiations on that; it has been some time since this type of challenge has been had, and it is possible that the rulebook must be consulted."

"What an event that would be," Dora says, freeing the rest of us to act out our astonishment. The rulebook is not often consulted. It is in the care of the city guard, as an organized third party, who neither duel nor regulate our dueling.

"It would indeed," my father says, pleased that there are such interesting goings on for once. It is no wonder that he and others turn to organized hunts outside the city; the duels of their echelon are organized and dispassionate, removed from the fraught theatrics that our tournament was so recently, and from the sordid sort of drama that we are a part of now thanks to my brother.

"Would we be permitted to attend?" Ottavia asks, wide-eyed. I cannot tell if she is excited or frightened, though I don't know if I have seen anybody in this room frightened. Only myself. Is it possible that others are afraid as often as I am, or has their spark tempered that out of them? I try to imagine my mother afraid as I have been and almost laugh out of turn. At my side, Lorenzo shifts slightly; I must have made some small noise. I pick up my wine again.

"As members of society, yes, but also as duelists who this would directly affect as well. Indeed, you would be compelled to attend," my mother says, her eyes resting on me for a moment, though I could not say why. Perhaps noting my adornment, realizing that I'd taken the time to go to my rooms and perhaps speak to my maid. My former maid.

"This is all so dreadful but also fascinating," Ottavia says. She smiles appealingly at my mother. "I have given such poor showings in duels, Katarina is the one to school me next, we've decided."

"Oh indeed," my mother says, arching a brow. Ottavia's near-deliberate ineptitude has not gone unnoticed, then. "Perhaps that approach will bear fruit. I am given to understand that Katarina has quite a lot of raw skill."

"I'm possessed of years of training and experience," Katarina says stiffly, defensively, and I have no means to tell her that what my mother means by raw is without spark. She must realize, I think, looking at Marco in appeal. Our mother is and is not insulting her; to speak so well of her at all is to elevate her above mere curiosity, indentured actor in one of our many theater companies, far below our station.

"It will be a boon to have Katarina in this contest, but also in the next tournament," Marco says. "She is quite formidable, despite her rawness." Katarina frowns a bit, head canted to him, but I think then she catches his meaning, or at least catches herself, and desists from trying to antagonize our mother.

The next course is brought out, small bites, and I think that this process will be even more agonizing if I *do* remain cautiously sober. The Golden Company was not Katarina's former indenture, and yet she is able to give a fair accounting of many of the members' skills, and speculate upon who will be chosen in order to face us. We assume that the contest will take the same form of the tournament, in rounds with duelists eliminated, but we will not be confident of further details until the terms are set.

We are all well-schooled in talking about nothing, which we must resort to presently enough, as we will know no answers to our questions until events progress. Word has already been sent that we will duel the company, and while so much of our society operates late into the night, no further decisions will happen now.

I am on perhaps my third cup of wine when Dora peers down the table and says "Fina, would you mind terribly taking a moment to show me that book we were talking about?"

"Oh of course," I say, standing, stumbling a little as I do so. I really must devise a way to increase my tolerances; nobody else is troubled by that amount of wine. Lorenzo reaches up as if by reflex to steady me, or prevent me from falling upon him, without breaking in his conversation with Luca. I murmur some thanks, but it isn't until Dora and I are free of the room and into the hallway before I realize that I am clear-headed once again.

Chapter Fifty-Eight

Lorenzo of House Valier

The tension in the room is hard to bear, and we all are doing our part with the etiquette game, but I am very glad when Dora and Serafina leave on a pretense. Their exit is noted, of course, but I'm not certain that anybody notices that I sober Serafina up before she steps away from the table. She is so desperately unhappy, that is plain, and there is much that remains undecided. Seated on my other side, Marco looks for a moment as though he might follow her out, but Tristan and Katarina are deeply embroiled in some conversation and he does not seem to want to leave his bride unsupervised.

Across the table from me, Luca sets down his wine and says "I know you're planning our practices already."

"Of course," I say. "To do otherwise would be foolish."

"But to plan too much without knowing the terms would be equally foolish," Armand says.

"Agreed, though also there are only so many conditions that we might plan for, even knowing the terms." We would none of us don armor, for instance. Or there are certain vials we might drink during practice, but those things are not typically allowed for within the terms of a duel. Just spark and skill and serendipity.

"Just need to account for a level practice floor and hope everybody's hands are steady," Luca says, and Tristan seems to catch that much and glares at him.

"If you are referring to—"

Luca waves a hand, though. "I am not, actually, what I was referring to is the only tournament death we've ever heard of. Your messy duel was in recent enough memory that I wasn't going to bring it up for *jest*, Tristan, honestly, you ought to know me better than that." He is incredulous but relaxed; we are not in public, he is not going to take it fully as an insult. I do see Katarina notes this with interested eyes; I wonder what she thought of us, before now. If she thought we were always fighting at the littlest slight, how much of it she thought was for show. If she assumed every dinner might be life or death, regardless of company. Marco would not have let her think that, though.

Tristan takes a moment, sips her wine. "I allow, I might be a bit sensitive still," she says. Not an apology, but Luca had not asked for one.

"We are all a bit more tense just now than we are accustomed to being," Ottavia says. Normally, Teodora is the one who would try to clear the air, so I do appreciate her effort.

"Just so," Tristan says, and she and Luca clink their refilled wine cups together in truce. Lady Galeazzo watches all of this with detached interest; she does not seem bothered about where her daughter may have gone, but instead is drinking in her son, and his gestures as he engages with all of us. I did not used to give much thought to whether I found my friend's parents likable, that is not something that I often trouble myself with. But now, I find myself deeply disliking Lady Galeazzo, which does come as a surprise to me. It was not long ago that I wondered how I might have turned out, were she my mother instead of the one I was born to.

Sterling is about to say something, indeed perhaps even starts to speak, when the front bell is rung and all of our attention is captured. A servant comes in mere moments later, out of breath though they ran quietly enough that their shoes were not heard upon the floors, and then lean to speak in Lord Galeazzo's ear, as his end of the table is closest to that door. He listens, eyes locked with his wife's, then nods, removes the napkin from his lap, and stands. "A messenger from the Golden Company," he says. "I'll be but a moment."

"Of course," Lady Galeazzo says.

We are unable to return to our banter, though, and sit quietly, drinking our wine and picking at the leavings on our plates, and it is this tense, quiet, scene that Dora and Serafina return to.

"What's happened?" Dora asks, immediately sensing the change in mood. Serafina looks to her mother, who does not turn to her daughter.

"We have heard back from the Golden Company," Marco says.

"Oh indeed." Dora slips back into her seat and picks up her wine. She is excited by this, fraught as it is. Though, now that I've taken a moment to consider, I also am excited by this. We are so easily able to slip into the banality of fighting the same people with nearly no consequences, for what difference does a wound make if it can be immediately erased? What is it that we are striving for, what does expanding our personal power gain for us? In our parents' echelon, duels can be to the death. Not ours. Either must serve the city, somehow. The city keeps the score.

"What did—" Serafina starts, and her mother cuts her off with a gesture, as though Lady Galeazzo can hear her husband at the front door. Perhaps she can; I am not aware of the nuances of her talents. From the hurt look on Serafina's face, which is quickly replaced by a more neutral expression, she isn't aware either.

We sit in silence for a few more moments, even Ottavia having the sense to keep herself still, and Lord Galeazzo comes back. "We have been invited to the central hall of the guard in order to consult the rulebook with the owners of the Golden Company," he says. "I told the messenger that we would make our way there." He clearly could not imagine any of us objecting to that, and indeed, neither could I.

Lady Galeazzo stands. "There we have it. We shall go immediately." We all stand, and then Marco says,

"My lady mother, I'm not certain that Katarina and I may accompany you."

"The Guard accounted for that," Lord Galeazzo said. "You may." Looking at Katarina's face, I cannot tell if she is pleased by this or not. I would assume not; she will have to be in the presence of those masters she fled. I do not know what the life of indentured servitude is like for theater companies, she did not speak of it in our prior acquaintance. But also, presumably, nobody will be fighting tonight, we will be setting terms and then a date for our contests.

We filter out to our carriages and when Serafina hesitates, Dora links arms with her and pulls her to get into the carriage with me and Luca. "You don't mind, do you Renzo?"

"Of course not," I say. Lord and Lady Galeazzo again had not given their daughter another glance, though also with Marco and Katarina in their carriage, they would hardly have had room for another anyway. They could not have treated her like this all along? Surely I would have noticed, Teodora would have noticed, somebody would have commented. Or perhaps the fact that she was not taking part in society due to Marco's maneuverings had protected her for all that time.

I glance at Dora, but do not know if she's understood any of this. Serafina is looking shyly at Luca, who is regaling her with one of his stories of near-escape of...something. It may be a real account, or he may be fabricating it to distract her. It is possible that this competition with the Golden Company goes very wrong, and there is nothing that we can do, at the moment, to alter that. Other than Armand, we cannot see the future, and even then, his vision is imperfect, shifting, sometimes irrelevant.

Chapter Fifty-Nine

Serafina of House Galeazzo

I have never been to the hall of the guard before. I'm not sure any of us have, but I always must assume that everybody else's experience is broader than mine. Perhaps Katarina has been here before, but her swagger is unchanged wherever she goes. I wonder if maintaining the same posture lends her confidence when she is unsure; it must. Or perhaps she is simply never unsure.

The hall is beautiful, but I don't know what an ugly building would look like. Everything in this city is cut from the same cloth, or at least what I have seen is. Large, ostentatious, stately even if not fully maintained. Our ceilings are unreasonably high and painted by artists known and bygone, our sweeping staircases always carven, our walls adorned. The hall, while perhaps less ornate, is no less stately. I peer upwards at the ceiling, and a starry firmament shines down on me, like and not like the sky we were just underneath when we exited the carriages. Celestial creatures hover there, as though the sky is their sea and that is where they swim.

The parents of the other dueling circle members are here now as well, for while it is everybody's choice to enter into this contest, it is the obligation of their house to be aware and show support. Rarely have I seen Tristan's parents, who are even more distant than my own, or Armand's mother, who is a widow. I am unsure of the circumstances of her widowhood; I can only imagine it was a duel. Or rather, it would be foolish to assume otherwise.

The owners of the Golden Company are like my mother, burning brightly. There are other members there, presumably who know Katarina, and I cannot tell at a glance how much spark they are possessed of, if any. I'm not certain many members of the stage are, I think that perhaps other vocations tend to purchase those indentures, but also I'm told it's possible a person might kindle a spark at any time. How often that happens, I also do not know.

The leaders of the guard are here, in full regalia that I have only ever seen before in parades and festivals, perhaps once a year or so, and not all of them at once. The lit lanterns chase yellow shadows up the walls as we walk through the corridors, and I look at the carvings in the wood here, twisted faces, pleading hands. There is a jail here, in the basement, and despite my horror should I hear anything from there, I find myself straining my ears for any voices that are not ours. I don't hear any, though.

The book is the only thing in the room, on a round pedestal in the center. The ceiling goes up even higher, opening up into the main bell tower. It dizzies me to look up at it, and I feel foolish when Dora puts her hand on my arm to steady me. I am so worried about Marco, about this contest, that I cannot keep my thoughts on it, and the guard hall has captivated them instead.

"We are here tonight to set the terms of contest for the duel regarding the theft of property from the Golden Company," one of the guard captains says. "The defendants are Marco of House Galeazzo and Katarina of the Company of the Canted Stage, now also of House Galeazzo. The wounded parties are the Primo, Secunda, and August of The Golden Company, who lost the indenture of one Valentino of the Golden Company. Katarina, you say you slew him in a duel?"

"Yes," she says shortly, as though she means to angrily expound on why she did it and how she would again, but is stopping herself. "Marco of House Galeazzo was witness."

The guard nods and looks to the owners. "You are not satisfied?"

"We are not satisfied," one of them says.

"What will bring satisfaction?"

They glance briefly at Katarina, and then my mother, and then the rest of us. "It would seem that Katarina of Canted Stage has found much support. However, Valentino was one of our stars, and has similar support. We will have a contest like one of your tournaments, between her dueling circle and an equal number from our company, of similar abilities."

"Do you find that fair?" the guard asks my mother.

"I find it overly dramatic," she says with a sniff, and one of the company members in the back laughs. Katarina shifts in a way that suggests she, too, would like to laugh, and Marco gives her a nervous, sidelong look. "But yes, fair."

"Then we will set terms and time," the guard says. They turn to the Golden Company owners. "Which would you have?"

"Terms," they say. My mother nods, tight-lipped, and they cast their gaze over us gathered. "Random pairings, drawn from a hat day of. Spark used at will. Third blood." Ottavia makes a dismayed little noise, and Sterling puts their arm around her.

"A fortnight," my mother says, and I could almost scream. Why not sooner, rather than the agony of waiting. But she's thinking of practice time, and to make sure of Katarina's capabilities. Maybe even Ottavia's. The Golden Company owners nod at that.

"If House Galeazzo's dueling circle wins, then the matter is settled and nothing more will change hands. If the Golden Company's dueling circle wins, then a person will be surrendered to carry out the rest of the indenture. It will be held on neutral ground," the guard says. "As Katarina's indenture has already been paid, she is not an acceptable choice."

The Golden Company owner's mouth twists very slightly in distaste, frustration. They wanted Katarina, then. They glance over the rest of us, and then back to my mother. "You have another child," they say, and my stomach turns to ice. I become aware of every breath in the room. "If your dueling circle loses, then your daughter will serve out the rest of Valentino's indenture."

She cannot agree to this. She must agree to this. They cannot agree to give up anybody else's children. It can only be me. She doesn't even look at me, though my father does. "Agreed," my mother says, voice clear and cold as a silver bell.

I don't mean to make a noise, to give any sign; I mean to be as still and stoic as can be. But Dora takes my hand and squeezes it and thus I must have failed. My head is still ringing with my mother's answer and I think that it must be time for us to leave, we have all agreed, and if we do not leave soon then I will faint on the floor here and embarrass myself and my house.

But my mother and father, and everybody's parents, are exchanging bows and curtseys with the Company owners, and the other company members are eyeing us but also retreating, and an adjournment must have been called and I simply did not hear it, and then somebody, Luca, has taken my arm on the other side and he and Dora are guiding me out. I am not crying, I know I am not making any noise, but I am stiff and stunned.

We are almost outside when Marco, just behind us, asks "Is she alright?"

"I think some air will help," Dora says. "It's quite a shock."

"Nothing's *happened* yet," I say. "I will be fine in a moment."

"Of course," Dora says.

The night air is cool on my hot face, and I stumble on the stairs but am still supported on either side. I want to shake them off of me, I don't want to show this weakness, and at the same time, I am so grateful for them. There is a bench in the courtyard by the carriages, and I sink into it when we draw near. I sit a moment, a few moments, just breathing, really only aware of my breathing. I'm not crying, I haven't been crying. Gradually, I realize that the rest of the dueling circle has also come outside, and are all standing around me. Even Katarina. Even Lorenzo. How many shocks must I endure?

"I'm sorry," I say, and Ottavia shushes me.

"It's *dreadful*," she says indignantly.

"We haven't lost yet," Tristan says, and her thorniness is strangely comforting.

"Anyway, win or lose, nothing appreciably will happen," Dora says briskly. I stare at her. "If you are suddenly claimed for indenture, that indenture can then be paid off, that's how they *work*. Your mother just wants this over with and is furious that she can't fight them herself. She isn't actually risking you, that would be too humiliating for her. Like she would let you on a stage in that capacity. And you saw them, they wanted Katarina."

I would be good at it, I think, Marco joked that I would be so good on the stage. But my heart is a bird trapped in my throat and I can't speak at the moment.

"Renzo, we'll start practice tomorrow, of course?" In all honesty, Luca sounds eager to start tonight. I did not expect this sort of support from the dueling circle; even after our practices, and the tournament, I still thought of them as Marco's friends and not mine. I see now that I was wrong, but I do not know when they became mine.

"Of course," he says. He looks at me, hesitates, and then offers his arm, perhaps at some sign from Dora. "To the carriage?"

"Your parents..." I trail off, and he shrugs, his face a mask of boredom.

"We'll send it back for them. It seems as though they intend to spend quite a lot of time talking."

"Why are they talking, if we are the ones fighting?" I ask, and Katarina laughs.

"Likely because they are not the ones fighting. They are unwilling, unable to divest themselves of involvement." She looks longingly to the street, or perhaps rather the possibility of where the street might take her, and then she and Marco go to their carriage. I allow Lorenzo to lead me to House Valier's carriage, and hand me up into it. Luca follows along, and Lorenzo steps aside a moment to speak with him before joining me.

We ride in silence for much of it, and then Lorenzo says, "At least Ottavia seems genuinely motivated, this time."

Even a month ago, I would have burst into tears, but now am able to just give a hurt little laugh. "That is quite something, is it not? I had thought for certain she would give her wedding as an excuse." I'm for a moment shocked that I would say something so crude, and to Lorenzo. "I'm so sorry, that was—"

He sighs. "No, you are entirely correct. Ottavia's motivation has been sorely lacking, always. She would prefer to be a pretty adornment, like your music friends." I have no answer to this, so surprised am I that he even remembered my so-called music friends.

We sit in silence for the rest of the ride to his house.

Chapter Sixty

Lorenzo of House Valier

I am relieved that Serafina is not sniveling on the carriage ride home; it is enough that we are embroiled in this for Marco and thus Katarina's sake. I am not confident that I could handle it appropriately, though it is curious to me that I would now care. A week ago I did not. Three days ago.

At my house, I alight, and then turn to hand her out. "It's best for you to get your rest," I say, not unkindly. "Our practices before the tournament were somewhat rigorous, but the stakes were lower. We need to do more."

"Of course I understand," she says woodenly. It must be a shock, I think, to become aware of being a pawn in two different ways in the course of two days. That our parents want us to marry, and that Serafina is the forfeit, should we lose the contest of duels. I do think Dora is right, that Serafina's indenture would then immediately be purchased, but also that Lady Galeazzo makes it seem entirely possible that it would not be. Would it be a relief, for Serafina, to escape her mother in either capacity? A marriage that neither of us wants, or an indenture in a trade she has not practiced and among strangers?

Once inside, she departs for the guest room where she has been staying. I hesitate about going to my rooms right away; I should like to speak with my parents, but also need to find the words. I go to the practice room instead, undoing my coat, the top buttons of my shirt. Perhaps while there I can at least see how better to hone all our skills, though we will of course be practicing at House Galeazzo. The practice room there has mirrors along the entirety of one wall, and ours does not. That on its own is hardly likely to tip the balance in any way, but I'm sure is a significant reason for Serafina's poise in her form.

I pause; I am unaccustomed to paying her compliments, be it in my thoughts or out loud.

I have seen strange machines at market, practice dummies that had clockwork in them, so that they moved and were not just stationary targets. But also such things came at tremendous cost, and I presume the repairs would also be tremendous, if one were truly used in as rough a manner as true practice would require. Still, I am intrigued by the thought, the change in approach that such a thing would require, even just the allure of having such a curiosity. What else, to spend one's coins on, after every drink has been sampled, gloves have been bought, swords adorned?

Truly, I hope that Katarina can give us insight on our opponents. The Golden Company is not her former theater, but she would surely have fought some of them before, or seen them fight, while I'm not certain they would have seen any of us. Just her addition to our practices might be enough to raise some of us to the next level, a person with new habits and strategies, honed without the presence of spark. Just sheer force of will, and skill garnered from practice and experience. It's admirable, really. I have little concept of how the other classes live; I think few of us do.

I have an idea of where each of us is, both with regards to skill and determination. And I know that there is always a further level to reach; the question is how one gets there, and the answer is not always clear, or simple, other than to keep trying.

I've paced the length of the practice room thrice in my ruminations, and leave it no more satisfied. House Galeazzo's mirrors might help Ottavia, I think. Katarina might help all of us. To third blood, though? Those are punishing terms leading to a punishing conclusion. It's one thing to do amongst one's own dueling circle, another thing entirely for settling a grudge, legal or moral.

I leave the practice room, and my parents are coming in through the front door as I reach the main stairs. "You left so soon," my mother says, not quite disapproving, somewhat questioning.

"Serafina was quite upset," I say. "And Teodora thought it best to remove her."

"The poor dear," my mother says sympathetically.

"Surely she has confidence that you will win?" My father asks.

"I'm not certain that she does, no."

"Well then. After the tournament, she should know that she is in capable hands," my mother says. She looks up the stairs, as though she is deliberating whether her presence might comfort Serafina or be a bother.

"Perhaps if I'd won the tournament, yes."

"Nobody expected you to *win* the tournament," my father says, and then laughs at the shadow that crosses my face. "There were a number of people there that outmatched you or had the potential to, it is simply where you are on your journey. There is no shame in it."

"As you say," I reply stiffly.

"My boy, you must learn how to laugh at yourself, and then nobody else's japes may hurt you," he says, giving me a rough, one-armed embrace. "You all did very well in the tournament except when you did not, and that is how it is every time that swords are drawn. You give in to the fight and you learn from it for the next time."

"Yes, my lord father," I say. He is correct, of course, in many regards. Nobody indeed expected me to win the tournament, not least myself. And it is always valuable to remove the social weapons that others might have against me. "I'm not certain whether she would prefer to be alone, Mother," I say.

My mother smiles, perhaps a bit sheepishly. "And she would never tell me to go away," she says. "She is too sweet for her own good."

"She handles herself well," my father says, clearing his throat. "It's astounding how rapidly she's advanced since reentering society."

"Yes, killing a man will do that for you," my mother says briskly.

"Even before that," he says. He looks at me. "You'll tell us, if you need any help in your preparations?"

"Of course," I say, though I'm not sure what help they could provide. Coming to practice with us, I suppose; any of our parents doing that would be a help. I would be very surprised if Lady Galeazzo did not make herself available to us. I also think that would be to Serafina's detriment.

"Drill and drill, those theater people will not have the benefits of tutelage that all of you have." My mother kisses me on the cheek and squeezes my shoulder. "Do get some rest."

"Yes, Mother." I watch them go up the stairs before retiring to my rooms. My mother hesitates, but does not knock on Serafina's door.

Chapter Sixty-One

Serafina of House Galeazzo

I do not yet have a maid at House Valier; I'm sure were I to mention it, I would receive effusive apologies and a maid immediately, and the longer I let the situation go the more I shrink away from the thought of it. I'd rather just dress and undress myself, hang my own clothes. But drawing my own bath is not something I know the mechanism of, and though fresh linens have been brought to me, I do not know when or on what schedule.

This is not to say I haven't been brought a bath, I have. But there is something about not knowing when that will occur or how to ask that I find uncomfortable. I also assume this particular guest room will not be my permanent chamber, but even that is up in the air. Whether I am betrothed to Lorenzo, or if I am not. Whether we will actually marry. His immediate response mirrored my own, which was no. No that is impossible, we cannot. I do not expect my mother to have sympathy for that, but I did expect his to. Lady Valier has always seemed so nice, and understanding, and for them to conspire so grandly regarding our futures without consulting either of us is just astonishing.

I look out the window, into the lantern-lit streets. The lanterns stay on all night, in our parts of the city. My hand finds the window-latch and I undo it, swing it open almost without thinking. It would not be too hard, I think, to climb down. Where would I go, then? Nowhere, I have nowhere to go. And I cannot, right now; not with this tournament of duels that we've accepted. I have responsibility to lives other than my own. I am a strong member of the dueling circle, and they need me. They need me to win, but also they need me in case we lose.

If we lose, will the Golden Company take me immediately, as I stand? In the clothes I wear, with the blades I hold? It seems likely. How do they live, those indentured by the theaters? Do the theaters have rooms there? I have never had to think about it. I would prefer not to think about it. I look out the window again, at the drop to the cobbles below. Perhaps it is far enough. But no, we might win. Even if we lose, my indenture would immediately be bought, Dora said. She must be right.

I have never felt so much despair and do not know what to do. I pull the window closed again, firmly, and latch it. I turn around in the room that has been mine, and the bed does its best to beckon but sleep has rarely been further from my mind. Instead I leave it, and walk to the library. There is escape there, as I said to Lorenzo so long ago. Or was that just yesterday evening? The one before? I cannot imagine what possessed me to say such a thing to Lorenzo. But he gave no sign of derision, for once, did not insult me. Instead, it seemed as though he had never before considered wanting to escape.

It's late enough that I see no servants as I make my way through the halls. Or, I make enough noise that they avoid me. The city's servants are in general very good at making themselves invisible from the members of the house, and I'm certain they take comfort in that invisibility. I know that I would.

The library is dark this time of night, of course, but I light a lantern to take around with me. I'm not certain of what I am even looking for; I think that it is soothing to just be here among these hushed shelves, breathing in the leather and vanilla smells of the volumes, occasionally stroking a finger down a gilded spine. It is quiet enough that I can hear my own breathing, and nobody will ask anything of me in here, right now, and that is enough.

Of course, the specter of my mother's voice whispers harshly in my ears, tells me I am wasting my time, that I should seek out dueling manuals, recountings of prior tournaments, exercises to perform and increase my strengths. I do none of that, shivering even as I have the audacity to ignore her imagined words. The book that catches my eye and finally has me draw something from a shelf has a bold red binding, a satin ribbon trailing from its gilt-edged pages.

It is not a very thick book, and seems to be a single play, lavishly illustrated. I almost put it back again immediately; I do not exactly wish to be reminded of the stage just now. But it is book that feels nice in the hand,

and I go to one of the plush velvet chairs that are tucked here and there in the corners, setting my lantern on the nearby table, and begin to leaf through it. It is a love story, something else that I am not in the mood for, but despite everything about this book being what I am trying to avoid, I find myself immersed in it anyway. It is about two young ladies who do not like their families' plans for them, and cut their hair and dress as boys and go out to sea to have adventures.

A sea monster has surfaced near their vessel when a voice near me, too near me, says "What are you doing?" It is due to my mother's teachings that I freeze rather than startle, and am able to seem outwardly composed when I raise my eyes to Lorenzo.

"I couldn't sleep," I say. He also has not yet changed out of his dinner clothes. "I might ask you the same, though I suspect your answer." He frowns, looking at the book in my hands. "Have you read it?"

He'd been about to say something, I realize, but stops and regroups. "I haven't."

"I interrupted you, I apologize."

He's still frowning, and I at first think he might just walk away. Then, he says, "I've been thinking on the Ottavia problem and your mirrors just keep coming up in my mind."

"My...mirrors?" I cannot understand what he means.

"In the practice room."

"Oh, those mirrors." I feel myself flushing a bit. "It's because the practice room was also where I took my dance instruction, when I had a dance instructor." I don't afford him the time to ask. "My lady mother decided I was too wrapped up in that, and neglecting my sword studies."

"I see." He pauses, and do I see the ghost of a smile? "And were you?"

I laugh, too surprised to restrain it. "Almost certainly. Marco promised me I wouldn't have to worry about all this." I try not to sound too bitter; right now, I am relieved that my brother is home and safe, and despairing of my mother's treatment of me, and I think that I am a fool for ever expecting her to behave otherwise.

"Did he."

"Yes, and I suppose I should duel him for breaking that promise, but perhaps I'll wait until after this business with the Golden Company," I say, with a smile and an air of bravado that I do not quite feel but that suits the moment, and might be amusing.

"I would offer to be your second for such a duel," he says quietly, and I'm briefly stunned, that he would offer me such support, I remember that the seconds in a duel might fight if something happens to prevent satisfaction in the primary duel.

"You just want an excuse to fight Katarina," I say, trying to imagine, and implement, the teasing note Dora would use. I mark my place with the book's ribbon and close it.

"You've caught me." He picks up the lantern before I can, and follows me through the shelves. "You could just take that with you," he says, as I replace the book.

"I think I'd prefer to visit it here." The library indeed has had quite the calming effect on me, even with Lorenzo's sudden appearance. This might be the most relaxed, and confident, I have felt around Lorenzo since before Marco left.

I think for a moment he might ridicule me for the sentiment, though, and stop myself from trying to explain further. I owe him no explanations.

Instead, he says, "Shall I walk you to your room?" and I am grateful that he said nothing more about our supposed betrothal, or even much about our upcoming duels. I seemed to actually have his attention, and not in his most recent harsh way. I don't know what to make of it.

Chapter Sixty-Two

Lorenzo of House Valier

I had not expected to find Serafina in the library; I half expected it to be my lady mother, though I could not have anticipated what she would have been reading either. Serafina was unusually frank with me; it is almost as though her fretting and worries reached a certain fever pitch and she has come through the other side, her capacity for concern burned out like a match. It is probably just the day's exhaustion, and tomorrow she will be more like her accustomed self.

Though I am also mistaken, thinking of her shy, hesitant demeanor of late as her accustomed mien. Before Marco took his leave without a by your leave, she was sweet and blushing, but not so cringing. That thought gives me pause too, both mentally and in the middle of one of my house's empty halls. Do I truly think Serafina sweet, so comfortably as that? She isn't sour, at any rate, as Tristan so often is.

It is tempting, to go out, and instead I do finally return to my rooms. I unbutton my coat, rack my swords, and then drink a cup of wine. We will start practice tomorrow. We will bring Ottavia up to an acceptable level, hopefully, to the best of our abilities, in the next two weeks. Ultimately, I suppose, it is out of our hands. But practice fights and practicing sword drills do more than improve individual skills, they breed confidence, and sometimes that is more valuable than any lesson that can be given.

I think at first that I will not be able to sleep, but a heavy slumber overtakes me almost the moment I've touched my head to pillow. Indeed, I do not wake up the first time my manservant comes in, to straighten whatever wreckage I've made of my clothes and accoutrements. I awaken the second time, when he comes in with a pot of coffee and a covered plate of breakfast, and sets them clattering on a table.

"Is it early or late?" I ask, squinting at the sudden daylight as he moves about, throwing my curtains open.

"Middling, my lord," he says. "Your lady mother said not to wake you too early, nor too late, and thus I split the difference."

I accept a cup of the coffee and drink it sitting on the side of the bed with my eyes closed. "And how does my lady mother seem this morning?"

"Busy indeed, my lord. She was on her way out to the carriage when she spoke to me."

I open my eyes at that. "And where was my lady mother going?"

"She did not tell me, my lord."

"No, I suppose she wouldn't." House Galeazzo, perhaps, but perhaps not. My parents have their own concerns, after all, beyond what has transpired due to Marco. I presume their concerns are to scale for their echelon's abilities. "Do you know if Lady Serafina is already up and about?"

"She is, my lord." He gives me a curious look, poorly masked, and I do wonder what the servants have said amongst themselves. It must all seem quite lurid to them, and maybe it is. My long friendship with her brother, and my behavior in his absence. Her appearing in the middle of the night, bloody and nearly dead. My ministrations. Her staying, despite her mother showing up in the manner that Lady Galeazzo always presents herself. Our unwanted engagement, not announced, but surely the servants know. They always know so much.

"Has she already had breakfast? Somebody ought to have awakened me." He gives no reply, to either. How would he know, if she has had breakfast? And I left no instructions to awaken me. He lays out my clothes as I wash up, and I drink another cup of coffee as I dress. I both do not know why I feel in a rush, and am acutely aware of how little time we have.

When I descend the stair, two of the maids are passing by, and they look at me and then exchange a significant glance before continuing on. Irritated, I almost call them angrily back to explain themselves, and then I hear a carriage being brought around out front, and continue out the doors instead.

Serafina is waiting there in practice clothes, watching the carriage but also glancing over her shoulder, and actually looks relieved when I appear.

I am not sure that I have ever seen relief on her face when I appeared, not even the night she came here after her misadventure.

"I assumed you would be coming down and so when they offered to bring the carriage..." she says.

"Yes, you were correct. I did not mean to sleep so late."

"I did not mean to rise so early," she says, smiling but abashed.

The carriage-driver is deliberately not looking at us, but I see his mustaches twitch in a smile, and I'm starting to suspect that the staff has made assumptions about Serafina and my association that are simply not true.

In the carriage, we do away with the necessity for stilted, false conversation. She gazes out her window, and I mine.

My mother's carriage is not at House Galeazzo when we arrive, and that is something of a relief. I get out of the carriage, remember just a moment too late that I ought to hand Serafina out. She did not wait for my assistance, though, and has alighted under her own power. I am unused to traveling with any of the ladies in the dueling circle, and have fallen out of that solicitous habit.

Tristan is already here, and Armand, speaking to Marco and Katarina. Armand says, "I thought to ask Iulio but didn't want to impose. Or to make Ottavia think that she is unwelcome."

"They won't let us switch out members now, I wouldn't think," Marco says.

"Perhaps if there were more copies of the book than the one that lies in state," I say, irritated again for no good reason, or for every good reason. They probably would not, in fact, let us switch out Ottavia at this point. She probably also would feel very wounded were we to suggest such a thing. It is interesting that Iulio and Armand have been keeping company again; I wonder how long it will last this time. I wonder if he knows already. "Regardless, we have two weeks in which to give Ottavia our undivided attention."

"Oh I do so love when I am the center of attention," Ottavia says, shedding her coat as she and Sterling come in. "Other than for this specific set of circumstances, of course."

"Of course," Tristan says. "You thought you'd retire early, and yet here we are."

"Perhaps this is what will make my legend," Ottavia says dramatically, then glances at Katarina. "Was that too much?"

"A bit," Katarina says, with a ghost of a smile. "But we are not here for theater lessons, after all. And teaching you stage combat would not be helpful."

"Not if they all already know it," Ottavia says. "Honestly, if you just spend all of your time fighting, how does anybody learn their lines?"

"Some people have more hours in the day than others," Katarina says cryptically, and that is when Luca and Dora arrive.

"This is starting to get suspicious," Tristan says in a teasing voice, and Dora laughs.

"I assure you it is anything but. No offense, Luca."

"None taken, Teodora," he says. "You are far too grounded for my tastes."

"Oh perhaps *now* I'm offended." She snaps her fan open, hiding her smile. "We all know it doesn't need to *mean* anything."

My eyes go briefly to Tristan, at the same time she looks at me. Surely somebody will mark that.

"Well to clear the air, Luca and Teodora can fight each other first, and I'll fight Ottavia and the rest of you can settle out how you'd like. Katarina, though, if you will...Ottavia perhaps needs the most improvement of those of us gathered."

"I understand," Katarina says, even as Ottavia makes a show of pouting.

"It isn't as though I'm *hopeless*," she protests.

"You indeed said you were exactly that just before our last tournament," I say. "Truly, I am not trying to be unkind for the sake of it, for if I was, this conversation would be far worse in tone."

"I know."

I remember, now, the day that Ottavia said she was hopeless is the day I threw Serafina against a wall and she slapped me. I cannot possibly apologize for that now, and at the time I thought that I was utterly correct. Somehow.

Chapter Sixty-Three

Serafina of House Galeazzo

The first time I saw Katarina on the stage, Marco brought me to the theater on a night our parents had concerns elsewhere, as they so often do. His dueling circle was a lower echelon then, and they were expected at fewer events. Our family had just renewed our box at the Company of the Canted Stage, at Marco's urging. My mother was inclined to let it lapse; she is not often a theater goer herself, any longer, though did quite a lot in her younger years, or when she was with child and desperate for diversion. There is a point at which nobody with honor will duel a pregnant woman, after all, regardless of terms.

Katarina's role was the second in command of a group of bandits in a forest, and at one point in the play, her character killed a nobleman's son while robbing his carriage. There were other deaths in the play, many of them, but I remember that moment starkly, I was just so shocked by it. The nobleman's son was out in his carriage with a girl that he was not allowed to be wooing, and was hesitating to hand over her jewelry, and Katarina's character ran him through and took the jewelry anyway. I do not know how they do it, make combat on the stage look like real swordplay. Especially not to an entire society who is consumed with swordplay.

But Katarina is one of the best duelists among us, even without her spark. She is *very* fast, even without her spark, as I discover the first time I fight her. She comes on exceedingly strong and with very showy blows, trying always to keep her opponent on their back foot. I try desperately to keep up with her from my own skill, and when I cannot, I use my spark for speed and she still gets her final touch on me before standing back to sneeze, muffling it with the back of her gloved wrist. After, we bow to each other and put our swords away.

Out of breath, I pull out a handkerchief and mop at my brow. "I'm very sorry," I say. "I knew I was losing, I should have just—"

"No, no, you apologize far too much." She gestures vigorously, and of course Lorenzo is nearby and from the corner of my eye I see him taking notice. Probably *everybody* is. But Katarina is a commanding presence.

"I beg your pardon?" She raises her eyebrows at me and I try again. "I don't understand what you mean."

"Other than what you've just done out loud, you're apologizing the entire time you're fighting." I stare at her and she draws her longer sword again, and then her posture becomes mine, what I've seen in these very practice room mirror time and time again. "You have a failure to commit, when you brandish your weapon, it's apologetically. So sorry, we seem to be fighting with swords here, isn't this a bother, I do hope that it's not an imposition should I land a hit." She doesn't mimic my voice, and for that I am grateful, I am quite abashed enough. "Now, draw your swords." I do. "Now, stand like me instead." She becomes herself again and I look at her, and then look at us in the mirror, side by side. I wish to look at the other's faces, see how they are reacting, and I force myself to concentrate instead. I've copied people's voices before, but this seems so much harder. "Almost. Stand up straighter, lift your chin just a bit...yes, there. That. Carry yourself like that."

"It feels strange." And it does; I can feel a number of tiny differences in which muscles are flexing or stretching, based on those changes.

"It will." Everything is quiet for a moment.

"Now give Ottavia the same treatment," Tristan says, and Katarina gives me a crooked grin before turning away.

"I am only one woman," she says. "But I will try my best."

"I'm not *nearly* as good as Serafina," Ottavia says, either a lie or a compliment, I'm genuinely not sure which. She must be of a certain level, else the dueling circle could not have reached this echelon. But also I've spent so much time under my mother's heavy criticism and without praise, that I'm unable to think of my swordwork as 'good.' Perhaps it is. Perhaps both are true. I won tournament duels and she did not. Dora did not either, though, and she is definitely also good.

"Surely you must have heard the lesson I just gave about being apologetic while swinging one's sword at somebody?" Katarina asks, cutting but in jest. "You have been so insulated by your society that you are unaware of what you look like."

I expect Ottavia, or anybody, to bridle at that. Instead, she says, "Of course, of course," hastening to stand next to me and also adjust her posture. "Better?"

"Your wrists are atrocious," Katarina says, in a disarmingly affable tone. "But otherwise, yes. Now can the two of you fight like that? Serafina, shoulders back."

We duel, and adjust, and duel, and the rest of the room falls away for a time. I've spent so much time in this practice room, and other than learning my basic forms when I was small, I'm not certain I've had such a productive session in a very long time. My newly-corrected posture feels odd at first, awkward, but as the morning progresses and I settle into it, I find myself thinking that it feels comfortable, and that the more I use it, the more assured I am as well. Some strikes and approaches make natural sense now,when previously they could not.

It's when Dora gently touches me on the elbow and offers me one of the little vials that we take when we advance that I realize how hot I am is not from the exertion. "Thank you," I say, out of breath. I feel so very alert and as though I am waking from a deep sleep at the same time. I've just finished fighting Luca, and though I did not win, I made him put forth more effort than he has had to before. We were matched on two touches for some time.

"Fina, I'm wildly jealous that Katarina did for you in three minutes what I could not in these last months," she says, catching me up in an embrace.

"I'm not certain you *could* have done that for me any time before now," I say, mindful of the glass vial in my hand. She releases me, and I pull the little stopper and down the liquid. It's bitter and it's sweet and I could not say for certain what color I thought it was, even though the glass is clear.

Ottavia is also downing a vial, with Sterling hovering nearby. Poor Katarina is sneezing again and Marco is trying to get her to take a handkerchief, frowning a little more than is necessary, I think, over the situation. Armand is also watching Katarina, but with a look on his face that makes me think he isn't really seeing her. Or, he is not really seeing her here and now, but rather a future possibility to do with her.

Tristan and Lorenzo are the only ones who are, at the moment, still in the midst of a practice duel. He seems, to my eye, to be going easy on her, and I wonder why. Then I realize that it's making her cocky, cockier, and she is overreaching. She commits to a long, lunging thrust that Lorenzo is just out of reach of, but when he tries to get what I assume is his final touch in, she tucks and rolls beneath his strike with surprising speed, even beyond what we typically see of one another, and she comes up inside of his arms and touches him just under the chin.

They remain like that for a bare moment, looking into each other's eyes, and I wonder what they see there. Then they break and step back, bowing, before sheathing their swords.

"That's a new trick," Dora says.

"It was very clever," I say.

"Clearly inspired by my backflip," Luca says. He's had the time to collect one of the open wine bottles and has the stems of three glasses threaded through his fingers, which he offers to Dora and I. We each take one, and he pours for us. Tristan and Lorenzo are still standing somewhat close to each other, talking. His back is to us, but I can see his face in the mirror, and I wonder why I am even looking. I have never seen him be as harsh with Tristan, or anybody, as he has been with me.

"Clearly," Dora says, then she raises her voice a bit. "Marco, do you know when we'll be fed? I'm absolutely famished.

"Soon, I imagine," he says, as a servant is coming through the door and stops to find us all looking at him.

"Lady Galeazzo invites the circle to luncheon," he says with a slight stammer as he recovers. I don't recognize him, he must be very new.

"As if summoned," Armand says, and the servant bows at him, confused, and backs out of the room again.

"Come now, Armand," Marco says. Katarina has finally accepted his handkerchief but tucks it away in a pocket as we retrieve our coats and settle our hair in the mirror, and finish off glasses of wine, before filing out.

Chapter Sixty-Four

Lorenzo of House Valier

I am very surprised both by how Tristan finishes our duel but also how, once we have done, she steps close again. "What are you going to do about Serafina?"

"I'm certain I don't know what you mean," I say.

"Well once we beat that theater trash, you'll be betrothed." She is not sneering, quite, but is implying a sneer.

"Neither of us wants that." I lean in to her slightly. "And if you wanted to discuss this, now is neither the time nor the place. I'm surprised at you, Tristan."

"The thought struck me," she says, and across the room, Dora asks Marco some question just as the door opens and a servant announces luncheon.

Tristan departs from me without a backwards glance, stealing Luca's wineglass from his hand and draining the remaining contents, and I can only shrug. Never before the tournament had she pursued any sort of partnering with me, and never since. I'd assumed she needed reassurance after the trauma of her wound, and that it was a combination of that and the wine. Perhaps it had been more, and I just didn't see it, and now she is concerned she waited too long. She needn't concern herself; I don't have an interest in anything serious with Tristan. I think what it comes down to is that, despite her disdain for the theater company people, Tristan does indeed love drama.

Lady Galeazzo is at the head of the table when we sit, probably no surprise. Serafina's posture immediately begins to close in on itself and then I watch her self correct. She still has color high in her cheeks from her advancement moments ago, and perhaps she's also thinking of her advancement the night of the duel that brought her to my doorstep, and she takes her seat to the lady's right. I sit across from her, as seems correct for our assigned relationship, and everybody else finds their places.

"Thank you so very much for hosting us, Lady Galeazzo," Dora says, as a servant comes through pouring the wine.

I'm not certain what Lady Galeazzo had intended to open with, but Dora surprises her into a smile. "You're very welcome, of course. I hope you find our practice space adequate."

"It's a *dream*, Lady Galeazzo," Ottavia says. She is also still a bit pink in the face from advancement, and I think there may have been some nudging under the table to prompt her. "The mirrors are so helpful!"

I look at Serafina right as she looks at me. Startled, she drops her gaze again and picks up her wine glass. I see Lady Galeazzo take note, even as she says, "Yes, they are quite helpful, aren't they? I hadn't considered that we might start a trend."

"I know I would be more inclined to practice if I'd had mirrors all along," Ottavia giggles, and then the first course is brought out, some sort of cold soup with a flower floating in the center of each bowl. I trust Lady Galeazzo to have the good sense to not weigh us down with a long and heavy meal, but also it is not my place to even ask. We are here at her pleasure.

"I'm not certain that is the case," Sterling says, looking at Ottavia fondly.

"We shall see, then won't we," Ottavia says, pouting prettily.

"Perhaps I'll get some for you as a wedding present," Lady Galeazzo says, and Ottavia flushes more deeply.

"That would be an honor," she says. Of course while *we* all expect her to recuse herself from dueling once she and Sterling are married, anybody outside of our circle would hardly expect that. Especially not somebody so advanced as Lady Galeazzo. I find myself wondering what *her* parents were like; rarely have I occasioned to visit the archives of dueling records, also kept at the Guard, but it would be a surprise if my mother didn't know. I have dim memories of my own grandparents, but each of them was lost in turn to illness that an apothecary or witch could not help, or to a duel, in the case of my father's father.

After the soup course is a salad one, and then some manner of airy mousse, and then an iced and fruited dessert. The wine flows freely, but of course there is the expectation of after meal naps, while the middle of the day is the hottest, and then in the evening more practice before dinner.

I don't know how long we can sustain all day practices like this leading up to this competition, but it seems more than reasonable to start this way. Perhaps three days on and then I will give them a break.

When all is cleared away and we are standing up from the table, I turn and bow to Lady Galeazzo. "Thank you, again, for your hospitality," I say, and from the corner of my eye, can see other bows and curtseys around the table.

"You are of course welcome," she says again, and even has some slight warmth to it.

"We don't want to presume too much upon your hospitality, though, and I do think for dinner we will venture out into the city. Marco and Katarina might do that if appropriately chaperoned, yes?"

"Yes," she says, raking us all over with her glance. "Between you and Teodora, I believe that is fulfilled."

"You wound me," Luca says, clownishly clutching his heart, and she regards him with some measure of astonishment. Trying to jest with Lady Galeazzo is a bold move, even for Luca.

"Perhaps better a spiritual wounding than one with steel," she says coolly, and departs from us.

"I do think that she is growing fond of me," Luca says. "That was very nearly a joke."

"You are a fool," Marco says, but he's smiling, and gives Luca a playful punch in the shoulder. Serafina is smiling as well, until she notices me glance her way and rearranges her features to be more neutral.

"You would do well to avoid a duel with my mother," she says

"You do not think she would be kind to me?" Luca asks, not quite grasping Serafina's tone.

"I know she would not be," Serafina says. "And it would not serve you well if she was."

"Spoken like your mother's daughter," Luca says, still jesting, and Serafina summons a smile that even I can tell is forced.

"Who else would I be?" she asks, and then Tristan yawns loudly, rudely.

"I'm so sorry," she says, in an elaborate tone. "It's just after such a meal, a nap must immediately follow."

"Of course," Marco says. "We all know where the rooms are, yes?"

"I think that we do by now," Dora says, even as Serafina hesitates.

"I believe your rooms are unchanged as yet," Katarina says to her, surprising me. But she had not been partaking in the banter, she had been watching and listening, taking it all in. She would of course realize that Serafina was no longer of this house but also not of mine yet, and unsure of her place in either.

"Thank you," Serafina says. "I had not heard otherwise, but there has just been so much happening it is impossible for every consideration to be handled."

"Of course," Katarina says. She must be aware of Marco's fondness for his sister, and want to emulate that. It is a surprise to me that I am following their conversation so closely, for what do I care, which room Serafina naps in, in her own house? What do I care, what she is told about it? But in spite of myself, I have taken note, even as Armand jostles my arm as if by accident and raises an eyebrow at me significantly.

"Why are we still standing around?" I ask. "Unless we want to decide where dinner will be now, and save time after practice?"

"Are we really going to go out, after being sweaty all day?" Tristan asks.

"We did after the tournament, too," Dora says. "Why would it bother you now?"

"You'll have time to wash up," I say. "How could I keep you from that?"

Teodora answers, interrupting as Tristan opens her mouth. "She just wants to complain."

"I do not," Tristan says. She seems more baffled than offended.

"You *do*, and while that is perfectly fine and normal, we are not going to make House Galeazzo feed the lot of us every meal here, and I'm certain we also ought not descend on House Valier unannounced, and with Marco and Katarina's limitations right now, going to a nearby pub or restaurant will keep them within the confines of the Guard's expectations and nobody will be in further trouble."

"I couldn't have explained it better myself," I say, and Dora smiles and unfolds her fan.

"You can't be expected to explain every last detail," she says, and Tristan smirks.

"I think that you might desperately need your nap as well, Teodora, if you're being so sharpish."

"I think that I might," Dora agrees serenely.

In the hall, everybody disperses fairly quickly, and Armand and I walk together towards the guest rooms. "Is everything well with you, Armand?"

"With myself, yes, I do think so. With Katarina I have a strange feeling, a thread that has been pulled out of the weave, but I have no more than a feeling just yet."

"Is there something the matter, or is just because you don't know her well?" I ask.

"I cannot say," Armand says with a shrug, and a troubled brow. "Nothing the matter today or tonight, certainly. Maybe nothing terrible, even. Just of note, or perhaps changed. I will think on it more, of course, but I wanted to mark it to you."

"Of course," I say, for even though I do not entirely understand, I am grateful for the observance. If I do not know to be wary of something, then I cannot be. "What of Teodora and Tristan just now, any insight?"

"Territory," he says, shrugging again.

"I'm not certain I understand."

"Tristan has a complicated heart," he says, and then goes into a guest room and shuts the door.

I'd thought for a long time that neither Tristan nor I wanted anything to do with each other's hearts. For that to change, now, is misfortunate timing.

Chapter Sixty-Five

Serafina of House Galeazzo

My rooms are unchanged but changed. My belongings have mostly been packed into trunks and sent to House Valier for me, but the furnishings are still the same. The curtains, the bedsheets, the mirror over the dresser. Do mirrors remember the faces that have looked into them, I wonder? Is it possible for them all to still be just beneath that silvery surface?

I give myself a little shake; certainly not, what a foolish thought. I lay my jewelry on the top of the dresser and put my swords and sword belts in the rack, hang my jacket. The bed is the same as well, of course, but I have not rested easily in it in some time. Now would not be any different. I am, physically, very tired. Emotionally nervous and my thoughts keep turning to the ever-burning question: what if we lose?

A tap at my door, and at my assent, Agnes creeps in. "I am so sorry to trouble you, my lady," she says.

"I hadn't thought I would see you!" I say. I am very glad to see her. "You have never been a trouble to me."

She struggles with herself a moment, and then says, carefully, "Lady Katarina does not share your generosity."

I sit on the edge of the bed. "Please, tell me."

"She...my lady is unfamiliar with having a lady's maid, and does not see the purpose. She is quite irritated by my presence, and I would happily leave her to her own devices, but for your lady mother, who instructed me to attend to her."

"Both are quite fearsome," I say in sympathy. I would not like to go against my mother in this matter, certainly. "I could try to speak with Katarina, though I'm not certain what change I might effect."

"My lady, I could not ask that of you," she says, her hands knotting together, casting her glance down and away. She lowers her voice further. "And I do think that Lady Katarina might have her reasons, other than unfamiliarity."

"Oh indeed?" I feel a slight thrill, as I am not somebody who is often gossiped with, or brought into confidence. "Do you think that it would help your cause, were I to know it? Before speaking with her?"

"Perhaps." Still she hesitates, and I am even more wildly curious, but do not wish to press her, lest she abandon the conversation. "I think she may be pregnant," she bursts out, in little more than a whisper.

"That would be a further reason to not want a lady's maid," I say, my thoughts awhirl. If Katarina is pregnant, does Marco know? Certainly not, he would not want her to risk herself dueling. Why *would* she, with such a ready excuse? "Very well, Agnes, I want you to know that it means a lot to me that you have trusted me with so close a secret."

"You don't need to—" she says anxiously, but I interrupt her.

"It will not come back to you, Agnes. Nobody will know that you told me this. It isn't even unusual that you came to see me, we have been very fond of each other." I stand, and I give her a quick embrace. "I'm sure you can busy yourself out of the view of both Katarina and also my lady mother, and I will make effort to speak with Katarina this evening. And if the worst comes to worst and my mother lets you go, I will entreat Lady Valier to take you on. I promise, you will be looked after."

"Yes, my lady," she says dubiously, and slips out again.

After that, I can hardly settle myself at all, much less enough to nap. I do try, but I toss and I turn and eventually I get up and settle my clothes again, comb my fingers through my hair and put it up again. I have a notion that Katarina, coming from a theater indenture, will hardly be in the habit of napping so much as we do. Which isn't to say she's used to any less physicality than our constant swordplay, but rather that those naps would not have been afforded to her.

I buckle my sword belts on and see if my suspicions are correct, though it takes me a few tries to find her. She is not one to sit in the garden, or in the library. No, she's back in the practice room.

I don't mean to sneak up on her, I'm simply accustomed to being quiet when I walk through the halls. But she has taken her jacket off and is doing some manner of drill with one of the dummies, and I do startle her when I come in, and she turns to me with a look of irritation before she rearranges her features.

"I'm sorry," I say. It is no matter to me whether she is wearing her jacket or not; I am not so familiar with her form to notice any slight changes an early pregnancy might have wrought. "I couldn't sleep."

"It's astounding, how many naps you all take," she says, sheathing her swords. "It's also astounding just how many hours you spend at sword practice. I didn't know that before, between the carousing and the parties, that you were so dedicated."

"I suppose you wouldn't have," I say carefully, for how *would* she know of our lives? In the theaters, beholden to curfew. "And in turn, I know very little of your life. I imagine it wasn't entirely consumed by rehearsal?"

"No, but enough of it certainly was. And tailoring costumes, and moving set pieces, and..." she trails off, smiling crookedly. "There are many separate worlds in this same city, I know that now, even if before I only suspected it."

"It's difficult to become aware of them," I say. "And I think it amuses the city to keep them separate."

"Yes, I do think it does," she says, picking up her jacket and shrugging into it. The way her shirt pulls, during those movements, allows me to give a little gasp, and say,

"Katarina, are you—"

She is on me immediately, close in my face, backing me up against the wall by the door. She isn't touching me, but she doesn't need to be. "Not a word," she says with a quiet, vigorous fury, her eyes flashing. "Not to your mother, not to your brother, not to your sainted Teodora, not a single soul. I am not so far along for it to matter one bit in what we are doing, and I will not be removed from these proceedings."

"I only think of—" I am more than a little shocked at her reaction.

"Think of *nothing*, for it is nothing yet. I will kill you where you stand, and you know very well that you stand no chance crossing sword with me." She stares into my eyes and I stare back, frozen. "Tell me you understand."

"I understand," I parrot back. She steps away immediately, and I can comfortably draw breath again. She has no spark, no command of it, but her physical presence cannot be reckoned with. Or I cannot reckon with it.

"I was so concerned, when my cousin took up with that fool, that she would get herself in this situation and ruin us. And now here I am." She gives a derisive little laugh. "Also living far above any station I ever dreamed. The turns life takes are inscrutable."

"They are," I say carefully, uncertain of her change in mood. "I am pleased for you, and also I will keep your secret. After all, we are sisters now, and sisters care for each other."

"I hadn't considered it like that," she says, something like wonderment in her face, as though I have disarmed her after all. "Thank you," she says after further pause, with what seems like genuine conviction.

Chapter Sixty-Six

Lorenzo of House Galeazzo

Afortnight is not enough time to prepare for a series of duels such as those we face, and also it is too much time, enough to risk becoming edgy and nervy. Some of us are already given to thorniness and bickering, and these stakes on that timeline do not help matters any, but we manage to train daily, we manage to not wound each other too deeply, in a physical sense anyway, and we arrive at the morning of the duels with the Golden Company.

It does not help that our theater opponents, by and large, are not of a level that would allow them to operate in our usual society, and thus we are unaware of each other's proclivities. There are popular stances and footwork and such that may never have reached them from us, and vice versa. I am extremely interested in these differences that we might find, and Katarina has been providing valuable insight, but of course it is impossible for her to know everything. Her shockingly good ability is also a bit of a worry; surely she cannot have been the only diamond in the rough.

But we are not fighting the owners, despite Lady Galeazzo very clearly wanting to, and they are the true powers there, the ones who are fully able to sit at society's tables. To her, they stole her son as surely as he stole their indentured property, and indeed, she feels her grievance stronger due to her place in society, and his. Though I suppose now Katarina is to be reckoned alongside.

After a breakfast that I eat and Serafina only silently picks at, eyes cast down, we ride a carriage to the theater. My parents are there waiting for us, everybody's parents are, and I wonder to what purpose they conspired to arrive early. The terms were already set, and could certainly not be altered by those not dueling. Not for lack of trying, I presume; Lady Galeazzo seems even more displeased than usual. Or perhaps that is just the demeanor of one who finds herself sharing a household with Katarina, who at a glance seems unbothered and perhaps even amused. She would be less amused were she to goad her mother-in-law into dueling her, but I suppose they are on a charted course towards that, all in due time. Perhaps Katarina would prefer that they duel already and get it over with. That seems to be her general demeanor, and while I have never fought Lady Galeazzo, I have fought Katarina, and she is breathtakingly formidable.

This round of duels is not open for spectators, properly, but many of the theater seats and boxes are full of members of the company, and families who hold tickets for those boxes. The duels were publicized, of course, as all manner of justice is, so their presence makes sense. I watch Serafina's face as she looks around and bites her lower lip briefly; she must have thought somehow that it would be a more private affair. Perhaps simply hoped that it would be.

We are ushered to the wings on one side of the stage, and across the expanse of the boards we can see the members of the Golden Company who we will be fighting on the other side. The stage lights are all burning bright, and Primo walks out into center stage, carrying a hat. They bow to those assembled, straight on first to the audience, left to their company, right to us.

"Though my impulse is, of course, to maintain the height of theatrics, those gathered are well aware of the tragic story that has brought us here today. Many of you were perhaps fans of our lost Valentino, and mourned his absence even as we now mourn his loss. We do hope that you find satisfaction with today's proceedings, as we do." There is scattered applause, and I look out into the theater. Past the lights, I do think that I can see all of our parents in the front row. Those damnable lights, they were a bother during the tournament too. An advantage that the Company people will have. "As you may well know, we have set the terms such that the opponents will be randomly drawn from this hat. The duels will be to third blood. Or yield," they amend, their tone elaborately solicitous, and there are scattered laughs. "And without further ado, if everybody is ready, we will draw our first fighters." They look from their people to us again, and the woman who seems to be something of a leader there nods, and I nod. "Secunda, if you will?"

She crosses the stage to him, and her footsteps make no sound of her passage. She curtseys deeply to the audience, but not to any of the rest of us, and reaches into the proffered hat with her face turned away. She draws one slip of paper, and the next, straightens them in her satin-gloved fingers, and then drops her eyes to them to read. "Luca of House Braggadin, and Felle of the Golden Company." Primo takes her hand, and they bow and curtsey to the audience in unison, and withdraw from the stage.

Luca drops Serafina's hand, which I hadn't noticed him holding, and hands me his coat. "Here we go," he says, tone serious but a twinkle in his eye. Felle is the woman who nodded, and strides straight-backed across the stage to meet Luca at the mark. They bow to each other, draw their swords, salute. She's smiling, just a little. I wonder what they think of us, these Company people. Spoiled rich brats who won't be so tough? Perhaps. Though it will be interesting to see how many of them are possessed of spark enough to use and how many are not.

It is rare that we duel to third blood, but all of us have done it, barring Serafina. The general convention is to maintain control and draw the blood lightly and wound inconspicuously. Not the face, typically. Reminding myself of that, I glance at Serafina again, the scar on her chin that I deliberately gave her. Has Marco asked her about it, yet? I don't think he's had opportunity.

The clash of swords immediately commands my attention. Luca has opted to fire up his spark, to move quickly and cleanly, and it would seem that Felle has some increased speed as well, though she is not moving in the same manner as he. Perhaps she took an apothecary's draught instead. They thrust, parry, riposte, once, twice, thrice, and then Luca draws first blood on the back of her hand.

"First blood," Primo says, in a neutral, if ringing, tone. They part, circle away, salute again. This time, Felle drives in hard, and Luca allows her to take ground, leading her almost all the way to the wings before tripping her. She stumbles, drops her main gauche, and does a one-handed cartwheel to dodge his next strikes, coming up with her main blade and a sharpened smile. She dodges like she's going for the main gauche and Luca doesn't fall for it, closing to meet the strike she actually commits to, and striking her shoulder. A pinprick blooms there, barely anything. "Second blood," Primo says, and Felle frowns.

She picks up her main gauche, they salute again, both breathing hard. She changes tactic, spinning her blades with a showy flourish, turning her back to Luca as she advances, ducks, comes in low. He blocks her long blade but not the other, and is blooded across the knee.

"Opposing first blood."

They salute again, but both stand stock-still, eyes locked. The entire theater is quiet enough that I can hear their breathing from where I stand. Luca's hair on the back of his neck, above his shirt collar, is dark with sweat; Felle's clothes and hair are both too dark to note any such sign.

Felle's eyes dart to the side and something about that makes Luca burst into action, even faster still than I've seen him move before, and she tries to throw up her blades to block but he slide stops low, coming even lower with his blades, and repays her for the knee strike.

"Third blood," Primo says. "Duel."

Felle and Luca straighten up and salute each other, and then put their swords away. She says something to him and he chuckles lightly, nods, and then they face the audience and bow, before turning their backs to one another and walking offstage.

His face is *very* flushed, and even as I hold his coat out to him, he's fumbling in the pockets for the draught we take when we advance. "Masterfully done," I say.

"My thanks." He pops the little cork and drinks it down, takes a deep breath, exhales hard. "That was invigorating."

"A nice opener," Tristan says.

"Let me see your knee," I say, and he waves me off.

"I would not have you spend your spark so early," he says. "It is barely a scratch and there is ample time."

"They're pulling names again," Serafina says quietly.

This time, it is August who carries the hat and takes the stage. They are not silent, as Secunda had been, and they plunge their bare hand into the hat with little fanfare. "Angelo of the Golden Company, and Ottavia of House Portela." There is murmuring in the Company crowd across the way; they want Marco, or Katarina.

"Not to worry, I'll be back soon," Ottavia says, fluttering her lashes and trying to laugh. Sterling runs a hand down her back, and they peck each other on the lips before Ottavia traipses across the stage to curtsey to Angelo's bow. He is quite a bit taller than her, broad of shoulder, with long golden hair pulled back. I recognize him as one of the leads.

They salute, and hardly had they lowered their weapons when he bulls forward. Ottavia is surprised, yes, but slips away lightly to the side and around, with the wide eyes of somebody dodging a carriage that has gotten away from its driver. She is too surprised, or overwhelmed, to strike before he has turned, but is able to meet him with a guard when he does, and regain something like composure, turning his blades away and dodging in to draw blood across his left forearm.

"First blood," Secunda calls.

Angelo shakes his arm, droplets of blood pattering to the boards, and they salute and start again. "She should be using her spark," Dora murmurs behind me, barely audible to my ears. Yes, she should. She should be moving faster, but perhaps thinks that it is not sporting if her opponent is not.

Angelo changes tactics, striking heavily at Ottavia's blades, using his size and strength to knock her back step by step. He knocks her long blade from her grasp and she grips her main gauche with both hands and drives upwards. He traps that with both his blades, twisting it away, and there is an audible crack that echoes through the theater and Ottavia cries out, face immediately ashen. "Yield, I yield!"

Angelo pauses. "Are you certain? There is no blood." I cannot see his face, but should like to run him through for that remark.

"I yield," she says again, clutching at her arm or her wrist, obscuring it in her skirts, shoulders hunched forward. Angelo looks upstage, to where the Company owners are.

"We have a yield. Duel to Angelo," Secunda says. So released, Sterling and I go to meet her as she stumbles stage right.

"Your weapons?" Angelo says. He's retrieved them for her and looks a bit confused, making me think that he did not, in fact, hurt her on purpose.

"Thank you," Ottavia says with effort, turning her eyes to Sterling. "Can you...?" They nod wordlessly, go and take the blades from Angelo, who seems surprised by whatever it is he sees in Sterling's face.

"Come, we'll get you offstage and find you a seat somewhere," I say steadily. "Surely somebody can bring you wine to help you forget this, once I've seen to it."

"I tried so hard," she says. She hadn't started to tear up before this.

"You did," I agree. "We all know you did. Come now, let me see what has happened, that I might fix it." We walk her offstage and there is indeed a chair somewhat nearby backstage, near enough that I hear Primo call for Tristan, and a Company member named Giorgia.

It is a bone, or bones, in Ottavia's wrist that has broken, and I think again how rarely I've had to heal broken bones. This and Luca's ribs. She is visibly struggling not to whimper when I handle it, and I am done soon enough. "See? There will not even be a scar," I say.

"I really haven't the taste for this any longer," she says plaintively.

"Well then it is lucky that you have your graceful exit planned," I say, kissing the back of her hand and standing from my crouch.

I had not been able to hear the duel progressing, but August says "Duel to Tristan" as I return to the wings. She and Giorgia are curtseying to one another, Giorgia bleeding from both arms, then turn and curtsey to the crowd.

Tristan returns to us with a haughty look of satisfaction on her face. "I'm surprised to see you so soon, Renzo, is Ottavia well?"

"Small bones," I say with a shrug. Armand offers me his flask, which I accept. Absinthe again. "Still no sugar?"

"It turns to dust in the pockets," he says, his tone a little askew, and that is when Secunda calls Katarina, who laughs when she hears the other name, Rugir.

"I have bested this one before," she says. Inexplicably, she pats Serafina on the shoulder before striding out onto the stage, her posture enlivened. It had not occurred to me, before now, that Katarina might miss the stage.

Chapter Sixty-Seven

Serafina of House Galeazzo

Though I thought I remembered Katarina's stage presence well, to see her on stage again is like she has cloaked herself in another mien entirely. It is not spark-driven, we are completely sure of that. It is through talent and training and years of experience. Her swagger brings her to her mark, and the corner of Rugir's mouth twitches, but he is otherwise outwardly stalwart. They salute, they bow, and then Secunda, who has not properly left the stage yet, says, "Katarina, I do believe congratulations are in order. Please pause a moment, and allow me to extend them."

I cannot see Katarina's face; the nature of the marks is that our own circle members have their backs to us at the start. But I do see the tension draw her up straighter, change how she holds her elbows. "That is not necessary," she says grandly and with great precision. "You do me quite the honor."

"First your nuptials, and now this...it must be quite the comfort, after your cousin." Secunda has been drawing nearer, without seeming to move.

"I'm certain I don't know what you mean, exactly." Katarina seems inclined to address the audience, rather than Secunda, and keeps turning her head. It is anathema for her to turn her back on either, it would seem.

"Have I spoilt your announcement? I extend my regrets for that, then. As well as my regrets for nullifying your participation in these duels, our honor cannot possibly allow you to fight here today." Next to me, I hear Marco draw in a sharp breath. Had she not told him, either? Though I am unschooled in the timing of such things, perhaps that is normal. To wait, until one is sure. Even with talented witches and midwives, pregnancy can be a fragile thing.

Katarina takes a step back from her mark, shaking her head. "I must appeal," she says.

Secunda smiles. "And I must refuse. Please, leave the stage." She clasps her hands and advances almost to the lights. "Please accept our regrets, dear audience, you will have to see Katarina fight another day in the future, when her situation has changed."

Katarina drops her swords back into their sheaths, her movements short and angry, but careful. She is not about to do anything that she might regret, in front of this audience, with the owners of the Golden Company and their formidable power. She bows to Rugir, who returns it again, confused, his swords still out, and then stalks off the stage, her jaw set. Marco slides an arm around her shoulders and though she does not shake him off, I see so clearly how she might, in a blurred copy before I blink and all is normal again. I shake my head just slightly; is this how Armand feels, at all times? Or was that my imagination?

"Katarina, you're—" Tristan and Teodora exclaim in chorused voices that would be joyful, comical, were it not for the situation.

"Please, now is not the time." She does not look at me; I fully expect an accusatory glare, reproachful words, but neither is forthcoming. It should not be a surprise, I think, that Secunda's spark may give her insight in such a thing. It is not unheard of.

August calls Sterling, to take Katarina's place. Ottavia has not rejoined us in the wings, which I think is unusual, as Sterling pushes past us. I go to see if she is still in the same place. Perhaps she just wants to be left alone to catch her breath, though it would rest more easily with me to hear her say so. But also I cannot imagine Katarina wanting to accept comfort from anybody, much less me, though I did not betray her confidence.

She is still in the chair, dabbing at her eyes with a handkerchief. She tucks it into her sleeve when she sees me coming, and makes effort at a smile. "I really should watch Sterling," she says, but does not move.

"You have seen Sterling duel before," I say. "And you will see Sterling duel again. It is no matter."

"I'm not certain I deserve your kindness," she says. "I haven't exactly been the most welcoming."

"You haven't been the least welcoming either, keep that in mind," I say ruefully. "You deserve kindness, and to take the time you need to recover. Are you well? Is there anything you need?"

"I just feel so unsteady," she says. "It was such a shock. I'm sure I'll be right again presently."

The sounds of the duel do not reach where we are, but the cutting voice of Primo saying "Duel to Umberto" does, and Ottavia is on her feet in a breathless instant and rushing to meet Sterling, who bears three scratches, yes, but none of them are of much consequence. They embrace, and Ottavia is visibly shaking, while Sterling murmurs against her hair.

There are so few of us left to fight, and so many. When Armand is called, the other side is audibly disappointed. They want Marco. The girl Armand fights, Elena, comes out with swagger and bravado, like Katarina, and after they bow to each other, and salute, I hear Armand say something, but I cannot quite make out his words. She falters, though, her face changing. "I've heard about you, you're the weird one," she says.

"Indeed," he says, affably enough. "Don't worry, though, you won't hurt me too badly."

"Stop *talking*," she says, snapping out at him with a strike that he is no longer standing there for. She is quick, though, and clever, and has some small spark that she calls upon for speed. Maybe also for flexibility, or she's able to contort like that naturally, I cannot say. Armand makes her work for each blood that she gets, only getting one strike on her before she takes the duel.

Marco's name causes a stir; his opponent is named Elena. He kisses Katarina before he goes, lingering just a bit, until she gives him a push to make him break off. She seems pleased, though. Perhaps smug. I wonder if anybody told him about our ridiculous 'kissing for luck' joke at the tournament but when would they have had the opportunity? Though also we've all spent so many waking hours together this last fortnight.

They bow to each other, and salute, and I almost can't watch. I have seen Marco fight before, of course, even before our recent practices. Last year's tournament. Uncounted times before that. But Elena is swift, her movements unexpected. There is something in her face that tells me that she cares for no risk to her person, in all of this, that she is in it or victory or death, even though death is not part of the terms.

"She wished Valentino had been hers," Katarina murmurs. "As she was not selected to be my opponent, Marco is the next best target." Elena gets first blood as Katarina says that, and for a moment, from the way he clutches his chest, I think that it is worse. But no, they break, he straightens, and salutes. I breathe again, and then they close again.

Marco is on the defensive, always. When I do glimpse his face, he is surprised, but concentrated, not alarmed. But he never gets a strike in. Elena gets second blood through his wrist with her main gauche and flicks the tip of her long blade across his face, right under his eye. I wonder if she missed it on purpose, or simply wanted to make a point.

The duel is called and they stand like statues there, her blade still through Marco's wrist, and he glances to Lorenzo, his expression carefully schooled but his eyes a bit too wide. Lorenzo is already crossing the stage, swift as when the other man broke Ottavia's wrist, and Elena has the good grace to wait, unlike the person who injured Tristan in the tournament with the blade through the leg.

When I feel Dora's hand on my shoulder is when I realize I had started onto the stage as well. "Let Lorenzo work," she says. "Marco will be all right." I look at Katarina, who is also watching keenly, but has not moved. Does she trust in Lorenzo so, already? Or does she not trust herself to not cut Elena down, if she is within reach?

The audience has been quiet. The Golden Company members have been quiet. I hear Lorenzo say something, brisk, businesslike, and Elena withdraws her blade as Lorenzo is burning his spark into Marco's wound, and there is a brief, swift, patter of blood to the stage and then it stops. Marco holds up his hand, flexes it, and that is when there is applause. Lorenzo still has his hands on him, though. Lorenzo's spark is still flaring.

That is when Secunda again slinks out onto the stage, catching Elena's arm as she is about to sheathe her main gauche. Secunda brings the blade close to her face, sniffs audibly, clicks her tongue softly. "Elena," she says in crooning disappointment. "Really, Elena?" Elena struggles against her grip, which seems both pointless and also unwise.

"What is happening?" I ask, since nothing else is immediately forthcoming. Secunda hears me, turning to catch my eye briefly, her smile terrible, before shifting her focus.

"Katarina, would you kindly join us on the stage?"

"Of course," Katarina says steadily, going out. She stops a little short of Lorenzo, who has now let go of Marco, stepped away slightly.

"Katarina, we are *so* sorry to bring this up so abruptly, so callously, but how was it your dear cousin died? Poison?"

A pause, either from shock or stagemanship, I cannot see her face as she turns a bit, both to address Secunda and the audience at once. "Yes. She poisoned herself when she heard that her love, Valentino, was banished from the city after stabbing Marco of House Galeazzo in a quarrel."

"And were you witness to this?" Secunda has her head cocked just slightly, as if to listen better. "The poisoning, I know you were there for the stabbing, as it was you who got Marco of House Galeazzo to a witch woman in time."

"I—" Katarina sneezes once, sharply, and there are some scattered laughs. "Yes, I was witness to it. I saw her drink the coffee, but did not realize she had poisoned it until she swooned, and I found the paper packet."

"Interesting that poison now comes to the stage. It was not in our negotiation of terms." Secunda clicks her tongue again, shakes Elena slightly like a scruffed kitten. "Houses, I extend the Golden Company's *sincerest* apologies, and I ask you now: ought we continue these duels as originally agreed, or should we cease that course immediately and take another tack? And, if we agree to cease and renegotiate, is it necessary to bring the Guard into our business again?"

A few glances amongst the front row, and my mother stands, with Lady Valier. "We might renegotiate ourselves," my mother says.

"What say we settle this with one final duel?" Secunda says. "We have seen such shows of prowess from both your side and mine, and needed to upset the balance anyway. Would this be acceptable?"

"It would be, yes," Lady Valier says. There's a slight movement on stage, and both Marco and Katarina move to support Lorenzo, who had been standing at ready, waiting, but who had staggered just slightly.

Secunda drops her hold on Elena and reaches out, resting her hand briefly on Lorenzo's cheek. "These lights are dreadful, aren't they?" she asks in a near human tone. "After having spent *such* spark, and you aren't used to them..." She looks back to our mothers. "I think, unfortunately, were you to select good Lorenzo as your champion, he would not be up to it just now, after so valorously saving his friend before he felt the poison's bite."

"It is no matter, Serafina will carry the evening," my mother says, to my utter panic.

Chapter Sixty-Eight

Lorenzo of House Valier

The feel of the poison, after I heal Marco's wound, is nothing like anything I have felt before, with my spark. I know I can't leave it, though, and I persist, and push myself. I have a thought that it might be to my detriment, as I have yet to fight, but we are doing this for Marco after all. Marco and Katarina and yes, Serafina, and it will be all for naught if Marco dies to a poisoned blade. I am hardly aware of what else is being said around me, even once I have done with the healing and am loathe to walk away from Marco while the Company owner is standing so closely. What I might do to prevent any ill action on her part, I cannot say, but it is still my feeling.

Katarina sneezes somewhere slightly behind me, and I turn my head toward the sound, catch sight of Marco's watchful gaze, hear Secunda say 'renegotiate.' It is very hot on the stage, with the lights, and I do think that I have advanced, but my feeling of utter drainage, of exhaustion is sudden and my hand will not raise to my pocket for my own little vial. Instead, I nearly overbalance myself, just standing still, and feel Marco's hands on me, and Katarina's.

Secunda reaches out and cups my cheek in her gloved fingers, and even through the satin I feel the thrum of her spark. She touches mine, just slightly, steadying me as she goes on about the stage lights, which are and are not the problem. The poison was the problem. I am not poisoned, but it took so much for me to rectify it...

Then I hear Lady Galeazzo say "Serafina will carry the evening," and I think, no, but it is fitting for Serafina to be the one to seal her own fate.

Secunda meets my eyes briefly, winks, and then looks past me to the wings. "Serafina, do you accept Lady Galeazzo's offering?"

I cannot turn to see her at the moment, but I have seen her struggle to master her feelings and voice the correct words, and after a pause, not too long a pause, Serafina says "I accept, and do hope that with my lady mother's blessing I might do our house proud." Her voice is steady, mostly; there is a very slight quaver when she says 'mother.'

"Splendid!" Secunda clasps her hands. "Why do we not disperse for a brief intermission, and meet up again in half an hour? Audience, you will find refreshments in the entryway. Duelists, you will find them in the halls off of your respective wings. No fraternizing." She wags a finger and there is the expectation of laughter and again, she receives some in reward. Primo and August have also come out onto the stage, and the three of them bow and the curtain drops.

Marco and Katarina start to help me offstage, but I disentangle myself from their grasp. "Thank you, but I am all right now." I am a little clumsy with the vial, but get it drunk down. "Or I will be all right, with refreshments."

"As you say," Marco says, watching me closely. Katarina says nothing, and her face is not open to me. Once we are nearly back to the wings, Serafina breaks loose of Dora and falls upon her brother with a fierce hug. He is surprised, and then returns her embrace. "I'm all right, Fina," he says soothingly. "Renzo made it so I am all right. I didn't even feel the poison."

Katarina casts her gaze upwards at the rafters for a moment, and then looks to me. "In all sincerity, thank you," she says.

"I couldn't see letting us go through all of this and then seeing him felled onstage," I say dryly, but she understands that it is an attempt at levity and smiles. Serafina releases Marco, and looks at me, her eyes wet.

"Thank you," she says.

"As I just explained..."

"Just accept it, Renzo, you're a hero several times over," Dora says merrily, coming and hooking her arm through Serafina's, and mine. "Now let us get drinks and eat finger foods and bolster Serafina's confidence that she might beat whoever it is that they pick for their champion, for they certainly did not say."

"I'd missed that," I say, frowning.

"Yes, I think that was part of Secunda's aim," Dora says. "It is no matter, knowing will change nothing for us. Serafina is strong and fast and clever, and the best she has ever been."

"Am I?" Serafina says, blinking quite a lot.

"*Yes*, silly girl, my goodness." We follow along with Dora, and the rest of the circle falls in with us. Tables of refreshments have indeed been set up, finger foods, afternoon tea foods. Little sandwiches and cookies and other confections. Teas and infusions and alcohols.

My apothecary's draught has already helped me regain some of my strength, and Armand hands me a drink that smells both floral and alcoholic. He nudges Serafina's elbow, and when she looks at him, startled, he presses a glass upon her as well. "What is it?" she asks.

"Nothing of consequence, if that's what you mean," he says. Then he turns his head as though somebody has called his name and wanders off. I shrug and drain the glass.

Serafina watches him go thoughtfully. "Secunda must realize the favor that she has done me, keeping us away backstage like this where my mother may not tread?"

"I wouldn't phrase it like that," Katarina says hastily. "It is not a *favor*, she calculated it in this manner for a reason. Be careful what you say to them."

"Of course," Serafina murmurs, confused again.

"It would be ever so dreadful if your mother inserted herself back here," Ottavia says. "You'll forgive me for saying."

"There is nothing to forgive. This isn't about her." One could almost believe her, I think. A dove resolving to fight an eagle. Perhaps. If ever I doubted she loved her brother, I have been proven wrong now several times over. Did I ever doubt that, or was I just angry that he loved somebody else more than he loved me? The complications of my abandonment have become an embarrassment. Perhaps they were all along.

The refreshments are very nice, though Serafina only has two drinks, and then nibbles on a cookie. Her nerves, I assume. Dora guards her from getting too deeply into conversation, but also from getting too deeply into her own thoughts, keeping things brisk and light until the signal comes to us from the stage that it is time.

For a moment, Serafina does not move, and I think that the final disaster will befall us without her ever going onto the stage. Then Dora touches her elbow, lightly, and we return to the wings.

The house lights are down already, and just one light is shining on the stage at the moment. Primo, Secunda, and August are all on the stage. Serafina pauses just past the curtain, and Primo raises both of his hands.

"Now, the moment we have been waiting for, the final duel. The decider of our grievances. Serafina will fight Angelo, satisfying all of our honor and putting this matter to rest."

I am watching Serafina, we all are, and I see the slightest of shudders pass through her, across her shoulders. Angelo is already walking out onto the stage to the cheers of his fellows. Serafina glances over her shoulder at us briefly, and Dora begins our applause, Luca pushing the envelope by doing a piercing, fingers-in-his-teeth whistle.

More stage lights come on, softly lighting Angelo and Serafina as they reach their marks. Serafina curtseys, deeply, and Angelo bows an equivalent match. From her posture, and from the slight quirk that I see pass through Angelo's brows, he knows that she is terrified. He knows what is at stake.

But they are in motion already, Angelo driving forward once they've saluted, Serafina on the defensive, but steady. So far she is steady. His movements are different from when he fought Ottavia, he must have also taken one of the alchemist's draughts that some of them favored.

August calls "First blood," and I'm not certain what's happened yet, even, though their positioning makes it so when they break, Serafina is facing us, breathing hard, blood trickling down her cheek.

They begin again, and again, Serafina is on the defensive, always. She is drawing him around the stage, though. Taking his measure, perhaps, except then second blood is called and as they salute again I just think, why not yield, you silly girl. I have a feeling that if Angelo lands third blood, it will be disastrous, and I do not know if I will have the spark to heal something large and catastrophic, after handling Ottavia's break and then Marco's wound and poison. Perhaps I can. Perhaps it will be easier, since I healed her from the brink once before.

But she does not yield and they begin again.

Chapter Sixty-Nine

Serafina of House Galeazzo

The moment our weapons first kiss off each other, I know that Angelo is an order of magnitude stronger than me, and has also done something to make himself faster. He does not seem to be one of the Company members who has spark to burn, it is something else. A small, quiet part of me that I don't have the time to sit with is pleased that I am not immediately overwhelmed the way Ottavia was, and driven around the stage, but in addition to his strength, he also has further reach, and I am on the defensive more than I would like to be. Even so, I hear August call "First blood" and then the sting in my cheek catches up, the feeling like tears of blood slipping down my skin.

We find our marks, salute again. I start to draw on my spark, remembering Ottavia's fight and how she didn't. Did she forget? I cannot take the time to think about that now, he is pressing again, and I am again on the defensive. I deflect and riposte, surprising him into a grin. He gets even showier in his fighting, strikes at my blades even more strongly.

I block one blow almost too late, crossing my blades to take the strike, my fingers tingling as I push him off, and he slips his main gauche in, gets the tiniest little nick just above my collarbone. That one is less fast, I feel it as it occurs.

"Second blood," August calls, in the otherwise silent theater.

We break, salute, our breaths echoing, motes of dust kicked up from the stage and down from the curtains, catching the light around us here and there. I cannot lose, I think. I cannot go through with whatever is after this, if I lose. I've left my sword up in salute a bit too long, but he has mirrored me, which is proper. I put my shoulders back, as Katarina tried to drill into me. How have I forgotten so soon? I take a final deep breath, draw on my spark more strongly than I ever have before, consciously. I cannot lose.

Then we are in motion again; Angelo tries again to simply overpower me and this time I have his pattern, it was a mistake for him to repeat it. I stop his first strike, and then in the rush that I have seen Katarina perform, I disarm his main gauche, knock away his main blade, and one, two, three, blood him in the chest, neat swift shallow cuts, finishing so close I might kiss him were that my intent. It is not.

Silence again, so quiet, I cannot even hear our breaths for a moment. I can only see his wide, startled eyes, not unlike Nunzio at the end of our ill-fated duel. But I haven't killed Angelo. I have, however, won.

"Duel to Serafina," August says, and even then there is a pause, and then the applause starts. I have to remember, consciously, to let my spark die down again. Angelo retrieves his main gauche, and salutes me, and, shakily, I return his salute, and curtsey. He bows to me somberly, and then a smile sneaks across his face.

"You surprised me," he says.

"I surprised myself," I say, and then I am gathered up in a cloud of lavender and it is Dora come onto the stage, and then Marco embracing me as well, over and around her arms. "Please," I gasp, but laughing, joyous. They have taken me nearly off my feet, but finally release me, and I find myself face to face with Lorenzo, much closer than I expected, and I stumble, surprised, and he reaches out to steady me.

He's looking into my eyes, really *seeing* me more wholly than ever I have known him to, and he raises his hand to my face, brushes his thumb across my cut there, the sting is gone. Then he cups my cheek, and strokes his fingers down to my chin, and then we are kissing and it is genuine this time, not for a game, not for luck, not to go along with a joke. The rest of the world falls away and I know only the pressure of his lips against mine, tipped up to him, and the strong support of his arms around me, gathering me to him.

We part, eventually, and I am a different kind of breathless. And I am reminded of our audience. My *mother* is sitting there and my eyes are drawn to her unwillingly, iron to a lodestone, and she has a look of triumph on her face unlike any I have ever before seen. But this is not her triumph, it is mine, no matter what she thinks, no matter what credit she might take.

Lorenzo is still holding me, I did not expect that. I did not expect any of this, and I look up at him again. "I have treated you badly," he says in a voice that does not carry, though the stage, the theater, is designed to throw voices.

"Not now," I say, and emboldened by everything, I kiss him this time, firmly, rising up on my toes a little in order to reach, grasping the front of his coat in my hands. Kissing him is not like kissing Teodora, or Luca. There is another, deeper feeling here, a meaning that I am grasping at, that I have never experienced before. Yes he has treated me badly and no, now is not the time to address that, just as it was not the time when he woke me up demanding that I fight him. There will be a time, but it is not now.

Secunda's voice interrupts again though. "They say journeys end in lovers meeting." We part, and Lorenzo releases me this time. I turn towards Secunda, and Primo and August are again by her sides. "Our honor has been satisfied. House Galeazzo, do you feel the same way?"

"We do," I say, before my mother has the chance to. There is a pause, though, and then my mother also says,

"Our honor has been satisfied." I turn to look at her, but even now, she isn't looking at me.

Secunda claps her hands, and then raises them to those of us gathered. "Disperse, then, and go about your business! May we never revisit this misfortune."

Lorenzo grasps my hand and draws me offstage. We pause again, in the wings, and he touches my other small wound, draws his fingers across it to turn it to gold. He has healed me a handful of times, and never has the feeling thrilled me the way it just has. I keep expecting everybody else to come and interrupt us, to urge us out into the streets, out to a tavern, for a victory celebration but it is just Lorenzo and I, and I keep forgetting that I am thinking of anybody else. I do, very suddenly, crave the open air, and I take Lorenzo's hand and pull him along with me. He lets me do it, of course he could stop me, but he does not.

The street is glittering in the street lamps with rain that fell unwitnessed, and the scent on the air is heady with flowers and possibility. I stop and take it in, take deep breaths, so many weights suddenly lifted from me.

"You're crying," Lorenzo says, not disgusted this time. He's looking at me in concern, in wonderment.

"I've taken altogether too many of your handkerchiefs," I say, laughing now as well. "I've entirely lost track."

"At least two," he agrees, drawing me near again, as if suddenly he cannot bear for me to be more than an arm's length away.

"Though I gave you the first one," I say.

"You did, and it was a masterful stroke," he says. The carriage is very near to us, was it there all along, and he reaches for the door.

"I would prefer to walk," I say.

"As you did that night, when you went to the market with Teodora?" he asks. His voice draws me up a little, but I am hardly the one with the most offenses, if we are comparing ledgers.

"You already know why I lied," I say, closing the carriage door firmly and stepping away. He follows.

"I do. And I do not blame you."

"Good. Because I am not apologizing." He laughs, surprised, and we fall into step together.

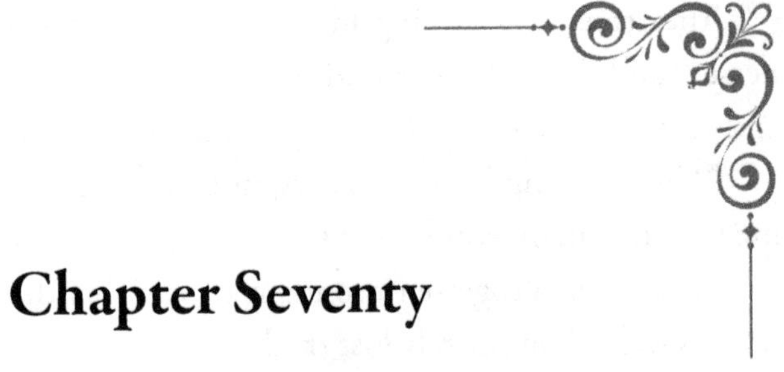

Chapter Seventy

Lorenzo of House Valier

We wander through the streets, intoxicated with one another. It is ridiculous, I think, for her to have been here all along. For me to have treated her in the manner I did, punishing her for her brother's abandonment, when we might have comforted one another. It is ridiculous, that now she is all that I want to love and to cherish, and I wonder if we have been bewitched somehow and I wonder if it matters. Serafina is free of her mother, her brother is free of previous consequences, and Katarina has her prize.

We pass innumerable fountains, it is impossible not to, and at one of them, I stop. It is not my favorite, but it is one I had heard the story of. The carvings in it are a cascade of metal fish, discoloring under the constantly running water either through age or design or both. The edges of it are broad, broad as sitting-room chairs, and I gesture Serafina to sit a moment. She does, arranging her swords and skirts, looking at the water falling, and then looking up at me in question.

"This is not a fountain that one tosses coins into," I say. "Or flowers or charms or trinkets. This is a fountain that one kisses at."

"Oh is it?" Serafina asks, wide-eyed, blushing prettily.

"It is." I take her hand, and kiss the back of that first. She has the most diverting way of tipping her chin up as I lean in, and even a day ago I had certainly not thought I would be passing time kissing Serafina. We spend enough time at the kissing fountain that a patrol of the Guard come past, and at the scrape of their boots we separate. They see our stations and give us a nod before continuing on, but that moment has passed and we continue on as well.

There are no carriages apparent, when we finally go through the gates at my house. Whether that means my parents are in for the evening or still out, I do not trouble myself, as kissing Serafina against the wall just inside the gate has again become more important. She giggles a little against my lips, but when I step back, does not explain herself. My eyes look for the smear of blood she left on the wall, that night, but it has been cleaned. It strikes me, then, how close to losing her I was, before I ever even knew that I might love her.

Do I love her?

Does she love *me*? How could she possibly?

There are no servants apparent as I follow her up the stair, and then she stops short and looks to me. "I don't know where to go," she says, somehow both pleading and commanding at once.

"We will be undisturbed either way," I say, and take her hand to lead her to my rooms.

Once there, I shut the door behind us, take off my swords, put them on the rack. Serafina seems to be taking in the furnishings, the things I have on my dressing-table. The books on my writing desk. I hesitate, unusual for me to ever feel the need, and I approach her again, put my hands on her waist. "Is it what you expected?"

"I didn't know what to expect," she says, casting her eyes down shyly. She bites her lip, and fumbles at her sword belts, and I still her hands with mine.

"Let me." She lets her hands fall loose, and I unbuckle her sword belts, put them in the rack with mine. She waits, still but quivering just slightly, and I think that she must be used to having a maid undress her. It was a temptation on the way here, more than once, to push her against a wall and ruck up her skirts, but never had I done such a thing, and she should not have tolerated it. This, though.

I am careful with her buttons and lacings, unlike the last time I had occasion to place my hands on her clothing. I kiss the back of her neck, I kiss her collarbones, scarred and not, I kiss her belly. The fabric whispers to the floor around her feet, and she steps out of it, still in her boots. She sits on the edge of my bed without my bidding, and I pull them off for her, roll her stockings off as well, kneeling in front of her still dressed, kissing her knees and the insides of her thighs, before I stand up to disrobe myself. Serafina lays back on the bed with a sigh, and I watch her long lashes as she blinks up at the painted pastoral scene on my ceiling.

I slide onto the bed next to her, dragging my fingertips across her hips, up to her breasts, kissing her again as she moans against my mouth. We are both so warm, flushed, as she finally, breathlessly says "please" and what can I do but comply?

I roll on top of her, position myself, careful of my weight, of how fast and hard I bear down on her. She rocks her hips up in to me in the same way that she tipped her face up, arching her back, and I catch sight again of the pale scar I left on her chin.

"What's the matter?" she says when I falter, catching at me with her hands. "Why are you stopping? Don't stop."

"I just—"

She puts her hands on my face, pulls it in close to hers. "Don't stop." I don't stop; her order, her desire, is enough to bolster my resolve. She cries out softly, shuddering deliciously, and I don't stop until that has happened twice more, thrice more, allowing myself to reach my own finish.

We lie side by side for a time, our breathing ragged. Once the pounding of my heart has calmed down, though, and Serafina's breathing eased, I turn to her, to explain, or perhaps to ask forgiveness, and find she has already fallen asleep. I cannot blame her; the events of the day, of the last weeks, have all had their culmination. I should get up, get dressed in nightclothes, locate a nightgown for her, any number of things, and instead I stay watching her sleeping face until I also drift off.

I wake up to Serafina dropping my sword belts on the bed next to me and saying, "Get up."

"What is this?" I ask, though I think I know. She is wearing one of my shirts, perhaps the one I most recently shed, the tails of it coming part of the way down her thighs. The light outside my window is the blue that comes before dawn's rosy hue.

"You treated me badly, and wanted to fight me over it. I refused. But now, I think, the balance of things has shifted significantly. Your actions weigh heavily upon you, and I cannot simply forgive you. But I can fight you now." She is calm and serious, not angry, not tearful.

"Very well," I say, slowly getting up. "I will put pants on, though."

"As you will," she says, her voice steady, but her face turns a bit pink, and I hide a smile.

"What are the terms?" I draw my swords, and she draws hers.

"We have seen quite enough blood lately, I think. Or, I have. Just a touch, please."

"One touch?" I ask.

She nods, resolute. Her hair is sleep-mussed; Teodora had braided it up so nicely. "One touch, and our honor on the matter is satisfied."

"I agree to the terms." We salute, and she surprises me by moving in first, rapidly. I block in time, with my main gauche, and she uses my own trick to twist it away to the floor with a clatter. I parry her attempt to touch me then, and she spins away. She's keeping her shoulders back, the way Katarina taught her, she is no longer apologetic, and being unable to beat Serafina is not something that had ever occurred to me. Allowing her to win also never occurred to me. It would be a tremendous insult to do so, and render these proceedings unsatisfactory.

I narrowly miss touching her with my rejoinder, and then she has the flat of her long blade under my chin, coldly, gently. She is smiling, slightly, and we are looking into each other's eyes, when my manservant Georgei comes hurriedly into the room, probably drawn by the clash of swords. He gives a short, wordless exclamation and withdraws again immediately, thumping the door closed behind him.

"My apologies, my lord, I thought—" he calls hurriedly. Serafina withdraws her blades.

"Please, Georgei, forget about it. There is no need to wake the whole household." If we have not already, I think. It hadn't occurred to me either time I was involved, or nearly involved, in a bedroom duel. I look at Serafina, who is turning pink again, but also has her hand over her mouth, suppressing laughter. "I suppose we ought to get dressed," I say.

"Yes, I should not like to meet your lady mother like this," she says, laughter subsiding a bit.

"I will say, I don't mind being woken up like this," I say.

"Thank you," she says, and I catch her hand briefly as she starts to turn away and see to her clothes.

"Thank *you*." There is so much more to be said, and discussed, and understood, but for now, it is enough.

I am able to dress far more easily than she is, and am doing up the laces on her dress when my mother raps on my door. "If you've quite stopped being dramatic, may I come in?" she asks lightly. I do wonder what Georgei said to her, and if she expects to find me on the floor with my throat opened. Serafina has done that to a man once, after all.

"You may come in, my lady mother," I say.

She does immediately, obviously having waited with her hand on the door knob. As always, she is the picture of collected grace, but there is a tension that runs out of her when she sees that we are unbloodied, when she senses no spark in the air. "You have my apologies, for disturbing you so early," she says. Serafina curtseys, her face schooled into a pleasant mask, but by this point, I can see plainly when she is conflicted about something, or terribly embarrassed. It is unavoidable that she is wearing the clothes that she dueled in yesterday, and I am not.

I bow, to show a united front. "And you have our apologies, for disturbing the household. We had a final matter of honor to be settled, and the finality of that moment is when Georgei happened in to start my day."

My mother, now smiling curiously, looks from my face to Serafina's, and back again, letting the moment draw out. "I see," she says. "And has your honor been satisfied?" she asks Serafina.

"It has," she says steadily. "Thank you."

"Very well then. I shall see you both at the breakfast table." My mother looks at me again, briefly, knowingly, and withdraws.

"I should go and bathe," Serafina says.

"I will make certain that is arranged for you," I say, proper, correct, and then push her up against the back of the door and kiss her thoroughly before releasing her to the morning.

Chapter Seventy-One

Serafina of House Valier

Though nobody of honor will fight her, Katarina does still come to the society dinner. It is the first time that all of us, freed from various bonds and grudges, sit together around a table in a house's meeting hall, drinking wine and watching other arrivals, standing to observe scuffles as they break out.

It is something of a surprise that Ottavia is here as well, and though none of us comment, she at one point bursts out with, "I was going to stay home but the idea was so *dreadfully* boring, can you even imagine?" We laugh, Tristan less kindly, Dora more.

"Nobody asked," Tristan says.

"We hoped you would realize that," Dora says soothingly, as she raps Tristan on the wrist with her fan. "Nothing has changed."

"Everything has changed," Ottavia says, giving both me and Katarina significant glances.

"For the better," Marco says peaceably, kissing the back of Katarina's hand. I'm not certain the wild look in her eyes will ever settle, but she does, at least, seem to be fond of my brother. Does she love him as much as I, or Lorenzo, think he deserves? Perhaps not, but that is not our business. Have they since also announced that she is with child? Yes.

Across the room, I watch my mother arrive, and Lady Valier go to meet her. She glances around, picks out Marco at the table, and then sees me watching her. Her expression is unreadable to me, as always. Have I met her expectations? Have I made her proud?

Lorenzo takes my hand and I turn to him. He looks into my eye, kissing my knuckles, and when he looks at me like that, it is as though the rest of the room falls away. It is dizzying to feel so loved, and supported. "Do you want to fight anybody tonight?" he asks.

"I do, actually," I say, after a moment's consideration. I look at the rest of the table, who is and is not paying attention. "My brother."

"Me?" Marco asks in a comically wounded tone. "And what is your grievance?"

"Your abandonment. I left the matter to rest for so long that I might not be adding insult to injury, but now is the time to resolve it."

"Am I allowed to pick Lorenzo as my second?" he asks, already standing and removing his coat.

"No, he's mine." Lorenzo helps me off with my coat.

He turns to the table in appeal. "Luca?"

"It would be my honor."

"What are your terms, then, my dear bloodthirsty sister?"

"No blood," I say thoughtfully. "Third touch."

We face one another, and he bows to my curtsey, and then we draw our swords and salute.

Acknowledgements

Here, at the end of the longest book I've written (so far!), I have some special thanks

To Lennon, for proofreading this.

To Jazzi, for making me aware that yes, this was a romance, and also the leads are dopes

To my Eternal Gratitude people on Patreon: Brian, Heather, and Sheryl

About the Author

Jennifer R. Donohue grew up at the Jersey Shore and now lives in central New York with her husband and their Dobermans. She works at her local public library where she also facilitates a writing workshop. Her short work has appeared in *Apex Magazine, Escape Pod, Fantasy, The Deadlands, Fusion Fragment*, and elsewhere. She is the writer of the Run With the Hunted novella series and the Learn to Howl werewolf trilogy. She posts @AuthorizedMusings.bsky.social and you can subscribe to her Patreon for a new short story every month:https://www.patreon.com/Jennifer-RDonohu[1]e

Further work by Jennifer R. Donohue

Exit Ghost

The Drowned Heir

Between the Blood and the Sun

The Learn to Howl Trilogy

Learn to Howl

Baying the Moon

The Company of Wolves

Other books in the Run With the Hunted series

Run With the Hunted

Run With the Hunted 2: Ctrl Alt Delete

Run With the Hunted 3: Standard Operating Procedure

Run With the Hunted 4: VIP

Run With the Hunted 5: Insert Coin to Play

Run With the Hunted 6: Burned Asset

Run With the Hunted 7: The Casino Job

---

1. https://www.patreon.com/JenniferRDonohue

9 781945 548369